HYBRID

Nick Stead

To

S. J.

With bite!

N. Stead

A Wild Wolf Publication

Published by Wild Wolf Publishing in 2016

Copyright © 2016 Nick Stead

First print

ISBN: 978-1-907954-49-8
Also available in an ebook edition

www.wildwolfpublishing.com

I would like to dedicate this book to my amazing family for their support and belief in me over the years, especially my mum for encouraging my love of stories from a young age and my cousin 'Lady' Sarah for getting me started on Hybrid all those years ago.

Also to my friends who I'm lucky enough to be able to say are too many to name, but you guys know who you are. Special mention goes to Charlie for really boosting my confidence with all the positive feedback and helping with the book launch, Sarah for helping me survive through school, college and more recently LARP, and Lauren for all those horror movie nights which helped keep me inspired to work on my own stories.

I would also like to thank my fellow writers and friends at Huddersfield Author's Circle for all their support and feedback on my work.

And finally, thanks to Alex and Squeaky for pointing me in the direction of Wild Wolf Publishing, making my dream of being published a reality at long last.

Nick

Prologue

The late autumn sun glares down upon the land, creating pools of light and shadow amongst the tree trunks and in the undergrowth. A chill wind whispers through the woods, a hint of what is soon to come in the winter months. Shivering, you quicken your pace, eager to be home, listening to the sound of your own footsteps crunching through the blanket of leaves that covers the floor.

Clouds lazily drift across the sun, casting yet more shadows through the trees. The woods suddenly seem a hostile place, as if something is lurking in the undergrowth, something that doesn't belong, something deadly. You can't shake the feeling you're being watched. You thought you were alone but can you be so sure? The woods hide many creatures, but the sense that something other than the natural wildlife is crouching in the shadows cannot be ignored. You can feel eyes following you as you walk, eyes that do not belong to any known creature on the planet. Fear begins to take its deadly hold, slowly tightening its grip upon your heart and squeezing until it becomes painful, until you feel your heart will stop. But what is it you fear the most? Do you fear the death that you feel awaits you, the pain, the unseen creature itself?

Movement alarms you and you begin to run, fearing for your life. Whatever it is, can you outrun it? Unbidden, images flash before your eyes, all those horror movies you've seen, the horror stories of man-eating animals you've heard, and your own lifeless body lying broken and bloody on the ground, hidden by the leaves, slowly rotting away and fed upon by the creatures of the woods. Fear spurs you on to a greater speed.

You're being followed now; you can hear something behind you but what is it? Through the panic, you're dimly aware that it doesn't make any noise running through the leaves, yet you can hear some creature behind you. Something darts out in front of you, causing you to cry out. The bird quickly seeks refuge in a nearby tree, followed by others of its kind. You stop running and double up with laughter, laughing at your own fear, allowing your imagination to get the better of you. Birds. It was only birds.

You start to walk again, still laughing and shaking your head at your own stupidity. But something still isn't quite right and you pause again. The world is still and silent. Shouldn't those birds be singing now? With a shrug you continue walking. Who knows what goes on in the minds of animals? Perhaps they fell silent in fear after you startled them.

Clouds are massing in the sky overhead, black and threatening, casting the woods entirely in shadow. There's no denying the hostility of the world around you. Maybe there is something other than birds here after all.

Leaves crunch behind you. Not your imagination this time, you are definitely being followed. But is it human or animal? Both seem equally as frightening.

Your head whips round in an attempt to spy the stalker, but only plant life meets your eyes. Another sound – it's in front of you now. And gone when your head spins back round to meet it. A human couldn't move that fast… The thought isn't very comforting. Can you outsmart the creature in its own habitat?

Running again, you see movement in the shadows: a darker shadow than those cast by the trees, weaving between trunks, keeping pace with you. Definitely an animal of some description but not one belonging to Britain. A quick glance is enough to tell you it's bigger than any other predator native to the country and your fear intensifies. You lose sight of it, the black shape seemingly melting into its surroundings, but you keep running, knowing it could be moving in for the kill.

Precious time trickles by but the creature is gone. Just as you think you're safe and begin to slow, a shape steps out from between the trees. But it isn't an animal this time. Shock and confusion brings you to a standstill and you face the stranger, chest heaving as your body craves more oxygen.

A man stands before you. There is a feral look about him: his dark hair is a mess, long and unkempt, and long stubble covers his face, just short of a couple of day's growth needed to be called a beard. His wild eyes belong to a madman at first, but as you watch they become cold and merciless, like the eyes of a killer, before seemingly growing warmer, more human perhaps. You cannot hold his gaze for long, for you can feel a great hunger burning in them, always there despite the changes you just witnessed. He is barely wearing any clothes, naked from the waist up. What rags remain around his legs are torn and covered in filth, and you can't be sure but they appear to be stained in blood. His eyes are narrowed while he surveys you, his top lip curling slightly to bare sharp yellow teeth, pieces of raw flesh caught between them. On any other man it would be described as an expression of contempt, but in this case it appears to be more of a snarl.

I look at you and I smell your fear. It calls to me as the hunger eats away at my insides, urging me to hunt. I see it in your eyes now, the fear is taking over. So hungry. And yet, something holds me back this time. Memories rise from the murky depths of my mind, corpses rising up from their watery grave. Memories of the human world. How long has it been now? Weeks? Months? Years? I don't know, but I remember... And I want to be part of that world again. I take a step towards you, so close now that you can smell the stench of flesh and blood on my breath. You're praying it's the blood of animals, but deep down you know that it is not. You want to run, but you seem to be glued to the spot. You find you want to know more about this strange man, in spite of yourself.

I try to speak but it's been so long, all I manage is a grunt. Frowning, I embrace the memories now, searching for the forgotten knowledge, trying to find the secret to forming the words to this forgotten language, the key to this forgotten world. It's been so long, but I remember a time when I was a part of that world, and finally my tongue forms words I thought I'd buried along with my past.

I tell you not to fear for the little good it does. I will not harm you. So many things I tried to forget, but I will never be free of those memories. Words cannot describe the horrors I have known, nor the torment I have endured, but I find the need to tell someone, and I shall seek to relate them to you as best I can. I've been alone for so long, isolated from the world, no longer a part of your world but not a part of theirs. I tried turning to the natural world for a time but I do not belong there. Your world fears me, my world turned their back on me, and I am alone. I long to be part of man's world again, to see my family if they are still alive. Maybe it's too late for that now. Have I outlived them all, everyone I knew in my former life?

I have been haunted by these memories for so long, keeping them locked inside my skull for what seems an eternity, but now it is time to release them. I have to tell someone; I cannot go on any longer like this.

It starts to rain. Thunder rumbles across the sky and lightning streaks through the clouds. Come, I will take you to shelter where you can listen to my tale while the storm rages. Please? I don't want to be alone any longer.

You look at me, distrust evident in your eyes, but pity stirs your heart and, though you should know better, you follow me to a cave, carved long ago into a rocky outcrop somewhere near the heart of the woods. You help me start a fire and settle down on the floor opposite me, with only the dancing flames between us. Now, where to begin? I search my memory for the right place to start. Everything is so confused, but thinking is slowly becoming easier. You act as a catalyst,

7

reminding me of the life I once had, and slowly the memories begin to make more sense, form some kind of order. Yes, the tale, or at least the part of which I will tell this day, began in a small Northern town in Yorkshire, here in Britain. I must warn you that my story is not for the faint of heart or those with a weak stomach. I will make your skin crawl and your blood curdle, and I swear to you it is all true. So long have I lived in secrecy, but a new era is dawning, I feel it, and the age of the undead is almost upon us. For it is their world to which I should belong. Most men are ignorant of our existence, yet exist we do. So then, now you are sitting comfortably, it began in my hometown at the beginning of September, in the year 2003. I was still at school then, and we must start with the last day of the summer holidays just before I was about to enter my final year at high school, preparing to take my GCSE (General Certificate of Secondary Education) exams at the end of the year.

Chapter One - My Entrance into Lycanthropy

The lights were still on red but the green man had just disappeared and they would change in a matter of minutes. I'd never had much patience, and I certainly wasn't going to wait for them to change again, so I sprinted across the road before the traffic started moving. A car had already been creeping forward, and just as I ran out the driver had decided to put his foot down. I couldn't stop in the middle of the road once I'd decided to go, so I kept my head down and sprinted onwards, feeling my glasses slide down my nose. The driver beeped his horn but didn't bother to slam on the brakes, and I barely made it across. I gave him the finger as he drove away in disgust.

I pushed my glasses back up my nose and walked away, calm despite the fact I could have been in the back of an ambulance by then, staring Death in the face. As I walked I entertained thoughts of the alternate realities theory, thinking if it were true I was probably long dead in at least a hundred alternate universes already. As a teenager I was somewhat reckless and I took stupid risks, and somewhere I was sure I'd paid the price. The thought didn't trouble me, mortal as I once was, since we were all headed for the grave eventually. I knew my time would come and it didn't matter to my younger self whether that was in hours or years.

Most of the girls at school were obsessed with eating healthy and their figure. I used to think, why bother? I saw no point in being so careful to avoid Death all your life when he would catch every one of us eventually. People talked of uncertain futures and being unsure of where they were going in life. As a human I knew where I was going. I knew where we were all going. I just didn't know how any of us were getting there or how long it would take. But regardless of how often I contemplated my mortality, I don't think I truly believed my life would end anytime soon. I didn't fear Death, and I didn't expect him to catch up with me for many years to come. I was still young and care free, and so very much alive. My dark thoughts turned to those more typical of a teenage boy as my feet automatically carried me towards home, which was just as well since I hadn't really been paying attention to the route I was taking.

Before I knew it I was walking down the drive to our house, and only then did I notice both cars were missing, meaning my parents were out. Dad was probably at the gym, but I had no idea where Mum could be. She wasn't shopping because she had just sent me out for a few supplies, and she wasn't working, since she worked in the same school my sister and I went to and it was still the summer holidays, albeit the last day. Not that her whereabouts really mattered. Having the house to myself for the afternoon was all that mattered to me back then, since it meant I could watch horror movies rated eighteen or play online games without being interrupted. Dad didn't like me watching horror films as it was; he thought they were 'morbid', and had once said they were 'poisoning my mind'. But I was fascinated with the horror genre and I wasn't going to miss out just because he couldn't understand it.

I felt in my pocket for the house keys and unlocked the door, trying to decide what to do with my hour or so of freedom as I dumped the bags in the kitchen. But I was soon disappointed to find I wasn't alone after all.

Amy, my younger sister, lay sprawled across the sofa watching TV with the back of her blonde head to me. I'd just assumed she'd be out with Mum when I'd seen the cars missing. She didn't bother to look round when I walked past, but she shouted out "Nick smells!"

At twelve years old she was a typical girly girl and the very definition of 'dumb blonde'. There was plenty of sibling rivalry between us which the raging hormones of puberty had taken to new heights, and we would often wind each other up. Sometimes it was on purpose, sometimes it was just from the tension of spending so much time under the same roof, but whether intentional or not we would argue often. Yet in spite of all her annoying qualities, she was still my little sister and I loved her, even if there were times when I felt like I wanted to throttle her.

I sighed and looked at the shopping. There was no way I could watch an eighteen DVD with Amy home, since she took great pleasure in grassing me up to our parents whenever she caught me doing something they'd forbidden. There were plenty of other films I could have watched but I decided my time would be better spent on the computer while it was free. However, fate wasn't on my side. Our internet connection had always been somewhat temperamental and it soon became clear that it wasn't going to connect.

Sulkily I ran upstairs, thinking I might watch one of my horrors rated twelve or fifteen after all, or maybe I'd have some time on the Playstation, but first I went into the bathroom for a quick pee. I looked up at the mirror over the sink while I washed my hands, wondering why nothing ever seemed to go my way. Green eyes tinged with brown stared back at me from behind my glasses. They were deep set, under brows that were fairly thick and slightly curved, somewhere halfway between straight and rounded. To my teenage self my lips felt a little too big for my liking, though not ridiculously so like some celebrities. But at least everything else was in proportion.

The overall effect meant that, relaxed, my face was quite serious looking, but more often than not it was grinning when I was out with my mates, or when things did go my way for a change. My face used to be round when I was younger but as puberty went on it was getting to be a little more angular, becoming the face of a young man rather than a boy. Puberty still had a long way to go, however. My beard hadn't started to come through yet and my voice was only just starting to drop.

I glanced back down at the sink to turn the tap off with my long, skinny fingers. I'd always been skinny despite the fact I had a good appetite. There was a little muscle on my arms and shoulders though it didn't look that impressive when I had such a skinny frame. I often wished I was better built, my bones thicker, and I could only hope they would change with puberty.

The muscle on my hairy legs was more impressive. They were skinny too but I had big calves, the legs of a runner. I might not have been one of the strongest guys in our year group at school but I was certainly one of the fastest.

We weren't a particularly tall family but I would have said I was about average height for a fifteen year old. I kept my dark hair short, mostly so I didn't have to do anything with it, or as short as school allowed. In a certain light it looked almost black, but it was actually a dark brown. Back then I thought black would look cooler and intended to start dyeing it eventually, though I hadn't tried any dye as yet.

Black was the preferred colour for my choice of wardrobe too. I generally only ever wore gothic t-shirts with snarling monsters, grim reapers or snakes preparing to strike, that sort of thing. I did have a few animal ones but the gothic shirts were my favourites. I also had a few band shirts that I loved. And I typically wore my black jeans everywhere, even in the height of summer. The only time I wore anything slightly different was when Dad insisted I change into something smarter, or at least less 'morbid'.

I ran my hand through that dark hair, still undecided what to do, but when Amy shouted out something else I headed back downstairs instead. Taunting her seemed like fun at that moment.

As I entered the lounge I could see she was watching one of the music channels, her greenish blue eyes glued to the screen. She had no taste in music as far as I was concerned, often subjecting me to modern pop, dance and hip hop. It was all rubbish to my ears. Much as I loathed the songs blaring out of the TV, I walked past the sofa and flicked her long hair, knowing she really hated that.

"Nick!" she shouted, and kicked out as hard as she could, catching me on the leg.

I laughed and stuck my tongue out at her.

"Just piss off, you're pathetic!"

"So where's Mum?" I asked.

"At the doctor's idiot, she told you God knows how many times before you went to town."

"Oh yeah," I said, then groaned and fell back onto the other sofa. "I'm bored!"

"Me too. Hey, get me the phone, I want to try something."

I looked at her suspiciously. "You get it."

She tried her little girl act, making a cute face designed to melt people's hearts. When that didn't work she gave me a look that said bring it or die.

I sighed and gave in, like I usually did when she asked me to do something. She never did anything for herself, seemingly of the opinion that boys were no more than slaves. The way Dad doted on his 'little princess' probably had something to do with that attitude. A pretty girl, she had Mum's looks and would no doubt grow into a beautiful woman some day. She already had all the boys chasing her in school, and I had no doubt she'd end up with a rich husband when she grew up, who would take over my role of running round after her.

She smirked as I brought her the phone and dialled the numbers one to ten.

"What are you doing?" I asked her.

"Just wondering what happens if I ring one, two, three, four, five, six, seven, eight, nine, ten," she replied.

The smirk vanished to be replaced by a look of horror. I thought I could hear a woman's voice on the other end of the phone but I wasn't sure. However, she soon started laughing again.

"What? What happened?"

"You try it."

I did. A recording of a woman's voice told me the time.

"What's so funny about that?"

Amy was in a fit of giggles then. I shrugged and looked at the phone, grinning as an idea struck me.

"Hey, I wonder what'll happen if I dial six, six, six! Think I'll get through to Hell or maybe the Devil himself?"

The laughter died in her throat. She gave me a look of disgust.

"That's the most pathetic thing you've ever said, geek."

12

I shrugged again and dialled the number, unsure of what to expect.

The phone clicked as it tried to connect but nothing else happened. It made a weird buzzing noise but when it became clear nothing more was going to happen I hung up. Amy rolled her eyes at me so I just laughed.

Later that day I sat in the back of the car, Mum and Amy in the front.

"How'd it go at the doctors, Mum?" I asked.

Her greenish brown eyes glanced back at me in the rear view mirror as, with a warm smile, she replied "Fine, thanks Nick. It was just a routine check up."

Mum was great. She could be strict when she needed to be, but most of the time she was pretty good about letting us do what we wanted. We shared a lot of the same interests and I'd always been much closer to her than I was to my Dad. She liked a lot of science fiction and fantasy, whether it be books, films or TV shows, and she did appreciate some horror as long as it wasn't too gory.

As previously mentioned Amy got her good looks from our Mum, including her blonde hair, but Mum wasn't a dizzy blonde like her daughter. She was an intelligent woman and could be very perceptive at times, which wasn't always a good thing if we were trying to hide something from her. She also had good fashion sense like many women, something else she shared with her daughter, but she didn't feel the need to spend a fortune on designer labels like some. Amy, on the other hand, had no sense when it came to money and had been known to spend birthday or Christmas money within days of receiving it.

Unlike Amy, Mum kept her hair a bit shorter, around shoulder length. She wore glasses for driving but they suited her, and she looked just as beautiful with them as she did without. In fact she looked good in almost anything she wore, whether it be jeans and a t-shirt or a dress.

Amy's McDonald's Happy Meal dominated my senses. Much as I hated McDonald's, I was so hungry I could have eaten anything. The smell of it snaked up my nose, and I watched hungrily as she ate, deliberately eating slow and savouring every mouthful just to wind me up, twisting round in her seat so I could see the fake look of ecstasy on her face. My stomach rumbled and I thought longingly of the meal waiting for me at Leisure X.

I'd arranged to meet up with Lizzy in town and we'd walk to Leisure X (a large complex complete with cinema, restaurants, pubs and an arcade, amongst other things) where we'd be meeting the others. Lizzy was one of my best mates. I'd known her since the first year of high school, when we met in a Science lesson and she'd invited me to sit next to her, since I was alone and she felt sorry for me. I wasn't the most popular guy in our year. I'd always been something of an outcast, alone in the playground at primary school, bullied by the rest of the class. Things hadn't improved much since I'd moved to high school, but at least I was no longer completely alone. Practically all of my friends were girls, but beggars can't be choosers. They could be annoying at times when they chose to discuss all the boring subjects girls like to talk about, but they could also be a good laugh.

I was so distracted by my hunger that I didn't notice when the car came to a stop.

"Come on Nick, are you going or not?" Mum said.

"Oh yeah, cheers," I mumbled, grabbing the jacket I'd slung on the backseat for later, then climbed out of the car.

Lizzy was waiting by a small shop on the main road, her long, bushy, light brown hair tied in a ponytail to keep it out of her blue eyes. She had a round, pretty face though she was quite slim, and despite her good looks I didn't see her in that way. We had always been like brother and sister and always would be.

"Don't be too late back," Mum called out as she drove off. I pretended not to hear and waved goodbye as I walked over to Lizzy and we started heading towards Leisure X, which was on the outskirts of the town.

We came to a stop at the side of the road, waiting to cross. There was a lot of traffic for the time of day. It was evening, well after the rush hour traffic.

"Bollocks to this, we ain't got all day," I muttered impatiently, and before Lizzy could stop me, I stepped out into the road.

I hadn't seen the car speeding towards me, but Lizzy had. She grabbed my arm and pulled me back onto the pavement before it was too late.

"Jesus, Nick! You're gonna get us both killed one of these days."

"We'll die someday anyway. Maybe I will end up splattered across somebody's windscreen, I don't care. Or maybe I'll be flattened on the road by a bus, squashed roadkill," I said, grinning.

"Yeah well, just don't get yourself killed while I'm around 'cause I'm not ready to die trying to save your sorry arse yet, okay?"

"Says she who keeps threatening to slit her wrists," I shot back.

"That's different," she replied.

"Yeah, it would be."

"Anyway, me and the others are taking bets on how you're gonna die. My bet's on a car hitting you, alcohol poisoning, or maybe you'll end up in a padded room if Death doesn't get you first."

I laughed at that. "Cheers, I guess there's hope for me yet. So what film are we seeing tonight?"

"I'm not bothered. There's only a couple of good films out at the moment. I'm easy either way, whichever one you guys go for."

It was a choice between two horror films; a werewolf one or some kind of a ghost story. My vote was for the werewolf one. Werewolves had always been my favourite horror movie monster.

"Oh, big news," Lizzy said excitedly. "This really hot guy just joined the bowling club."

Bowling had been one of Lizzy's biggest hobbies for as long as I'd known her. Both she and her brother were members, and regularly played in tournaments. I had a feeling her parents were on the team too and it was a real family thing, but I wasn't certain. I'm sure she told me at some point but I forget now.

"Yeah?" I said, trying to sound interested, though I really didn't want to get on the subject of her latest crush. She had her girlfriends for that sort of talk.

"Yep, and I plucked up the courage to ask him his name. Yay me!" she told me.

"And?" I enquired.

"He's called Ryan. He's eighteen though. What do you think, too old?" she asked.

"It's only three years, go for it." I said, before quickly changing the subject. "So, can you believe this right-wing Christian nut wants to put a ban on pretty much every horror movie out there? I guess a lot of them go against their beliefs and whatnot but come on, nobody's making them watch."

"First I've heard of it" Lizzy replied.

"Oh yeah, I just happened to overhear it when Mum and Dad had the news on t'other night. Some guy who's big on the whole Christianity thing. Said he didn't even believe in Halloween!"

"Personally, I've never really believed in God or the Bible."

"Nah, me neither. God never did owt for me when I needed Him. If He exists, He doesn't bother to listen. No, I believe in my own mortality and that's it."

"So stop taking risks with your life, you idiot," she said.

I didn't reply to that and we resumed the journey in silence.

We arrived at Leisure X to find the others waiting for us, six of us in total.

After arguing for a while, it was agreed that, as I had arranged for us all to come, I could pick the film. There was no debate in my mind: it had to be the werewolf one. Unfortunately, the only showing wasn't until ten o' clock that night and it was only seven. We all agreed it was time to get something to eat, then we could hit the arcades while we were waiting for the film. I'd make some excuse up for being home so late to tell my parents. It was hard enough to persuade them to let me walk home. There was a good chance they'd ground me for being out past midnight, especially as we had our first day of school the next day, but I was willing to risk that.

We ate in one of the restaurants, after waiting what seemed an eternity for the food to come. I wolfed down a steak and chips, then settled back while the others finished eating, my hunger finally satisfied.

In the arcades after our meal, I battled it out against David, the only real male best mate I had, on some fighting game. I had known him since primary school, and we had spent many afternoons locked in battle on the latest console games, both evenly matched. That day I was winning.

He swore furiously as I knocked his character to the ground and proceeded to beat him to a pulp while he was down, smashing the buttons in a desperate attempt to get back up and give as good as he was getting. A bead of sweat rolled down from under his light brown hair, which he wiped away before it could trickle into his blue eyes. His hair was trimmed short but not shaved as short as I kept mine back then. He was of a similar build to me and in a real fight we would probably have been fairly evenly matched too, though I think he was maybe a little stronger than me, while I was definitely the faster. He was probably fitter as well due to his love of football, something I'd never really got into. I did have a kick about with him from time to time but I had no real passion for any sports.

On the machine next to us, Fiona and Lizzy were on the dance mat. Lizzy would have been equally as happy on the fighting game with me, or shooting down enemies of some description, or racing, but Fiona's favourite was the dance mat. She wasn't really a gamer like the rest of us. Her long brown hair was bouncing up and down as she switched from arrow to arrow almost effortlessly, her brown eyes full of joy from behind her glasses as the game awarded her A grade after A grade, regardless of the song. She was another girl gifted with good

16

looks. I know you must be thinking how lucky my teenage self was to be surrounded by so many hot girls, but they really were all growing up to be beautiful young women.

Of the girls in the group, she was definitely the fittest, partly because she did gymnastics and dance. She had a nicely toned body and though she was white, she had quite dark skin as if she had a permanent tan. David had a major crush on her but unfortunately for him the feeling wasn't mutual. She loved him as a friend but her heart was currently owned by a guy who'd been in the year above us before he left school that summer, and she had eyes for no one else.

Fiona scored highest on most of the dances they did but Lizzy just managed to beat her on the odd song, with more exclamations of "Yay me!" each time. It had been her saying for as long as I'd known her. Fiona was a good sport, congratulating her for each victory without coming across as patronising.

The last two of our group, Ava and Becci, were shooting down zombies.

Ava was the scientist among us. She had always been a strange kid but then she came from a strange family. It was rumoured her mum slept in a coffin, though how true that was I didn't know. Both she and her mum were goths but they were also vegetarians, so I doubted they took the vampire thing too seriously. She had shoulder length hair dyed a dark red that summer but the colour often changed, as much as school would allow. However, unlike a lot of goths I knew, she wasn't particularly pale. She was a little chubby but not so overweight I would describe her as being fat and, though she wasn't stunningly beautiful, she certainly wasn't ugly.

Becci I always thought of as slightly insane, but then, so was I which meant we got on well. She was also obsessed with sex. Once she told us she'd had sex with her boyfriend in front of the webcam while both of them were pretending to be boys, just to turn on a gay guy she'd met in a chat room. And I believed it. It was the sort of thing she'd do. One of the craziest things I ever saw her do was during a PE lesson when the girls were playing rounders, while we boys played cricket. Ava was her best friend, but they had been put into different teams so Becci had crawled down the banking army style, stopping whenever the PE teacher looked her way, frozen there until she looked away again.

That might have been effective if she was camouflaged, but the PE uniform for both boys and girls was a maroon rugby shirt and blue shorts. And yet somehow she managed to crawl down the banking without being seen, even though logic should dictate it was a doomed mission from the start.

Once on the field where Ava's team were playing, she crept over to where her friend stood. The teacher caught her halfway there, and I couldn't hear what was said since we were on the furthest field from the school building, but Lizzy had filled me in. The teacher had asked Becci what she was doing out there, and stupidly Becci pointed to the banking where she had come from and said "I'm supposed to be up there Miss."

Our game of cricket had been all but forgotten whilst we watched that particular crazy episode.

Like Ava, Becci was also something of a goth, though she was much slimmer than her best mate and she wasn't a vegetarian. It wouldn't surprise me if she did try vampirism but she hadn't as far as I knew. She certainly had the pale skin for it.

She too had a habit of dyeing her shoulder length hair on a regular basis but she'd kept it black for some time that year, and she also had quite a plain face.

The arcade kept us busy until it was time for the film. We bought tickets and popcorn before going in, heading straight for the back row. I ended up between Lizzy and Fiona. David had made sure he was sat on the other side of Fiona so he could comfort her, not that she needed it. I felt a bit sorry for him. I'd never seen him that way with a girl before and it seemed like some cruel twist of fate that the one girl he had really fallen for was already in love with someone else. That was exactly why I'd never had an interest in relationships as a teenager, feeling sex was all I wanted.

We threw popcorn at each other, laughing and talking about school, what we'd done during the holidays, and in Becci's case, sex, sex and more sex. When the film started a bald man in front turned round and glared at us. We grew quiet after that, mainly because of the muscles rippling beneath his shirt. Apart from him, the cinema was all but deserted.

The film itself was great. It was well written with a decent plot, and what my younger self would have described as awesome visual effects. But what really made it for me were the werewolves. They were half men, half wolf creatures, resembling everything I thought a werewolf should be and more, not like the kind of werewolves that barely changed, which I always said looked more like wereapes. Any werewolves that were little more than hairy men with a slightly bestial face were a disappointment, and if they didn't meet my expectations it often ruined what would otherwise have been a good werewolf movie for me. But that movie had everything I wanted to see, including some great blood and gore effects. It was one of those rare horror films that I found so good it filled me with an excitement, almost sexual in its intensity. I felt so alive in the cinema that night.

The others were enjoying the film on some lesser, more normal level. Had we known what was soon to come, we may have been screaming like the characters in the film, but even if a psychic had told us our future, we wouldn't have believed it. My life as a care-free, mostly average teenager was about to come to a brutal end. How I long to go back and change the path fate was about to set me on, but of course these are only memories, and no matter how completely I might lose myself in the telling of them to you, I am powerless to change my own past.

We emerged from the cinema to find the world in shadow, the sun having long since set as we whiled away the hours in Leisure X. It was a mild, dark night and a full moon hung overhead like a dead eye, the only light save for a few street lamps. I remember it well. There was a cool breeze, so I put on my jacket as I stared up at the night sky. That feeling the film had filled me with intensified and I felt more alive than ever, gazing up at the glowing white orb. Clouds suspended it like the muscles of some great face as it held me transfixed in its blind, milky gaze. I was dimly aware of one of the others talking but I was so caught in the moon's spell that I wasn't following the conversation, until one of them placed a hand on my shoulder.

"What?" I asked distractedly. The clouds began to drift across the moon until it was hidden behind a wispy eyelid, throwing the world further into darkness and breaking the spell. The moon had never affected me so before. I'd always felt drawn to it, but never to that extent. I put it down to the after effects of the film, and the time of night itself. I always felt more awake in the late hours of the night, regardless of what phase the moon had reached in its cycle.

"Hey, are you okay man?" David asked.

My friends were looking at me worriedly.

"Yeah I'm fine, just thinking I guess," I shrugged. "So a full moon, huh? Scary after seeing the film, don't you think? Coincidence or what? That werewolf could be waiting for us just round the corner. If we're lucky it'll kill us before it rips us apart, or if we're even luckier it might turn us!"

"Give it a rest Nick," Ava replied, ever the scientist. "Werewolves exist only in film. The only thing we have to fear is lunatics who think they are wolves, and as you used to do taekwondo there isn't much harm they could do."

Despite the strangeness surrounding her family, she was in the top class for nearly every subject and she did have a real passion for science. As we neared adulthood and were encouraged to think on what career paths we wanted to follow, she had decided she wanted to be an astronomer – space had always fascinated her.

"Why would anyone want that?" Fiona asked with a shudder. "Why would you want to turn into a man eating monster?"

Why? Good question. I never really knew why. It was the actual ability to gain the more powerful wolf form I wanted, to become a wolf or at least a wolf man creature, not the death that always came with it in the films. With that power I could deal with the bullies that had taunted me for so long for a start. But why a werewolf specifically, and not some other supernatural creature, or a comic book hero like most guys, I had no idea. To Fiona, I just shrugged. "We all have our dreams."

"Come on, before he starts howling," David said.

"I feel like howling right now. Weren't the werewolves great? Not like all these crap hairy men with fangs that some directors are so fond of," I commented enthusiastically as we set off back into town. "I mean, they could make them more wolf-like! The ones in this film were perfect."

"Nick, werewolves are a myth or a legend, call them what you will, but the fact is, they aren't real and so no one knows what they look like. You could be called a werewolf," argued Ava.

"I wish," I muttered. "Legend has it that they are humans who turn into wolves, so in the films they should use real wolves! Or at least make them look wolfish, like we just saw."

"It is hard to get real wolves to act like humans though," Lizzy commented.

"Ah, but that's the point. Legend also has it that their minds become wolfish as well as their bodies so they act like wolves! All they've gotta do is film a wolf hunting but use a computer or something to make it look like they're hunting humans," I argued back. "That's why in many werewolf stories, the werewolf wakes up the next day with no memory of what happened the previous night, because they weren't in control."

"Whatever," said Ava, unconvinced.

The conversation turned once again to Becci's favourite subject, namely: sex.

Somehow the subject of whether I was a virgin or not came up. Becci didn't believe I'd done it.

"You've never even had a girlfriend!" she said, her shoulder length black hair falling in curtains around her pale face.

"So? That doesn't make me a virgin," I replied.

"Yeah Becci, you should know him well enough by now. He doesn't do relationships! Heartless, aren't you mate? You wouldn't know love if it punched you in the face," David said.

"Aye," I agreed with a grin, taking it as a compliment. I dreamt of being famous one day, for what I didn't know, but it would be something to do with horror, so that's how I wanted the public to see me: heartless and sick, with a twisted sense of humour. I didn't know what I'd be famous for, but I already had ideas about my image. Sometimes, if I was feeling really bigheaded, I would fantasise I could change the world, though for better or worse I didn't know. "It's true, I never felt nothing for no one, not in that way. Besides, why bother with a relationship? Do or say whatever it takes to get 'em into bed and move onto the next one."

The others laughed, though Fiona and Lizzy, and possibly David too in light of his feelings for Fiona, didn't agree with me.

As we walked, I kept darting behind the girls trying to make them jump. It didn't work but I tried anyway until Lizzy said "Will you quit fooling?"

I stuck my tongue out playfully and laughed. Then I looked ahead at the road we were walking down and wondered if the myths about werewolves were really true. After watching the film, I wanted more than ever to believe they were and that I would someday be one, young fool that I was.

The eerie feeling that someone or something was behind us cut through my thoughts. I froze and turned around. There was nothing there. I turned back to my friends who had stopped and were looking at me questioningly. I told them to look around. Nothing. Not surprisingly, they thought I was making it up and rolled their eyes. They carried on walking. I followed, uneasily.

Suddenly, a man appeared at the side of the road, out of nowhere. The cloudy eyelids above parted to reveal a slither of the pale orb they'd shut out. A beam of moonlight fell on the stranger, revealing a little more of his dark form. He had black hair and he was wearing a leather jacket, black t-shirt and blue jeans. He had his head down and he was groaning in agony. He ran past us and Fiona asked "Hey, shouldn't we see if we can help?"

I shook my head.

"Some things are best left alone," I said simply, trusting my instincts on that one, and the others agreed. Fiona shrugged and after that we thought nothing of it, thinking he probably had really bad stomach ache or something, and so we carried on walking.

Just minutes later, after crossing the road and rounding the corner onto a new street, we came to a standstill again, this time because there was something waiting in the darkness at the end of the road, stood just out of the light of the street lamps. We couldn't make out what it was as it was stood in shadow, but we could see its two eyes and it was almost as if we'd frozen in place from their icy glare. They were cold and merciless, the eyes of a killer, a predator, though not necessarily evil. They told enough about the creature to know that we were in trouble. I gaped at them. They told me something else about the creature, something my friends wouldn't know. But the only thought running through my brain after learning this information was that it couldn't be. Not here. Not in England. And yet it was.

The night's great eye had completely opened once more and the street was bathed in moonlight, making the creature's eyes glow menacingly. Now surrounded by moonlight rather than shadow, it revealed the identity of the beast, the identity which I had already guessed at from the colour and shape of its eyes.

A wolf stood there at the end of the road, blocking our path. From its size I guessed it was a grey wolf, or a timber wolf if you'd prefer. Canis Lupis. This particular specimen was black rather than grey and it was quite large for its species, though not unnaturally so. I assumed it was male since it was so big and muscular.

"Erm Nick, what do we do?" Fiona asked me nervously. I stared blankly at her for a moment, my brain still reeling at the wolf's very presence. I had known they were wolf's eyes because of all the books I had read on wolves and all the pictures I'd seen. I had seen many wolves in the zoo but knew none were left in the wild in Britain, the last one having been shot some centuries ago. Which was why I was so shocked to find myself face to face with one in the town centre, of all places. Of course they were looking to me for what to do, since I was supposed to be the expert on wolves. I recovered enough from the initial shock to weigh up our options.

"Come on mate, do we run or what?" David asked.

"No!" I replied, snapping out of it. "No, if we run he's only gonna give chase. Erm, maybe back away slowly."

"Maybe?" David snorted. "That's the best you've got?"

I glared at him and he fell silent. We began backing away as I had suggested, keeping our eyes fixed on the wolf, waiting to see what he would do.

At first I thought it was working as the wolf never moved, but just as we were about to turn back round the corner he charged us.

"Oh shit, run!" I yelled.

The others didn't need telling twice. We broke into a sprint, desperate to escape the predator that had decided we were prey. And yet no ordinary wolf would attack a human. I had to assume he was either rabid or weakened in some way that meant he couldn't hunt his natural prey. Weakened enough that he had been forced to turn to a much slower animal, one that made for an easier kill. I hoped for the latter explanation. If he was rabid one bite would kill us, not to mention he would easily run us down. If he had been weakened we might stand a chance of escaping.

As the fastest of the group, I easily pulled ahead of my mates, pushing my body to its limits. Ava was the slowest but it was Becci who was stupid enough to turn round, wanting to know if the wolf was closing in. She didn't see the lamp post until it was too late and she crashed into it, winded as she slid to the ground.

Realising what had happened, I swore loudly and turned back the way we'd come. I had no idea what I was going to do when I got to her but I had to do something. I couldn't just leave her there for the wolf to feed on. Wordlessly, Lizzy came with me. The others never even slowed down.

I ran as fast as I could but I knew I was never going to make it back to her in time. The wolf was just too fast, he would be on her in minutes. Becci had been dazed from the collision with the lamp post but she had recovered enough to realise what was happening. She watched as the wolf drew level with her, screaming in terror. Yet the wolf kept on going. He was coming for me!

"Bollocks!" I screamed; a really heartfelt curse. I might have been willing to risk my life crossing the road, thinking I didn't fear death. But when it came right down to it I was terrified. In that instant I didn't want to die, not yet.

As soon as the wolf was past her, Becci managed to pull herself up and run in the opposite direction, leaving me to my fate. But Lizzy wouldn't leave me.

She desperately cast around for something to defend ourselves with. There wasn't much on the ground, just a few small stones. She grabbed one and threw it at the wolf as hard as she could. The beast barely even flinched and he never once wavered from his chosen target. And then he was upon me.

I threw out an arm to protect myself, for all the good it would do. The wolf grabbed hold but his teeth didn't sink as deep as I expected. It was almost like he was being careful with me. His fangs ripped through the sleeve of my jacket but they barely raked the skin underneath, leaving only a slight scratch. I fought free of the jacket and let him have it, hoping it'd distract him long enough for me to escape. It hung limply in his jaws like the carcass of some small animal, until he dropped it and advanced forward again.

The beast leapt on me, knocking me to the concrete and sending pain flooding through my body. Something in my chest throbbed. I brought my arms up again in an attempt to keep his jaws away from my throat, or I knew it would all be over. My hands tried to grasp hold of something. His fangs sliced through the now exposed flesh which stung with the pain, and blood ran down, quickly weakening me. I strained against him with everything I had but it wasn't enough. His jaws were drawing closer and closer to my throat until his fangs pierced my flesh, even with my hands being sort of in the way. I let go and tried hitting him for all the good it did. He didn't even seem to feel it.

"Run Lizzy, there's nothing you can do!" I managed to shout through the pain and the terror. I guess it's true what they say, you find out who your real friends are in these situations. She was the only one who'd stayed to try and save me. But it was too late then; there was nothing she could do. There was no sense for both of us to die.

When I first felt the wolf's fangs slide in I thought I would die. The fear was soon gone and only the pain remained. No matter what awaited me on my final journey, be it some form of afterlife, reincarnation or oblivion, I was no longer afraid. I closed my eyes and waited for death to come. But death did not come. The pain intensified but I felt the fangs slide out again as the wolf rose off of me with a yelp.

Lizzy, God bless her, had not run after all. She had given the street a proper search for something, anything, that she could use as a weapon. And she'd found half a beer bottle.

The wolf twisted round, trying to get at the wound in his shoulder where she'd plunged the glass deep inside until it had hit the bone and could go no further. He couldn't reach it and turned back to us, growling angrily. With a slight limp he charged again, this time at Lizzy, but something spooked him and he veered off course, now unmistakably fleeing. We didn't know what had scared him but we weren't going to stick around and find out.

Lizzy helped me to my feet but I couldn't stand unsupported at first so she let me lean on her. I felt bruised and battered from being knocked to the ground, and the blood loss was making me dizzy. My chest felt like it was on fire and I wondered if the wolf had managed to crack a rib.

"Come on Nick, we have to get you to a hospital," she said, helping me walk.

"No hospitals," I gasped through the pain.

"Nick, you're covered in blood! You need a hospital," she told me. "Those wounds might need stitching."

"Not my blood," I lied. "Most of it's wolf after you stabbed him."

"Come on or you're going to die and I'll lose my bet," she joked. "I never thought it'd be death by wolf."

I started to laugh but it hurt too much. "Just get me home."

"I still think you need to get those wounds checked out."

"No hospitals!" I snarled through the pain. "Please."

I could tell she wanted to argue but my house was nearer than the hospital and we currently had no signal on our phones to call an ambulance, though she checked several times. She didn't want to leave me there in case there were any other wolves on the loose, so she had no choice. She probably planned to come in with me and ring an ambulance as soon as we got through the door but I was adamant I wasn't going. It was stupid and childish, but I knew a hospital would lead to too many awkward questions, and my parents would probably never let me leave the house again if they knew there was a predator out on the streets. How I would hide the extent of my injuries I had no idea, but I thought I could hide more of the night's events from my parents than I could from the hospital staff.

"I suppose you're going to tell me we can't go to the police either?" she asked after a few minutes.

"That's right," I answered.

"They need to know there's a dangerous wild animal on the loose," she said.

"Well leave an anonymous tip if you must but with that wound you dealt him, I don't think he's gonna survive for long," I told her. "Unless a vet were to remove that glass it's not coming out and more than likely it'll get infected, trust me."

After a while the pain became bearable and as strange as it seemed a little of my strength was returning. I told Lizzy I could manage to walk the rest of the way unaided. That seemed to satisfy her that I didn't need a hospital after all.

We reached the point where we would need to part ways if Lizzy was going to go straight home. She still wanted to make sure I got home safe but I was insistent I'd be fine and she should take care of herself. I was only five minutes from my house so she let me go, but I knew she didn't really want to. Before she went I asked her to make sure the others didn't tell anyone about the wolf attack.

"Those four ought to be too ashamed of themselves to talk to anyone about what happened," she said, but assured me she would as she turned away towards her house.

I walked up past the school, trying not to think about the fact that I'd be trapped within its walls just hours later. Then I passed the playing field on the opposite side of the road, not much further down the street, where dog owners frequented with their furry friends, and football matches often took place. The field was bordered by hedges and on the side nearest my house there were trees and some other kind of vegetation all kept safe behind a spiky metal fence.

It was somewhere within that vegetation those same predatory eyes we'd encountered just a half hour ago were watching me. When I first saw them I think my heart stopped. Despite what I'd told Lizzy about the wolf's wounds, he'd come back to finish me off. And though I'd regained enough strength to walk unsupported I was far from strong enough to run. I was doomed and I knew it.

I struggled down to a kneeling position and prayed I would find something to defend myself with as Lizzy had done. But the only things cast aside on the pavement that time were empty crisp packets and chocolate bar wrappers, nothing of any help whatsoever. As I searched the wolf leapt for me a second time, but there was another yelp similar to when Lizzy first wounded him. A dark fluid which could only be blood was running down the fence. Lucky for me he must have impaled himself on the spikes. Maybe because of the wound he'd not been able to clear the fence properly.

I stood and looked around at the wolf I expected to see, but it was not a wolf's limp form on the metal railing the animal had launched himself over and had indeed impaled himself on – it was a man's! The man hung limp over the fence, silhouetted against the moonlight, blood gushing from his wounds, staining the railing red. The perilously sharp spikes had pierced his chest about where his heart would be. I looked closer and realised it was the man who'd passed us earlier that night, although he was naked now. Was I becoming delirious with blood loss? I decided it was time I got myself home quick before I grew too weak again and the night got any weirder. With a slight shiver at the sight of him I finally staggered away, puzzled at what had happened, because after all, as much as I wanted to believe werewolves were real, I knew they were not. Though I was sure it had been the wolf lying in wait for me on the other side of that fence, not a man, and yet there he was… I was unable to think properly, feeling dizzy again from the blood I was still losing through the wounds which seemed to be very deep.

Somehow I managed to stagger the rest of the way home. I was in agony again as I walked, mostly from the pain in my neck which was far worse than anything I'd ever experienced before, and soon the mystery was forgotten. I let myself in and struggled up the ladder onto my bunk bed, muttering into the darkness before sleep took me and grinning to myself at the thought of it.

"I guess I did reach the Devil after all."

Chapter Two - I was a Teenage Werewolf

The next day I spent in bed lost in nightmares, oblivious to Mum and Dad's concern when they saw the blood stained sheets and pillowcase; and their panic when they could not wake me; and their puzzlement as to where the blood came from, for I did not look to be wounded.

Dusk came and I awoke. I staggered downstairs, still dressed in the clothes from the previous day, just as my parents were discussing whether to make an emergency appointment at the doctors, but they were too relieved I'd finally come round to ever make the call. They were so busy worrying and fussing over me that there was never any lecture about being home late. Mum made me supper but I could feel bile rising in my throat at the mere thought of eating, so I returned to my room, intending to go back to bed.

I vaguely remembered the night before but I thought it had been a nightmare as the wounds had gone. There were no cuts on my arms and there was no longer any pain in my chest. My body didn't feel bruised at all and there didn't seem to be any puncture wounds in my neck. The blood on my clothes, sheets and my skin was the only evidence I was aware of that it had been real, but still the impossibility of it all made me think the blood must have been from no more than a bad nose bleed.

Something drew me towards the window upon reaching my room. There I saw the full moon for the first time that evening, the last full moon of that month. I knew I should go back to bed, the bile threatening to rise up at any minute; I could feel it churning inside and imagined it bubbling inside its pit, frothing up like a green raging river. I could almost sense the vile taste in my mouth. But I couldn't pull myself away. I started pacing from side to side like a caged animal, and this soon turned to a stalk. I vaguely wondered what was happening to me. The moon seemed to be having an even greater effect on me than the night before. Could it be my dreams were finally answered?

What happened after that is hard to remember, but I will try and describe it to you as best I can, based on other experiences. It was like the one time I had been drunk at a friend's house. I wasn't really aware of what was happening, or if it was real or not. Only the present existed; I couldn't even remember what had happened seconds ago. The pain. I remember the pain. It was the only thing I was really truly aware of. It came suddenly, a great wave of it, drowning me in its great angry sea. I think I may have been screaming, but it might have been too intense even for that. If I was making any sound it must have been drowned out by Amy's music, which she often had on in her bedroom full blast. That night was no different, despite the fact she knew I was unwell. As it was, no one came to check on me, thank God.

I also remember feeling hot, as though I had a fever. I opened the window, hoping the breeze would cool me down, but no sooner had I done that than the next wave of pain washed over me and sent me crashing back into its angry waters, making me bend over in agony, clutching my stomach where it was worst. That's probably when I noticed my hands. My nails were lengthening and becoming sharper, like claws. Fur was sprouting on them and my whole body itched as the fur spread. My pet snake was watching me from his tank as my weak, pathetic human teeth became deadly, razor sharp fangs and, as I looked at my reflection in the window, I saw my eyes turn amber like a wolf's, noticing my eyesight improve as a result. My ears became pointed and moved up to the side of my head and my nose became black as my snout grew outwards, my hearing and sense of smell improving drastically when this happened. The snout caused my glasses to fall off, where they lay at my feet.

My clothes tore off as muscles bulged, shifting around underneath my skin. The structure of my legs completely altered, causing me to fall onto all fours, and my spine extended as a tail grew, while other bones painfully changed size and shape. I was vaguely aware of a crack and I realised I was stood on my glasses. My hands and feet had already hardened in becoming paws and I could barely feel them there, beneath my pads. The transformation complete, I felt the predatory mind of a wolf within which became stronger under the influence of the full moon. The wolf mind pushed the human one aside and took over my body. Before the human part of me was buried deep inside the wolf, only to return at sunrise, I sensed the cold intelligence rising up beside my own, and was surprised to find more than instincts there. And then the human part of me was all but gone and only the wolf remained.

I had not eaten all day and I was ravenous. Sniffing the air, I determined there was no food around in that room, and I felt uneasy at being trapped in there. So I bunched my powerful muscles and leapt through the open window, just managing to catch a back leg on the sill and knock several ornaments off, though none of them smashed. I landed on the grass in the back garden and pricked my ears for sounds of prey, sniffing the air once again. I growled irritably, finding no scents of interest – or at least none that were fresh. There were only old scents left by animals, humans, and fumes from their great, roaring machines that constantly chased each other through the day. I started to walk down the street, enslaved by my own hunger, the need for food greater than any other.

Padding along the pavement, a fresh scent carried to me on the breeze, accompanied by the sound of human footsteps. A woman walked by on the other side of the road and glanced at me, but mistaking me for a large stray dog she carried on. She was in her fifties and her breathing was quick and uneven, almost a pant. Obviously unfit, and very much overweight, her clothes stretched tight around the bulge of her belly, she would be an easy meal. Any human would tire much quicker than a wolf but I wouldn't have to waste much energy on this hunt.

I advanced across the road, lips curling back in a snarl, fangs bared. She looked back upon hearing that bestial warning and froze, realising something was amiss. Recognition of my true wild nature seemed to hit her, for she screamed and ran down an alley. I pursued, fast enough not to lose her yet not fast enough to bring her down immediately. It was the thrill of the chase that made the kill more satisfactory.

The sweet smell of her fear and the sound of her hammering heart spurred me onwards. I was playing with her, letting her think she had escaped certain death, only to discover me ahead or to the side, or just behind. I could have kept that up all night if I wanted to but she was tiring already and the hunger had grown unbearable, so I pounced on her, knocking her to the ground. As I stood over her, I heard something and turned, trying to determine if it was a threat. She took the opportunity to lash out while I was distracted. The blow didn't hurt me but it caused me to turn back to her, growling.

There was a strange scent on the air, but it did not matter to me then. I was intent on my prey and, as I sunk my fangs into the soft flesh of her neck and ripped out her throat, blood spewing out onto the pavement and spattering my body, the bloodlust took me, making me oblivious to the world around. The life in her faded, her heart and body stilled, and she died. I howled in triumph and then savaged her body, tearing through her clothes and skin and feasting upon the soft, sweet flesh beneath. I grabbed a piece of flesh in my jaws and pulled until tendons snapped and it came away from the bone, still warm in my mouth, the blood making it slippery. I swallowed and it slid down my throat and into my stomach, slithering down into the dark pit to be bathed in acid.

After I had stripped the limb of its flesh, I bit into the side of the stomach, nuzzling into it with my snout in search of offal, richer in blood and providing more sustenance. It didn't take me long to find my prize, and I surfaced from the deep, dark hole I had made with a kidney between my teeth, gulping it down greedily, blood splashing the concrete, leaking down the side of my mouth and staining my fur red. The intestines came out next, as they were blocking the way to everything else. I pulled, and slowly they slid from the hole like a slimy, giant, grey worm. Passers by might have seen them dangling from my mouth and mistaken them for a string of sausages in the jaws of a stray dog.

Once I had laid them to rest alongside the kidney, the way was clear to more of the organs and I had soon eaten my way up to the heart. Blood squeezed out of it and along the veins in a mockery of life as my jaws clamped down on the dead muscle. More blood was forced out as I pulled and sought to rip it from the tubes chaining it inside its bony prison, the ribcage. Finally it came free in a shower of blood, staining the concrete red and splattering my body, the crimson spots almost lost in the darker parts of my coat.

Once I had picked the corpse clean, I dragged it into the nearest garden and buried it deep down in the earth where nothing else would find it. I knew little of the human world, my knowledge limited to the little I had glimpsed within the human's mind during my awakening, but I knew enough to know that if dead bodies started turning up, the hunter would become the hunted, and I would be prey to the angry mobs who would not rest until they had spilled my blood. That done, I decided to explore my territory and look for my pack. I would belong to the same pack as the werewolf who had bitten me, my blood brothers, and their blood called to me, stronger than the call of the moon, almost as strong as the hunger that had driven me moments before.

I sent up another howl into the night to inform my pack of my whereabouts, and stood listening for their rallying howl, calling for me to return to them. But only silence greeted my ears. That puzzled me. Why were they not replying? Had they left this territory for a better one? But that made no sense, for they would not leave without me. They would howl for me and wait for my reply for at least three nights to determine whether I was lost and returning, or whether I had left to join another pack, or even start one of my own. And yet I had found no sign of them so far that night and I had heard nothing. Had they, then, been killed? Or forced to flee from death? But even stranger was that there were no howls from rival packs, defending their own territory. I was uncertain what to do and howled again to tell them I was here and that I was ready to take up my place in the pack's hierarchy and help them with day to day pack life, such as the hunt, raising pups, and defending the territory. Still the night was silent so I decided to move on and try to find their scent, or any other hint of where they might be. While doing so I could also familiarise myself with the territory.

I had not gone far when a dog barked at me. I caught its scent and knew it to be a male Yorkshire Terrier. It was also clearly someone's pet, as it was in a kennel with a chain that stretched just far enough for it to come to the end of the drive where I stood. As far as he was concerned, this was his territory and I was in it. He was barking a warning for me to go away. My keen senses detected no movement within the house belonging to his human masters. They were either asleep or out somewhere. I had no love for dogs, despite the fact we had originated from the same lupine ancestors. They had allowed themselves to be enslaved by humanity, and I had only contempt for them. The day a human tried to tame me was the day to give up on life, for I would not allow myself to become a slave, not to anyone, but especially not to humans. They were so arrogant, thinking they owned the world. If I could only find my pack, we could remind humanity they didn't rule the Earth as they liked to think. They'd even tried to conquer nature. I wanted to remind them they are not gods, they are mortals like the rest of us, whether we walk on four legs or two, and I was going to start with that dog. So I lunged without giving him any warning, my jaws, flecked with blood and spit, opened wide, revealing the deadly fangs within, already bloody from the previous kill. I must have been a fearsome sight, for the dog's growls became whines and he tried to cower back in submission before I attacked, but even if I had intended to spare him, it was too late – I was already in mid-leap.

The lunge was so powerful that we smashed into the small kennel, which splintered from the impact. I closed my jaws round his neck and picked him up, shaking him from side to side like a dog with a rabbit. I heard his spine snap and he went limp but still I shook him, in the grip of the bloodlust, his blood gushing into my mouth and spraying the surrounding broken wooden planks.

When I finally dropped him to the ground, he was not completely paralysed despite the broken back. Still able to move his front legs, he scrabbled at the ruined wood, trying to get away. I gave a low, threatening growl as the bloodlust took me once more and lunged again, ripping open his belly and spewing his guts all over the floor, making his upper body writhe in pain. Despite the fact I had already made a kill, my hunger was not yet satiated, and I would not wait for him to die. I started with the stomach, which lay at my feet, gripping it in my jaws and swallowing it down eagerly, even though it was still attached to the dog. The tubes attaching it soon ripped as they caught on my teeth. I ate the other organs that had spilled out: the kidneys, the liver, the spleen, the intestines, the pancreas. The dog was in its death throes when I started stripping the bones of their flesh, what little of it there was on the small, skinny frame, and it died soon after I had devoured the left leg. The right leg I ripped right out of its socket and chewed at until it was all but gone. Strange noises in the night were enough to persuade me to leave my meal. There was little left anyway, and there was still time to hunt yet.

I emerged from the wreckage and slunk away into the night, ignoring the urge to howl and mark the place with my scent. I didn't bother to hide the remains of the dog as I had with the human, for I knew a dead pet would attract less attention. And I was more concerned with the possibility of an immediate threat.

When I was far enough from the kennel to feel safer again, having not heard, seen nor smelt anything else unusual that could possibly pose a threat, I continued to explore my territory, pausing every now and then to howl for my pack. The night was almost spent when finally I received a reply. But I did not recognise the howl as one of my pack members, who I would instinctively know by scent and sound, even though we had never met before – the werewolf who had awoken me had passed that vital knowledge on, though I knew not how. Cocking my ears in that direction I determined it was a lone wolf, female, containing all the confidence that went with a high rank; an alpha I decided, but fairly young, at least physically. Her voice did not betray her mental age, which could be centuries for one of our kind. The howl was brief and soon ended, and filled with excitement I howled again, straining my ears in desperation for a reply. My pack seemed to have deserted me but this was a chance to start a pack of my own, and gain the security a pack brings. The howl came again, brief as before and from a distance. I could tell that the wolf had moved from her last position so that rival packs could not easily find her, but I had some idea of where she was, and as I replied with another howl after that to tell her of my interest and my intentions, I knew we would meet whilst still hiding from rival packs. She replied again, having moved slightly closer, and I pinpointed her current position and set off in that direction at a run.

However, I soon came to a stop, feeling that I was being watched. My hackles rose in alarm and once again my lips curled back in a warning snarl. Yet my sharp hearing caught no sounds of movement, my night vision finding nothing, my acute sense of smell picking up no dangerous scents... But I knew whoever or whatever it was could be downwind of me. I decided to take the risk that time, so intent as I was on finding the alpha female. Trying to shake off the feeling, I slunk into the field of the nearby primary school, knowing that if I was being followed I could crawl into the neighbour's gardens where a human could not follow me, assuming it was human. If it was anything else I could deal with it; only humans posed a threat to me for they came with their guns and hunting dogs and brought the death which only humans bring. Their dogs I could handle, but their guns I could never defeat. Little did I know there was someone in the field with me.

I padded over the grass, towards the hill at the other end where there was a fence I could easily jump over and a ring of bushes which I could slink through, my thick fur coat protecting me from thorns. But upon reaching the middle of the field shapes materialised from the shadows and I suddenly found myself surrounded by people with guns who were creeping towards me from the edges of the school grounds. How I had not detected them before I did not know. I saw the glint of silver from their belts, most likely a selection of silver knives, and instinctively knew that the silver was meant for me. They must have been following me most of the night and I guessed they knew I was more than just a wolf, though I hoped they didn't know who I was, otherwise my life was over.

I glanced around for an escape route but found none, so, growling, I turned on one as if to attack him and started forward, but as he readied himself to shoot me I suddenly turned and ran in the opposite direction, moving faster than they'd anticipated and so making it past them, knocking one over in the process. This bought me some time and I ran flat out towards the hill. And, though they shot at me before I got there, dirt spraying up around me from the bullets, I did reach the safety of the hill without being hit. I kept on running, afraid then and only dimly aware of where I was going; over the fence into someone's garden, under a hedge and *back onto the street, over the road, narrowly avoiding one of the human's rushing machines, hearing the sounds of pursuit, doubling back to try and confuse them...*

I heard a noise and turned my head to see where it had come from while still running, lest it was the hunters, whoever they were, and that's when I bumped into the young woman. She was obviously annoyed because she picked me up and threw me, sending me flailing through the air until I hit a wall. I slumped to the ground, stunned slightly, and lay there panting. She killed the people hunting me effortlessly, her movements too fast for me to follow, but when she'd finished they lay in a heap, some with broken necks, others with gaping wounds in their chest or stomach, blood seeping out onto the ground. The girl glanced at me, then she turned her back and walked away.

Chapter Three - New Friend in all the Madness

There was a graveyard not too far from the school field, which was where the woman was headed. After recognising her for what she was, I picked myself up from the ground and followed, head down in submission, feeling I owed her for saving my life and that she was my leader then. I was still adamant I would not be anyone's slave, but at least her kind were worthy of being called alpha and forming an alliance with.

While I walked behind her, I remembered the lone wolf I had been searching for and paused, trying to decide where my loyalties lay. I decided to at least howl to her again and see if she replied. I called for her, but when I paused to listen for a reply I was surprised to find the woman had stopped. She approached me with all the confidence of an alpha female and she was growling. I lowered my body in submission, showing her the respect her position deserved. She stood before me, still growling in displeasure.

"Idiot!" she snarled in the wolven tongue, known to all canines. "Those who hunted you found you because of your howling. It was me who returned your howls in the hope you would find me before they found you, but I hoped in vain. You were lucky to escape with your life tonight."

Understanding dawned and I growled an apology. Things were beginning to make sense. The reason I had found not even a hint of my pack was that they had all been wiped out by the same group of humans who had tracked me to the field. The one who bit me must have been the only survivor, attempting to strengthen his pack in numbers again before they died out. I was disappointed to learn none of my kind were in the area, but grateful to my leader for coming to my aid. She watched as I began to put the pieces together and then started walking again, satisfied I would be more careful from then on.

Upon reaching the graveyard she lay down on a grave to rest. Still angry at her for throwing me, and wanting to test my superior as all lower ranking wolves will do, I was about to attack her again while she was off-guard, though I knew I could never beat her in a fair fight.

I crouched down like a coiled spring, ready to pounce. I didn't get much further before the fur on my head was yanked upwards and I was suddenly eye to eye with the woman.

"Try that again and you'll be cat meat!" she hissed.

Growling, I looked up at the sky. It was becoming lighter as dawn approached and I could feel the human growing stronger again. It would not be long before I changed back.

The woman followed my gaze and made a run for shelter in the mausoleum. I turned to go in with her but at that point the transformation took hold.

I froze while it took place, and grunted as the pain washed over me once more.

As the fur shrank back into my skin the itching returned. I watched as my paws elongated to become fingers while my pads disappeared, and the claws became blunt and shortened to form fingernails once again. The bones in my hand were shortening, my dew claws sliding back down as a result and forming opposable thumbs. I was forced to transfer my weight to the flat of each hand, the digits now too delicate to support it, and the bones no longer able to bend in the same way.

I felt my tail disappear and the bones in my upper limbs lengthened, particularly my femurs, so that I could no longer stand comfortably on all fours and had to shift to my hands and knees. I felt my ears slide back down the side of my head and though I could not watch that time, I knew they were no longer pointed since my hearing was suddenly not so sharp. I felt my fangs become blunt and shrink back to human teeth, making my gums itch, while some disappeared entirely, having no place in the shorter, human jaw. My sense of smell dimmed and I knew my eyes were human once again. The human mind was pushing its way up through our consciousness, and I was forced to retreat, awaiting the call of the moon once more.

I opened my eyes and found myself on my hands and knees. The first thing I was aware of was the hunger, all consuming and so powerful I could have eaten anything, even another human. I felt a craving for raw meat, and my mouth watered as I thought longingly of the beef joint in the fridge back home.

The last thing I remembered clearly was staring up at the moon. Everything became confused after that, but the few snatches of memory I could make sense of were memories of the impossible. Other than the pain I had endured, I couldn't remember the details – my memory had recorded the fact that I was changing into a wolf, rather than the actual change itself; the transforming bones, changing limbs, shifting muscles. After that everything was blank. Much as I wanted to believe it were true, my head was swimming as if I had hangover and I decided I had probably been drunk again. Bile was threatening to rise from the depths of my stomach, sickness replacing the hunger, and I swallowed hard in an attempt to keep it down.

I realised there was blood in my mouth, and stringy pieces of flesh caught in my teeth, like a rabbit in a trap. My brain had barely had chance to register that fact before I finally became aware of what my eyes were showing me. The first thing I noticed was my vision was much clearer than before – perfect in fact. Where the world should have been completely blurred from a few inches away from my face, it was as clear as it had been before I had become short sighted and in need of glasses, maybe even clearer. I didn't question this miracle since

I hated glasses anyway. I looked around and finally took in my surroundings, becoming more confused by the minute.

Beams of sunlight pierced the clouds in the sky above, shooting down from the heavens like arrows and falling on great grey stone slabs, some rounded, others shaped like crosses, almost as if the light were a holy connection between Heaven and Earth. It didn't take my confused brain long to realise what they were. Tombstones, rows upon rows of them, marking the graves where the dead lay in peace, oblivious to my presence. Or perhaps their spirits were rising up on those beams of light, climbing them to God's Kingdom. I wouldn't know until it was my turn, but if some form of afterlife existed, which I believed it did, I doubted it involved God.

The grass beneath my fingers was cold and damp with morning dew, and as I looked at my hands I saw they were covered in dirt and what was unmistakeably blood.

My stomach heaved and I couldn't prevent the foul eruption that time. I retched so hard I thought the muscle lining of my stomach would rip, spilling blood and guts onto the ground until the life drained from my body and I joined the dead. Thankfully it ended before it came to that. My stomach settled to an angry gurgling and minutes later I was able to stand.

The hunger returned with a vengeance, so powerful that I had to fight hard against the urge to dig down into the dirt in search of the rotting flesh lying in the graves. I was slave to that hunger, and it had me back on my knees before I realised what I was doing. I quickly stood again, sickened by my actions.

Wiping my mouth with the back of my hand, I shivered in the cool morning air and only then realised I was naked. Embarrassment flushed through me and I quickly moved my hands to cover my groin. Fortunately, the final resting place of the dead was silent, except for birdsong, seemingly beautiful and sacred in one of the few places in the world to know peace. Peaceful as it was, I knew I couldn't stay there. My parents were sure to notice I was missing before long, and I had to go to school, even if I didn't want to. I'd already missed one day; there was no way Mum would let me miss another.

Movement caught my eye, coming from inside the mausoleum. There was a young woman there, a vision right out of a history book. She looked to be in her early twenties but her black dress was from a bygone era. There was no modern touch to the style of her shoulder length brown hair, and those brown eyes glinted with the cold and calculative mind of an ancient predator. Very pale and slim, she wore no make up or jewellery, yet there was an unnatural beauty about her, as if she wasn't human. Her features and her body were too perfect to be human: a form that was almost godly. But there was nothing holy about this creature. She lay on a coffin almost hidden in shadows but strangely didn't seem out of place there.

Aware of my presence, she beckoned to me and, despite my nakedness, I was drawn towards her, my legs moving forward before my brain had time to intervene. However, she didn't seem to mind the fact I was naked and handed me some trousers and a t-shirt without question, as if this was something she saw everyday. I didn't ask where she'd got the clothes from. I probably didn't want to know.

Turning away, I quickly dressed, too dazed under the influence of her spell to ask any questions. I was barely aware that almost every inch of my skin was as dirty and bloody as my hands.

When I turned back to her my mind had cleared of the hazy shroud she had placed on it, and though she was still beautiful, I was ready for it that time and it didn't hold me entranced. I could see that she wanted to sleep, and given our current surroundings, the fact that she had chosen a coffin in shadow, protected from the light, and the effect she had upon me when I first laid eyes on her, I could guess what she was. And if I was right, that meant I had to accept the fact that my memories were true, and not some kind of hallucination brought on by alcohol. The possibility of that excited me, but I felt cheated that I couldn't remember what it was like to experience the world with a wolf's superior senses. It would explain why my vision had improved overnight and the blood in my mouth, which, young and naïve as I was, I assumed to be the blood of animals I had hunted under the full moon. After all, most wolves avoid humans, let alone hunt them.

As you probably guessed already, I knew a lot about werewolves, having researched all the different myths and legends way beyond the point of obsession, but how many of those myths were true and how would this change my life? I knew that there would be changes – the hunger and craving for meat were testament to that – but exactly what would change I couldn't be sure, for not all the myths agreed on the same thing. For example, some myths seemed to agree silver was the way to kill a werewolf, while others said any mortal wound made by any weapon would do it. I wanted to know what to expect.

I felt slightly resentful towards this strange woman for placing me under her spell: I didn't want to be used, but if she could control me so easily there was no telling what she could force me to do if she really wanted to. But if she was really what I suspected her to be, I felt sure she would have all the answers, so I pushed those feelings aside.

And besides, whatever she'd done to me was temporarily keeping the hunger at bay, which could only be a good thing after it had almost had me digging up graves.

The woman seemed to sense I was burning with questions and began by introducing herself.

"My name is Lady Sarah of Wilton," she said.

"Nick James Stead." I replied. Somehow it just seemed right to give her my full name, even if I didn't have a grand title like she did. "You can call me Nick."

"You are newly turned," she observed.

"So it's real then? I am a werewolf?" I asked, eager for her to confirm it for me.

"Indeed," she answered. "And there is much you need to understand, for these are dangerous times to walk among the undead. I will tell you the tale of your origins, for there is much truth in it, and also the origins of those who hunted you this night. Listen well, young wolf, and if you still have questions afterwards you may ask them of me, and I will answer as best I can."

She paused to gather her thoughts as I waited impatiently for the truth behind the werewolf myths I knew so well. Just as I was about to start asking my questions she began the tale. There was a weight to her words as she began to recount this piece of epic history and I listened attentively, my love of stories keeping my questions at bay.

"From the dawn of mankind war has raged; bitter struggles for power, led by those who would seek it. So it has always been and so it will always continue to be, for the heart of man is corrupt and always longing for that which is out of reach: wealth, fame, immortality. Those men that would chase such are never satisfied, no matter how many tales are told of their deeds, no matter if they hold all the gold in the land: they always hunger for more.

"The rise and fall of such men is remembered even to this day, but the one this tale concerns sat the throne of Arcadia in Ancient Greek times. His name was Lycaon, and it is believed it was he who was the first of your race.

"Lycaon's shadow already engulfed the region of Arcadia, but the sights of this tyrant were fixed ever outwards, beyond the border of those lands. Driven by the same greed that afflicts all men with a thirst for power, he sought to conquer and further extend his reach. And as is so often the case, power bred arrogance, and in his arrogance Lycaon fancied himself the equal of the gods. This mortal man took it upon himself to test the great god Zeus by serving him human flesh at a feast, to test whether Zeus was truly omnipotent. But gods are not so easily fooled and in doing so Lycaon sealed his fate.

"Doomed to roam the Earth as a wolf with the rise and fall of every full moon, through Lycaon this new curse was unleashed upon Arcadia. For Zeus cursed him with a terrible lust for human flesh above all other prey, and the power to spread the curse to some of those he wounded, but failed to kill. Those descended from apes were safe from the hold of lycanthropy, but those born of wolf, including Lycaon's own bloodline, of which he sired many as legend would have it, would soon join the tyrant's great and terrible pack.

"A curse this was intended to be, but to a man such as Lycaon it was viewed a blessing. Possessed with greater speed and strength than any mortal creature, and the equal of many beasts even in human form, none could stand against the savagery and power of these supernatural predators. Lycaon and his kind learnt to transform at will, though the transformation at full moon remained involuntary. Most men ran before them, and cowered and hid, but his prey could not escape him and the streets ran with blood. Some rebelled, as is man's wont, but those with the courage to fight fell to the jaws of their oppressors. Savaged and mutilated, they suffered brutal, bloody deaths. That first pack alone would doom millions, either bringing death to its victims or passing on the curse to them.

"And so the curse spread across the land like a plague as Lycaon extended his rule ever outwards, fancying himself a god now of the mortal realm. There was no cure to lycanthropy except death, and to kill a werewolf was no easy feat. Only a fatal wound to the heart or the brain could stop these beasts, the curse providing them great healing capabilities that could repair all else. Not even time could tame Lycaon, for the constant regeneration of tissue during each transformation rendered him immune to the same ravages it inflicts on mortal men.

"So began the Age of Wolves, a dark time for those still human. Had Lycaon remained in power, man might have passed into the void, forever lost in the shadow of the new werewolf race. But as powerful as Lycaon had become, his downfall was inevitable.

"Man's salvation came not in the form of the blood and steel of heroes reclaiming the lands they had lost, but in tooth and claw as the werewolves turned on each other. Lycaon spent so much time looking outwards from the borders of his lands that he failed to see his once loyal pack mates turning to their own quests for power in their own names, not his. When he finally realised he'd lost his grip on Arcadia and other areas of Greece, it was too late. Werewolves turned on each other and hundreds died.

"There the curse might have stopped and died out, for tales of the monsters terrorising the country had spread beyond the borders of Greece, and people learnt to avoid the unholy place. The werewolves might have eventually wiped each other out in the power struggles they were now locked in amongst themselves, had some of the newly turned not tried to escape.

"Often forgetting what they were for their minds during the full moon were those of wolves rather than men, some tried to flee the curse which only served to spread the cancer to other parts of the world.

"But werewolves are not the only race of undead to walk this earth and vampires too suffer from the same corruption as man, since human we once were. Though other werewolves followed in Lycaon's footsteps, attempting to use the power of the curse to claim lands for themselves, the vampires joined the struggle for power and in doing so prevented any chance of werewolves rising to dominance again. And in the midst of it all men, defeated but not broken, rose up once more and seized their chance while we undead were weakened in the war we waged on ourselves. Thus were born the group who named themselves the Demon Slayers, and they fought against us with a new determination, bent on our destruction. We were forced to ally against them and a great battle was fought, yet it was too late, we were too weak from the battles already fought among ourselves. The Age of Men was restored and our numbers swiftly fell, never again to hold such influence over the land. We were forced to flee into the wilderness and the shadows, our desire for power forgotten in the bid to simply survive. But the Slayers were not content with merely driving us out of their lands and they continued to hunt us down.

"In power once more, men learnt to prevent our numbers ever rising again, staking the bodies of the dead so they would never rise as vampires, and burning any at the stake believed to be werewolves. Many lives were lost, including those of mortal humans and wolves mistaken for your kind. Men are ruthless, and the Slayers' resolve to eradicate us was absolute. So it was our numbers dwindled yet further.

"Slowly over the years men forgot why they feared the night. They forgot the nature of the predators that stalked the long hours of darkness. Man turned to science, and the undead became no more than myth and legend to them. Only the Slayers remembered, and in the shadows the bitter struggle rages on, except now it is we who are on the verge of extinction, while the Slayers' numbers continue to rise."

She fell silent and looked at me expectantly for the questions she knew I still had. There was a lot of information to take in from her tale, but the first thing my brain had excitedly latched onto was what she'd said about the werewolves learning to transform voluntarily.

"So if those first werewolves could learn to transform at will, does that mean I have the power to transform whenever I want as well?" I asked her.

"You do, but it is something you will also have to learn for yourself, as they did. I can help teach you but not now. However, the full moon will always hold power over you, and there are other things that can bring on the transformation as well. Strong emotions can induce it, for example, and things that call to the wolf's mind, such as blood, so you will need to be careful."

"You keep mentioning the wolf's mind, what does that mean?"

"When the wolf was awoken in you it was not just the ability to change form you gained. You also have a wolf's instincts, but the brain's way of coping with this is to separate the two personalities of human and wolf. Your inner wolf is a part of you, yet separate, for the time being at least."

"Okay, and what did you mean about humans who are descended from apes being safe from turning into werewolves but not those 'born of wolf'?"

"Some humans evolved from wolves rather than apes, despite what science would have you believe. Only those with wolf blood in their veins can become werewolves, and it has to be a high enough percentage at that. Also, those who can become wolves do not always do so from one bite, though I do not know why. If it was as easy as biting everyone you want to turn into werewolves, your race would not be on the brink of extinction."

I considered that and thought over what other information had been in her tale. "You said something about me being hunted while I was turned. So that was the Demon Slayers?"

"Yes, and they would have killed you had I not been there. We can only hope they do not know who you are and where you live, for if they do then all hope is lost.

"As it is, I had thought your kind were already extinct, for it is years since I have heard the howling of your brethren beneath a full moon, years since I have seen you hunting in the great packs that once roamed the forests... I fear you may be the last werewolf and the one who turned you did it as a last desperate act; for there are few lupine descendants capable of becoming werewolves left now, the Slayers saw to that. A pity he perished on the same night he made you. You are either the last, or one of the last, of a dying race. Perhaps there are a few remnants of the great packs that still haunt sacred places, though even if there are I fear for you all..."

"Well that's comforting," I said, but she didn't seem to hear me, seemingly lost in thought. I wanted to ask more about werewolves and the Slayers, but I had no way of telling the time and I knew I couldn't linger too long in the graveyard if I wanted to sneak back home before my parents could notice I was missing. So I settled for two final questions, waving a hand in front of her face to get her attention again.

"And the Greek gods, are they real too?" I asked, out of curiosity more than anything. "Was it really Zeus who created werewolves?"

"I cannot say for certain whether any gods or deities truly exist, but I believe it was more likely to have been a witch who cursed Lycaon. There have been witches who wielded that kind of power over the centuries, though they too are in decline in this modern world."

I nodded and asked my second question, to confirm my suspicions about who this strange woman was. "And you're a vampire bard or storyteller or something, then?"

"Nothing so common," she hissed. "A vampire yes, but royalty as a human."

I realised I should have known that from her title but before I could apologise she had already begun the tale of her own transformation into one of the undead.

"It happened in 1356 on All Hallow's Eve, which you now call Halloween. I was born into monarchy, a princess to one day rule as queen. I had just lit a jacko lantern and was preparing to go to my father's banquet when a window came open. A gust of wind blew out all the candles and as I went to shut the window, I noticed a full moon outside. I gazed at it for a minute, before sitting back down on my bed. Then I saw the shadow of someone behind me and I spun around, but he grabbed my mouth so I could not scream. His eyes were hypnotising and as soon as I stared into them I fell in love with him, becoming spell bound. He was so handsome, even when his canines grew longer. He gently turned my head to the side, baring my neck, and sunk his canines into my jugular vein, drinking every drop of blood in my body. And as I died in his arms he bit his finger and let one drop of his blood drip into me. I felt younger, stronger and fresher than I had felt for a long time.

"There was a knock on the door and I fell to the ground as he made a quick exit out of the window. I never knew his name.

"I then slept for a month as I was changed forever into some kind of monster, forced to walk the earth in darkness forever, drinking the blood of innocent people. At first life was easy as no one suspected anything was amiss. I was a princess, and nobody questioned why I had begun to sleep through the day and live through the night.

"My first few victims were slaves in the castle, but I realised their deaths would not go unnoticed for my father would need to replace them, so I would feed on the peasants in nearby villages. I took my parent's place on the throne and ruled over them for some time, until I was forced to fake my death to avoid suspicion.

"After that I found ways to live as I had become accustomed to living among humans, not quite part of the mortal world but not completely isolated from it. Yet as technology became more advanced people were becoming suspicious, and the Slayers were ever adding to their ranks. I was driven into hiding, and now I must hide in such places as this graveyard and hide my victims. I don't even have my own coffin.

"But enough now, I must sleep as I did not feed tonight and I shall need all my strength for tomorrow when there will be more Slayers, always more of them and less of us... You should go home and rest as well."

"Yeah okay, thanks for explaining stuff to me."

She didn't reply, already lying back down on the coffin, so I left her to sleep in the mausoleum and made my way home as quick as I could, aware that the blood and dirt on my skin could lead to awkward questions. Fortunately, it was still too early to encounter anyone and I was able to climb back up to my bedroom window without being seen. I scrambled through and climbed into my bunk bed where I pretended to be asleep, knowing Mum would soon come in to get me up for school, my mind buzzing with all that had happened and all I had learned. But in spite of all the information Lady Sarah had given me, it would be some time yet before I fully understood the true nature of this curse. Perhaps deep down I already knew it was not merely the blood of animals staining my skin, with the reference to Lycaon's own craving for human prey in the vampire's tale. Or perhaps I really was too young and naïve to consider it could be anything else. Even if I suspected, it was a truth I did not want to face, so caught up in the excitement of my new powers as I was. So I returned home that morning with the innocence of my youth, such as it was, still in tact, while in an unmarked grave the body of the woman I had killed lay forgotten: she who was but the first of many in the months to follow.

Chapter Four - Back to School

I had returned just in time, for no sooner had I climbed into bed than the door opened and my Mum called out "Come on! It's time for school, you'll be late!"

The thought of going back to school wasn't a happy one but I had little choice, so I climbed down from my bunk bed to shower and get dressed, pausing to wait for my parents and sister to go downstairs. I couldn't let them see me in my current state. How could I explain to them why I was covered in blood and dirt? Despite the clothes Lady Sarah had given me, it was still visible on my bare arms, feet, hands, and my face. There was no sane explanation. If I told them I was a werewolf I was looking at a one way trip to a padded cell, restrained in a straitjacket for all eternity. It wasn't exactly what I planned to do with my newfound immortality. For immortal I had to assume I now was, from what the vampire had said about Lycaon.

I'd had time to mull over what Lady Sarah had told me, and it seemed being a werewolf had both its advantages and disadvantages. It was hard to see why it was called a curse if I'd only killed animals, which seemed no worse than buying meat from the supermarket. Since I was already a carnivore it didn't seem to make any difference who took the animal's life. As long as it was only animals I could live with that, and despite the part of the tale about Lycaon's craving for human prey more than any other, I had experienced no such feeling. The hunger was there again and I did crave meat, but it was just a feeling of being famished as if I'd not eaten in days, not a hunger for human flesh specifically. And meat had always been my favourite food, particularly beef, so that didn't seem strange to me. The craving for meat might partly belong to my newly awoken lupine nature as well, but there still didn't seem to be anything to suggest my tastes had changed.

Not aging was going to be hard to explain to my parents over the coming years, and I didn't really want to spend an eternity trapped inside a teenage body. For one thing, it'd mean I'd never be able to drink legally, something I'd been looking forward to. And I'd never be able to see eighteens at the cinema. But maybe there was some way round that, maybe I'd find a way to age myself. Maybe Lady Sarah would know someone who had the power to make me age a few years, just so I could finish puberty and reach adulthood. Maybe I was just being optimistic.

Still, the enhanced senses and greater agility, strength and speed would make me unbeatable in any sport, something I would enjoy, and no doubt it would have its advantages in the world of video games as well. I was going to enjoy thrashing David next time we met up after school, both on the Playstation and in the real world when he wanted a kick about with the football. It was something else Lady Sarah had alluded to in her tale, and I'd already noticed the difference for myself; I could clearly hear everything that was going on in the world outside, even hear snatches of conversation from neighbouring houses, but unused to my new powers at that time it was just a confusion of sound.

Even stranger was the sharp sense of smell. It was weird after years of relying on sight and sound as the primary senses. Mostly it was just a jumble of scents like the overwhelming wave of sound, but I could pick out a trail left by one of Amy's friends who had come over a few days ago. At least, I assumed it was her friend. I couldn't really understand what my nose was telling me yet; I needed the wolf's mind to help me out there. All I knew was the scent didn't belong to my parents or my sister. And was it my imagination or was my eyesight better than a human's? Things were definitely clearer than when I'd worn glasses, but maybe I'd just been due for a new, stronger pair, I couldn't be sure. With the enhanced hearing and smell, it made everything strange and I knew it would be a while before I became accustomed to the changes. It was like I'd woken up and found myself on a different planet, everything alien and unnatural.

As for the wolf's mind, I could feel it somewhere within my subconscious, watching warily from the dark place it hid in, watching and waiting. And learning. I got the impression it was trying to learn more about humans from me. It was strange, I could feel both parts of my mind and yet they were both separate: one animal, the other human, and yet both me. A reminder that I was no longer human, but neither was I wolf; I was something else, something in between, a hybrid of the two perhaps. I didn't want to dwell too much on that. I hoped somehow I could still live in the world of humans, if I could just learn to control the lupine side of me. I wanted the best of both worlds.

Still musing, I hurried into the bathroom when I was sure my family were out of the way downstairs, helping themselves to breakfast. I spent longer than usual brushing my teeth as they were still stained with blood, as was my body, and there was dried blood under my fingernails. Showering took a lot longer that morning. I'd never really liked washing but for once I found myself glad of this part of modern hygiene, feeling more comfortable for cleansing myself of the dirt caked on my skin and the death smell I'd only been vaguely aware of, unpleasant to my human self.

46

While I was getting ready for the day, I couldn't help running through in my mind all I could remember of the previous two nights, and contemplating how much my life had changed in such little time, though for better or worse I didn't know. As I had already decided for myself, it seemed there were advantages to my being a werewolf. But with the threat of the Demon Slayers not only my life, but the lives of my family, could be at risk if they ever found out who I was. I was going to have to be careful, something that reckless side to my teenage self would have trouble adjusting to.

The reference to a werewolf's greater healing abilities seemed to also be true. I was somewhat pissed off to find my toenail had grown back; I noticed it when I was showering. I'd gone through a lot of pain to have that damn thing removed when it was ingrowing, more than once, and every time it had promptly grown back and inwards like before, until I'd finally had the roots killed. It had caused me that many problems, I'd always said it would be easier to cut the whole damn toe off and even then it would probably find a way to grow back, with the nail on, ingrowing. So I wasn't too happy to find my lycanthropy had restored it, as if I'd never had the surgery.

After I'd cleansed myself of the blood and dirt, I returned to my room only to notice the torn clothes I'd been wearing the night before. I'd never even thought about them and I swore, wondering how the hell I was going to hide them and whether Mum would notice they were missing. Dad wouldn't, since he took little interest in the shirts I wore and he never did the washing, but Mum would most likely realise I was a pair of jeans down. And she probably would notice the absence of one of my gothic shirts. I'd have to think up an excuse later, as long as she didn't see that they'd been ripped apart which would be even harder to explain. If my school bag had been in my room I would have just stashed them in there until I had chance to throw them in a bin somewhere out of sight of prying eyes, but it was downstairs in the study. In the end the best I could think of was to hide them under my bed for the time being and hope Mum didn't go under there for anything before I had chance to dispose of them.

I also placed the ornaments that had been knocked off back in their places on the windowsill, thinking at least they hadn't been broken. My room needed a good clean as usual (which was my own fault for being too lazy to keep it clean and tidy) and it was easy to see where each one went from the circles in the dust.

My glasses presented more of a problem. I couldn't have carried on wearing them even if I still needed them to see, as they were too cracked to do any good and the frame was also damaged from being stood on. It was too much to hope no one would notice the fact I wasn't wearing them. As I dressed and ran downstairs I desperately tried to think of a believable story to explain the sudden absence of them, but whilst I was usually good at that sort of thing, this was one situation where my mind was frustratingly blank.

I jumped the last two steps and landed as I always had done since an early age, cat-like at the bottom, crouched with my knees bent beneath me, back arched, one hand out to steady myself, the other resting on my knee, my long fingers bent into imaginary claws. And similarly, going up the stairs I had a tendency to either run up on all fours, or crawl at a leisurely pace, imagining I was something more powerful than a human. I think these habits started as something I imagined a werewolf would do, when I used to think behaving in ways I thought a werewolf should behave was as close as I'd ever get to living my fantasies. How wrong I'd been.

It was strange, but I felt more alive than I had in years, more alive even than after the film on the night I'd been bitten, as if the blood that had drained from my kill and stained my body had somehow added to my life force, the life draining out with that blood somehow transferring into my own bloodstream, giving me more energy, more life. I found that ironic, since I was now classed as one of the undead.

I walked into the kitchen in high spirits, stomach gurgling and still craving flesh. Dad liked me to make the tea and coffee as one of the little jobs he thought I should do to help out round the house, and to that end I headed for the fridge to grab the milk. Mum opened the door just as I stepped up behind her, and I could smell the enticing aroma of the beef joint. My mouth watered and without thinking, I practically dived at the raw meat, snatching my prize while my family watched, open mouthed with surprise. I was about to rip off the plastic skin when Mum recovered enough to ask me what I was doing. I looked at her, then I looked back at the meat in my hands. I'd reacted purely on instinct. If aspects of the lupine side of my personality were going to creep in to my everyday life I would have to be even more cautious than I'd first thought. And it was unmistakeably part of the wolfish side to me that had reacted, since I'd never even considered eating raw meat before. Perhaps my tastes had changed slightly, but I still wasn't worried. It seemed I would enjoy my steak a little bloodier than before I'd been turned, nothing more.

I laughed, making it out to be a joke, and carefully placed the beef back in the fridge, trying to ignore the craving. Amy rolled her eyes and gave me a look that clearly said she was ashamed to be my sister. Mum shook her head too and Dad looked like he was going to shout but in the end he, too, shook his head and turned away in disgust.

He'd never understood my need to pretend to be a werewolf. And it was something I could never explain to him. It was something I'd never understood myself but I'd never questioned it. Why had I always wanted to be something else so much? I didn't know. But from an early age I enjoyed playing games with my sister, or the few friends I had, that involved me pretending to be an animal. I'd always loved werewolves and other shape shifters. I'd always wanted to be something else, be it an animal or a horror movie monster. But never someone else. I blamed the years of bullying for creating the desire to be something more powerful than a human. Or maybe it was the fact I'd never been truly human to begin with. If it was true some men had somehow evolved from wolves as Lady Sarah had said, I was clearly one of them or, according to her, it wouldn't have been possible for me to become a werewolf, even after being bitten. Of course, that thought was not one I could share with others, but to me it seemed to make a lot of sense for some of the traits I'd always had and my obsession with werewolves to begin with. Maybe it even went some way to explaining why I'd been so tormented by bullies in the first place, if on some level they'd sensed I was different from the rest of them. But even if I could have shared those ideas with Dad, he still wouldn't have got it. He barely understood me as it was.

Physically my Dad and I shared a few things in common though. I got my dark hair from him and, at least when I'd been mostly human, we'd had similarly bad eyesight, though his eyes were dark brown. I don't think he hated wearing glasses like I had, as he was always changing the frames so he had the latest fashion, whereas I couldn't have cared less what frames I'd had, I just didn't want them in the first place. He kept his hair shaved short like me and he was always clean shaven. He wasn't much taller than either me or Mum. If I had another growth spurt I might just be taller than him. But he didn't need physical height to tower over us. He could be really intimidating when his anger and aggression got the better of him, and it might as well have added another foot to his overall height because he seemed so much taller for it.

It wasn't just the frames of his glasses that he liked to change often; he was always buying new clothes. He was a bit of a snob and insisted on having the latest designer labels, refusing to buy clothes in the sale because he thought he was too good for them.

He had a fairly plain face, not ugly by any means except for when anger made it that way, but not strikingly handsome either. He wasn't as skinny as I was; he was better built and more muscular since joining the gym. He also played golf every Saturday which had helped keep him in shape over the years.

"So what's for breakfast?" I asked Mum, changing the subject before anyone could say anything else.

"You're feeling better then." It was a statement rather than a question. "You had us all worried yesterday, must have been that twenty four hour bug that's going round. And you know what's for breakfast Nick, it's just the usual."

She sounded slightly exasperated when she told me about breakfast. I asked the same question every day in the hope that just once there'd be something other than cereal, which I'd always hated. So most of the time I went without eating till lunchtime, unless it was one of the rare occasions when Mum did a cooked breakfast. Then I'd eat as if I'd been fasting for months. But that day I was so ravenous, I had to eat something. I still couldn't bring myself to eat cereal, but there was no way Mum would let me have anything else while I was at home. Maybe if I set off early for school they might have bacon or sausages in the canteen. I'd never had breakfast there before, mainly because it meant going in early and I hated school, but I had to do something to satisfy my hunger. It had already had me on my hands and knees ready to dig down to the rotting corpses beneath my feet; there was no telling what else it would do if I didn't eat something soon. It would only get stronger, and if I gave into the craving for meat and started to hunt in broad daylight, the Slayers would soon put me down as if I was no more than a rabid animal, judging from what Lady Sarah had said of them.

"Hey, how come you're not wearing your glasses?" Amy asked while I silently cursed her. I thought I was going to get away without having to explain that one after all. I still hadn't come up with a good lie. What to tell them? I couldn't say I'd got contacts, since that would have involved a visit to the optician and probably my parent's permission for the prescription. It was a believable lie for my friends who wouldn't know any different, but I needed another excuse to tell my family.

"I dropped them and they broke," I said, choosing to give them a partial truth.

"So what are you going to do now?" Dad said angrily. "How are you going to manage at school? It's your GCSE year; you can't afford to mess it up!"

He was always shouting at me, usually for little reason, but I understood it that time. He regretted having not done so well in his own exams all those years ago and as a result he was stuck in a job he hated, though the pay was good. He didn't want me to make the same mistake.

"Well they were giving me headache anyway," I replied, fighting to keep my voice calm. Whenever he had to shout I couldn't just stand there and take it, I had to argue back and that usually made matters worse. I couldn't afford to set him off that morning though. As a teenager I was more concerned with the thought of being grounded, thinking myself lucky they hadn't done so for staying out late the night I'd been bitten. Nobody had really mentioned it other than Mum asking if I was feeling better. The blood had never really been mentioned either; Mum just washed the sheets and it was forgotten. But there was also what Lady Sarah had said about strong emotions being able to bring on the change, and it seemed I couldn't afford to let my anger get out of control. "I think my eyes are getting better. I'll just have to sit near the front and ask my mates to read anything I can't make out."

It wasn't the best lie I could have thought of, but it would have to do since I hadn't had time to think it through. I decided that was a good time to grab my bag and return to the privacy of my room to pack it for school, where I could avoid any more awkward questions.

I closed the door behind me and leant against it with my eyes closed, wanting to shut out the strange new world I had found myself in, but the thin piece of wood wasn't a strong enough barrier against the barrage of sound that pounded against my sensitive eardrums. Moments later the argument started downstairs.

"What the hell was that all about? Did you see the way he was looking at that joint?" Dad said.

"I don't know, John. Probably just his idea of a joke. I'm sure it was intended as a harmless bit of fun, that's all," Mum replied.

"Well I don't like it! And you don't help, Emma! It's your fault, encouraging him all the time, letting him watch those bloody horror films! And what about his glasses? How's he going to cope at school without them? He's so bloody clumsy; he's only had that pair for a few months!"

"Keep your voice down John, he'll hear you," Mum hissed, too quiet for a human to hear. No mention of Amy so I guessed she'd retreated to her room too. They rarely argued in front of us, though we could often hear them shouting at each other anyway. It was usually Dad who started it.

"And it's alright blaming me, if we banned him from watching that sort of thing he'd only go and watch more films round at his mates'," she said. "Be grateful he doesn't watch eighteens yet! He's nearly sixteen; we can't stop him watching anything under an eighteen. Besides, it's not real and he knows that. He was always into monsters, even before he was allowed to watch horror films. He'd probably still be the same, even if we didn't let him watch them. As for the glasses, there's no point staying angry over it. What's done is done. We'll just have to take him in for a new pair. If they were giving him a headache then he may need a new pair anyway; we might as well get his eyes tested again while we're there."

Dad grunted disbelievingly but let it drop for the time being. My stomach was gurgling again and I quickly packed my bag. I retrieved the ripped clothes from under my bed and hid them under my books while I was at it, then I ran back downstairs and pulled on my shoes to leave for school, in the hope of getting a decent breakfast.

"How come you're off to school so early? Keen aren't you," Dad asked, as if nothing had happened. He seemed to have his temper under control again and he sounded almost jovial, but it was strained slightly, as if he was forcing it.

I shrugged and told him I'd arranged to meet up with my mates before school started.

"See you tonight then," he said, satisfied with my answer.

"Yeah, see you all later."

I walked out of the door before anyone could say anything else. I didn't want any more awkward situations, and the hunger was becoming unbearable.

I could feel his eyes on me as I set off down the street, probably watching from the window. I felt a sudden urge to run, not for any particular reason, just because I could, but Dad would know something wasn't right if he saw me running to school (running home sometimes maybe, but never to school, even if I was late), so I forced myself to keep walking at my normal pace. I was sure I'd read somewhere before that wolves like to run. It reminded me nothing would ever be the same again. Was the wolf going to affect every aspect of my life? It seemed so.

Lost in thought once more, I hardly noticed where my feet were taking me, until I suddenly found myself in the canteen, surrounded by the smell of food. I was relieved to find they did indeed have bacon and sausages.

The dinner lady gave me a scathing look when I asked her to pile my plate high with the meat, as if to say there was no wonder our generation were growing fatter by the day, despite my skinny frame. But she didn't comment as she served ten rashers of bacon and five sausages. Almost visibly drooling, I nearly forgot to pay with the distraction of food playing games with my senses, controlling my mind. Another dinner lady on one of the tills shouted out and I paid up. That was all my lunch money gone and the plateful of meat wouldn't fill me. I'd have to hope I could find Mum later and get some more money off her, or go hungry, which didn't seem an option that day.

I sat down at a table on my own and made quick work of my breakfast. There weren't many others in the canteen at that time; school wasn't due to start for another half hour, and it was the quietest I'd ever seen it. Possibly a good thing, since it would have led to yet more awkward questions. I didn't normally eat much at school – the food was that bad. But that day I didn't care, I was just glad of the meat to fill that empty feeling in my stomach. I soon finished the plateful and washed it down with two cups of water from the jug on a table next to the wall, the only free drink available since I didn't have any money left for anything better. Then I reluctantly headed for my form room minutes before the bell rang to signal the start of school, when the corridors would become awash with a river of students, fighting and pushing against each other, channelled between the two walls towards their own forms.

The classroom door was unlocked so I let myself in and took my seat at a table at the back. There were four rows of tables going down the middle, each made up of two tables pushed together, and four single tables on either side. I sat at the end of one table and my fellow classmates soon joined me. Becci sat next to me.

"Feeling better today, Nick?" she asked me.

"Yeah, a bit," I said. "Actually, I feel great. Pity we're stuck in school today, wouldn't it be great to go see another movie? It was a right laugh. We have to do that again sometime."

Becci shifted uncomfortably as she remembered the night of the cinema. It wasn't until later in my life I was able to retrieve the memories from the first few months after becoming a werewolf, which is how I am able to recount them to you now, but back then everything was confused, and if I vaguely remembered anything it was hard to make sense of it, and it was even harder to sort out the real memories from the nightmares. She was about to say something else but thought better of it and kept quiet. If I'd remembered the way she'd run off and left me to die the night I'd been bitten, especially when I'd risked my own life to help her, I don't know what I'd have done.

There was a reckless energy inside of me, and while it was a positive energy at that moment, I felt it could turn negative at any minute. It's hard to describe to a mortal, but it was like I'd been struck by a bolt of electricity and now I was charged with it, and I just had the sense that it could change my mood as quickly as Dad's had that morning. I felt that if anybody angered me I might do something stupid, something that might lead to the Slayers discovering what I was. And according to Lady Sarah, if that happened my life was over. I didn't even know if I could trust her, but what reason was there for her to lie to me? As unbelievable as some of it was, I was already experiencing things to evidence some of the information she'd given me about my kind. Whether the rest of what she had told me was true or not, I had to believe it, because if I didn't and I was wrong, I was doomed. And even if the Slayers didn't really exist, if I started acting strangely I might end up in a padded room or worse, and eventually someone would discover the existence of the undead. And I doubted whether humanity would be understanding enough for me to remain a free man. At the very least they'd keep me locked up, but I knew they could well take my life if I was perceived as enough of a threat to the world.

An uncomfortable silence had fallen between us and I decided it was time for a change of subject.

"So Becci, would you ever fuck a corpse?" I asked, grinning.

"You're sick," one of the girls in front said, having overhead me.

Becci, on the other hand, looked thoughtful for a second, before replying "It depends on whether it's a fit corpse and how long it's been rotting. Might be a problem for a woman though, if the corpse was limp. I don't see how it would be possible."

"It'd be possible if it was in rigor mortis," I said and we both laughed. Others were looking at me, wanting to know what was so funny, but I doubt they'd have got the joke, even if they'd been listening.

She was about to say something else but just then our form tutor, Ms Brooks, entered the room, cutting our conversation short. Silence fell as she sat behind her desk, ready to take the register.

After she had given out messages from the Head of Year, she handed me my new timetable and planner, the rest of the class having already been given theirs the day before. I scrawled my name on the front of the little book they referred to as a planner, which was like the school's own version of a diary, with little enthusiasm, feeling I was signing away my freedom for another year. While I was momentarily distracted, Kerri seized her chance, snatching my bag from under the table.

Mischief resonated at the very core of her being, and it was this that led her to dig through my backpack in search of the most treasured possession she knew I would be carrying around school. With her prize clutched in her thick, chubby fingers, she dropped my bag and tauntingly danced out of reach, heading for the other end of the room. In a rush of anger, I stood so quickly I knocked my chair over, ready to give chase, but Ms Brooks quickly intervened before things got out of hand.

"Kerri, pack it in, Nick, sit down," she said calmly, her tone betraying a hint of impatience and a warning in her eyes. Most of the time she wasn't too bad as teachers went, and she was friendly enough, but she could control the class when she needed to.

Seething with anger, I glared at Kerri, my lips curving slightly to bare a few teeth in a partial snarl, remnants of the wolf I had been just hours earlier. Some part of me tried to make itself heard, reasoning that a trouble maker like Kerri wasn't worth starting to slip down the disciplinary slope before school had even truly begun, yet it was all but drowned out in the roar of emotion rushing through my veins. This annoying girl had taken the one source of escape available to me from bullies like her and the school itself, a horror story I was reading at that time. I spent most of my spare time reading back then, preferring to keep my head down and lose myself in a good book, in the hope I would go unnoticed by the rest of the school. Kerri knew how much my books meant to me and my reaction only fed her need for mischief.

"This is your verbal warning you two, I won't ask again," Ms Brooks said sternly.

Still I grappled with the desire to cross the room and physically retrieve my book from Kerri's thieving, grubby fingers, but finally my reason won out, if only because of the thought that losing control could cause me to transform, and the anger subsided enough that I picked up my chair and sat back down as I had been told. Kerri was slower to respond to our form teacher's authority, causing Ms Brooks to lose her temper.

"That's it Kerri, give me your planner. Now!" she shouted.

Finally Kerri gave in, handing me back my precious book and accepting the negative comment without complaint. After a verbal warning, the first stage of the disciplinary system was a comment in our planners, two of which in the same lesson led to detention. Detentions led to isolation where you had to work all day in silence, cut off from anyone else as the name suggests. Next came suspension, and eventually removal from the school, though if the offence was bad enough teachers could skip the lower levels of the system. Much to the dismay of her teachers, Kerri hadn't quite given them cause to kick her out yet, though she was getting closer by the year.

Though I appeared outwardly calm again with my book returned to me, I could still feel the anger just beneath the surface. It had surprised me. Yes Kerri was annoying, but she had never invoked such a strong reaction in me before over something as petty as running off with my book, especially when I hadn't even been trying to read it at the time. The feeling I'd had moments earlier that I might do something stupid had been justified. I realised with a jolt I'd been ready to fight with her over it, right in front of a teacher! And much as I hated Kerri at such times, she wasn't worth that. I'd have been straight in detention at least and probably grounded at home by my parents, neither of which were particularly appealing prospects to my teenage self. The anger had been stewing inside me for years; anger at Dad, anger at everyone who bullied me, anger at myself for not doing anything about it. But I'd always kept it in check. Suddenly it seemed to have intensified, no doubt as a result of the wolf awoken and lurking within, and I knew I was going to have to work harder to keep it under control. I didn't want to think about what could happen if I didn't rein it in, but I knew my survival depended on how well I learned to do just that.

Form was nearly over by the time Kerri had been dealt with, and I realised I didn't know what lesson I had first so I quickly studied my timetable, to find it was Maths. So when the bell went, signalling the end of form and the beginning of the first lesson, I walked out of the room with Becci and picked up the macabre conversation from where we'd left it. While most classrooms were on the ground level, all the Maths rooms were on the same corridor up a flight of steps, and the IT rooms were just above them.

"Well Becci, you can fuck me when I'm dead, I don't care. If I'm lucky I might even be able to feel it in the afterlife."

"Nick, I wouldn't want to touch you dead or alive," she told me.

"You keep telling yourself that Becci, you know you want me really. I mean come on, a fit guy like me, I'm just irresistible. Every girl in the school wants me really, and just wait till I'm famous, they'll be fighting amongst themselves to be with me! Every girl in the world will want a piece of the action, and I'll be all too happy to share. And for every girl who doesn't get a chance in this life, you can guarantee it'll be in her will that the coffin has to be left with me so her corpse can receive my personal attention."

56

The girl who'd been sat in front of us in the form room must have overheard again because she decided to interrupt. "Do you have to be so sick? Why can't you have normal relationships like normal people?"

"'Cause I ain't normal. Anyway, love is over-rated. I don't do relationships, everyone knows that. All love causes is pain and sadness, it's a useless emotion. From what I've seen, relationships are a waste of time. Just get 'em to bed and move on, saves a lot of pain and heartbreak. That's all relationships are good for. A relationship with a corpse, now that's my ideal relationship. All the sex you want without the arguments, and you don't have to sacrifice things for your lover, you can have everything your way. Isn't that anybody's ideal relationship if they were being honest?"

"You're insane," she said, a look of sheer disbelief on her face. "Love is real. It can make you stronger, give you something to live for. It isn't useless, it can do a lot for the soul. You'll see someday."

"Ha, yeah right. I'll stick to the shagging side if it's all the same to you, whether they're dead or alive."

"I have to agree with Nick on that one, sex is the best part of it," Becci said. If everything she'd told us was true, she was talking from years of experience.

At that point we had just climbed the stairs and were entering the Maths corridor. It was time to go our separate ways. I was in the fourth classroom along, while Becci and the other girl were in the fifth.

The day dragged after that. I wouldn't bore you with the details even if I could remember them, though it was the start of the year which probably meant we were just going through what we'd be studying in the months to come. I switched off while teachers droned on, everything I learnt back then long forgotten. It didn't help my concentration that I could hear what every other teacher was saying on that corridor with my new enhanced senses, and even worse was the sense of smell. We weren't meant to eat during lessons but that didn't stop most of us, and the hunger soon returned, the smell of various different snacks calling to it until it built in power and I could focus on little else. French was the best lesson I had that day. It was one of the few lessons I had with Lizzy, and talking to her distracted me from the hunger.

"Hi Nick," she said as she walked into the classroom with Fiona and took her place at the desk behind me, Fiona taking the seat next to me. "I wasn't going to come in today but I thought I better do just to check you were still alive."

The three of us burst out laughing at that, before Lizzy grew serious again.

"Seriously though, you're okay after the other night aren't you? I can't believe the others ran off and left you like that." She shot an angry look at Fiona who stared fixedly at the table, avoiding our gaze, and I realised that's what Becci had been hiding. If my memories were clearer I might have said something, but as it was I decided to let it go. Besides, I was still very aware of the potential consequences of letting my emotions rule me, and I couldn't afford to give the anger I'd felt that morning any cause to resurface.

"Yeah I'm fine thanks, it wasn't as bad as it looked. They were just flesh wounds, that's all," I lied.

"Good," she said. "I can be angry at you now then."

"Why, what have I done now?" I asked indignantly.

"You could have text to let me know you were okay you dick, you had me worrying all day when you didn't show up yesterday!" she said. "I tried ringing but your phone was off and I couldn't get through to your house phone."

"Ah, sorry about that. I just needed a good sleep afterwards so I was in bed most of the day. Never even thought to turn it on," I replied.

"You're clueless sometimes, you know that?" she said but left it at that. Mostly she was just glad I was okay.

Talk turned to a website we all played on. It was a virtual pet site, where you created your own pets and then you could battle with them, amongst other things. There was also a chat room and you could create your own guild, which was kind of like having your own website within the website. You could do whatever you wanted with the front page of your guild if you had the technical know how, and other players could join and talk on the message boards. We used our guild for roleplaying mainly.

We were interrupted by our new teacher's attempt to start the lesson. Usually we would have had the same teacher throughout our GCSEs but Mr Andrews had left at the end of Year Ten.

"Fine morning class," she began in a thick French accent. "My name is Miss Dubois and I am taking your French this year. Today let's talk about, er how you say, hobbies from the summer. Did anyone do anything nice they are wanting to share with the class?"

As she talked she wrote her name on the board and underneath she made a heading 'My Summar', to a chorus of sniggers at her bad English. We began chatting amongst ourselves again as if our teacher hadn't arrived to the lesson yet.

"I dunno if I'll make it on tonight," I said to Lizzy and Fiona, not bothering to keep my voice down. "Dad's going through another of his bad years and you know how he is with me being on the computer 'too much'."

"What do you mean another of his bad years?" Fiona asked. She hadn't been round to my house as often as Lizzy and didn't know my family very well.

"Every couple of years he just gets angry for no reason," I explained. "It lasts for about a year, and then he's back to his other self who can be a good laugh when he wants to, like fucking Jekyll and Hyde or something. That's okay while it lasts, but then we have to suffer another year of his mood swings. It's like this constant cycle with him."

"Your Dad's always been nice to me when I've been round," Lizzy said, as if she thought I was exaggerating.

"Of course he is, you're not family," I replied bitterly. "He puts on the friendly act for the rest of the world, but he takes it out on me and Mum when it's just us. Not his precious Amy though, she can't do owt wrong."

I thought gloomily of the bad atmosphere waiting for me back home, after school. Even if I returned to find him in a good mood, it never lasted long during a bad year. He was unpredictable, like a mad dog, his mood changing in the blink of an eye. Mum had often said to him he needed anger management and he'd even agreed with her, but he'd never been.

"That sucks, Nick," Fiona said.

"It's okay, I know I'm a huge disappointment to him. I don't give a damn anymore. In a few years I'll be free of him anyway."

That was my one comforting thought whenever things were bad at home, but sometimes that day seemed an eternity away. I often thought about just running away from it all, but I couldn't leave Mum and Amy behind. They needed me. We needed each other whenever Dad was going through another bad year, even Amy, despite the fact she was very rarely a target for Dad's anger.

We were interrupted again by Miss Dubois, whose voice had been drowned out in the classroom chatter. The lights flicked on and off and silence was restored as we all looked round to see what she was doing.

"Merci," she said and resumed the lesson, but moments later we had begun talking again.

She returned to the light switch but of course, while it might have worked to restore order among primary school children, it had no further effect on a room full of teenagers.

"I will have more quiet!" she shouted in an attempt to assert some authority. Someone threw a paper aeroplane which hit her forehead and fell to the ground. She was fuming but she didn't have the presence of some teachers in the school, and no amount of shouting was going to control our class.

Most French lessons would be like that over the year, but I wasn't complaining. It became a chance to talk to Lizzy and Fiona for fifty minutes, which felt like a nice break to the tedium of the school day.

Lunch break came and went. Fortunately, Mum was in her office when I went to see her, and she gave me some money without question. Then it was back to being bored out of my mind in the afternoon's lessons.

When the bell finally rang at the end of the day, most of the energy that had filled me that morning had died. The feeling of being so alive was long gone. Whatever I had done the previous night, it had finally begun to take its toll, and twenty four hours without sleep had left me exhausted. I wearily stumbled back towards home and collapsed onto my bed when I was back in the safety of my room, listening to my parents rowing about something else. I couldn't stay there long, much as I wanted to. The hunger was already growing to the point of becoming overpowering again, and I knew I had to stay awake long enough to eat.

Having changed out of my uniform, I only ventured downstairs when the argument died down and I heard the sound of the door slamming and a car starting up outside. I was glad to find Dad had gone to the gym, meaning we could eat dinner in peace.

"Ah, I'm glad you've come down Nick, I need to talk to you about dinner. We've got chicken in breadcrumbs, spaghetti bolognaise, or that chicken in red wine sauce you like," Mum said.

I shrugged tiredly. "Whatever's easiest for you, I'm not bothered."

"Are you okay, love? You look tired, early to bed tonight."

Normally I'd have argued against an early night, but I was too tired even for that. "Yeah, I'm fine, just tired like you said. Didn't sleep last night."

"How did you cope without your glasses today?" she asked.

"Fine. I think my eyes are getting better again, I could read everything on the board no problem."

"I still think you should see the optician."

I just grunted at that.

"Okay, well you can have the chicken in breadcrumbs because that cooks at the same temperature as ours. What do you want with it?"

"Whatever."

"How about a jacket potato and peas, is that okay for you?"

"Yeah, that's fine. Two pieces of chicken please."

I sat and read more of the horror story Kerri had run off with earlier that morning while I waited for dinner to cook. Half an hour later it was ready and I ate in silence. Not long after I'd finished eating I went back to bed and welcomed the sleep as soon as it enveloped me.

Chapter Five – Nightmares Awaken

The ground rushed by beneath my feet, twigs snapping and burying themselves in the dirt. My breath steamed out before me and I was panting with the effort, sweat soaking my fur, running over my skin. A thread of drool dangled from my lower jaw and fell to the ground, an explosive vibration for the invertebrates beneath the soil. My prey was just ahead and I was closing the distance between us with every bound. She was beginning to tire: I could hear her heart pounding against her chest, her lungs gasping for air, and no doubt her muscles were burning, in need of oxygen.

I leapt over a fallen log and swerved between the trees. She veered to the left and I almost skidded trying to follow her, my claws digging into the dirt, making deep grooves as I sought to keep my balance. Fast and agile as I was, wolves are not built for sharp turns.

She was slowing now and I was almost upon her. I pounced and knocked her to the ground, growling hungrily. Too ravenous to bother killing her first, I ripped the flesh from her back and swallowed greedily, blood spraying my face. When I'd eaten what I could from around the ribs and the spine and the base of the neck, I rolled her over, wishing she'd stop screaming. The shrill sound hurt my sensitive ears.

She didn't fight back when I rolled her over, but she covered her face, sobbing and screaming and struggling to suck in air, still in need of oxygen after the chase. I ate everything from inside her belly until she was hollow. I moved upwards to the flesh round her throat. She was still screaming, despite having no lungs or vocal cords left to scream with. Finally I reached her face.

Her hands were still in the way, so I bit them off and ate them, more blood spraying out, covering us both, and continued to chew the limbs until the arms were all but gone. The bloody stumps waved uselessly at the sides of her head, unable to reach any higher, and I went to rip off her face, but what I saw stopped me. It was pale and covered in blood and dirt, barely recognisable, but still I had seen enough to know who it was. The eyes were wide and staring with horror and shock, the jaws were stretched as far apart as they would go, still sounding that unearthly scream. I backed away in horror, retching, no longer a wolf but human now, my body tainted with her blood, my mouth dry and foul with the mixture of vomit, saliva and more blood. We were both screaming now, and I couldn't bear to look at her mutilated body. The mutilated body of my sister.

I awoke screaming and drenched in cold sweat, my bed wet with it. I fought with the covers, fighting to free myself from the last remnants of the nightmare, until Mum came rushing in.

It took a while before she could calm me, how long I don't know. I only know that the terrible images refused to go away, the haunting scream still echoing in my head, the taste of blood somehow still in my mouth. Mum rocked me in her arms like she had when I was young and the screams died in my throat. I closed my eyes against the shadows as if they contained more horrors, and forced my mind to think of other things. I never used to have nightmares before I'd been bitten, not even bad dreams. It seemed now I was half wolf the lupine part of my mind was determined to interfere with my dreams, bringing horror to my human mind. It served as a reminder of the transformation I was undergoing, not only physical but mental too. I shivered with the memory of the dream and the thought that nothing would ever be the same again. I would never be the same again.

Once she was sure I was back in reality, free from the realm of darkness within my mind, containing my own horror and fears, and even my own private Hell, she went back to bed, leaving me alone again. I couldn't face sleep; I could feel the nightmare lurking on the edge of my subconscious and I didn't want to go back there. No matter how tired I had been the day before, or how tired I would be at school, I couldn't go back there. I lay there in the night, feeling alone and afraid, no longer human yet desperate to remain in their world. There was no one I could talk to, except for maybe Lady Sarah, but I'd only met her once and I didn't trust her enough yet to confide in her too deeply. Besides, she didn't seem like the right person. From what she'd told me, if it was true, she'd been a vampire for centuries. Would she remember what it was like to be human? She might not understand. She'd probably tell me something like I wasn't human anymore and I had to let my humanity go. But I still felt human, even though deep down I knew then I was something else. And I had wished for this through most of my childhood. Still, it was only a dream. It didn't mean anything. I still believed I hadn't taken another human's life yet and I certainly had no intention to. I told myself it was only a dream.

My nightmares fled with the break of dawn and my fears were forgotten as I got ready for school. Two nights without sleep had left me feeling drained, empty. I was running on automatic, feeling like a zombie. My brain was too tired to work properly, but I'd bullied it into thinking long enough for me to decide to go and visit Lady Sarah again. Though I could not talk to her about the nightmares, there were other things I wanted to know. For one thing, she hadn't really told me much about the Slayers. I needed to learn more of what I was up against in case I ever came across them. From what she'd said they'd already been hunting me in wolf form, even if I couldn't remember it myself. I only hoped they didn't know who I was, for my family's sake, as well as my own.

The hunger wasn't as bad as it had been the morning before and I went without breakfast. I refused to eat cereal but I didn't want to go to school early again. Dad had left early for work that morning so I wouldn't have to listen to any more arguments, or be careful what I did and said to keep the peace, if only for Mum's and Amy's sakes. Most of the time he worked at home, but occasionally he had to go to other parts of the country. I wasn't sure exactly what he did, something to do with training people I think. I know the company he used to work for dealt with insurance, but other than that I hadn't taken enough interest to find out exactly what his job was.

While Mum and Amy spent ages straightening and brushing their hair and God knows what else, I sprawled out on the sofa and relaxed. I'd been fighting sleep all night and I was exhausted. I didn't have the strength to fight back when my eyelids started to droop. The next thing I knew, I felt myself falling back into that dark place in my mind. I could feel the wolf there, its dreams becoming my nightmares. I tried to crawl out, back towards the light, but the need to sleep was so great, struggling against its pull proved impossible, and every time the light was visible, it pulled me back down until it was swallowed up by the darkness again. Fear threatened to take a hold of me once more when I found myself in another nightmare, but before it could go far enough to cause the same horror as the previous one, I was awoken with a start.

Mum shook me awake. It was time for school, and for once I was glad. At least in lessons I wouldn't be allowed to sleep. There'd be someone there to keep me awake and I wouldn't have to face the terrors again that day.

We were running late, partly because of my nap and partly because Mum hadn't been able to decide what to wear for work, a typical woman. It was raining outside so she decided to go up in the car and gave me a lift. Amy had already walked up with her friends.

Moments later we arrived at school and I headed straight for form, only to find it was deserted. In my zombie-like state I'd forgotten it was Wednesday, which meant our year had assembly. Groaning, I doubled back and stumbled into the hall.

Chairs were arranged in rows with a gap running down the middle. Each form sat together, taking up two and a half rows, with the form teachers sat at the end where they could keep an eye on their students. One of the Deputy Headmasters or the Head of Year usually took the assembly, and that day it was led by our Head of Year, Mrs Redgewell.

"Morning everyone," she began. "I'd like to take this opportunity to welcome you all back after the summer, as we enter the most crucial year of your time with us here."

She proceeded to remind us of a few school rules and we were given a message about the amount of litter round school. I don't remember all the details, bored and not really paying attention as I was.

"Now, let us pray."

Praying seemed pretty pointless, and even if there was a God to listen, I doubted He wanted to hear from me. I was pretty sure the undead weren't His creation. But I put my hands together and bowed my head anyway, intoning the words of the Lord's Prayer as we'd been taught.

With that the assembly was over and I had French, followed by Science. Like Miss Dubois, Mrs Brewins was new to the school and she had no idea how to control a class. Except instead of flicking light switches she stood there at the front of the class with her finger over her lips for silence. When she finally decided we weren't going to get any quieter, she started the lesson, shouting above us all to be heard. Even if we'd been listening we wouldn't have learnt anything. We were meant to be doing Biology first, and then later in the year we'd study Chemistry and Physics, or so she told us. Cells were the first thing we'd be looking at, and she was trying to explain how they worked but was failing badly. Apparently she used to be a farmer and I couldn't help but feel she should have stuck with farming.

After that we had Geography, and then the lesson I had been dreading – English.

I had been taught English by Miss Aughtie for three years running, and to my teenage self it had been torture. She certainly knew how to control the class. Most people were that scared of her, they didn't dare talk at all in her lessons. Those who risked a quick chat while they were working were easily silenced by a single glare. Every school has a teacher everyone hates and fears, and for us it was Miss Aughtie.

Geography came to an end all too quickly and the bell sounded like a death knell. With a heavy heart, I walked down the corridor and into her room, feeling her eyes on me as I walked to my desk.

I couldn't help but feel I'd rather face the nightmares again than spend fifty minutes in a room with her. I was convinced she was a witch from the moment I first laid eyes on her in my second year. She had long mousy coloured hair and her brown eyes seemed to pierce right through to the soul whenever she glared at you. They were always so hard and cold, filled with hate. Her face was permanently twisted in a grotesque expression of contempt for everyone around her, both students and colleagues, like a living gargoyle. She had that bad a reputation, even students who had yet to meet her could be controlled with just the threat of being sent to her.

I sat with Ava. There was a strange scent in the room, one I'd been able to smell with my human senses the year before, but it was stronger as a werewolf. It's something I could never really describe, though Ava once said it smelt like sweaty socks, stale water and wet dog all mixed together. I'd learnt to tune it out with my human senses, but to my newly enhanced senses it remained strong and unpleasant throughout the lesson. The curtains were drawn to shield our eyes from the sun's glare, but even in the sudden dimness of Aughtie's classroom my sight remained sharper than ever, and I wondered if my night vision had also improved. I could clearly see Aughtie's eyes on me in the gloom, but I kept my head down and tried not to draw attention to myself, which was always the wisest course around our most hated teacher. It seemed she still bore a grudge against me, after I'd dared complain about her to Mrs Redgewell for giving us too much homework in Year Nine.

She made us read while she took the register. I read some more of the horror story. Ava was reading some science fiction novel.

When Aughtie finished the register she looked up to find someone reading a kid's book.

"My nine year old nephew reads more challenging books than that!" she said. She was always going on about her nephew, and how great he was. I couldn't help but feel sorry for the kid, my mind always conjuring up images of him being made to study Shakespeare already.

She proceeded to tell us she didn't ever want to see us reading childish books again since they weren't challenging enough for us, and next time it would be a detention. Something inside me rebelled and I amused myself with the thought of bringing in a picture book for the next lesson. I didn't like being told what I could and couldn't do, especially not by a tyrant like Aughtie.

We were then told to put our books away and she launched straight into the lesson and the poems we'd be studying for the first term, along with the essays to be submitted as part of our coursework.

The workload was piling up before we'd even begun. Most teachers would use the first couple of lessons as a gentle start to the year, but Aughtie had us all writing down notes as she went through the first poem we'd be studying.

Ten minutes in and we were disturbed by three Year Seven girls wandering the corridor outside. Aughtie hated any kind of disturbance to her lesson above all else and stormed straight out to challenge them.

"What are you doing out here?" she asked angrily. "Why aren't you in class?"

"Sorry Miss, we got lost."

"That's no excuse to be wandering around while lessons are going on. Why didn't you ask someone for directions? Planners, now!"

One of the girls began to cry at the strictness and lack of understanding, and above all else the unfairness of the unreasonable woman confronting them. Tears were commonplace amongst the younger students.

"The Science corridor is back the way you came and to the left, now get out of my sight!"

The door slammed as the first years practically ran from the room, one of them still sniffling, and the lesson resumed. There was an atmosphere in the class after that little episode but none dared speak out in defence of the girls. I certainly felt a renewed hatred for Aughtie and the way she treated us all. I'm sure the others did too.

I was so tired by that point. And it was so warm in her room that day, even though summer was coming to an end. My eyelids were drooping again, so heavy I could barely lift them. I forced them open a couple of times but it was no good, I just couldn't fight the sleep that was creeping over me, though I knew at any minute Aughtie could explode if she noticed I wasn't paying attention.

Unable to resist it any longer, my eyelids dropped and locked into place, and I drifted off to sleep while the lesson carried on around me as normal, trapped inside that dark place where the nightmares lurked.

The ground rushed by beneath my feet, twigs snapping and burying themselves in the dirt. My breath steamed out before me and I was panting with the effort, sweat soaking my fur, running over my skin. A thread of drool dangled from my lower jaw and fell to the ground, an explosive vibration for the invertebrates beneath the soil. My prey was just ahead and I was closing the distance between us with every bound. She was beginning to tire: I could hear her heart pounding against her chest, her lungs gasping for air, and no doubt her muscles were burning, in need of oxygen.

I leapt over a fallen log and swerved between the trees. She veered to the left and I almost skidded trying to follow her, my claws digging into the dirt, making deep grooves as I sought to keep my balance. Fast and agile as I was, wolves are not built for sharp turns.

She was slowing now and I was almost upon her. I quickened my pace, readying myself to pounce.

A gunshot came from somewhere behind me. The sound rang in my ears and the smell of the gun powder reached my nostrils. I turned round to find someone aiming a rifle at me, and moments later they squeezed the trigger and a sharp pain in my chest told me they had found their mark. I yelped, turned, and ran, the hunter becoming the hunted. There was no sign of my quarry having ever been there, but that didn't matter now.

The hunter pursued me. Who it was I didn't know, since they wore a mask, and there was no scent to give me any more information. But that didn't matter. All that mattered was the hunt. And now I was the prey and the only thing that mattered was my survival.

I ran flat out, easily putting distance between myself and the hunter. I was moving too quickly for them to get another clear shot, and they didn't waste their bullets. I could hear their heavy footfalls behind me, but no human can outrun a wolf, let alone a werewolf.

Blood was flowing freely from the bullet wound, soaking my fur, and I was slowing, growing weaker. Fear had my heart pounding, but that only helped the blood drain away quicker. The world was starting to spin, I was growing dizzy, and finally I collapsed.

Somewhere behind me, the hunter slowed, raising the gun a third time. I lay in the dirt, blood pooling beneath me, my breathing heavy and laboured. I was suddenly a mortal wolf, with no way of saving myself from the death that surely awaited me. And the hunter knew it.

Cautiously at first, they drew closer, perhaps to gloat in their victory or perhaps because it would be easier to kill me with a single shot if they were stood over me. Confident that I wouldn't be rising from what was soon to become my final resting place, they quickened their pace. I could feel the hunter's excitement, the finger squeezing on the final shot, and I was powerless. I looked into the cold and merciless eyes and knew that I was going to die.

The hunter removed her mask and confusion and shock clouded my brain, while fear twisted its deadly knife in my guts. For I knew that face well. It was Aughtie.

I awoke with a start to find Aughtie stood over me, glaring down. Memories of the nightmare fresh in my mind, I yelped as if I was still a wolf, and shrank back from her glare, covering my head with my hands as if it would protect me from the deadly shot.

My classmates laughed while Aughtie screamed her rage, until she shouted for silence. The laughter died immediately.

When it became clear my life wasn't really in danger, I relaxed and let her get on with it. She ordered me to stand and give her my planner, but as I rose to obey I felt the sharp, stabbing pain in my gut that signalled the start of the transformation. I couldn't hide the pain, doubling over in agony as it continued to throb from within.

"Get up!" she screamed. "You are not getting out of detention by playing sick, now give me your planner!"

I didn't hear anything else that was said as I was lost in the pain, an internal battle raging in my head. I just about managed to hand her my planner, but then to my horror I noticed the fur growing out of my hands and panic gripped me. I had to regain control or I was going to transform right there in the classroom, but I had no idea how to stop it, so new to my powers as I was.

Luckily Aughtie hadn't noticed the fur. If it were any other teacher I'd have run out of the lesson without bothering to ask permission, but it just didn't seem an option with Aughtie, such was her power over us.

"Please Miss, I think I'm gonna throw up. Let me go to the toilet and I'll stay behind in break." I fought to keep my voice calm despite the sheer state of panic, which wasn't helping. It was only making the change happen quicker, and I felt sure that a whole room full of people witnessing me turn into a wolf meant my life was over, with or without the Slayers somehow becoming involved.

At first I didn't think she'd let me go. Once Ava had asked to be excused and Aughtie had told her she could wait, since there were only ten minutes left of the lesson. Of course, when you need to throw up waiting isn't really an option so she couldn't help puking on the floor. It was only then Aughtie let her go to see Matron, and then she had the cheek to ask if anyone in the class would clean it! I'd refused, since it was her fault.

She glared at me, and I felt sure she'd pull the same stunt she had with Ava, but then she surprised us all by saying "Make it quick; if you're not back in ten minutes I'll have you in isolation!"

Relieved, I ran for the boy's toilets at the base of the Maths stairs. There was a first year in there, but he took one look at me and ran out. I stared at my reflection in the mirror, afraid that the transformation would be noticeably visible, but my features had barely changed. Whatever had scared him, it wasn't the change. My friends might have noticed a slight difference, but a stranger wouldn't.

My eyes had just started to turn amber. They still looked mostly human but they were definitely tinged with amber, rather than their usual brown. My nose had changed shape slightly, but again not enough to make it unrecognisable as human. Judging from the pain, changes had happened internally, but the only real visible change was the fur that had started on my hands, which felt like it had now spread along my arms and across my chest.

I closed my eyes and took a deep breath. Lady Sarah had said the transformation could be brought on by strong emotions, and I supposed that included fear, so I needed to calm myself. It wasn't easy but somehow I managed to conquer the fight or flight response my body had so suddenly gone into, and as I calmed the fur sank back into my skin, and the pain quickly eased off.

Minutes later I walked back into class, fully human again and free of fear. I was surprised the nightmare had affected me so badly. The previous one during the night had scared me, where I had killed my own sister, but I still didn't really fear my own death, even after the experience of being attacked by the werewolf who turned me. Yet the wolf evidently feared death, for that could be the only reason why I'd started to change. The dream had scared it and it had tried to take over, wanting to run. It was a strange dream, and I wasn't sure I really understood it, but my best guess was the wolf had caused me to dream I was hunting someone again, so I'd fought back, creating a hunter to stop it killing anyone else. Aughtie had been stood over me towards the end of the dream, and aware of her presence I had given the hunter her face. That had to be it. But why it had felt so afraid by the dream I didn't know. It was intelligent enough to know it wasn't real, so why it had felt the need to run was a mystery to me. I could feel its fear, even once I was sat back down. I decided to make it another topic to question Lady Sarah about. It had been a dangerous situation, and I felt I needed to speak to her sooner rather than later. There was no guarantee it wouldn't happen again that day, tired as I was. Forgetting she needed to sleep through the daylight hours, I resolved to visit her after the lesson, through lunch break. After Aughtie had finished shouting at me, of course.

The lesson dragged by. Aughtie had me sit right by her desk so she could keep an eye on me while she was going through the first poem with us. Five minutes before the end she informed us we'd have homework to do, in the form of an entire essay to be done in two nights. Other teachers might have given us something that would take little more than ten minutes, or none at all during the first week while we eased back into school life after the long summer holidays, but not Aughtie. She delighted in giving us as much homework as she possibly could, and she expected six pages of A grade material, otherwise you got it back to do again and again until she was satisfied with it. And she always under marked our work. Ava had found an essay submitted as part of a GCSE exam and it had been given an A. We could just tell by reading it Aughtie would have given it a B. I could hear my classmates complaining under their breath so Aughtie wouldn't hear, but I was too preoccupied to join in the grumbling. I just hoped I wouldn't be kept too long into lunch break so I could make a quick trip to see Lady Sarah.

Finally the bell sounded to signal salvation would soon be at hand, but first I was made to stay behind ten minutes while Aughtie screamed at me some more, then she let me go with a comment in my planner. It would have been detention, but another teacher had been in to see her and suggested to her that perhaps that was a bit harsh for so early on in the year. I silently thanked him and hastily left the room before she could change her mind.

If I left without telling anyone I probably wouldn't be missed, but I went back to form anyway and found Becci there. I told her I was going home for lunch in case anyone went looking for me. We were meant to get permission to go home, and with Mum working at the school, if anyone did notice my absence they would know I didn't have it, which meant I'd be in big trouble. Even at lunch break, you could get isolation just for leaving the school without permission. But I wasn't sure if Dad would be back home by then so even if I asked Mum, they would know I'd not gone back. I would just have to hope no one questioned it if I was missed.

Though I usually stayed at school for lunch, Becci believed me without question. I didn't waste any more time after that: I left form room and walked straight out of school, hoping no one would see me who knew Mum. There were no teachers around so there was no reason why Mum should find out, unless Amy grassed me up, but she was probably in her own form.

I reached the school gates without being stopped and I passed through them, into freedom. It was tempting to skive the last two lessons, but that would be pushing my luck too far. It was too much to hope that word of my absence wouldn't reach Mum. That was the main disadvantage of her working at the school. With any of the teachers I could get away with it if I forged a doctor's note, as long as I didn't do it often enough to make them suspicious. But Mum would of course know if I was faking appointments or not, and I didn't want to end up grounded; it'd be no computer games and no internet for a month if I missed any lessons. Back then I used to think I'd never survive if I was deprived of either my games or the Net, so for the most part I kept out of trouble.

I soon reached the graveyard. It was not until I approached the mausoleum and saw her sleeping form that I realised I'd risked isolation for no reason. I swore at myself. I should have known better: she was a vampire, of course she'd be asleep during the day! She lay there on the coffin, cold and still as death. Asleep she was like a corpse and could easily be mistaken for one, her skin deathly pale, so very cold to the touch, and her breathing to human ears non-existent. If not for my greater sense of hearing and the fact I already knew what she was, I would have believed her to be a corpse. But I could hear her breath like a faint breeze sighing through her body, and her heartbeat, slower than it should be for a living human so that no pulse was detectable. And never once did she move; not a flutter of her eyelids nor a twitch where I touched her arm curiously. Her lips seemed darker than they did when she was awake, almost as if they were darker with the hue of death. Maybe this was a defence mechanism her kind had evolved so that humans would not disturb their sleeping form, believing them to be one of the dead. Maybe her kind were less likely to be killed when sleeping and at their most vulnerable this way. Or maybe it was some other reason connected to her being one of the living dead. I didn't know what the real reason was then and I still don't know now. I never asked her, though whether vampires themselves know, I'm not sure of that either.

I didn't think I could have awoken her even if I'd tried, and I really didn't want to face an angry vampire after Aughtie's lesson. My ears were still ringing with my English teacher's screams of rage. So I left Lady Sarah to sleep, slightly disappointed, and knew I'd have to wait till dusk to talk to her.

Since people thought I'd gone home for lunch, I couldn't go back to school for another forty five minutes when break ended. Fortunately I had a packed lunch that day so I wouldn't starve, and I sat on a tombstone while I ate it, watching birds fly past overhead, lost in thought. It didn't take me long to finish eating and I read some more of my book to pass the time, though I stayed alert to my surroundings for sounds of anyone approaching, ready to sneak out of the graveyard if there was any risk of being seen.

Once I was back at school, the afternoon passed unusually quickly. I had Maths and then PE, which, as I'd predicted, was a lot easier with my new powers. We'd be playing football for the first term, and then moving onto rugby. I'd never been much good at football, probably because I didn't practise that often. Whenever I played with David he always won. Not that day though. He was on the other team, and was unable to believe it when I tackled the ball off him every time and went on to score five goals. We won easily, and afterwards he wanted to know how I'd gotten so good all of a sudden. I told him I'd been practising over the summer, and made a mental note to make it look like I was having a bad day once in a while so people wouldn't get suspicious. I'm not sure if he believed the lie, but I didn't see why he had any reason not to. Whether he did believe it or not, he let it drop.

Home time came and I decided to do a bit of research while I waited for nightfall when I could go and talk to the vampire. And the longer I spent talking to her, the less time I had to face the nightmares that sleep would bring. I hoped she'd be more willing to talk this time. There was so much I wanted to know from her.

When I got in, I dumped my bag in my room and went straight to the computer, only to find Dad was on it. Unable to contain my frustration, I let out a loud, impatient sigh.

"I need to get on there. Got homework to do," I told him.

"Well it's tough, I'm using it for work."

"How long are you gonna be?" I asked him sulkily.

"As long as it takes, Nick!" he said, losing his temper.

"But it's important!"

"So is this!"

We were both shouting at each other then, fists clenched, anger burning in our eyes. I would have loved to punch him right in the middle of his ugly face, knowing I could do a lot of damage if I really wanted to, thanks to my superhuman strength. But I knew whatever I did to him would hurt Mum and Amy too, and I didn't want to see them suffer.

With a deep breath I backed off, relaxing my hands.

"Let me know when you've finished," I muttered, walking away. Why did somebody always have to be on the computer when I needed it?

Luckily I didn't have long to wait before he finished. I searched through countless myths and legends I'd studied before, searching for any truth in them, trying to learn more about myself. A few of them showed signs of traces of the truth, but I couldn't find any myths detailing everything Lady Sarah had told me or that I'd experienced for myself, and while there was plenty on Lycaon, there were no legends of a time when werewolves reigned. I had to wonder again whether she'd been completely truthful with me or not, and whether I should trust her.

Amy came in while I was searching, took one look at the screen and said "You scare me sometimes. Why can't you be normal like everyone else?"

I didn't answer and she left me to it.

I gave up after a while and searched for chat boards supposedly run by lycanthropes. I loved the internet and the sense of freedom it gave me. I could be anyone or anything I wanted and no one would know any different. I had passed myself off as a werewolf before in chat rooms full of people claiming to be real life lycanthropes. I'd always thought they were all nutters like I was, obsessed with werewolves to the point where they wanted to undergo the physical transformation, or even to the point where they believed it to be true. But now it had become a reality for me, I had to wonder. How many of them had really been werewolves, just looking for others of their kind to talk to and learn from, much like I was then?

I had many different identities on the Net, many different usernames on various different websites, and several email addresses. I was sure it would be safe to ask around without the Slayers being able to trace anything back to me if they worked out I was for real. But I wasn't taking any chances so I mixed truth with lies, claiming to be researching the subject for a school project. It generated a lot of interest in the lycanthrope chat rooms I joined that day, but a quick scan through their replies told me they were all human.

After a while I gave up and went on the virtual pet site I played on with Lizzy and Fiona. Lizzy was online and we spent some time roleplaying before Dad came and kicked me off, lecturing me about the amount of time I spent on the Net. He was adamant I'd ruin my eyes and damage my hands if I spent too long on games. He complained if I spent most of the day reading too, lost in a good horror story, or if I was watching horror movies, saying I didn't get enough fresh air. I think he just enjoyed making my life Hell. Everything I enjoyed doing he didn't approve of, and if it wasn't for Mum I'd have never been allowed to do any of those things. He'd probably have locked me out of the house just so I spent some time in the 'fresh air' if Mum hadn't taken my side. I always argued there was no such thing as fresh air anymore anyway, since humans continued to pump it so full of poisonous fumes.

Dinner was ready not long after I'd come off the Net. Mum had done the beef joint, but there would soon be more raw meat to tempt me when the hunger returned next full moon. Since that morning after my first transformation the hunger seemed to have died down to the point where it was no stronger than it had been before I'd been a werewolf. Just before becoming a werewolf I used to complain about being hungry all the time and often claimed I was starving, but that had been nothing compared to the hunger straight after the transformation, when I'd truly felt famished.

After I'd eaten dusk wasn't far off and I decided it was time to pay Lady Sarah another visit.

My parents didn't like me wandering the street alone after dark so I was forced to sneak out through my bedroom window. I told them I was feeling ill again and I was going to bed so as not to be disturbed, then once I was in the safety of my room I climbed out the window. It would have been awkward if I was still human, but my greater agility made it easy. I wanted to jump down, but if anybody saw me they'd know I wasn't human, falling from that height with no broken bones, so I climbed.

It wasn't long before I stood amidst the tombstones for the second time that day. I hadn't met anyone on the way to the graveyard, and the streets beyond the gateway to the resting place of the dead were empty. The graveyard itself seemed deserted, save for the silent inhabitants beneath my feet. I hadn't expected any of the living to be there, except for maybe animal life, but I was disappointed to find Lady Sarah wasn't anywhere to be seen. She wasn't in the mausoleum and she wasn't in the graveyard. There was no trace of her. Perhaps if I understood how to follow scents I might have been able to track her, but I had only been a werewolf for two days, and while the wolf might know how to use my enhanced senses, my human mind couldn't make any sense of what my nose was telling me. I was only just adjusting to the greater sense of hearing.

Disappointment turned to anger. How could she just leave me alone in the world without explaining everything fully? She must know how difficult it was to adjust. I was willing to bet becoming a vampire wasn't all that different to becoming a werewolf, and yeah, it might have been a long time ago when she'd had to deal with it, but she had to remember what it had been like. She might not have mentioned it when she'd told me her own tale, but she could have had help adjusting for all I knew. It seemed unfair that I had to do it on my own. I needed help and if she wasn't going to give it freely I decided I was going to force her to help me, somehow. I might not be able to find her that night, but if she couldn't be there for me when I needed her in the hours of darkness, she'd have to face the sun's deadly rays. I swore to myself I would find some way to wake her the next day, and then she'd have to answer my questions. My survival depended upon it. I had to learn to control the transformation but I needed someone to help me do it.

It was happening again, my stomach ached and I could feel the itching where fur was beginning to grow. Fortunately this time there was no one to see, but I dreaded the thought of it happening again in school. What if I couldn't stop it next time? I desperately needed the vampire's help and she had to know that, so where the hell was she? I kicked a tombstone in frustration with all my strength and yelped at the sharp pain in my toe, which helped stop the change. The tombstone came off worst though. I'd kicked it so hard it uprooted and fell over, the stone cracking and crumbling where my foot had connected with it. Snarling as if it was all the tombstone's fault, I left the graveyard to wander the streets for a while, not wanting to go back home and face sleep. The night was still young, but if I went home my parents would only make me stay in bed after I'd said I wasn't feeling well, and tired as I was, I really didn't want a repeat of the previous night, or the nightmare in Aughtie's lesson that had scared the wolf bad enough to induce a transformation.

I wandered aimlessly long into the night and returned home only when it began to rain, after checking the graveyard one more time. The rain didn't bother me, but if I came back soaking wet Mum and Dad would know I'd lied to them and they'd want to know what I was doing out at night.

The next day I returned to the graveyard but Lady Sarah still wasn't there. There was no way she was walking around in daylight. Had she left the graveyard? The terrifying thought occurred to me that perhaps she had left the town, leaving me all alone. The night before when I'd calmed down and had time to think things over I'd decided she'd been hunting, but she couldn't be out in direct sunlight. So she'd either chosen somewhere else to sleep, moved on to new hunting grounds, or worse, the Slayers had her. And if the Slayers had her and she talked, they'd find out who I was. I still didn't really know whether I could trust her or not.

She wasn't anywhere to be found that night either, or in the days and nights to follow. Practically a month passed and still I hadn't seen her. What little sleep I had was full of nightmares, but no more to cause another transformation, and slowly I was growing used to them, no longer waking up screaming, no longer afraid. No one had any reason to suspect I was no longer human, and despite not being able to find Lady Sarah, everything else was going great. I knew it wouldn't last forever and something would go wrong eventually, maybe even sooner than I was expecting, but the need to find her became less urgent. Still, I checked the graveyard every time I was passing by, with no luck. And before I knew it the moon was growing fatter, the wolf growing stronger, and I would be completely alone this time. If the Slayers hunted me again there would be no Lady Sarah to come to my rescue, and so I was forced to put my trust in the wolf to keep us alive through the night. Intelligent as it was, judging from what Lady Sarah had said they had already outsmarted it once. If they did so again and she wasn't there to save me, I was doomed.

Chapter Six – A Blood Moon Rises

September had become October and the moon was almost full. Autumn was well advanced and with my superior senses I could feel, more so than a human, that winter would soon be here.

The morning before the full moon dawned bright and clear. It held no hint of the gruesome events that would take place that night.

I hadn't been able to sleep again, and it wasn't just down to the nightmares. I was restless, unable to lie still enough to sleep. I'd tossed and turned until eventually I gave up and decided to risk watching an eighteen, needing something to occupy my mind. I had to turn the sound right down so nobody heard it and I watched in the dark. But that was okay, I'd always liked the dark. It held no fears for me, not even as a young boy, and I enjoyed watching horror movies with the lights off, feeling it added to the atmosphere. Even though it was a film I'd seen many times before, there was a certain thrill about watching the film in the dead of night while everyone else was sleeping, knowing at any moment a character might scream too loudly and wake someone. It set my nerves on edge, making me listen hard at every little noise, trying to determine if someone was coming. If I disturbed Dad there'd be hell to pay, and Mum wouldn't be too pleased either. I didn't much care at that point. The same reckless energy I had felt before, just after the full moon of the previous month, had filled me again. The film had finished about an hour before daybreak and I'd been back in bed, feigning sleep long before Mum had come in to wake me.

That morning I stood in the bathroom looking at my reflection, wondering if anything about me had changed. I felt different inside somehow, and I knew it was the moon's cycle affecting me, but I was surprised to find my appearance had barely changed. The eyes were still my own, brownish green, full of laughter and warmth and human emotion, if a little bloodshot from the lack of sleep, so different to the eyes of Lady Sarah. And somehow that didn't seem right. My face was still the same, though round the eyes it looked bruised, the sleepless nights beginning to tell. There was nothing lupine about it, however. Not yet anyway, not till later that night. My ears were still rounded, despite my mind telling me that wasn't right. Every time I heard a noise I instinctively wanted to swivel them like animals do, but they were in the wrong place on my head. I kept feeling the need to sniff the air, even though I still couldn't understand everything my nose was telling me. It did seem like my canines were slightly longer and more pointed than usual, but maybe that was just my imagination.

School went slower than usual that day. I couldn't concentrate on my lessons. Not that I ever paid much attention, but that day my thoughts were somewhere else, running through the woods somewhere, chasing something, like in the nightmares. Only in my daydreams, while the wolf was certainly influencing them, I was still in control. During the day the prey was always animals.

I wanted to run and when it was time for PE I enjoyed it more than ever, though I had to fight the urge to drop to all fours, no matter how much more comfortable my brain kept trying to tell me it would be.

We were already overrun with coursework and we had PD (short for Personal Discipline) that day, a free period for the teachers to sort out detentions and isolations and things, as well as signing off credits in our planners, given out to reward good behaviour. PD was spent in form, and it wasn't timetabled; it took place when we should have had another lesson, but the time and day changed each week so that we didn't miss the same lesson all the time. Lower years were meant to read through PD when they'd sorted out everything with the teachers, but with the GCSE exams drawing closer by the day we could use the time to catch up on coursework. I was too distracted to do any work and sat gazing out of the window, watching the birds fly by and fighting the instinct to hunt.

The hunger hadn't returned which surprised me. I'd been content with a normal sized meal at lunch. Yet I still wanted to hunt. I felt like a caged animal, stuck inside that room.

"Haven't you got coursework to do, Nick?" Ms Brooks asked me, breaking through my thoughts.

"Yeah, I should probably do some but I really can't be bothered today," I said.

"That's not the right attitude, Nick," she told me, sternness creeping into her voice while Becci sniggered.

I shrugged and went back to staring out of the window.

Evening came. I sat watching TV with my family, but I was restless again, even more so than I had been through the previous night. I kept shifting position on the sofa until I felt the need to stand and pace.

"What's got into you?" Amy asked, giving me a look that said she thought I was a weirdo.

I paused and glanced at her but didn't answer, resuming my pacing.

"Nick, will you stop pacing?" Dad snapped. "You'll wear the floorboards out! Be still."

"I'm not a dog, I don't have to obey you," I snarled. An anger sparked inside, both from human and wolf.

"Don't talk to me like that! I'm your father," he bellowed. "Go to your room! Now!"

"I've had enough of you anyway," I spat, and turned my back on him. I left him fuming and began to climb the stairs when the first wave of pain crashed against me, a faint slither of moonlight filtering through from one of the bedrooms. I faltered halfway up and fell to my knees, gripping the banister to keep from falling all the way down. It wasn't quite as bad as the first time, but it was still agony as my whole body began to shift shape. I wanted to curl up into a ball and wait for it to pass, except that it didn't work like that. I remember this transformation clearer than the first, though I'm not sure why. When the fur began to sprout from my skin, I knew I had to reach the safety of my room before the pain reached the point where it was too intense to move.

I gritted my teeth against that internal agony and began to crawl up the steps like I had so many times before, but that time I wasn't pretending to be a monster. Limbs were shifting before my eyes. My fingers were shortening, sucked back into my hand, pads forming and fusing them together, while the nails lengthened and became claws. It was a painful process that felt like my bones were being ground together, melting away until they reached the right length. And I hadn't even set eyes upon the moon yet.

My thumbs lost their dexterity, becoming dew claws, and the bones in my hand elongated until each dew claw was too high up to be of any real use. Similar changes were already beginning in my feet. True wolves have no dew claw on their rear legs, however, so my little toes, being the least developed, were fast disappearing, and each foot needed to lengthen significantly to allow me to stand on all fours.

It took all my physical and mental strength to keep myself moving upwards. Though in reality it was a short distance, the staircase seemed to stretch ahead of me, so far that it might lead to the very stars and the moon that caused the agony.

Nearing the top, another wave of pain racked my body and I had to dig my claws into the floor to keep from sliding back down. Deep scars were gouged into the woodwork, but I had other things to worry about. Movement was aggravating the pain, and I knew I had to reach the sanctuary of my room soon. Just two more stairs and then across the landing and I'd be there, just had to push myself a little harder…

My claws still digging into the wood, I used them to heave myself up to the top where I paused, panting from the effort. My tongue hung out like a great fat worm over teeth that were fast becoming fangs. My gums throbbed where new teeth were growing at the back, while pain shot through the teeth already in place as they elongated, the ends becoming thinner and thinner until they came to a point. The canines were the most unpleasant, and they grew to the point where they pressed painfully against my gums, no longer fitting comfortably inside my mostly human mouth. It seemed the changes were random, for I was sure it hadn't happened in that order before.

I crawled towards my room and collapsed inside, painfully twisting round to shut the door. My clothes suddenly felt too tight and I struggled out of them as best I could before they ripped apart like the previous month. My t-shirt came off fairly easily but without opposable thumbs it was impossible to undo the fly on my jeans. Somehow I painfully managed to wriggle out of them but I knew I was going to have to get into the habit of stripping off before the change started in future. If I'd left it just a few minutes longer I didn't think they'd have come off in one piece. My underwear I was less worried about since I had plenty of socks and boxer shorts, and I doubted anyone would notice another pair had gone missing.

I lay sprawled out on the floor as the other changes took place, bathed in the moon's light. It felt more comfortable to stretch out my limbs while the bones continued to elongate or shorten as necessary, but I wanted to curl up again when the pain intensified in my gut. It always seemed to start there, and it didn't seem possible that it could increase any more, but it had. My blood boiled and my muscles rippled, but it was nothing compared to whatever was happening inside my stomach. I think I read somewhere wolves have a shorter gut so as to be able to digest raw meat. Maybe that explained the feeling that my intestines had been twisted and tied into knots, and the way they slithered like snakes beneath my skin. The greater amount of acid necessary for killing the bacteria in raw meat was probably the reason behind my stomach seemingly being turned inside out. That's what it felt like anyway. I'd been lying on my stomach, but I had to roll over onto my back. Despite the pain, I sensed I was growing more powerful. I could feel it coursing through my veins, all the more potent with the anger Dad had caused.

Breathing soon became painful. Each breath was shallow and quick as if I were dying from a hole in my lungs, and I didn't want to think about what might be happening to them. My heart felt as if it were being squeezed while it sought to beat and pump the blood around my body. Sweat trickled down my changing form as I writhed on the floor, levering myself up on my elbows when my back caught on fire, some kind of change happening to the spine, only to fall back and then rise up onto my shoulder blades as a tail grew out from the end. I wanted to scream for it to end, scream for death to come and take me, save me from the pain. But my vocal cords had changed and I was unable to make any sounds other than those of an animal: grunts of pain, snarls, growls, yelps.

My face stretched outwards until it formed a snout. My skull felt like it was splitting down the middle as the anatomy changed. My ears migrated upwards. The optic nerves behind my eyes changed so that my night vision improved, though I could still see in colour, unlike true wolves. The whole of my head was being rewired like a computer, being transformed into a completely new machine, one programmed to hunt and kill.

More wolf than human, I rolled back over onto my stomach where it had become more comfortable, and risked standing on all fours while the final changes took place. If I thought the world was alien before, it was nothing compared to what it was then. But I didn't have much time to explore that world, with its even louder sounds and greater scents, for the wolf had been waiting all month for the chance to hunt, and now its time was come and it would wait no longer. Like a dormant volcano it erupted into my consciousness, its thoughts flooding my brain, as alien as the world around. How could it be a part of me? And yet it was. It pushed me aside and I was drowned in its dominating mind until I lost sight of the surface of our consciousness. Forced down into our collective sub consciousness all went black. There I lay in wait, dead to the world, waiting for the sun to bring me back to the living.

I stood in the room, waiting for the final changes to completely finish, scenting the air and pricking my ears for a hint of prey. The hunger was already taking hold again. There were three humans in the building with me, each one an easy meal. No, Lady Sarah had opened my eyes to reality. I had to be more careful when hunting. Their screams would be heard in neighbouring houses, and I would soon become the hunted.

But I could find no way out that night – there was no opening in the glass wall for me to jump through as there had been before and, if I shattered the glass, the noise would bring humans, and probably the Slayers too.

I paced the length of the room, looking for a way out. I stood up on my back paws, resting my front paws on the windowsill for a better view of the glass standing between myself and freedom, trying to find why there was no opening this time where there had been before.

Finding no reason why the opening was not there, I was about to look elsewhere for an escape route to freedom and the endless hunting grounds the town offered, but then I noticed a handle which had been pushed up last time when it was open. To my delight I discovered that, if I nudged it up with my snout and pushed against the glass, it swung outward. Wasting no more time, I leapt out into the night.

An hour later I had been prowling through my territory looking for suitable prey but I had so far found none. The streets were deserted, with not even a cat in sight. There was human life to be found for those who knew where to look, however (and I had learnt much in the past month from the human, gently probing its mind so as not to arouse suspicion, for I knew it didn't trust me). But even without that knowledge all I needed was to follow my nose.

Thanks to the human I knew the route to the town centre well, and once I was there it didn't take me long to find my prey, gathered in large herds flocking to their nightclubs and bars. Once I was inside the buildings would become slaughterhouses; I would massacre them and feast on their flesh until morning light. Or I would if it wasn't for the fear of the Slayers. But not only that, the sound blaring out from the buildings repelled me. A battering ram against my ear drums, it was strong enough to rip through them and deafen me. It hurt my sensitive ears and confused my brain. And in my confusion I snarled and snapped at thin air, as if I could silence the sound somehow, until fear had me running from the pain. And so I ran back to the quiet streets I had already explored. Away from the noise, I came to my senses and realised I was back where I'd started: no prey to hunt and growing ever more ravenous.

Hunger and desperation drove me to scavenge from a bin outside one of the nearby houses from which I could smell rotting flesh. I would have preferred fresh meat, and I craved human blood for it was part of the curse, setting me apart from true wolves. But it was either that or go hungry.

I knocked over the bin, spilling its contents, and found a half eaten roast chicken which I wolfed down, pardon the pun. But the rest was just scraps that could not even be considered a small snack, and not wanting to stay in one place for too long, coupled with the knowledge that the other bins would most likely be the same, I was driven away from the town towards the farmer's fields.

I wandered the fields until I came upon a large herd of sheep. They had not scented me as yet and I remained downwind of them, selecting which one to take.

83

Sadly there were no tender lambs at that time of year, but I picked out the youngest in the herd and stalked towards her.

As I advanced closer the sheep scented me and bleated in panic, and I heard a sheep dog bark from a kennel not far off near the farmer's house. It wouldn't save them.

Before they knew what was happening I had lunged at my chosen victim and had crushed her neck in my strong jaws, her blood leaking into my mouth and dripping to the floor.

I quickly dragged the sheep to the edge of the fields, back near where they became streets, and ripped open her soft underbelly.

I was so hungry I stripped her bones completely of their flesh and began to devour the soft organs. I swallowed the kidneys whole. The liver I bit in two. One half slid down my throat while the other fell to the ground, lying there like a lump of jelly before I swallowed that down as well. The stomach I bit into and licked at the contents that oozed out, a green liquid mixture of acid and enzymes and half digested grass.

I greedily devoured the other organs, then I slipped away before the farmer followed the slight trail of blood I had left and discovered me with the body of one of his sheep. I didn't want to find myself staring at the wrong end of a gun's barrel again.

But I was still hungry and I desired human flesh this time. It would have been easier to return to the field and take another sheep, but I could not risk the farmer finding me, for I would surely be shot. So I took to wandering the streets once more.

I was lucky to find a fresh trail of a male human youth of the age of seventeen. I followed the trail, drool and blood dripping from my jaws, and was rewarded when I found him walking alone.

Too hungry to play with him first, I pounced and knocked him to the ground. The human landed heavily on his back, I on top of him. He screamed but I quickly slaughtered him by crushing his head, forever silencing him. His brains oozed out onto the street while I hungrily lapped them up.

I ate the more appetising parts until the hunger was satisfied, then I buried the carcass in the nearest garden as I had the previous month.

After that I decided to seek out the vampire who I had found before, as she was my leader. Had she been one of my kind I would have sought her out first so that we could hunt together, but I knew her kind were for the most part solitary, and preferred to hunt alone. And besides, I was strong enough and fast enough to hunt alone too. The human had been searching for her, but though I had learnt much from it over the past month, I didn't understand every thought running through its half of our mind. A month wasn't long enough to learn an entire language.

So it was that I came to the graveyard in which she resided and, like the human, found no trace of her. Not even a scent trail for me to follow.

The night was still young and I had nowhere to go. Alone but well fed, and content for the moment, I decided to settle down amongst the graves, feeling it was as safe a place as any. I slept there for the rest of the night with an ear cocked and an eye half open, and my nose pointing upwards into the wind, ready to bolt if the Slayers showed up again. The human had always been a light sleeper and I was no different. I would awake at the slightest hint of danger.

Close to sunrise, I returned to my room where I could transform back to human in safety.

Over the next two nights I would hunt again and take more human victims. The vampire was nowhere to be found, but I didn't run into the Slayers either. On the third night, the full moon set for the final time that month and I was reluctantly forced back into the depths of our mind, while the human dominated us again.

Chapter Seven – All Hallow's Eve

After the full moon the month passed slowly, without event. Mum took me to see the optician, who couldn't explain why my vision had suddenly corrected itself, though nothing bad came of it. The scratches I had made in the floor had been blamed on next door's cat, who had somehow got into the house earlier that day. The cat's timing couldn't have been better. I'd managed to dispose of my torn socks and boxers again before anyone found them and it raised awkward questions. I had still been unable to find Lady Sarah, but there'd been no other close calls since the beginning of the transformation in Aughtie's lesson, and finding her didn't seem so urgent. Halloween was on its way, my favourite night of the year. I used to love the excuse to dress up as monsters and scare people, and in all the excitement Lady Sarah was forgotten.

Fiona would be trick or treating with one of her friends from the year below us, Jessica, and she invited me along. I'd had other plans, thinking I'd find some way to set up the ultimate scare for anyone who was brave enough to approach our house, but I hadn't been out trick or treating for a couple of years so I agreed. I already had a costume in mind for the night, though I thought it was a pity I couldn't control the transformation yet.

If only I could control it so that I could change far enough to become something half human, half wolf like in the movies, everyone would think it the ultimate Halloween costume. I wouldn't take it so far that it wouldn't pass as a costume, just enough to make it effective. However, since I didn't even know how to become a full wolf at will – which was probably easier because, as I'd found out in Aughtie's lesson, once the change had begun, it was hard to stop it – or whether it was even possible to do that, I would have to settle for the grim reaper costume I had already chosen. Which was just as well, considering how reckless a part way transformation would be, no matter how far or how little I took it, but at the time it seemed a good idea, if only I'd known how.

Halloween was a Friday that year, so my parents had said I could be out later than usual, as long as it was a reasonable time and I stayed with Fiona and Jessica. I had the feeling it was going to be a good night.

The day passed slowly. I had double Graphics periods three and four, which was another lesson I had with Lizzy.

I took my seat beside her and she wasted no time asking me what I was doing for Halloween that night. I told her about my plans with Fiona and Jessica to which she complained "Well she never invited me!"

"Oh, that's odd. You haven't fallen out over owt have you?" I asked her.

"Not that I know of," she replied. "I'm off to a party anyway."

"Well maybe that's why she didn't invite you if she already knew," I said.

"Would've been nice for her to ask though," Lizzy grumbled.

Silence fell while the register was taken, then our first piece of coursework which we'd handed in a week earlier was given back to us.

"I got an A⁺, yay me!" Lizzy said.

"Nice one!" I looked at my own work as it was handed back to me. "A B? There must be a mistake. I mean look at that, clearly graphical genius!"

"Yeah, dream on Nick", Lizzy told me and then after a pause she said "Graphical? Is that even a word?"

"Probably not in the context I used it but you know what I meant," I laughed.

We were instructed to make a start on the next piece of coursework. We would be making pop-up books on any subject we wanted, and now all the design work was out of the way it was time to begin making the actual product. I'd chosen to do mine on dinosaurs, another childhood obsession, and Lizzy had chosen to do hers on Disney's Winnie the Pooh.

Lizzy withdrew a pair of blunt scissors she carried in her pencil case for Graphics. She pinched the skin of her wrists and tried to cut the flesh, which always worried me even though I knew the blades were too blunt to actually do anything. They barely cut through paper.

She was weird like that sometimes. I didn't know why she did that or whether there was anything going on at home that made her act a bit melodramatic at times, since we never really talked about that kind of thing. After all, that's what girls do, talk about all their problems. I might have hung around with girls but that didn't mean I was one. As far as I knew she never tried to slit her wrists with anything sharp enough to actually do the job so mostly I just left her to it, assuming she wasn't really serious about suicide.

"Want me to fetch some scissors?" I asked her.

"Please, these are useless," she replied, giving up on her wrist.

Once I'd grabbed all the tools we needed to get to work, I sat back at the desk and picked up a pair of school scissors, ready to attack the sheet of paper in front of me and do something vaguely creative.

"You know you're holding those scissors the wrong way again, right?" Lizzy asked me.

I looked at my hand and realised I'd put my fingers through the smaller hole that was meant to be for my thumb, and my thumb through the bigger hole that was meant to be for my fingers.

"I can't believe you still do that. Some days I swear it's like you don't know how to be human. I know you love werewolves Nick, but there's being a fan and then there's being obsessed," she said.

That was something else I'd done all my life, though not on purpose. She was right: it was like some days I didn't know how to be human. There were times when human activities even felt awkward, and that was before I'd been bitten. Once more I found myself wondering, if I was truly descended from wolves, whether that had something to do with my strange behaviour over the years. A lot of activities required of me as a human seemed to go against my instincts, like running on two legs. Even before I'd been bitten there were times when I felt it would be more comfortable to drop to all fours. I'd always assumed it was just wishful thinking but it seemed maybe there had been more to it. Of course I couldn't tell Lizzy any of that, so I just laughed and agreed with her.

After the lesson I spent lunch with Lizzy. We ate in the canteen together before heading back to her form, slower than usual because we were busy talking. I heard a loud sigh behind us and someone exclaimed "It's like waiting for a bus!"

The next thing I knew, two boys had pushed their way past us, shoving me into the wall. The last time this had happened in Year Ten it had angered me, though I'd kept the anger well hidden. Then minutes later I was doing my best to laugh it off with Lizzy, who again had been with me at the time. She'd asked me "Why do you let them push you around?" I'd shrugged and she'd let it drop. That day, however, the anger was uncontrollable.

It broke free of its chains and escaped through my mouth in an animal roar of fury. A red haze descended over my eyes, a sea of blood, with the two boys the only clear things left in my sight. I was only dimly aware of the shocked look on Lizzy's face, but I was very much aware of the mocking expressions on the faces of the two boys, who were laughing at my reaction. Their laughter cut through me like knives through my flesh, wounding, scarring, fuelling the hate. It made me bleed like I had throughout my childhood when they taunted and laughed and mocked, all of them, and I was suddenly sick of it. I growled and charged at them, their laughter soon turning to surprise and then to a smug confidence, and finally to horror when I was suddenly on one of them, moving too quick for them to react.

One of them had short, dark brown hair but I can't remember his face. He wasn't particularly tall or bulky but he liked to shadow other bullies, where he could taunt his victims whilst remaining safe in the presence of his larger counterparts. The other I knew well, for he had been determined to make my life Hell since he first laid eyes on me in Year Seven. Like the stereotypical bully, he was an ugly son of a bitch built like a thug, and though he looked dim-witted he was surprisingly intelligent. His short hair was a dirty blonde, his eyes a blueish grey and cold, full of laughter and cruelty, set in a round face dotted with freckles. And he was the one I wanted to hurt most, make him pay not just for everything he had done to me, but for all those years suffering at the hands of bullies just like him.

Before I knew what I was doing I had him by the throat, pinned to the wall, and my fist was drawn back ready to beat the crap out of him. And I would have done if it hadn't been for Lizzy and the other boy trying to pull us apart. My grip was so tight I was choking him, and I didn't take kindly to the interruption. Feeling Lizzy's hands on my arm, trying to pull me away, I snarled and turned on her, ready to lash out. The anger melted away as soon as I saw the hurt look on her face that I would strike her. I looked back at Jamie and realised he was turning blue, struggling to breathe. I relaxed my grip and turned away indifferently, while Lizzy whispered in my ear "Have you gone mad? Aughtie's coming! When I said don't let them push you around I didn't mean go this far. Jesus, Nick, you looked like you were going to kill him!"

I didn't answer and we hurried back to her form room in silence, before Aughtie could question any of us. She kept giving me worried looks through the remaining lunch hours, and I was glad when lunchtime ended and I could escape her. Deep down I knew she was only looking out for me, but I had enough problems without her worrying and starting to ask awkward questions. The brief encounter had been unlike me and she knew better than to believe my reassurances that everything was okay. I didn't want to have to start avoiding her but it seemed like I might not have an option in future, unless I could learn to control myself better.

Jamie was in a few of my lessons, including the two I had that afternoon, but he avoided me. He'd obviously been shaken by my sudden display of violence, though he tried his best to hide it from everyone else. By the end of Period Six I forgot the anger and the hate, locking them away in the dark place in my soul, my thoughts turning to Halloween as I filled with the excitement it brought.

Later that night I'd changed into my skeleton outfit, complete with scythe, and was waiting for Fiona to call. A few young kids came trick or treating with their parents while I was waiting. Every time the door closed Mum and Amy kept going on about how cute they were. I sat there rolling my eyes, bored and wishing Fiona would hurry up.

Movement on the edge of the carpet by the wall caught my eye as a spider scuttled along. Amy hated spiders and I was feeling mischievous that night, and in need of some fun while I waited for my friends.

"Hey Amy!" I yelled. "I've got something to show you."

"So? I don't care about anything you've got to show me, geek."

I'd caught the spider on my hand and it was running along my knuckles, trying to escape.

"Oh no you don't," I muttered, and nudged it back over onto my palm. Finally it lay still, quivering. I closed my fist and ran upstairs.

Amy was in her room and the door was closed so I knocked. She glared when she opened it to find it was me.

"Trick or treat," I said and opened up my hand. Exposed to the light, the spider started making a bid for freedom again.

She screamed and ran into her room, slamming the door behind her. I forced my way in and she screamed again, running to the furthest corner and scrabbling up her bunk bed to be as far away from the spider as possible.

"Mum! Tell Nick, he won't leave me alone!" she screamed, while I doubled up with laughter.

"Nick! What are you doing to your sister?" Mum shouted up.

"Nothing, Mum," I said innocently.

Footsteps on the stairs and Mum came through the open door. Nobody ever believed me.

"He's got a spider, Mum," Amy sobbed, bursting into fake tears.

"Stop teasing your sister and get rid of it Nick," she told me, handing me a tissue to kill it.

"It's got a big fat body, should squish nicely," I said, and crushed it in the tissue, opening it back up to prove it was dead. "Look, you can see all the juices have come out."

"Nick, don't. Do you always have to be so disgusting?" Mum asked.

I pretended to look thoughtful for a moment before answering "Yup. Besides, it's Halloween. Get into the spirit of things."

Mum rolled her eyes and walked out, bidding me to follow and leave Amy in peace. Minutes later there was a knock at the door. Fiona stood in the doorway with Jessica and her little sister Hannah, who I eyed with distaste.

"You didn't tell me there'd be kids," I said. I hated kids. Hannah was dressed as a witch with a green face, wearing a pointy hat, a cape and carrying a broomstick. I could hear Amy's exclamations of how cute she was in the background.

"Sorry, Mum made me bring her along," she told me.

"I'll put up with a kid just this once, but I hope you know this is seriously damaging to my image! The King of Horror can't be seen with kids," I said, using the title I'd come up with for myself for when I was to become famous. "Unless maybe he's torturing them."

Mum overheard. "Oh Nick, don't say such things."

"So what are you two meant to be?" I asked, ignoring Mum. Both were wearing their school uniform with shirts pulled out and ties hanging loose (the teachers were really strict about our uniform; shirts had to be tucked in otherwise we risked a comment and ties had to be fastened tight and to the right length), and they'd painted freckles all over their faces. They had their hair in pigtails.

"Naughty school girls," Fiona answered.

"Well you didn't need to dress up for that," I laughed.

After promising Mum I wouldn't be too late home and that we'd stay together, we set off down the street.

I had a great time, knocking on doors with the scythe which looked really effective, scaring young kids out with their parents and revelling in the praise for my costume, as people told me how cool it looked. Even an old lady thought it was a great costume, though most of the older residents didn't celebrate Halloween. One miserable sod tried telling us he didn't have anything to give us, so I wanted to play a trick on him but Fiona said we'd get into too much trouble, and I let it go.

After a couple of hours of roaming the streets, we decided to head back to Fiona's house. For one thing, we needed to get Hannah home. Fiona had promised her mum she'd have her back before eight.

We were walking down Fiona's street, eating the sweets we'd collected. Me and Fiona were walking together in front, Jessica and Hannah behind. Fiona was telling me excitedly about a dance tournament she had coming up in the next couple of months or so. I feigned polite interest and encouraged her that she was almost guaranteed first place, but I switched off when talk turned to her boyfriend and how she believed him to be the one. She'd already picked out her prom dress even though it was still months away and she had him making plans on their entrance. There was a prize for best entrance as well as the obvious title of Prom Queen, and I knew she would love to win either. Any girl would.

We hadn't gone far down the street when Hannah cried out from somewhere behind. We turned round to find her in a heap in the bushes, fighting to get up, her cape caught in the branches. I don't know if it was all the sugar I'd eaten in the sweets, the excitement Halloween held, for me at least, or the wolf blood running in my veins, making me feel more alive in the darkness, but I burst out laughing and couldn't stop, even after Fiona had untangled her little sister and we set off walking again.

I had fallen behind, still laughing, when I happened to glance down the street and saw something to still my heart. The laughter died in my throat.

Shadows moved at the end of the street and it was gone, but I knew what I had seen. I'd noticed a definite improvement in my night vision like I'd suspected there might be that day in the dimness of Aughtie's room, and now my eyes could penetrate the darkness where human eyes could not.

Uncertain, I stood thinking. We'd be safer at Fiona's house, though if it was what I thought it had been Fiona could be in danger if we led it back to her family. For I was sure I had seen a human figure in the shadows. It had to be a Slayer; who else would be following us? Unless my eyes deceived me and it had been a large animal wandering the streets. Was I just being paranoid? I couldn't take the risk. And if it had indeed been a Slayer and they knew I was the werewolf they'd been hunting on the night of my first full moon, they may well use Fiona and her family to get to me. I wouldn't let that happen.

The others looked back at me, realising I'd fallen behind. Before I could do anything, shadows moved down the side of the house nearest to the others. Another one? Almost too quick for me to follow, far too quick for human eyes, the thing struck. Glued to the spot, I could do little more than watch in horror as it held Hannah in a death grip. It was human in form but I knew then it was far from human.

He looked like a pale man dressed like a goth, complete with full length black leather coat and leather boots, and long hair blacker than the night atop a face twisted with eternal hunger, almost bestial. His nose was slightly flatter than it should have been, like a bat's, and his eyes burned with that hunger. His canines elongated as I watched until they extended over his bottom lip and came to a point halfway down his chin. Even his ears weren't human; they were slightly pointed which again put me in mind of a bat. Time seemed to slow as I watched him open his mouth wide and lower his lips to the little girl's neck to give her the kiss of death. His fangs pressed against the skin right where the jugular vein rested beneath, about to pierce it and plunge into the bloodstream to suck the precious life from her.

The other humans still didn't know what had happened. Suddenly a stranger had appeared in their midst and they still hadn't recovered from the initial shock. I had, yet I still hadn't moved, indecisiveness preventing me from reacting.

At the first pinpoint of blood on her neck I knew I had to do something before he killed her. It quickly became a thin trickle as the fangs slid a little deeper, threatening to become a fountain if the wound wasn't healed over soon. If it were any other kid I don't know if I would have left them to the vampire, but as it was she was Fiona's little sister and I had to do something. Didn't I?

No. I didn't. The memory of the night I had been bitten had chosen to return to me and suddenly I remembered it clearer, the vampire's attack bringing it all back to me, and I remembered my friends leaving me to die. And Fiona had been one of them. Why should I risk my life to save her sister? She'd left me to die. But could I live with myself if I did nothing while Hannah approached the point of death with every drop the vampire drew from her veins? I felt I didn't owe Fiona anything since she'd run and left me to my fate, even if she was supposedly a friend. I could simply turn my back on the three of them and let the vampire gorge himself. It would be a tragedy, a little girl killed at so young an age, but these things happen. Predators feed on prey. It's always been nature's way, even if the predator in question was unnatural. And she had to die at some point anyway, mortal as she was. If I interfered the vampire may simply kill me and still feast on Hannah, since I doubted he would drink the blood of a werewolf when it was human prey he craved. Could I really leave her to die though? A little voice from the darkest depths of my soul kept screaming *but Fiona left you to die!* I ignored it. Whatever I have become over the years, I wasn't completely consumed by darkness so early in my lycanthropy, and the light was winning.

I roared a challenge at the vampire. I didn't really know what I was doing. Panic had driven me to distract him in any way I could, and it had been the first thing that came to my mind.

The vampire's head whipped up, anger at being disturbed when feeding etched into his bestial features. He snarled and I thought he really was going to kill me, but tossed Hannah aside like a rag doll, hissing "You!"

I backed away, conscious of the blood leaking from the wounds in the young girl's throat, knowing it had to be stopped. Fortunately I'd stopped the vampire before he'd made the wounds deep enough to be fatal.

"Fiona, stop the bleeding!" I yelled before the vampire was on me. Fiona staggered backwards slightly as if I'd slapped her round the face and looked around dazedly. Finally she had the sense to tear a strip of material off her shirt and press it to her sister's neck.

The vampire pinned me to the ground by the throat. I struggled to free myself, thrashing around like a maddened animal, all to no avail. He was too strong, and though I landed a couple of blows on his arms and chest, he refused to move. I realised I was powerless to do anything if he decided to kill me and gave up fighting him, letting myself relax, waiting for death to come.

"You," he repeated.

"Have we met?" I asked, studying his face. I was sure I'd remember a face like that.

"Not in person, but I've heard so much about you," he said, leering at me. "You spoilt everything. So young, so full of life, so sweet... She's mine and there's nothing you can do about it."

"You'll have to kill me first."

"Maybe I will," he replied.

He tightened his grip on my throat. Breathing became harder and I started to choke. Instinctively I started to lash out again and thought I had caught him a lucky blow on the side of the head when he fell off me, but someone held out a hand to let me up and I realised it had been they who had saved me. I took the hand and they pulled me to my feet, coughing and gasping for breath. Once I'd recovered I looked at my rescuer and was surprised to find it was Lady Sarah.

"Where've you been? I've been looking for you!" I rasped, my throat feeling a little sore. Before she could answer I was aware of Fiona's and Jessica's eyes on me and wondered what to tell them. They looked at me uncertainly, so I said "Hey guys, this is my, er, cousin Sarah, and this is one of her friends. It was meant to be a joke but he took it a bit too far."

I glared at the vampire who lay on the floor where Lady Sarah had struck him down. I don't think they believed me, so I suggested they take Hannah home while I spent some time with my 'cousin'. They didn't argue and as soon as the door closed behind them I turned back to Lady Sarah, waiting for an explanation.

"My friend needed help. It was no longer safe for him to feed in his usual hunting ground so I brought him back here," she said to me, before turning to him. "And I told you not to hunt children! Will you ever learn your lesson? It would still be safe in your own territory if you did not prey on children so often. We have enough with the Slayers hunting us; we do not need the police on our trail as well. And you know preying on children always makes them search harder for the killer. By rights you should be dead by now."

He looked away from her as if he knew she was right, but would never admit it. When he looked back his face had changed; he looked like Lady Sarah, a human with a face too perfect to be a mortal man, who had been around the same age as her when he'd been turned. He got to his feet and studied me, the hunger gone from his eyes now. Without it, his eyes were very different to Lady Sarah's. They were much more human, as if, like myself, he had recently become undead, and he dressed so differently to the Medieval vampire too.

"Sorry about that mate, I guess I let the hunger get the better of me," he said. I was too surprised by the difference between his speech and Lady Sarah's to reply. "If we were still living in the Middle Ages like Lady Sarah here, I would be Sir Vincent of Desmodontidae, but since we're in the new millennium you can call me Vince."

He held out his hand. I took it dazedly, unsure by the turn of events.

"Vincent chooses to live amongst humans when he's not hunting," Lady Sarah told me with obvious disapproval. "Most of us leave the human world behind after a decade or two, if not sooner."

After a pause she added, almost sadly, "Though I do miss All Hallow's Eve."

"Well I'm glad you're here, I've been wanting to talk to you," I said, snapping out of it.

"Not here, you never know who might be listening," she told me.

When she led us back to the graveyard I hesitated before telling her about the past couple of months, still unsure whether I could trust either of them. Particularly Vince, after the close call with Hannah. Yet there was no one else there for me and I couldn't survive alone; I needed to understand more about the new world I had been plunged into. So I told her everything that had happened since we last met.

"Understand this," she said when I'd finished. "Dreams are more than mere random thoughts and images conjured up by the brain in a semi-conscious state. Yes, sometimes they have no meaning, but sometimes they are much more than that. Dreams can be images from the past, present or future, though what you may see in the future may not necessarily be what comes to pass. Do not disregard any of your dreams, for some of them may have a meaning. However, with you it is more complicated. Some of the dreams will come from the human part of your mind, while others come from the wolf. Some may hold meaning for one but not the other. The wolf may already know about the potential power of dreams, therefore it was scared by what it saw in the dream about the hunter, and the fear was enough to trigger the change. As for teaching you to control it, I promised to help where I can and I will, but it is really something you must learn for yourself."

Over the next hour Lady Sarah talked me through becoming a wolf at will. I can't really explain to a mortal how it's done or how she taught me to do it. All I know is, somewhere in those sixty minutes I concentrated on transforming into a wolf, willed it to happen, and finally it did.

Of course, to transform that meant I needed to strip off, so I could dress again when we'd finished and return home. The vampires sensed something of my discomfort at being naked in front of them and stared fixedly at my face. I cupped myself to protect my modesty as best I could while I was still human. But I soon forgot my embarrassment once the transformation began.

The first time I began to change, the pain, while not as powerful as at full moon, became unbearable and I lost control long enough for the fur that had begun to appear to melt back into my skin. The few bones that had begun to change in size and shape returned to their original form. I had to learn to distance myself from the pain to keep the transformation going. I soon found it became easier once I was more wolf than human, because my body seemed to want to keep going, and after several attempts I stood on all fours, experiencing the wolf's superior senses with the human part of my mind for the first time. I also had to learn to remain in control once in wolf form, as the lupine half of my mind was much stronger and I could feel it clawing its way up into my consciousness, crawling up out of the darkness in my soul. It was exhausting work, mentally and physically, and I felt the hunger as powerful as during a full moon. The vampires had to keep catching small prey to keep me going, though it was far from enough to satiate that unnatural hunger.

Once I had mastered the change, I had to learn to control it to the point where I could stop it at any time, without it reversing straight away. That part was much harder. My body wanted to be one form or the other, and whenever I stopped the change halfway it wanted to either return to human or keep going to wolf, depending on which form I was closest to. It took a further hour before I could stop the transformation at any point without losing the changes that had already taken place. Lady Sarah told me this would help give me complete control over my form at all times except for the full moon, so there would be no further problems if I started to turn again in public.

After the worst of the pain was over it was a great experience for me. Part man, part wolf, I flexed my hands before my eyes, barely able to believe this was my body. I enjoyed the feeling of power, the knowledge that I could crush those who had bullied me for so long without any real effort. You must think I'm mad by now. Maybe I am.

By that point it was getting late and I knew my parents would be ringing Fiona's family if I didn't return soon. I was ready to collapse among the graves when we'd finished, hungry and tired, but I had to go back.

"A word of warning now you have mastered transforming at will," Lady Sarah said as I turned to go. "Be careful with the amount of time you spend as a wolf, for if you spend too much time in this form then the wolf in you will grow too strong. If that happens you will begin to forget everything human, and slowly the human part of you will fade away until there is nothing but the wolf left, forcing you to live out the rest of your life as an animal. If you are with me or Vince most of the time when you are transformed you should be alright, for we will remind you of your humanity and so keep the human part of you alive. But be sure to balance the time you spend as wolf and human."

I nodded and tiredly made my way home. There hadn't been time to ask Lady Sarah any more, despite all the questions I still had, and I was curious about the new vampire who had been mostly quiet once we reached the graveyard. I knew I would find them again the following night.

Chapter Eight – A Monster Is Born

"So did you have a good time?" Mum asked me when I got home.

I nodded wearily and went straight to the fridge. I was craving meat again, raw and slippery and dripping blood, and I didn't want to think about what the hunger might drive me to do if I didn't eat something. I realised I'd spilt some blood from the small carcasses Vince and Lady Sarah had been supplying me with, but since it was Halloween no one questioned it, assuming it was fake blood staining my skin.

"You can't be hungry at this time of night," Dad said disbelievingly. He had a beer in his hand, sat in front of the TV in the dining room watching football. From his tone of voice I could tell he'd been in a bad mood, though with the help of the beer he was bordering on at least being friendly if I didn't piss him off.

"I haven't eaten," I replied, while looking for a pack of beef I knew we had.

"Didn't Fiona's parents give you anything?" Mum asked.

I shook my head. I found the beef slices we'd bought in for sandwiches and ripped open the packaging, immediately feeling better as I gulped down several slices of the meat. "I don't suppose you could cook me something could you please Mum? I'm starving."

Dad's anger fired up again. "No she can't, why don't you do it yourself? You're old enough!"

"It's fine John, we've got a spaghetti bolognaise that'll just go in the microwave for two minutes."

"He has to learn someday Emma," Dad said, almost sulkily.

"I bet you never cooked for yourself when you were my age, you bastard," I muttered under my breath. He was always having a go at me, but never at Amy, even when she asked people to get her a drink because she was too lazy to get it for herself. She was the favourite and he made no attempt at hiding it. It didn't matter what I did, nothing was ever good enough for him. Sometimes it felt like he was so disappointed in me he was ashamed to call me his son. That was alright, I refused to call him Dad unless I really had to. Someday I'd find a way to sever the blood link that bound us and I'd be free of him forever, but until then I had no choice but to live with him.

Minutes later the spaghetti bolognaise lay on a plate in front of me, steaming and sizzling with the heat from the microwave. Mum had been watching Eastenders with Amy, and she left me to my meal while she went back to the TV in the lounge. I ate in silence, ignoring Dad completely. If he spoke to me I grunted or gave one word answers. I knew how much that annoyed him, and he soon gave up trying to engage me in conversation. As soon as I'd finished eating I retreated to my room and switched on the Playstation. I was feeling better after the meal. The weariness had all but left my body and the hunger, while not completely satisfied, had subsided enough that the craving for raw meat was then only a vague suggestion from somewhere deep in my brain directly linked with the wolf's thoughts and instincts.

About an hour later I settled down for another sleepless night, my mind full of vampires and Slayers and a burning desire to know more.

No matter how much I wanted to see Lady Sarah again and learn more, as fate had it I didn't get chance to talk with her until nearly a week later.

My thoughts were on the night, determined as I was to visit the graveyard, but I had to survive through the day first. The first two lessons dragged by, uneventful and dull. Then break came and Lady Sarah's teachings were to be put to the test.

I walked into the Geography room, Fiona just behind me, to find a girl called Lucy flat against the far wall, pressing hard against it as if she was trying to force her way through. Jamie stood in front of her with his back to me, holding something near Lucy's face in an outstretched hand: the source of her terror. She looked up as I came in and screamed my name. Jamie turned and smirked at me, his eyes glinting cruelly. The scare I'd given him the previous week had evidently worn off and he wanted to get back at me.

Lucy relaxed slightly once Jamie had turned towards me. I wasn't entirely sure what was happening, but after the way she had been pressed against the wall, I wasn't sure I wanted to know what he had in his hand.

"And what's he gonna do? You want to see it too Nick? Will it make you scream like a girl?" he taunted, advancing slowly like a predator stalking his prey, holding the thing in one hand, cupping the other over the top to hide it from view. When he was close enough, he extended his arm until it was inches away from my face, taking away the other hand at the same time to reveal the source of Lucy's fear.

I looked at it and almost laughed with relief. I don't know what I thought it might be, but it was something I could deal with.

The biggest house spider I had ever seen sat in the palm of his hand, its body covering most of the palm, its legs resting right on the edge. And that was its size crouched. When I showed no fear, he turned away and moved back over to Lucy, perhaps aware that she had relaxed. She shrank back again in horror, eyes screwed up tight, wishing she could fall through the wall and escape. She screamed my name again.

"Don't waste your breath, he ain't gonna do nothing. Come on then weakling, you gonna try and stop me? Oh I forgot, you can't 'cause you got peas for muscles," he said. He began to address the room which had gone deadly quiet, putting the spider down on the nearest table where it remained crouched, as if awaiting its chance to escape. "Do you know he needs a crane to lift a pencil?"

Rage was building up inside me, coursing through my veins and making them throb painfully. I wished I could've come up with some clever retort but the anger was fogging my brain. I felt the itching on my skin from the growth of fur and realised the pain was from the change, not the anger. I tried to build a barrier in my mind against the rage, which was giving the wolf enough strength to take control. I could feel its mind and its hunger, its thirst for blood, for the kill. My fists were clenched tight with the effort and I think some of the pain and the anger must have showed on my face. Jamie didn't know what was going on. He took my actions to mean I wanted a fight. In truth I did. I managed to keep the wolf at bay for the moment, managed to reverse the slight changes that had already begun, but just for a few seconds the wolf and the human had almost become one. I had wanted to hurt Jamie for a long time, make him pay for the pain he had caused me over the years, and both parts of my mind wanted the same thing. I might have controlled the change but I couldn't control the anger, and I could feel the wolf clawing its way through the thin barrier in my mind, breaking its way through and roaring for blood.

"You'll take that back," I shouted.

"Now look who's the big man," he laughed. "What, you gonna fight me now? You and who's army?"

"You were the one who needed an army last week," I sneered.

I took a step towards him. He stood his ground. Adrenalin and testosterone pumped through my veins. I took another step. He wasn't laughing any more, but I could see the cruel light in his eyes now he had a reason to hurt me. There was a spark of anger there too, in response to the reminder of when he'd been at my mercy on Halloween. I was about to complete the final distance between us when I felt someone gripping my arm. I looked around to find Lucy had hold of me.

"No, Nick! Don't break the rules now, you could be thrown out and you'll fail your GCSE's. Just get rid of the spider, that's all I wanted."

Rules! To Lucy rules were like the law that governs you humans, the law that had already begun to mean little to me by then. Such laws were laid down by human society, for humans. But I was no longer human. I had proven that on the Halloween night when I became a wolf at will for the first time. And then came the realisation: I was bound by no laws. Not even the ultimate law to which every living thing must obey, the law of time. I alone in that room could wander the depths of time and never once feel the pain it inflicts on mortals, unchanged by its ravaging claws. I still felt very much a part of the human world, still longed to be a part of it, but I was slowly drifting away. And as the distance started to grow, with it came the realisation of my own immortality. I still clung to the human world, but bit by bit my fingers were slipping away from the edge, only to plunge me into the deep, dark, uncertain void that awaited below. I felt young and alive and rebellious. I had eternity, could feel it stretching out ahead of me with no definitive beginning or end, infinite years open to me to explore as an outsider, an outcast, if death didn't claim me first. And there before me stood a stupid mortal boy who dared to taunt me. Me, an immortal creature more powerful than he could ever know. I could have broken him so easily, could have brought him a death so terrible even his parents wouldn't recognise him. It sounds arrogant now, but back then, in that moment, with the realisation of what I had become came contempt. It was a mindset I would fall completely into in the coming months and I would have to learn again to respect those who died for me, those whose lives I took for the continuation of my own. I believed myself to be above them as humans think they are above the cattle they slaughter, but in time I would be proved wrong.

"To Hell with the rules," I snarled as I broke free of her grip and closed the final gap between me and the bully.

"Get out of my face, freak," Jamie growled and pushed me back.

The world around me ceased to exist, and all that mattered was the small space in reality filled by my opponent, though I was vaguely aware that someone had begun the old playground chant which was soon taken up by everyone else in the room. Everyone except for Lucy who stood looking worried, unsure what to do.

"Fight, fight, fight, fight."

"Why, you afraid?" I said and pushed him in return. Angry as I was, I forgot to measure the strength of it, or maybe I just didn't care.

Either way, Jamie would have fallen over if the wall hadn't been in the way. He was thrown against it and cracked his head painfully.

"Fight, fight, fight, fight."

With a roar born of anger and pain, he pushed himself away from the wall and charged at me.

The chant was getting louder. Jamie was almost upon me. I took up a defensive stance ready to absorb the power of it, when a cold, stern voice suddenly brought silence to the room.

"What's going on in here?" the voice demanded to know. It was Aughtie.

Jamie stopped just short of me, anger draining from his face, and pushed me aside, looking innocent as he slid over to his mates. "Nothing Miss, I was just showing Nick this spider I found."

"Well there's no need for all that noise, sit down and wait for Mr Turner in silence. Now!"

Nobody argued. We took our seats and Aughtie left, muttering something about how her nine year old nephew was better behaved. The bell must have gone but I hadn't heard it over the sound of my heart pounding angrily against my chest. The wolf withdrew, but the lust for blood hadn't been satisfied and my rage was far from spent. I didn't think I could sit through Geography when both the human and the wolf in me wanted to hunt. I needed to take my anger out on something. I found myself staring at the spider and squashed it with my bare hand on the tabletop. That felt a little better but not much.

Lucy had been unable to decide which she feared most, Aughtie or the spider, and in the end she'd compromised, sitting at the table across from me. Once she saw that it was dead, she came back over to sit in her usual place next to me, though she begged me to move the remains, which was easier said than done. It might as well have become one with the table; I'd flattened it that hard that it was stuck there, a mess of tangled legs and exoskeleton in a pool of its own blood. I thought it a pity I couldn't do the same to Jamie.

After Aughtie had gone, he twisted round in his seat to face me and mouthed "This isn't over."

I gave him the finger just as Turner walked in the room, and he turned round to face the front.

Geography was always a dull lesson, and Turner's voice usually put me to sleep, but that day I was restless. It took all my self control to sit still, time dragging by until finally the bell freed us from boredom. I couldn't face Aughtie's lesson after that, and even though I knew skiving one of her lessons was more trouble than it was worth, I did it anyway. I didn't really care, I just wanted some way to vent the anger.

So when the bell went I waited until everyone had left the room, taking longer to pack my bag than usual, and slipped out of the classroom into the flow of students. I let them carry me down the English corridor, past the room I was supposed to be in, feeling confident I wouldn't be seen in the throng. Some idiot tried to push past me and I would have hit him if there hadn't been too many people in the way. Not that I cared about who I hurt at that point, but movement was restricted in the tightly packed corridors and I knew I wouldn't get in a decent blow.

We reached the end of the English corridor and the tide split two ways. I had to fight against the current of students to get in the right direction. The next corridor was much wider and things calmed down after that. Nobody tried to stop me when I walked over to the door to freedom, teachers assuming I was either going to PE or cutting across the car park to avoid the corridors, my fellow students not caring. And yet I felt like I was being watched as I approached the school gates, and when I turned and looked back, I was sure I could see someone watching from the windows on the IT corridor, the highest point in the school. I thought I could just make out the shape of someone stood there, or was it merely shadows?

Whether the dark shape belonged to student, teacher, or was something else entirely, I was beyond caring. If that was a teacher up there then news of my skipping lessons would soon reach Mum, but I didn't care. They'd ground me, but I no longer cared about that either. It'd probably be a month without the internet, video games and TV. So? I'd wait till everyone was in bed and then I could play on them for as long as I wanted. It wasn't like I could sleep anyway. Besides, I had other things to do. It would be winter soon, I could feel it in the wind which grew colder and stronger by the day, and that meant the vampires would awaken sooner. I'd be able to spend more time with them and hopefully learn the answers to all my questions and much more. It was a pity there were none of my own kind in the area, if there were even any left in the world, but from what I knew of vampire and werewolf mythology, in many ways we weren't that different anyway. Assuming what I'd read was true.

I soon forgot the possibility of someone watching me once I was through the gates. Outside of them it seemed like a whole different reality. The school was teeming with humans, full of their fears, their worries and stress, their depression and sadness. But in the world I found myself in, nature surrounded me, and it was somehow more calm and tranquil, even though it was a world full of fear and hunger and death, and the urgent need to survive. Actually that wasn't strictly true; mainly roads and houses and other man made things surrounded me, but around those nature still existed, in hedgerows and bushes and trees, defying man, refusing to be ruled by him. I felt isolated from humanity that day, even though I still longed to be one of them, because I had seen eternity lying before me and I knew I would outlive them all. If live was the right word for it. My heart still beats, my lungs still breathe, my brain still thinks, yet I am undead, neither dead or alive. But I felt alive. What was I? I didn't know then and I'm not sure I know now, even with all that I have learned since then.

The wolf was still pushing for the change. I knew better than to transform there in the middle of the street, where anyone could be watching. I needed somewhere quiet and secluded, hidden from prying eyes.

It was to nature I wanted to go, to escape the world of man for the moment, but the nearest woods were not within walking distance in the time I had (or at least not while I was human in form) and the fields were too open for me to be able to transform safely. No, it was deep into the heart of man I had to go, to the part of it which was dead, a place I knew well. Within the town centre there were several side alleys leading away from the main street, where abandoned shops had been left to crumble and rot into ruins. It was to there I was headed, confident that I would meet very few people, and even if I did, there were many places to hide.

Fifteen minutes later I stood in the corner of what had once been a hairdresser's, partially hidden behind the last surviving section of the brick walls. The change was still fighting to take a hold of me, and finally I gave in to it, embracing the pain, enjoying the feeling of my weak, pathetic human body becoming a powerful animal built to kill. Through the rage it was harder to think and to plan ahead, something I was going to have to learn to do if I was to survive the new world I had been thrown into, but I had sense enough to undress first and hide my clothes and my school bag where I could retrieve them later when it was time to become human again. A tramp walked by while I was still changing. A part of me wanted him to see the shifting mass of flesh and blood, stretching and melting and knotting together to form a completely new shape, but that would mean I had to kill him and no matter what I was feeling at that point, or how angry I was, I would not take a human life. Hurt them yes, but I didn't really want to slaughter them needlessly. Crouched behind the ruins, he didn't notice me. I completed the rest of the change witnessed only by the birds overhead and the bugs swarming across the floor, seemingly in an attempt to flee from the unnatural predator in their midst. Soon the boy was gone, and in his place stood the wolf.

When I had learnt to change at will with Lady Sarah the previous week, I hadn't been given much chance to truly experience the new form with the human part of my mind. I wanted to feel the power in my muscles and jaws, feel those teeth ripping through prey animals, bringing a brutal, horrific end to their life. I wanted to kill. Or was that the lupine half of my brain, influencing me, wanting to satisfy its lust for blood? It didn't matter. I wanted to feel the warm blood bathing my tongue and seeping down my throat. And I wanted to see my reflection, whether it be in a mirror or a stream. Somehow all this still felt unreal. The pain, that had been real. But now? I knew it was real, but it didn't quite feel it. It felt more like a hallucination created by insanity or drugs, or both. I wanted to see my reflection, feeling that would force my brain to finally accept the full reality of it. I didn't even know the colours of my own pelt, only that it was not one solid colour, but a mixture of greys and browns and blacks, judging from what I could see by twisting my head round.

While I stood experiencing all the wolf's superior senses, my sensitive ears picked up the sound of someone approaching. It wasn't the tramp again: the footfalls were lighter, and I guessed they belonged to either a woman or another teenager. Whoever they were, I couldn't stay in the alley. I might pass for a large stray dog in the dark, but I was certain in broad daylight most people would know I was a wolf. As the person came closer, I slipped away into the shadows of the two complete, but deserted buildings that stood at the mouth of the alley. They were approaching from the opposite end, and once I was past the buildings, I found myself on a quiet side street. From there I was able to make my way to one of the quiet country roads leading away from the town, into neighbouring villages. The fields were full of long grass, and there I could hunt without hindrance. Anyone who drove past would not be able to see me from the road, and if the farmer or anyone else entered the field I could be gone long before they reached the place I had been. The only threat of discovery was posed from above, but if I heard a helicopter or a plane I crouched low enough to the ground to be sufficiently hidden from view. Hidden enough that they would not know I was a wolf.

I hadn't been in the field long when I clumsily caught and killed a rabbit. Unused to my new body as I was, I didn't quite move with the same grace and agility as I had under the full moon with the wolf in control.

I crushed it in my jaws and shook it with a ferocity that was not my own, feeling the blood spill down, soaking the fur around my mouth, staining it with the life I had taken, stolen even. I began to choke as it gushed down my throat, awakening me from the bloody fantasies the rage had created. That wasn't me. I wasn't a killer. I didn't thirst for blood, not like the wolf. I spat out the carcass in disgust, the dead limbs hanging limply by a few tendons, soon to grow cold and stiff in the grip of rigor mortis. It was barely recognisable as a rabbit then, my jaws having destroyed the fragile framework of bones and flesh. Shattered bones poked out through the skin and blood and organs oozed from a gaping hole my teeth had made in the stomach. The wolf hungered for the fresh meat, but it was separate from me. I decided then I didn't want that life of a predator, and I would avoid becoming a wolf unless I had to, or was forced to under the full moon.

Hunger drove me to pick up the animal again and devour it whole in one quick gulp. Since I'd already transformed, I didn't have much choice but to obey the hunger lest it become so powerful it drove me to do something more horrific. The rabbit wouldn't satisfy it, and I was forced to take another life, a sheep that time in one of the neighbouring fields. I surrendered my mind to the wolf then, letting it feast so I didn't have to face what I had done. Yes, it was as I had said before, only nature, predator feeding on prey, but if I hadn't changed I wouldn't have needed as much meat to satisfy the hunger. I would have probably had burger and chips for lunch, as there was little choice in the canteen, but only one life would have been taken to feed many. As it was, I had taken two lives to feed myself, just because I had been angry. I had no problem with taking animal life myself if it was necessary, but that day it hadn't been and I felt ashamed. I might be immortal, but I didn't have to leave the human world yet, did I? There was nothing stopping me living there a little longer, until the curse forced me to move on, and I could still let myself believe I was human for a little while longer. Even if I did currently have a wolf's form, I didn't have to behave like a beast. I knew eventually I would have to abandon humanity completely, when it would become noticeable that I did not age, but until then I had to believe I could remain there for at least another couple of years.

Once the wolf had fed I washed away the blood in a nearby pond. The day was cloudy and overcast, and I couldn't see my reflection as I had hoped before the kill, though I suddenly wasn't so sure I wanted to look into the water's edge and see the killer staring back at me. From there I made my way back to the alley and returned to human form. Impossibly, I felt hungry again, but there was no time to eat anything else. I'd just have to pray it didn't get the better of me.

After I had dressed I knew I should return to the school, though I was enjoying my freedom too much to want to go back. The fifth lesson would be starting soon and I was already heading for trouble without skipping another lesson as well. I really didn't want to think about what Aughtie would do when she found me. She'd know I'd skived since she'd seen me in Geography the lesson before, and I'd be regretting it when she was through with me, but I didn't want to face her that same day. In the end, it was only the thought of the look on Jamie's face when I didn't show at the school gates after sixth period that made me go back. For that was where we would finish it. He would wait for me, and if I didn't show I would be called a coward and the bullying would be worse than before. And worst of all he would win. The thought of that made me sick, and the anger boiled up again inside.

If I was going to fifth lesson, that meant I had to go to form too, otherwise I'd be marked down as absent for the afternoon. Form period was due to start in ten minutes. It was a twenty minute walk back to the school from the town centre. I sprinted at what would have been a fast pace for a human, but felt slow to me after experiencing the wolf's body, and I made it with two minutes to spare.

"Is it true? Are you really gonna take on Jamie after school?" David asked me the minute I stepped out of the classroom, where he'd been waiting for me, his form group having been let out a couple of minutes earlier than mine.

I nodded in reply, unable to speak, an angry growl erupting from somewhere within.

"Are you out of your mind? Have you gone completely insane or something? You're no match for him, you'll get your face smashed in! He's built for fighting; no offence mate, but you ain't built for that."

"We'll see," I said quietly. David looked at me doubtfully but let it drop and we walked the rest of the way to our next lesson in silence.

Three thirty came and the bell rang out through the school. Kids poured out of the building that had imprisoned them for the past few hours. Usually groups of friends would be stood around talking, waiting for more of their mates to join them so they could walk home together, creating a seemingly endless sea of faces stretching across the front of the school grounds, covering every inch between the school itself and the gates and wall with its blue railings running along its length, a feature which only added to the feeling of imprisonment. Bullies tormented their victims. Loners and the friendless, neither popular nor victims, snaked their way through the crowds to walk home alone. But not that day. News of the fight had spread, and most of them crowded round to watch. I soon found myself in the middle of the crowd, stood waiting, clenching my fists and gritting my teeth in a silent growl, feeling that anger again but not letting it take control enough that it would make me go too far. I had no intention of transforming in front of everyone.

There was no sign of Jamie as yet.

I looked round at the sea of faces, many unrecognisable and yet still they had come to watch. My mates were at the front of the crowd. David was there, almost laughing at my nerve. He knew, or he thought he knew, that Jamie would beat the crap out of me, and he still thought I was mad. Lizzy and Fiona were there looking worried.

Listening to the crowd, I knew very few were there to support me. Most favoured Jamie, though a few believed in my abilities at taekwondo, which I might have bragged about when I was mortal. I might have stretched the truth a bit, making it out that I'd gotten to a higher belt than I actually did before giving it up. It had earned me a bit of attention from the really hot girls for a short time, making me out to be harder than I was, and some of the guys even hung out with me. That is, until one idiot decided to see if it was true and punched me in the stomach. I'd claimed I could block any punch that came at me from any angle. Once they knew I was lying they turned their backs on me and it was back to being invisible, seen only by bullies, my true friends, and others like me who had no one else to talk to.

Finally he decided to show his face. He swaggered over to me, the crowd parting to let him pass, flanked by two of his mates who took their place at the front alongside my own friends.

"So you decided to show your scrawny face then? Didn't think you had it in you," he sneered, before addressing the crowd again, revelling in the attention as he had in class earlier that day. "Hey, have you seen his muscles? No? That's 'cause he hasn't got any. Do you know all his mates are girls?"

David scowled but kept his mouth shut. No matter how mad he thought I was, he knew his own limits and he wasn't going to make the same mistake.

"Did you come to talk or to fight? This ends here and now. Show us your own muscles, or are you all mouth?" I retorted.

He turned back to face me, anger stamped across his ugly face and I knew I'd pushed him too far that time. He was done with talking. Even if I'd been human I wouldn't have been afraid, the anger leaving no room for other emotions. As it was, I was confident in my own powers. He was only mortal, what could he do to hurt me? I was stronger, faster, more cunning. I'd felt the wolf's mind on a few occasions, and we may not trust each other, but knowledge had involuntarily passed between us. It had learned of the human world and I had been given a glimpse into the world of a predator successful enough to inhabit everywhere on the planet, or at least until man had come along and hunted them to near extinction. I'd learnt from the wolf. It knew a lot more about fighting than the human part of me, though how I couldn't say, since it had only been awoken a couple of months ago. Some of that was instinct, some of it was more.

Jamie's mates took up the chant first, and it spread through the crowd like wildfire.

"Fight, fight, fight, fight."

Jamie spat on the ground at my feet. I snarled and took up a fighting stance. He whispered something else, too quiet for the crowd to hear.

"You're pathetic. You're nothing. You're shit."

I didn't waste my breath on a reply and I didn't waste any more time. Rage was building. I really wanted to hurt him then, and the knowledge that I could so easily break him and tear him to shreds gave me confidence. Yet it wasn't enough simply to know that. I had to show him that. I wanted him to leave me alone, sick as I was of his constant taunting. The thought of the pandemonium if I transformed before them all, and the fear, the sweet smell of fear, and the damage my teeth could do was all too tempting. I entertained the thought longer than I should have, long enough to consider if I could somehow get away with it, though I knew really it was a crazy fantasy. And even if it were possible, there were no guarantees I wouldn't lose control and kill people. I wouldn't risk that, especially with my friends present.

"Fight, fight, fight, fight."

The chanting had grown so loud I was surprised the teachers hadn't come out to see what was going on and break it up. Even after school they could give comments out, and it'd be suspension for fighting.

"Fight, fight, fight, fight."

I threw the first punch, deliberately slowing it, making my movements more human, aiming for his ugly face. He ducked and laughed at me. "Is that all you got?"

He aimed a kick at my groin. With a casual sweep of my hand I knocked his foot aside and used his momentum to swing him round, as I had been taught in taekwondo, ridiculing him. His face grew blotchy, the anger becoming more powerful, testosterone and adrenalin in the air, pumping through our veins. He'd been expecting an easy fight, probably planning to play with me like cat and mouse. I'd seen it all before. If he'd found his mark, he'd have pushed me to the ground while I was doubled over with pain, and then he'd have proceeded to beat me while I had no chance to fight back. This was no longer play. I think he was surprised that I'd lasted so long already, but he did a good job of hiding it and he wasn't going to let it get the better of him.

I caught his fist as he aimed another punch and squeezed until I felt the bones splintering beneath the skin. He cried out in agony. I continued to crush the lump of flesh and blood until he fell to his knees from the pain, his face screwed up with it, tears streaming down his cheeks. Then I jerked him to the ground and released him. He curled up in a ball, crying like a baby, cradling his hand which was possibly damaged beyond repair. The thought didn't bother me. Whatever I'd sworn to earlier that day, about taking innocent life and not behaving like a beast, it had been swept away by the rage. Besides, humans were more bestial than any other animal on the planet. Only humans kill for pleasure. What I had done earlier that day with the rabbit, I would come to realise that was more human than wolf, and I was more in the world of humanity now than I had ever been. The wolf had wanted the blood to satisfy hunger, not to satisfy anger. But those were things I'd come to realise later. During the fight there was no room in my head for thoughts. I was too busy enjoying Jamie's pain, and the gasps emanating from many in the crowd, including David; everyone who had expected me to lose. Some people were starting to cheer, all those who had ever been bullied by Jamie in some shape or form. They were enjoying his downfall nearly as much as I was.

I stood over the pathetic mortal boy that lay at my feet and kicked him in the stomach.

"That's for every victim you've every bullied in your miserable life," I snarled, loud enough for everyone to hear. Many cheered.

I aimed a powerful kick at his groin, enough maybe to damage that too.

"That's for Lucy."

I aimed yet another kick at his head, hard enough to split it open and render him unconscious. The crowd fell into shocked silence. Jamie had never gone that far with any of his victims.

"And that's for me."

Satisfied, I turned my back on him and the crowd parted for me as they had for Jamie, too shocked to say anything. But that didn't matter. The anger spent, I was ready for home where I would enjoy my victory in the haven of my bedroom. No doubt I'd pay for that day. At the very least I'd be grounded, possibly suspended, and maybe I'd even be in trouble with the police. I don't think I meant to hurt him so badly, however much I might have dreamt of it that day. It was hard to control this destructive power I had been given, and at times I forgot myself in the grip of anger, forgot to measure it, make my blows soft enough to feel like the strength of a human. It's hard even to this day, but it is a skill I have learnt over time.

I didn't really care what punishment lay in store right then. No one would ever bother me again. It might even make me popular. Yet in that moment I realised I didn't want that. I didn't want everybody talking to me just because I had beaten the hardest boy in school, which in doing so made me the hardest boy in school I supposed. They would only be after my protection. They'd only want to know me because I was suddenly cool. Or maybe I wasn't after taking it too far. Maybe they'd all fear me. In any case, I just wanted to be left alone, something people wouldn't think twice about from then on.

Chapter Nine – Born of Death

I spent the evening with my corn snake. I'd named him Alice after my favourite rock star, Alice Cooper. As much as I loved him, I wished he was a huge boa constrictor like the ones used in his namesake's rock shows, and I swore one day when I had the room I was going to own a snake that big. For my schooldays, Alice was big enough, and whenever I was feeling down or depressed, I liked to sit on the sofa bed underneath the top bunk where I slept and simply hold him. I enjoyed the feeling of his soft, smooth scales brushing across my skin, and I would lose myself in thought while he slithered over my arms. It made me feel better, and when I was angry it helped to calm me.

I'd started to notice other animals reacting to the wolf they seemed to sense within me, like the bugs that had swarmed across the ruins of the old hairdresser's when I'd transformed that day. I'd been worried it would cause similar problems with Alice, and whether I'd have to give up my pet if he was too afraid of me for me to continue to keep. But even though my scent had probably changed, the snake still seemed to recognise me as the same boy who'd raised him and he seemed as relaxed around me as ever.

By the evening I was past being angry. I felt a grim satisfaction at the thought of the pain I had caused Jamie, and the pain he might at that very moment be going through while doctors sought to mend the fractured bones. The fist may have been beyond repair, and that made it all the more satisfactory. I had sworn not to take innocent lives, but Jamie deserved all that he got. I felt no remorse for what I had done to him. But I couldn't help thinking about the rabbit and the sheep whose lives I had taken, and I wished I could bring them back. Their deaths felt pointless.

"Ha, some predator I am," I muttered sarcastically. I watched Alice, admiring the way he moved, so swift and silent, the perfect predator, cold blooded and emotionless. Not like me, a human with a wolf's form, not yet a killer.

Darkness slowly descended upon the land while I sat there with Alice, and when the shadows swallowed up the light I put him back into his tank and climbed out of the window.

Lady Sarah and Vince were waiting for me when I reached the graveyard. Lady Sarah stood between the graves, barely moving, her dark form engulfed in shadows from a distance. She looked like a sentinel, keeping watch over the graves, or a dark angel perhaps, waiting for the next burial so she could lead the soul into the afterlife. Vince, on the other hand, was sat on a coffin with his feet up, resting one arm on a tombstone. Something glinted in the moonlight, and I noticed a silver pendant that I hadn't seen before, with something engraved into it, some kind of symbol. It didn't mean much to me, just a shape. Tied next to the pendant was a large fang. I would have said it was a wolf's or a large dog's, but it was too big for an average canid. A werewolf's? But what would he be doing with a werewolf's fang? Maybe he'd taken it from some long dead enemy. He also wore gothic rings on his fingers that definitely hadn't been there before, silver moulded into skulls and bats, stolen perhaps from a victim. He could have passed for a mortal.

"But how did you know I was coming?" I asked, confused.

"We heard you coming from the minute you set out from your home and recognised your footfalls," Lady Sarah answered.

Vince laughed. "A zombie could hear you coming! You've got the loudest, heaviest footsteps I've ever heard among all the ranks of the undead I've known. The whole point is we're silent predators, light on our feet and too fast for mortals to follow. You're gonna give us a bad reputation!"

I laughed too but I didn't really get the joke. Vince seemed to sense my confusion because he said "God, you've got a lot to learn boy. Zombies have the worst senses among the undead. We have heightened senses, but their hearing could be worse than human depending on how much they've decayed."

"Hey, give me chance! I've only been undead for two months," I told him.

He shrugged, still smiling with one fang visible, and shifted his gaze to Lady Sarah, expecting her to answer my questions. I would have said she looked out of place next to us two, dressed like present day mortals, but given our surroundings she looked more at home than either me or Vince, in her old fashioned black dress, something she could have been buried in. Vince looked like he belonged in a mansion somewhere with servants surrounding him, the way he was lounging around, while I still looked like a mortal boy, and I looked lost among the tombstones. It was not a place for kids.

"So," I said. "Is this a good time to talk?"

She nodded. "What troubles you?"

"Well, I've been thinking, and if I'm caught in the middle of a war I want to know more about the Slayers. For one thing, if they hunt undead, why do they call themselves Demon Slayers and not Undead Slayers? And do demons really exist, or are we demons to them?"

She held up a hand to stem the flow of questions. "Yes, demons exist, though there are few on Earth now. Once the Slayers slaughtered demons as well as undead and they viewed us as one and the same – though we are, of course, different to demons – but the demons withdrew against their onslaught and returned to the deepest pits in Hell from whence they came. As I said, there are few on Earth now. Only the most powerful or the most reckless prey on mortals. Most are content with the souls of the dead, or at least they will be until the Slayers are defeated. So, to return to the Slayers, they named themselves the Demon Slayers. And they still think we of the undead to be demons to this day."

"How are we different from demons?" I asked, soaking up everything she was telling me and hungry for more, my curiosity far from satisfied.

"Demons belong to Satan, if he really exists, or at least to Hell which is real, while we belong to no one but ourselves. Demons were never human, as we once were, and demons are living creatures, while we died to become what we are. The only thing that links us is our immortality. We can be destroyed, but we cannot die of natural causes, therefore we are not mortal. Demons do not age either. But enough of demons, you wanted to know more of the Slayers, and I shall tell you."

"Hang on a minute, you just said I died when I became a werewolf. I didn't die! I'm pretty sure I'd remember something like that," I said.

"You died Nick, as all among the undead have. Otherwise your kind would not be classed as one of us. We are born of death. You died, but the wolf brought you back. Unlike the rest of us, your kind still have living bodies, though the body is changed after death. Yet you are still somewhere between living and dead, as with the rest of us. We vampires may give the illusion of life, yet our bodies are dead. We do not need to breathe, though most of us do out of habit, and we produce no waste, or any of the other things living bodies must do. Most of us are re-animated corpses, the most obvious of these being zombies. Werewolves are the exception. Do not ask me how it works because I do not know. How the wolf brings you back, I know not. How the dead can be made to walk again, I know not. I know only that it happens, as the three of us are proof. Now, what would you have me tell you of the Slayers?"

"And not too many questions this time, we have to feed before daybreak," Vince interjected.

I glanced at him and nodded before turning my attention back to Lady Sarah. I thought about what I needed or wanted to know the most and tried to remember what she'd told me before about the Slayers, which had been brief and created more questions than it answered, when an image came to me. A memory, gone as quickly as it appeared, but not one of my own. Or at least not one belonging to the human part of my consciousness. Had the wolf chosen to show me that or had it been a mistake, something I'd happened upon while searching my mind? Either way it didn't matter. The memory was important. It concerned the Slayers, and from what Lady Sarah had said when we first met about people chasing me, I guessed it was from that very night. It wasn't very detailed though; some things in the memory were strangely blurred.

The memory was of a group of hunters, undoubtedly the Slayers, stood in a circle around me. They were all aiming guns directly at me and wore silver daggers at their belts. But their faces were strangely distorted, the eyes the only clear feature, full of cruelty, malice and hate. The only explanation I could think of for this was that eyesight wasn't as important to the wolf as its other senses. It could learn more from scent and sound than it could from sight. Besides, maybe all humans looked the same to it in the same way that members of other species look the same to us, beyond having different coloured fur or skin, sometimes the only distinguishing feature to a human eye. Not that it mattered, what interested me the most were the silver weapons.

"Okay, if any damage to the heart or brain kills a werewolf that means the myths about silver aren't true, so how come the Slayers have silver weapons? Surely they know any weapon can kill us if we're wounded in the right place?" I asked.

"They know all too well but the Slayers are traditionalists and like to use silver, and I believe it is also considered as something of a trademark among them. They like other members of the undead to know when one of their numbers is killed by them," she told me.

"What do you mean so we know they were killed by them? Don't tell me there's other mortals out there hunting for us," I said, feeling a little overwhelmed.

"There are rogue hunters out there. They don't count themselves amongst the Slayers. Usually they find out about the undead by mistake. The Slayers will try and persuade these people to join with them, but some don't agree with their methods so they hunt alone. You have little to fear from lone hunters, who can usually be dealt with. It is we vampires who must fear, for we are vulnerable during the day and it doesn't matter how many come after us. We're powerless to defend ourselves. And that's when they strike, in the daylight hours while we sleep.

"There aren't many lone hunters out there now as most mortals refuse to believe in us, ignoring the proof that we are more than mere myth and legend, and those that do learn the truth either become Slayers or find ways to explain away our existence. Few take it upon themselves to hunt us alone."

I thought this over while Vince yawned and shifted position on the coffin.

"How many Slayers are there?" I wondered aloud.

"That is one question I cannot answer. They have a base in every major town and city, and a leader for each base. Slayers in neighbouring villages and small towns serve the base nearest to them, and patrols are sent out into the surrounding area of each base in their everlasting quest to wipe us out. They have some kind of overall leader. Each city may have a force of up to a hundred at their command, maybe even more in the bigger ones, though not all of them remain active. Volunteers patrol the area around where they live and kill most of the undead they come across. Occasionally they take some alive for questioning. If they discover one of us too powerful for them to kill in a small group they call in reinforcements. Other Slayers never take part in the killing as far as I know. I can only guess at what their purpose may be, but I believe some of them are scientists, striving to learn more about our kind and more efficient ways to kills us, while others handle the weapons, making sure their army is well equipped."

I was shocked by what she'd told me. I hadn't really taken the threat of the Slayers all that seriously up until that point. I'd taken risks, endangered us all perhaps, without a second thought. Yes, I'd known I had to be careful, but I'd still taken risks. Earlier that day I'd taken a risk when I allowed the anger to drive me to transform. I'd taken precautions, but if I'd have known how big a threat the Slayers posed I would not have transformed at all. Or maybe the day would have still played out the same due to my sheer recklessness, who knows? I didn't really know myself. When I'd fought Jamie, I could have easily changed before his very eyes, enjoying the fear it would have caused, the chaos, and I could have done far more damage than I did. It had taken all my will power to remain human and keep myself from hitting him with all the unearthly strength I now possessed. I'd never been that reckless when I was human. I didn't really know myself what I was and was not capable of anymore. I was growing unpredictable, and I knew it was something I now had to learn to control if I was going to survive.

Despite the shock to learn just how many Slayers there were, my curiosity was not yet satiated. I suddenly didn't want to know anymore about the Slayers; the grim reality Lady Sarah had just revealed was enough to cope with for the minute. But I did want to know more about vampires. I asked Lady Sarah how powerful they really were, how many of the myths were true.

She smiled at my curiosity, and replied "Most of the myths are true. There are many vampires in this world and you need to understand that we are not all of the same power. All animals fear us, as they do your kind. None of us can walk in direct sunlight, and it's true we can be killed by a stake through the heart or decapitation, but anything that destroys the heart or the brain usually works.

"Garlic does not hurt us but holy water is as an acid to all our kind because we are of the eternally damned, as are you. Crosses can cause burns, though how severe they are depends on the power of the vampire - the more powerful we are, the less harm is done. I am not all powerful in the vampire world though it may seem so to you, but the vampire who made me thus was one of the most powerful of our kind and so I am more powerful than most."

"What powers do you have then, exactly?"

"I can become a wolf or a bat if I wish and I can control the weather to a certain extent. I also have a certain telekinetic ability, but this is not rare among us. A few of the most powerful of our kind can even control the mind of any being, but this is a rare gift. Most of us can hypnotise our victims, however. The difference being, hypnosis only creates suggestion in the mind of our prey and can be broken by those powerful enough, while complete control cannot be resisted."

"So what defines your power? How is one vampire more powerful than another?"

"It depends partly on the power of the one who made the vampire in question, and partly on the age of the vampire. Our powers increase with time, but some of the weaker ones will never be powerful enough to change form or even use hypnosis. Why this is I know not. Perhaps the story of how we came to be would offer some explanation but that is one story that seems long forgotten."

"So in a fair fight I'm guessing a vampire would beat me. In the tale of Lycaon you mentioned our kinds used to be at war before the Slayers forced us to ally against them. Are we still allies or do I need to be wary around some vampires?"

"The struggle between our kinds lasted for centuries before men fought back and, out of all that bloodshed, the Slayers were born. We were forced to ally out of necessity but many vampires were never happy to fight alongside a race they mistrusted, and in many cases hated. Many have always been of the opinion that you are little more than beasts, thinking of us as better than your race. Some of us see you as allies and a few even equals, but the older vampires who still remember the battles long past nurture the most hatred for your race. You would be wise to be wary of us."

"So what about you, do you consider us as equals?" I asked.

"You would not be here if I didn't," she replied with a predatory smile. "I may seem old to you, yet you are new to our world and in time you will no doubt find I am young compared with many other vampires. The war between our kinds was long before my time."

"Is that it now?" Vince asked me. He'd been silent throughout the conversation. I'd almost forgotten he was there. "Only, I'm starving and I need to hunt."

"That's it," I said. Vince looked relieved. Lady Sarah showed no sign of emotion, or at least not outwardly, but I was sure I saw relief in her eyes too.

Though the two vampires must have been fairly close friends, since Lady Sarah had gone to Vince's aid and brought him back to the place she currently called home, the solitary hunters split up as they took their leave. That left me to wander the streets alone as well. I was restless and didn't want to go back home straight away.

The night dragged by, and in my boredom I was tempted to transform again, convincing myself I could beat the hunger. I'd go home and eat just enough meat from the fridge to keep it under control or maybe I'd find some roadkill to scavenge. I knew it wasn't worth it though. From what Lady Sarah had said, the Slayers were constantly out looking for our kind, and for all I knew they could be watching me. As it was, I'd been lucky not to have any more encounters with them since my first full moon.

I doubted they were following me that night as I was sure I'd hear them. But until I learnt to pick out different scents like the wolf did, they could hide behind a wall and spy on me, and I would never know they were there if they didn't make a sound.

The streets were practically empty, apart from a few homeless people I came across and drunks staggering home from the pubs. It occurred to me the Slayers might not even need to be hidden to watch me. They were just humans. They could be anyone. They could have been disguised as any one of the homeless people I passed and I'd never know. They could be the neighbours who bid me good day when we passed, or one of the doctors or nurses in the surgery, or part of the police force. Perhaps I was in even more danger than I'd realised before. The drunks were for real though. I might not have mastered my enhanced sense of smell yet, but I knew the scent of beer and when I passed them I could smell it on their breath, beer and vomit.

I was growing paranoid as I walked aimlessly, feeling their eyes on me. I decided it would be safer to go home after all when Vince stepped out from the shadows in an alley. I hadn't heard him coming and he startled me.

He laughed. "Wow, I must be good to stalk a werewolf."

"You don't make as much noise as a human, I didn't hear you coming," I said sulkily and carried on walking. He fell into step beside me.

"Any excuse. You probably didn't hear me over the sound of your own footsteps! You walk like a human, you gotta learn to move quieter. In fact if you were mortal I'd say your footsteps were heavy, even for a human. Your body isn't as clumsy as a mortal's anymore, learn to be lighter on your feet. Anyway, never mind sound, what about scent? I never met a werewolf who couldn't smell a vampire."

"I'm still learning, okay?" I told him, slightly annoyed. "I might not be human anymore, but I still feel human. And scent is just confusing. It's too powerful, I can't understand it. I might be able to pick out the odd smell I recognise from my mortal life, or I might be able to work out what a certain scent is, but I can't understand everything my nose is telling me. And I have no idea how wolves work out gender and age and all that shit from an animal's scent, 'cause I sure as hell can't do it."

"There's still time to learn all that. The wolf can help you. You can learn a lot from him, and you need to if you're gonna survive. I don't mean to sound like Lady Sarah, all dark and dreary, but the Slayers are a real threat. I've seen too many of our kind die, all killed by the Demon Slayers," he replied.

"The wolf doesn't trust me and I'm not sure I trust it, but I don't wanna talk about that. Lady Sarah's talked a lot tonight, but you haven't said much. How did you become a vampire?" I asked him.

"Well, I'm not much younger than Lady Sarah, just that I choose to live among mortals, so I wear clothes that would fit in with the era and use the latest slang words and stuff. I was born in a village not far from where she would soon be learning to be a princess, but I was just one of the many peasants and it would be decades before we met. There aren't many years between us. It was on the eve of my twenty fifth birthday when the vampire came and changed my life forever. I'd spent my time up until then dreaming of being someone. I wasn't satisfied with the simple life I led like most of the other peasants. I wanted to live in the castle we could see in the distance. Sometimes I would dream I was royalty, other times I would dream of being a knight. All that was to change when he came. He took my life and gave me eternity to roam the night, somewhere between living and dead. The same vampire who made Lady Sarah what she was, when he was passing through our village. I'll never know why he made me this way. For Lady Sarah it was lust. Not love, no matter what she believes, otherwise he would have come back to her. But for me? I've been looking for an answer for years, and I don't think I'll ever know unless I find him again.

"A vampire myself when I awoke, I found I couldn't feed on those I had known for so long and so I moved away to another village. I spent a lot of my time on the move, never content to be in one place for too long. I never stayed anywhere for longer than a few nights, and everywhere I went I brought death and misery. I never had anything to fear except the sun and a few angry mobs, led by the superstitious. I think they blamed me for the deaths because I was the outsider, rather than because they knew what I was.

"Then the Slayers became a real threat, becoming more organised and closer to the present force we have to deal with. They hunted me from village to village. I should have died back then, if it hadn't been for Lady Sarah. She happened to be in the same place as me, having just faked her own death, and she sensed my presence. We were made by the same vampire, descended from the same bloodline. She heard me crying out for help when the Slayers overpowered me. They had me pinned to the ground ready to drive a stake through my heart and then cut off my head to make sure I didn't return. I knew I was finished if no one came to help so I called out to anyone or anything that might hear and take pity, and thanks to the blood we share she was drawn to me.

"She killed a couple and the rest were frightened off. We went into hiding after that and we have been friends since, though we didn't stay together for long. Most vampires prefer to live alone. Few have friends in the human sense of the word, though they may have allies. Now I live in the mortal world, renting apartments, going to nightclubs where I find my victims and lure them out. I go to the movies when I feel like it, that kinda thing. And I only sleep in graveyards when I have to. There aren't many of our kind that choose this life now. Most prefer to live in graveyards like Lady Sarah, since it can be riskier living among mortals. Not to mention a lot of the older ones are stuck in the past. But it has to be said, graveyards are certainly one of the safest options these days. In a graveyard if someone finds your body in the day when you're sleeping they don't think much of it. In an apartment they get the police involved and you wake up in a strange place, then the Slayers find out about it. Sometimes you wake up to find you're in the middle of an autopsy, and that hurts like hell. I got into some trouble again a few weeks ago and if Lady Sarah hadn't come to bail me out once more, I would have died. I'm in her debt. It's the blood that links us, otherwise she wouldn't have bothered coming at all. As for the one who made us, I don't think we'll ever see him again."

I nodded, unable to think of anything to say. "So what's that around your neck? That symbol, what does it mean?"

"This is the only valuable thing my family ever owned. Life was hard. Dad died when I was young and he passed this onto me. I wanted to sell it, hoped it might give us enough money to make things a little easier, but Mum wouldn't hear of it. So I've worn it around my neck ever since in memory of my father. As for the symbol, I haven't a clue what it is."

Silence fell between us as we walked the rest of the way home. He didn't say anything about the werewolf's tooth so I didn't say anything either. We reached my house and I climbed back up to my room while he carried on down the street, presumably to the room he was staying in, if he'd found one yet. Or maybe Lady Sarah had persuaded him to sleep in the graveyard until the danger passed, since that was where I'd found him that night.

When I lay down in bed I was more tired than I had thought and I soon drifted off to sleep. Mercifully for once the nightmares did not come, and I found peace through the remaining hours of the night.

Chapter Ten – Dark Revelations

I was allowed some time before the next full moon to forget the Slayers and the world of the undead to which I now belonged. But I couldn't escape their world forever and the curse was almost upon me again.

I'd been grounded by my parents and suspended by Mrs Redgewell for a whole week after the fight (a week off school even if I was grounded, why did everybody think that was so bad?), though I considered myself lucky that was all I got. There was also the detention with Aughtie for skiving. I was worried if Jamie's hand really was broken for good I'd be wanted for GBH in the eyes of the law, but it didn't come to that. His hand had not been damaged as badly as I had thought. Most of the bones were broken but not to the point where they could no longer be mended. His manhood hadn't been too badly damaged either, and his head would be okay, once they'd stitched it back together. The hand would take a long time to heal though. The thought filled me with a secret, dark pleasure.

Once I was back at school I had other things on my mind. It was worse that month: the lupine half of my mind was affecting me more than ever in the days leading up to the night of the full moon. The only way I found to fight this was to spend more time with my mates and have a laugh. It made me feel more human, and it kept the wolf at bay.

Amy seemed to get blonder by the day, but I was secretly grateful to her for giving me something else to think about. She was watching Eastenders with Mum, and before they started watching she read the description in the TV guide. It said something about two of the characters finally going out with each other, a man and a woman, but somehow she confused them with two brothers in the show.

"Err, that means they're gay," she said.

"No love, they're brothers, so even if they were gay they wouldn't be going out with each other," Mum told her, rolling her eyes when Amy wasn't looking. I think she despaired sometimes.

"Err, what if they had a baby?"

"What? How can two men have a baby?" I asked her, laughing. Mum had her head in her hands. I felt sure she would disown Amy eventually. She always maintained that her daughter wasn't really that blonde, she just pretended to be because she liked the attention. I wasn't convinced.

"Oh yeah, I forgot," she said sheepishly.

"Forgot," I repeated, disbelievingly. "Have you done sex education?"

She glared at me and Mum told me to let it drop. I shook my head and went upstairs, still laughing.

The next day I was telling my mates about it at break. We were sat at a table in one of the Science classrooms. Everyone who had been with me that fateful night at the cinema was there, and we were all laughing.

"That's nearly as bad as my brother's blonde moment," Lizzy said when I'd finished. "We were watching this thing on shark attacks and they interviewed this guy and Chris comes out with 'If he's got a wooden leg, is his foot still real?'"

We were in stitches again. Then we fell quiet and I started doodling on a piece of paper.

"So, have you decided what you're gonna be famous for yet?" Becci asked me, just to make conversation.

"Well it ain't singing," David laughed. "Have you ever heard him sing?"

"Piss off, you're no singer either. No, I dunno what it'll be yet but someday everyone will know my name. And someday everyone will want this signature."

We all looked down at the scribble on the piece of paper. My writing was scruffy at the best of times. My signature was barely legible. I voiced the thought for all of us. "Okay, so it needs a bit of work, but someday this piece of paper will be worth summat I tell you."

"Yeah, to the homeless who need it for the fire," David said. They burst out laughing. I had to laugh too, though I was convinced fame and fortune would be mine someday. It was like Vince had said about when he was mortal, I wanted to be someone. It wasn't enough I was probably the last werewolf on the planet. I wanted to be someone in the human world. I wanted people to know my name; I wanted fans and I wanted to be worshipped like a god. And a bit of money would have been nice too, but it was the fame that held the attraction for me.

"Well I might not be world famous but my dance tournament's next week," Fiona said excitedly. "I've been practising for weeks now, I can't wait!"

"You'll get that gold trophy easily, the others won't stand a chance," David told her, his eyes glazing over dreamily. I had no doubt he was imagining her prancing around in a leotard, showing off her amazing body as she went through her routine.

"Hey Nick, have you finished that English coursework yet?" Ava asked me.

123

"Yeah, I did it last night," I lied. I had been good at getting homework done on time once, when I'd usually complete it the same day it had been set. But I'd grown lazy over the previous year and started leaving it till the night before it was due in. That year I had other things on my mind and my grades were dropping, not that I really cared about school by that point. I was a werewolf, what did I need with good grades? I didn't need a job to survive, even though I'd probably end up doing something just to keep my conscience clean. I couldn't deny the attraction to a life of crime though. With my powers I would make a great thief. Or I could live as an animal, but I decided I'd rather have a job. I thought back to killing the rabbit. Despite what I'd thought at the time, afterwards I had to admit it was pretty cool being a wolf, but I didn't want to spend eternity in that form. I wanted the best of both worlds, preferably without the flesh that was needed to support the wolf's form.

I don't think Ava believed me. "Just make sure you get it in on time, you don't want Miss Aughtie on your case again."

"Who are you, my fucking mother?" I snarled. She looked hurt and fell silent. I had the feeling she was worried about her own skin as much as mine, since Aughtie had a habit of taking it out on the whole class, not just the student who dared disobey her. So I didn't feel bad at what had just happened. Everyone else was looking at me in shock. I never used to be like that.

They all left after that except Lizzy, most of them going to different classrooms, Fiona and David going to their seats. We actually had two teachers for Science: one was Brewins, the other was Mr Enderson, and he was far more capable as a teacher. He was much stricter and made us sit alphabetically. I was stuck next to a guy called Adam. There was something about him that meant I didn't like him much, something a little strange about him, though admittedly he probably said the same about me to his mates.

I turned to Lizzy and said "Why does no one believe me when it comes to coursework?"

"Well have you done it?" she asked.

"No, but that isn't the point."

She rolled her eyes but didn't reply. The lesson was just about to start and she left for her own classroom, glancing back at me when she thought I wasn't looking. She knew something wasn't right.

When I got home later that day I opened the fridge to find it packed full of beer for some football match Dad was watching.

"Hey Mum, can I have some beer?" I asked.

"Please," Dad said automatically. If it hadn't been for the football match he would probably have said more, but as it was he hadn't really been paying attention.

"Not on a school night, Nick," Mum told me.

"Aw, come on Mum, just one?"

She shook her head. "When you're eighteen you can have as much as you want but until then it's the odd one for a special occasion, you know that. Anyway, you don't need any beer, you just have to look at the stuff and it sends you giddy."

"Someone told me you sing better after a few beers," I said.

"No, what really happens is you think you're singing better but really you sound worse. It's like when you're drunk and you're looking in the mirror and think you're really good looking," Mum answered.

"I think that every time I look in the mirror anyway," I replied, while Mum rolled her eyes and Amy looked at me as if I was insane. To her I would never be anything other than a geek.

Mum was proved right though. Later on we were sat watching TV and I was giddy for no reason. Something made me laugh just as I took a swig of juice and I was forced to spit it back out again. Amy looked disgusted. That was nothing, when I calmed down again I drank the rest of the juice, spit an' all.

"Err, you dirty gyppo," Amy said, looking even more disgusted.

"It adds to the flavour," I replied and laughed.

It couldn't last though. Happiness and laughter are alien concepts to the damned.

That night I was hungry as ever and eager to hunt. I landed on the street outside to the sound of some sort of animal fleeing, but I soon found that it was a cat and hardly worth the effort of chasing. Such small prey was barely a snack for a predator as large as me.

However, I soon began to wonder if I would regret that decision before the night was over; I could neither smell nor hear any other creature in the town. Early winter had come upon the land, bringing harsh, cold winds, and rain that chilled to the bone, though it had yet to become snow. Fewer and fewer humans were out on a night, and there were none in the quieter areas of the town where I preferred to hunt; where I felt safer and could easily detect anyone approaching; where I could flee long before they reached me in case they were Slayers. The first night after my awakening had taught me to be much warier. I might hold humans and their slaves in contempt, but I could not deny the threat they posed and I had to learn to respect them for that, and accept the possibility that they could outsmart me if I let the contempt blind me.

Four hours of hunger passed. I was forced to move towards the centre of the town again, the only place where humans never failed to be. The problem was, they were all hidden away in the buildings filled with the loud noise they called music. I was learning more about the human world and I knew that if I waited long enough the drunks would come staggering out, some thrown out by the bouncers, some to cleanse themselves of the alcohol poisoning their bodies, the rest forced to go home when it closed, and then they would be mine for the taking. Yet the hunger wouldn't wait.

There was no one outside at that time of night, or at least no one I could take without being seen. It was too early for the drunks to appear and too late to try and pick one off on their way to these places. Resignedly, I started to search the bins again, this time outside a fast food restaurant, when I heard human voices. And they were heading towards me! I thanked fate for the meal being brought my way while I lay in the shadows, waiting. From listening to their conversation I learnt that it was the birthday of one of the girls in the group and they were going to the night club to celebrate. I detected five of them but I only needed to take one. Sometimes I had eaten more, but I only really needed one to make the hunger bearable.

Now I needed to find a way to isolate one of them and make the kill without being seen by the others. The question was: how could I possibly do it without revealing myself to them? If any witnessed it I would have to kill them too, and the more deaths, the greater the likelihood of discovery by the Slayers. I could think of no way to lure one of them away and was growing desperate. However, fate remained in my favour that night and I had no need to take chances; as they were approaching the nightclub one of the girls had forgotten something. Consequently she left the safety of the group, promising to be back in about fifteen minutes.

Seeing she was taking a different route back – probably shorter – down an alley, I slunk ahead of her and waited until we were out of sight of the others, checking that there was no one about. Satisfied it was as safe as it could ever be in such dark times, I emerged from the shadows and pounced on her. She was too shocked to scream at first and by then it was too late – she could scream no more.

I had begun to feast on my meal when I sensed another female human nearby, but in the grip of the bloodlust I became more reckless. Nothing mattered then except the warm flesh on the ground at my feet. The world around me ceased to exist until there was only the flesh that nourished me, and the hunger. Nothing else mattered.

And so I ignored her. I continued to feed, her footsteps coming closer and still I ignored them. At this point my muzzle was deep in a hole in the belly of my victim, drawing out the organs as I had always done, since the first night I had been released from my prison deep within the human's consciousness to hunt under the full moon. So lost in my meal, and the pleasure the fresh meat and offal brought, I

126

did not notice the girl to whom the footsteps belonged walking down the alley towards me, until it was too late.

She had not seen me yet – both myself and the carcass were hidden in shadows – but that was about to change. I only became aware of her when I rose from the hole I had made, the organs devoured, to attack another part of the corpse and rip through the soft flesh. And then it was, when my muzzle emerged from the hole, her sweet scent tore through the blood red veil in my mind, and in that instant we saw each other.

The quickest to react, I snarled instinctively, ears flattened against my skull. My lips curled back so that my blood stained teeth were bared, defending my kill. I was an impressive sight in the dark alley, terrible to behold. I was a demon in the darkness, seemingly much larger than any mortal wolf. She did what any mortal would have done, except maybe for the Slayers. She turned and ran. The bloodlust clouded my judgement. I wanted to go back to my meal, but the bloodlust also wanted fresh blood, fresher meat, since the corpse at my feet was already beginning to lose its warmth, though it would not be entirely cold for hours yet. Besides, some part of my mind was insisting that she could not be allowed to live. And the age old instinct in all canines to chase running creatures was trying to make itself heard in the confused knot of thoughts. I could not ignore it. I obeyed. I gave chase...

An hour later I stood in a small, shallow stream, allowing the icy cold water, numbing, yet refreshing, to wash over my paws and rinse away the blood from my claws. And I drank the clean, clear, pure water that I might quench my thirst and cleanse my bloodied muzzle. The blood mixed with the water: a dark red streak snaked down the stream. I licked the blood away that had splattered all over my body, congealing and thickening on my matted fur. There was something about that night that made me feel the need to cleanse myself of the last remnants of the lives I had taken, as if it were impure, staining my soul. But these were human thoughts. The human was beginning to affect me, and I didn't like it.

I stared down at my reflection in the water, looking into the amber eyes that stared back at me. What was I? Not human. Not wolf. A hybrid of the two. A monster? That was what humans believed. But did monsters have a conscience? A killer yes, yet I only took life so that I may survive, one of the oldest laws of nature, to which all living creatures are bound, predator and prey. And what sort of a predator feels... what? Remorse? No, it wasn't remorse. The human may have felt remorse when it killed the rabbit, but not I. What then? I didn't understand this. But I felt something after the kill, and if these feelings grew they would get in the way. What sort of a predator feels for the victims it feeds on? Whatever I was, be it monster or some poor confused creature that was never meant to be, I was flawed and it made me weak. These were the human's problems affecting me, and it had to learn to accept its fate. Our survival depended upon it.

127

Once the blood was washed from my fur and my mouth I splashed back through the water, my pads gripping the smooth pebbles on the stream's bed as surely as any human footwear. I ran back up the bank, leaving paw prints in the mud. From there I began to make my way back home. The hunt that night had led me to the outskirts of the town into the surrounding countryside, and I had travelled to the nearest patch of woodland, where the stream ran through, to be alone with my confused thoughts. I had plenty of time left before dawn so I prowled back at a leisurely pace, though I still remained cautious, sticking to the shadows.

I liked the woodland better than the town. I felt at home there. It was my natural habitat and at that time of year it had already begun to die towards the end of autumn and the onset of winter, only to be reborn again in the spring. The dead belonged there.

An owl hunting overhead saw me coming and darted away. Bats avoided me. Rodents fled before me. I even inspired fear in the ants and other insects; they suddenly emerged from beneath the leaves and surged across the forest floor, appearing in front of, and around, my paws, and swarming away from them. I ruled the night. None dared challenge me, except for man. But there, in the natural world, I was the top predator and the world was my territory, the ideal situation for any creature. So why did I feel so alone?

I paused to howl, confident the Slayers would not be able to pinpoint my location until I had moved on and the trail had gone cold. I sent my howl up into the night like a prayer, as if it could reach the very stars. It was a mournful sound that meant little to other creatures. Only my brethren would have truly understood, and they were all gone. The vampires would have understood the words behind it, gifted as they were with wolves, but not its meaning. They were too old to remember these feelings, and they were naturally solitary. Like all wolves, I wanted the security a pack could bring, yet it was more still than that. The human was beginning to feel alone, realising it was no longer like the others that surrounded it, and the loneliness was beginning to affect me.

Of sadness the howl told, and loneliness, and the longing for a pack. Of eternity, and confusion and isolation, a creature separate from every other living thing, born of two races but belonging to neither one nor the other. An unnatural creature, cursed and wretched, one of the damned. Was it to Satan I truly belonged? Lady Sarah had said not to the human, I had been listening, but she did not know the origins of her own kind, so how sure could any of us be that the story of Lycaon was the true origins of my kindred? We knew only the myths and legends that had survived through the generations in both the living and the undead. Were we Satan's children after all? Outcasts from Hell, thrown out perhaps when we refused to obey him, and in our place the demons were created. It was as good an explanation as any. Whatever we were, wherever we came from, we were not God's creation. Born of evil, our souls were stained, our blood tainted, and we were damned.

128

All this I conveyed in the howl, and up it went into the night, to the moon and the stars. If there was a God He did nothing, whether He was listening or not. He did not even reach out to receive it. The howl died away in my throat and was carried off by the wind before it ever reached its destination. I looked down at the woodland floor in this dead place. The skeletal trees were empty and lifeless around me now the creatures had fled in terror, the last of the autumn leaves rotting away, and I imagined I could feel the heat of the fires of Hell beneath my paws. Had the Devil heard the howl? Did he laugh at this lost, unnatural thing? Lost somewhere along the road to death, never to find its destination unless someone sent it there, but never to return to its beginning, at the end of life. Perhaps I was not undead in the true sense of the word like the vampires, but I was not exactly living either. I was not a natural creature, and to this world I did not belong, yet here I was.

With a sigh, I turned my gaze ahead of me again and made the journey back into the town, back to my home, to my empty room. Back to my family. Were they still my family? I was no longer one of them. What were they to this thing I had become? Prey, and I would kill them without a thought if the human didn't intervene. But not that night. I had fed well that night and I was content. I curled up in my room and waited for the sun to rise, curled against the cold and the dangers and the pain, and all these alien emotions.

The sun rose and my senses dulled, the pain came and went, and I found myself lying on my bedroom floor. I was restless once again. I needed to walk and clear my head. It seemed the wolf had left its imprint on my mind and my thoughts were confused because of it. It was hard enough to convince myself to walk upright, my brain trying to tell me it was impossible, still convinced my body was designed to be on all fours.

It was a Saturday morning, so there was no school to stop me going out once I'd dressed. I scribbled a quick note for my parents to explain my disappearance, making up some lie about going to meet a friend. I noticed there was no blood on my teeth that morning and my skin was cleaner, which was odd. The hunger was pounding away inside my belly; surely the wolf had felt it too. It must have killed and eaten something. Wait, yes, there were the tell tale pieces of flesh caught between my teeth.

Before I went out I took some meat from the fridge, sliced ham that time, to help ease the hunger, and then I took to the streets.

I didn't care where I went; I just needed to be on the move. I couldn't have kept still, not even for one of my favourite movies. There were a few people about and I avoided them where I could. I was soon driven to the more remote areas of the town on the outskirts, where the streets gave way to fields.

I walked aimlessly until my sensitive ears heard the sounds of a girl crying out in pain, somewhere in the fields themselves, out towards the woods.

I ran as fast as I could towards the sounds and as I drew close I heard a human voice, whimpering, and it sounded familiar. As I drew closer my heart stilled at the horrific sight that met my eyes.

A girl lay there twitching in a pool of her own blood, long brown hair covered in dirt, brown eyes filled with pain, her soft, smooth skin turning paler by the minute, and there was little wonder when I saw the extent of her injuries. The blood she lay in was pumping out of her leg which was completely torn open, most of the skin gone. Flaps of what was left hung loosely from the wound, muscles torn apart, the bone exposed. Severed blood vessels spilled out their precious liquid, and she had already lost a lot of it. With a jolt I realised she was dying. And I knew her alright; it grieved me to see her this way.

I'd considered her one of my closest friends in life and immediately hatred ran through me, directed towards the one who had done this, along with the fear that was flooding my body. She was dying and there was nothing I could do about it. I knelt beside her, trying to hide the fear and comfort her as best I could, thinking desperately there must be something I could do to help her. I thought about my mobile phone that was lying uselessly on my desk in my room at home. Could I reach the nearest phone in time to call an ambulance? Even though I knew she was already gone I refused to admit it, denying the fact there was nothing I could do.

"Fiona," I said gently, my voice shaking slightly. She had been talking to herself, mortally afraid, but I had not caught much of what she was saying. She didn't seem to know what was happening or where she was, but one fact couldn't escape her; she couldn't feel one of her legs and the realisation of this terrified her, despite her weak grasp on reality. I didn't even know if she realised I was there beside her, and if she did whether she recognised me. And then I noticed the other wound.

Just above her waist most of the skin had been torn away and the flesh beneath showed red raw. I could clearly see where something had bitten the flesh once or twice, as if it had been eating her alive. Something had attacked her. It wasn't as bad as the damaged leg, and maybe she'd have been saved if someone had found her sooner, but then I noticed both wounds had already become infected. Pus oozed from them, and the flesh was beginning to turn a horrible dark colour. I felt helpless.

"Fiona," I said again, more urgently this time. Her eyes rolled up towards my face, and was that a flicker of recognition? Yes, she realised it was me.

"Nick," she whispered and smiled weakly.

"Fiona, it's gonna be okay, you just wait here and I'll go get help, we'll get you to a hospital," I told her. I stood up to go for a phone but her hand gripped me with surprising strength for the state she was in.

"No! Don't leave me here alone," she pleaded. Her hand slipped back down to the ground as if the effort had drained the last resources of strength left to her. She was starting to panic, and the next thing she said would have been a scream if she had enough life left in her. "My leg. I can't feel my leg!"

"It's okay, just broken," I lied, tears leaking from the corners of my eyes. I blinked them away, not wanting her to see. "What happened to you?"

She coughed up a lot of blood and I thought she would die before she could tell me what had attacked her, and then she was trying to scream again. I calmed her, and she looked at me with renewed fear.

"Nick, you have to get away from here! Take me with you; we have to get away! It could come back at any minute. We're not safe! None of us are safe," she sobbed.

"What could come back? What did this to you?" I pressed. I had to know.

"Hard to remember, all confused," she muttered. I struggled to make sense of what she said next, for she muttered incoherently between the details, and even the details themselves were not that clear. "Something in the shadows, chased me, big amber eyes, cold, so cold, merciless. And its jaws, a mouthful of teeth chasing me, blood everywhere, not my blood, then it had hold of my leg and there was more blood. Mine."

"But what was it?"

She shuddered and struggled to answer me, but finally managed to gasp "I only saw it clearly once in the moonlight, the wolf. That's what it was. A wolf."

I was stunned. There was only one wolf left in our town. And she'd been attacked by this wolf that was not really a wolf at all. A werewolf. *Me!* I was sickened. Guilt and horror washed away the hatred and I couldn't look at her anymore. All this time I'd believed the wolf had been killing animals, and for all I knew it had fed on humans every time. Fiona might be the first, or she might be one of many. Either way it didn't make it any better. And the pieces of flesh caught between my teeth, *her flesh!* My stomach heaved and it was all I could do to fight it for her sake.

"Nick, promise me you'll kill the wolf if you see it and not let your love for them get in the way," she said with her dying breath.

But before I could give her any sort of reply her eyes rolled up into my skull so that only the whites showed, she twitched more violently while I screamed her name, and then the eyes came back down, empty, lifeless. *Dead.* She was gone and I was alone once more, horrified at what I had done, but the anger and the hate were coming back, and everything would be different now.

I roared like the monster I was. The wolf had killed one of my best friends, and though I refused to accept it was part of me, I shared the blame for Fiona's death. I wanted to see it die, and in my head I hunted it, wanting to confront it and to kill it, and then I would be human again, and at least no one else would get hurt.

It evaded me for a while and I sat there by my fallen friend, raging and cursing. Any who might have seen me would have considered me mad, but few ever came that way. There were none to witness my insanity.

I pursued the wolf to the darkest depths of my mind and there I confronted it, oblivious to the world around me.

Before I could attack, the wolf turned and stared at me calmly. It snarled and then did something that took me completely by surprise. It spoke in English!

"You wish to kill me and yet I have committed no crimes. I am innocent like any other wolf and deserve no more to die than they do. Yet you would save their lives and you wish to take mine. What gives you the right?" it challenged.

"You killed my friend," I roared at it. How dare it reason with me? In my anger I was the monster and it was almost human, but no, that wasn't right!

"I killed to eat like any other wolf. Besides, you share the blame and we both know it. We are one and the same. I am part of you."

"No! You're not me. I'm human!" I screamed. "I would never have done that to her!"

"But you did," it said, so calmly that I hated it even more. "You are no more human than I am wolf. The sooner you accept that, the easier life will be."

"Life? You call this life?" I said bitterly. "And even if you are part of me, it doesn't matter. You made me become a killer. You caused me to lose my soul!"

"Every wolf must kill to eat, like any other predator. I did no more than hunt and feed as nature intended. Besides, there are too many humans on the Earth. I am helping to keep their numbers down. Call it pest control if you will. As for your soul, can you be so sure you ever had one? You humans believe we animals, who are of flesh and blood as yourselves; who share a high percentage of DNA with you; who are living creatures just like you; you believe we do not have souls and yet you do. What makes you so special? What makes you believe that you are a greater species and that we are all lesser species below you, to do with as you please? You abuse us. You capture us and slaughter us for 'fun' and deny us of our rights. What gives you the right? What makes you so different?" it argued.

"You cannot speak or think," I snarled. "Besides, you could have eaten animals."

"I am speaking now, am I not? And what of my mind? You think there are only instincts there but we are bound together and you can see into it, and hear what runs through it. What then, are these that run through it, if not thoughts?" it said.

"You're different. You're a monster. You just told me we share the same blood, that you are partly human as I am partly wolf. Were it not for that you would be the same as other wolves and instincts would be all you had," I argued back.

"And how can you be so sure? The first time I was awoken within you I remember hearing your thoughts, though they meant little to me then as I had not learnt any words, but you were surprised, I think, at how intelligent I was. Back then I was wolf and wolf only, or as near a wolf as I could ever be. But you are right: I am different in that I hunger for human flesh, unlike true wolves. It is part of the curse. I could not feed on animals alone; the curse would not let me. We are both alone in this world. You will never be truly human again and I can never be truly wolf. You think you are the only one of us two to have suffered but you are wrong. I suffer too, and maybe death is our only comfort but we can only die together, we both know that. Even if you defeated me now I would be called back every full moon, or if I defeated you no doubt the vampire would call you back. Let us avoid a pointless fight for it will resolve nothing," it reasoned.

I remained silent but my rage and anger were even greater than before.

"You would still condemn me to death despite the fact I am a part of you," the wolf sighed.

"Yeah, if I could!" I roared and charged at the wolf, pouncing on it, trying to wrestle it to the ground though it fought back despite its words. And as we each fought for dominance it was possible my body shifted between forms when one of us gained control for a short time. Though whether or not it actually did so I cannot say, for of everything outside my mind I was unaware, including my own body and anything physical which happened to it. I could have been shot by a Slayer and I wouldn't have felt the pain.

I don't know how long the fight lasted inside my mind but the wolf and I were easily matched and finally we lay exhausted on the landscapes of my imagination, panting and bloody.

Then before I could do anything the wolf retaliated in a way far worse than anything I could do to it. It thrust its memories upon me and I was suddenly seeing the world through its eyes and hearing its thoughts, and reliving all the events since it was first awoken when I became a werewolf.

Chapter Eleven - Horrors Relived

The earliest memory, of first feeling the hunger inside that could never be satisfied. *I had not eaten all day and I was ravenous.* The first sight, that of the moon, my only master, and first sounds; *I leapt through the open window, just managing to catch a back leg on the sill and knock several ornaments off, though none of them smashed.* And more importantly to me, my first scents... *I growled irritably, finding no scents of interest – or at least none that were fresh. There were only old scents left by animals, humans, and fumes from their great, roaring machines that constantly chased each other through the day. I started to walk down the street, enslaved by my own hunger, the need for food greater than any other.*

The search for a victim, and finding the prey. *Padding along the pavement, a fresh scent carried to me on the breeze, accompanied by the sound of human footsteps. A woman walked by on the other side of the road and glanced at me, but mistaking me for a large stray dog she carried on.* Her sweet scent carried to me by a faint breeze, blocking out all the others.

I felt all of the wolf's emotions and feelings; the thrill of the chase, the pleasure brought by *the sweet smell of her fear and the sound of her hammering heart.* And the hunger, always the hunger. The bloodlust as I ripped into her and the aggression it brought on, making me savage her, again and again, until she was unrecognisable. The sweet taste of her flesh.

The search for my pack but to no avail. *I sent up another howl into the night to inform my pack of my whereabouts, and stood listening for their rallying howl, calling for me to return to them. But only silence greeted my ears.* The confusion.

The fight for territory and satisfaction at defeating the challenger. The bloodlust once more.

The excitement when my howl was finally answered. *I paused every now and then and continued to howl for my pack. The night was almost spent when finally I received a reply. But I did not recognise the howl as one of my pack member's, who I would instinctively know by scent and sound, even though we had never met before – the werewolf who had awoken me had passed that vital knowledge on, though I knew not how. Cocking my ears in that direction I determined it was a lone wolf, female, containing all the confidence that went with a high rank, an alpha I decided, but fairly young, at least physically. Her voice did not betray her mental age, which could be centuries for one of our kind. The howl was brief and soon ended, and filled with excitement I howled again, straining my ears in desperation for a reply.*

The memory changed and I saw how the Slayers had surrounded me, and how Lady Sarah had come to my rescue. The wolf respected her. This memory was brief and less detailed, and lost in the horror of the others.

It faded and a new memory began, much like the first. I felt the hunger dominating all my other feelings again. But there was something new this time, and I felt the wolf's mind, not just following instinct as in the first memory, but thinking like a human, calculating, looking for a way out of the room. *I could find no way out this time – there was no opening in the glass wall for me to jump through as there had been before and, if I shattered the glass, the noise would bring humans, and probably the Slayers too.*

I paced the length of the room, looking for a way out. I stood up on my back paws, resting my front paws on the windowsill for a better view of the glass standing between myself and freedom, trying to find why there was no opening this time where there had been before.

It had worked out for itself how to open my window! Fear gripped me. Fear at the wolf's intelligence.

The memory moved on and I was soon hunting again and tasting the flesh of a sheep.

But, though it seemed strange since reason said the sheep should have filled my stomach, *I was still hungry and I desired human flesh this time.*

As the memory moved on again, there was *a fresh trail of a male human youth of the age of seventeen.* It seemed in the memory that he was suddenly before me, and then he was on the ground, screaming, *but I quickly slaughtered him by crushing his head, forever silencing him. His brains oozed out onto the street while I hungrily lapped them up.*

There were more memories like that, memories of blood and death and hunger, but it also showed me the times in between the full moon, when it lurked just on the edge of my consciousness, waiting for its chance to break free. It had been quietly observing the human world it had found itself in and listening to my thoughts, probing my mind, and learning from it. It had learnt to understand our language, even if it couldn't speak it itself while in its own form. It had learnt many things, and it was all the more deadly for it.

And then... Another memory came, the final one in the wolf's onslaught, much more powerful than the others, overpowering in fact, so that I did not know whether I was human or wolf, and it became the present, more so than the others had, and I became the wolf. If I had thought the others seemed real I was wrong, they were like dreams compared to this, or like watching events through the wolf's eyes, but this was like living it.

Four hours of hunger passed. I was forced to move towards the centre of the town again, the only place where humans never failed to be.

However, there *was no one outside at that time of night, or at least no one I could take without being seen. It was too early for the drunks to appear and too late to try and pick one off on their way to these places. Resignedly, I started to search the bins again, this time outside a fast food restaurant, when I heard human voices. And they were heading towards me! I thanked fate for the meal being brought my way while I lay in the shadows, waiting. From listening to their conversation I learnt that it was the birthday of one of the girls in the group and they were going to the night club to celebrate. I detected five of them but I only needed to take one. Sometimes I had eaten more, but I only really needed one to make the hunger bearable.* The knowledge of this angered me, but it was lost in the memory.

Now I needed to find a way to isolate one of them and make the kill without being seen by the others. The question was: how could I possibly do it without revealing myself to them? If any witnessed it I would have to kill them too, and the more deaths, the greater the likelihood of discovery by the Slayers. I could think of no way to lure one of them away and was growing desperate. However, fate remained in my favour that night and I had no need to take chances; as they were approaching the nightclub one of the girls had forgotten something. Consequently she left the safety of the group, promising to be back in about fifteen minutes.

Seeing she was taking a different route back – probably shorter – down an alley, I slunk ahead of her and waited until we were out of sight of the others, checking that there was no one about. Satisfied it was as safe as it could ever be in such dark times, I emerged from the shadows and pounced on her. She was too shocked to scream at first and by then it was too late – she could scream no more.

I had begun to feast on my meal when I sensed another female human nearby, but in the grip of the bloodlust I became more reckless. Nothing mattered then except the warm flesh on the ground at my feet. The world around me ceased to exist until there was only the flesh that nourished me, and the hunger. Nothing else mattered.

And so I ignored her. I continued to feed, her footsteps coming closer and still I ignored them. At this point my muzzle was deep in a hole in the belly of my victim, drawing out the organs as I had always done, since the first night I had been released from my prison deep within the human's consciousness to hunt under the full moon. So lost in my meal, and the pleasure the fresh meat and offal brought, I did not notice the girl to whom the footsteps belonged walking down the alley towards me, until it was too late.

She had not seen me yet – both myself and the carcass were hidden in shadows – but that was about to change. I only became aware of her when I rose from the hole I had made, the organs devoured, to attack another part of the corpse and rip through the soft flesh. And then it was, when my muzzle emerged from the hole, her sweet scent tore through the blood red veil in my mind, and in that instant we saw each other.

The quickest to react, I snarled instinctively, ears flattened against my skull. My lips curled back so that my blood stained teeth were bared, defending my kill. I was an impressive sight in the dark alley, terrible to behold. I was a demon in the darkness, seemingly much larger than any mortal wolf. She did what any mortal would have done, except maybe for the Slayers. She turned and ran. The bloodlust clouded my judgement. I wanted to go back to my meal, but the bloodlust also wanted fresh blood, fresher meat, since the corpse at my feet was already beginning to lose its warmth, though it would not be entirely cold for hours yet. Besides, some part of my mind was insisting that she could not be allowed to live. And the age old instinct in all canines to chase running creatures was trying to make itself heard in the confused knot of thoughts. I could not ignore it. I obeyed. I gave chase...

I forced the human towards the outskirts of the town where it was more isolated, and pursued her into the fields, where I began to close in for the kill.

I ran forward until I drew level with her and grabbed hold of her leg with my jaws, pulling her down to the ground. This time I wanted to play. I let go of the leg which was already leaking blood, and waited for her to rise.

Minutes passed but she made no move to get up. She just lay there whimpering, so I grabbed hold of the leg again and reared up, tossing my head back. Her body was thrown up with me, and as gravity took hold and I fell back down onto all fours, with a jerk of my head I slammed her back down onto the hard, cold soil. I didn't put too much force behind it, however, not wanting to end it too quickly. I had not broken any of her bones; merely bruised and winded her. The movement had caused my teeth to rip right through her leg, down to the bone, spewing out more blood.

This time she rose and limped off, crying and screaming in terror.

Silently, I followed behind her until she collapsed again. The game was over: she had not the strength to continue. I sniffed at the leg, but it was the organs I really wanted, so I moved up to her stomach.

Weakly she tried to kick me, but I dodged easily and tore at some of the flesh from just above her waist, though I did not yet dig deep enough with my teeth to the organs beneath. I didn't bother to kill her first. She'd die soon enough and she didn't have the strength to fight back or run away.

I had only taken a couple of mouthfuls of flesh when I heard gunshot from somewhere within the town. They weren't shooting at me but it didn't matter. I wasn't taking any chances. If they picked up my trail I'd be shot down, and I wasn't ready to die yet. I abandoned the meal and ran for the cover of the woodland that I could smell nearby.

And so, an hour later I stood in a small, shallow stream, allowing the icy cold water, numbing, yet refreshing, to wash over my paws and rinse away the blood from my claws. And I drank the clean, clear, pure water that I might quench my thirst and cleanse my bloodied muzzle. The blood mixed with the water: a dark red *streak snaked down the stream. I licked the blood away that had splattered all over my body, congealing and thickening on my matted fur. There was something about that night that made me feel the need to cleanse myself of the last remnants of the lives I had taken, as if it were impure, staining my soul. But these were human thoughts. The human was beginning to affect me, and I didn't like it.*

I stared down at my reflection in the water, looking into the amber eyes that stared back at me. What was I? Not human. Not wolf. A hybrid of the two. A monster? That was what humans believed. But did monsters have a conscience? A killer yes, yet I only took life so that I may survive, one of the oldest laws of nature, to which all living creatures are bound, predator and prey. And what sort of a predator feels… what? Remorse? No, it wasn't remorse. The human may have felt remorse when it killed the rabbit, but not I. What then? I didn't understand this. But I felt something after the kill, and if these feelings grew they would get in the way. What sort of a predator feels for the victims it feeds on? Whatever I was, be it monster or some poor confused creature that was never meant to be, I was flawed and it made me weak. These were the human's problems affecting me, and it had to learn to accept its fate. Our survival depended upon it.

All of a sudden I was violently brought back to something vaguely resembling reality. I became dimly aware of the outside world again. But the memories seemed to have burned into my mind and I lay on the ground beside the corpse that had, just hours ago, been Fiona; innocent, young and full of life. She'd been so excited about her dance tournament, and with a guilty pang I thought about how I'd stolen the opportunity from her. She might have won a trophy or a medal and it would have made her so happy, and her family so proud, and I had taken it all away in just hours. I could forgive her for leaving me, Lizzy and Becci the night I'd been bitten. She'd just been frightened after all. Despite that particular incident I knew she'd cared about me, and this was how I'd repaid her. She would never have the chance to compete in her tournament, or to wear her beautiful prom dress she'd already picked out as she made her entrance on the arm of her boyfriend, the guy she believed was the one. She'd had so much ahead of her to look forward to, and now she would never enjoy any of it.

The images circled my mind like birds of prey, and one would suddenly swoop down, making me relive that particular horror again. Open or closed, for several hours all I could see before my eyes were the victims I had slaughtered.

And just as it seemed the torment would never stop, I was finally allowed a moment's respite and became fully aware of the world around me once more. I knew my family would probably be looking for me by then, wanting to know where I was and when I would be coming home. I forced myself to stand, preparing myself for the long walk home. I was unable to look at Fiona and turned away from her, muttering "Forgive me..."

Not that she heard. She was beyond hearing now. Did I leave her there? If I left her, her family, who no doubt already considered her missing, would have to face the anguish of not knowing what had become of her, for who knew how long it would be before someone looked out there? I doubted anyone would happen upon her, and the police would not do anything until forty eight hours passed since she was first reported missing. Yet if I was discovered with the body the police would want to question me, which I couldn't bear right then, and the Slayers might put two and two together, for surely they would recognise a werewolf's victim. Not that it seemed like a bad thing at that moment. If the Slayers found me they'd end it, and countless lives would be saved, though I doubted my soul would be spared. And then came the thought: oh God, would I take at least three victims every month for all eternity? Death seemed my only option, but I decided I didn't want to meet my end at the hands of the Slayers.

I stumbled away from her body in a state of shock. I began walking without taking note of where I was going and somehow found my way back to the town centre. My feet were automatically set on the path home but as I walked I heard someone calling my name, and so I paused and turned to find it was Lizzy.

"So what's wrong?" she asked me, walking over and sitting on a bench, motioning for me to do the same. I wasn't sure I could face her after everything I had just learned, but I had little choice so I joined her. If I'd just walked off she'd have only followed me. I had to say something before she would leave me in peace.

"Nothing," I said, trying to hide the flutter of panic. It was clear she'd already had her suspicions after the few uncharacteristic bouts of aggression she'd witnessed, but did she actually know something? She couldn't find out my dark secret. For one thing the knowledge could put her in danger.

"Nick, you've been my best friend for the last four years. I know something's not right. So what's wrong? You know you can tell me. I'm here for you anytime, whatever it is."

"Are you? Would you be here for me if you knew the truth? I don't think you would. I don't think anyone would."

"Of course I am. I'll always be here for you, no matter what."

I smiled sadly at that. The wolf only saw the darker, brutal nature of mankind but here Lizzy was proving there was more to them than that. I wanted to believe she would find it in her heart to forgive me for what I had done to our friend, maybe even pity me and try to help me find a way to control the curse. Maybe we could look for a cure. But I knew that could never happen. Even if I could tell her, she would no doubt run from me in horror and fear, and never once look back.

"I'm not the guy you think I am," I told her.

"What, you mean you're really a girl? Are you saying you're one of these transgendered people we've heard about? Because if you are that doesn't change anything, you're still the same person I've known since Year Seven."

I laughed despite myself, though it was hollow and filled with little humour. "Hell no, there's no confusion over my gender. No, I mean I'm not the guy you think you know. There's this other side to me that you would not like. I wish I could tell you about what's really going on but I just can't. I value our friendship and it means a lot to me that you've always been there for me when I've needed you. But you can't help me right now and talking about it will just make things worse. So leave it please."

She was worried for me – it was plain to see even without any supernatural abilities. But she did as I asked and we sat in silence for a few minutes until I told her I needed to be alone. She left me to it but kept glancing back as she walked away, still worried that things were obviously not right. Clearly I needed to make a better show of hiding it, but I was so lost in the horror and the shock of the wolf's memories, not to mention the building depression and the despair at the sheer hopelessness of my fate, that acting like my normal, happy self seemed impossible.

I made it back home without further interruption. Dad was out golfing as usual on a Saturday, but Mum was in. She'd been worried about me, though she didn't lecture me when she saw the state I was in. I looked worse than Fiona had when I first found her. Mum wanted to take me to a doctor, the last thing I wanted. I grunted something about feeling sick and needing to rest, then I retreated to my room to be alone.

I wasn't the same after that. I couldn't eat, the very thought of it sickening, couldn't sleep, since the nightmares plagued me worse then than ever, and refused to speak to people. I withdrew into my own mind, only to suffer reliving the horrors again. Outwardly I was an empty shell, just a shadow of the laughing, joking boy I had once been, but I was still in there somewhere, just enough of me left to function.

My parents gave up on trying to find out what was wrong and let me be. My friends soon did the same when the weekend was over and we were back at school. Maybe Lizzy had talked to them for me. I sat in silence in the classrooms, letting the teacher's words wash over me, not really listening. My grades were suffering worse than ever. Not that I cared. It all seemed pointless then.

When it was discovered Fiona was missing, they soon forgot about me anyway. Fiona had been a popular girl, and everybody was worried about her, none more than David. And finally when the police found her body, I wasn't the only one lost in a dark pit of my own grief, sadness and mourning, but unlike the rest of them I had guilt, depression, despair and horror to seal me in, along with anger and hate, with no hope of ever crawling out into the light. I had reached a point from which it seemed there was no return and the only way out was death.

Death. I thought about it often. What I wouldn't have given for the earth to open up beneath my feet and let me fall into Hell. I didn't fear Hell, if such a place really existed, and I didn't fear death itself. I wanted to pay for my sins. Did I have the nerve to end it myself though? I didn't fear death, and yet I didn't know whether I could commit that final sin. But to do so was to save countless numbers of lives stretching over eternity. And why should it be a sin anyway? God didn't care about me. It was my life after all, mine to take and do with as I wished. If I chose to end it no one would stop me. If. That was the thing. I didn't know if I could. Perhaps if I was pushed far enough over the edge I would, but there was still a faint desire to live somewhere in there. Maybe it lay with the wolf. It had shown me something of its suffering, but did it suffer enough to want death as much as I did?

Time didn't help either. Gradually the school began to forget. Fiona Young became just another name in the school's history, and only in those closest to her did she live on. And in my nightmares, which plagued me every time I dared to close my eyes, and that wasn't often. I spent every waking minute fighting sleep. It left me exhausted, constantly. In fact, time made it worse.

Fiona's death had been in the paper, and experts had come to the conclusion that she'd been killed by some sort of animal, canine, but they couldn't determine the species. They were saying the bites looked like the work of a large wolf or a dog. Most people seemed to be in favour of a wolf. Dogs had too good a reputation, whereas people have always hated and feared wolves. The rogue wolf, they were calling it, an escaped animal probably brought up illegally by someone with a taste for exotic pets, rather than a zoo. And then two more

142

deaths were discovered – the wolf's kills from the two following nights before it was locked away inside again for another month – and the media had got the whole town in a panic, as more bodies were turning up, people who had been missing since September.

The wolf had been clever enough to hide its kills to start off, what had changed? I didn't know and I didn't want to know. Maybe it deemed it pointless, once the first body had been left out in the open to be discovered. For all its intelligence, it hadn't considered the general public's reaction, or the reaction of the local government, at the greater number of bodies it left for them to find. For all I knew they were already planning to hunt down this monster and kill it. I'd never paid any attention to the news and I was ignorant of whatever they had promised to do about it. It didn't matter to me anyway. If they killed me it was for the better, and it would save me having to find the courage to do it myself.

And as we were plunged into the heart of winter in December, I knew time was running out for at least three more people that month, unless I found a way to stop it without ending my own life.

But how did I stop it? I had felt the wolf's strength. What could possibly contain that brutal force, driven by the primitive need to kill, to feed? My room wouldn't hold it, but I had to try something. It was either that or ask the vampires for better ideas, but I didn't know if they would understand. Lady Sarah wouldn't, I was sure of that, and while Vince chose to live among mortals, he had no problem with killing, of that I was also sure. He had told me to learn from the wolf; I didn't think he would understand why I wanted to stop it.

Whatever I was going to do, I had to decide on it soon. Time was running out.

Chapter Twelve - Hybrid

The temperature dropped and the land became bitterly cold in the days leading up to the full moon. The sky grew gloomier with the threat of snow showers above, though people weren't expecting much – snow was rare in our town. But the clouds overhead were dark enough to match my mood and temperatures were already below freezing.

Then the first of the winter snows fell; it drifted down in a gentle flurry from the clouds and landed delicately on the ground, dusting the land. At first that was all it did: powdered the fields at the back of the house and the streets at the front. It did not last long enough, nor was it heavy enough, to do much else. But the next day another snow shower fell, heavier than the first and lasting longer, the flakes swarming down like a plague of icy cold, white insects, and settled to form a pure white blanket.

At school there were snowball fights breaking out all over the field at break and during lunch time, and the unwary were pelted with snowballs in between lessons if they ventured outside. Everyone was making the most of the snow while it lasted and I'd have been enjoying it with everyone else, if it weren't for the knowledge of what I'd done.

The nights had been growing noticeably longer, something that worried me. It meant that when the time came I would have longer to kill. Would there be more deaths? From the memories the wolf had shown me, it seemed its hunger was insatiable.

But what was on my mind the most was the fact that I had not seen the moon for a couple of weeks due to the cloud cover, and I couldn't be sure which night it would be full – I could only guess. I'd looked on the Net for lunar calendars, but it seemed they could only guess too; not one of them could agree which night the moon would reach its fullest. It meant it was on my mind constantly, the unanswered question of whether it would be that night, or the one after, or the one after that. And all the while I was trying to think of a way to stop the wolf, and so far I had come up with none.

Then, the day of the heavy snowfall, it seemed I was to face what I feared the most.

As we approached Christmas, my mood was far from festive. After I finished school one day, I stayed behind to catch up on some homework, not because I was worried about my grades and whether I passed or failed my GCSE's, but in the hope of forgetting what was still to come that month, and the inevitable bloodshed. When I grew restless I knew what it probably meant and I took my leave.

Dusk wasn't far off when I walked home in fear of the oncoming darkness, despite the fact it was only four thirty. By the time I reached our drive minutes later, the little light penetrating the clouds was already beginning to fade, while another snow shower began. I looked up at the darkening sky as I came to the front door, wondering if there was a full moon hidden behind those clouds. For the sake of whichever poor soul who was fated to become my prey that month I hoped not, though I knew it had to come some time soon, and what difference did it really make whether it was that night or later in the week? I shivered and went inside.

No sooner had I stepped through the doorway than the pain started. Amy hadn't been home long either, since she'd been to the corner shop on the way back with her mates. She sat on the stairs sucking a lollypop, watching me. I groaned as pain ravaged my stomach and turned to run upstairs to the safety of my room. I still didn't know what I was going to do to stop the wolf but it was too late for that now. However, Amy had that taunting smile on her face. She stood up with her arms outstretched, blocking the stairway. She wasn't going to let me pass until I was begging her for it. I couldn't believe her timing. She was so bloody annoying when she wanted to be, and already I was sure I could feel things happening and I had to know, had to find out whether it was what I feared it to be.

"Shift," I grunted through the pain.

"Ask me nicely," she said in a sing song voice.

"C'mon Amy, move!"

"Ask me nicely," she repeated.

I didn't have time for this. Visible changes could start at any moment, and I really didn't want to transform in front of my family. Not so much because of the fear it would cause, it was more the thought of the wolf gaining consciousness only to find itself confronted with prey, trapped inside the building with them: an easy meal. Amy noticed my growing anxiety and was enjoying it all the more. Was my skin itching or was that my paranoid imagination? I was sure I could feel the crawling sensation that meant only one thing.

"Get out of the way," I roared and pushed past her. She slipped and fell to the floor with a sharp crack, where she lay crying. Whether I actually hurt her or not was anyone's guess. She could turn on the tears whenever it suited her. She was a born actress, a natural drama queen. Maybe the tears were real and I should have felt bad at the thought that I had hurt her, but I was too afraid of the moon, convinced as I was that it was full.

In the safety of my room, I examined the backs of my hands and ripped my shirt open, expecting to see the wolf's pelt spreading over my skin, muscles rippling beneath it, bones reforming. My hands were normal, my chest bare, the skin stretched across a human framework, and the pain was dying down. Not daring to believe it, I ran to the bathroom and looked in the mirror. I was shocked by what I saw.

It was human, but it was barely recognisable as the boy I had been. Human eyes stared out of a gaunt face, almost a living skull. Human, but not my own. The horror had affected me more deeply than I'd thought. The lack of sleep and refusal to eat, coupled with the stress my mind was under, weighed down with every negative emotion known to man, had caused me to rapidly lose weight. That was the first time I'd really looked at myself since Fiona's death. Looking at my reflection had left me feeling guilty, and I'd avoided it where I could. A trace of something in the eyes unnerved me, a hint of the unearthly hunger both human and wolf shared around the full moon. It was gone, and the eyes stared back at me, full of sadness, pain and despair.

I held that gaze as long as I could, and then finally had to look away. Truly I had died the night I was bitten and but a shadow of myself remained. Still, I had a faint glimmer of hope. I wouldn't transform that night, I still had time to find a way to restrain the wolf, keep it from killing under the full moon.

Over the next few days I clung to that hope with everything I had left, all the strength that hadn't been driven out of me by Fiona's death. I clung to that hope like it was the edge of a cliff, and I was scrabbling on the smooth rock face, trying to pull myself back up, save myself from the fatal drop below. Perhaps it was too late for that.

And then Thursday night, the thing I had been dreading was finally upon me. The restlessness, the pain as darkness fell, and finally the transformation when the moon found a break in the clouds and revealed itself to the world.

However, that night, and the following one, the town would be safe. For I was to be spared the horror of knowing I had taken more innocent lives.

Snow drifted down onto the wintry landscape, thickening the white blanket, lit up by the moonlight. Outside, it was quiet and still, peaceful, while the monster I was becoming lay writhing in pain, growing more powerful but currently trapped in a world of chaos in both body and mind. It seemed impossible that the two could exist so close together. And soon the chaos would break free, let loose upon the peaceful world that lay beyond, bringing death and destruction. Or at least it should have done.

The moon was slowly climbing higher into the night sky, passing into another layer of cloud cover, a layer that was growing thicker as more clouds drifted across, until there were few breaks left for its light to penetrate. And as the world was plunged into darkness, I felt the impossible begin. The change was reversing!

I had almost become fully wolf when thankfully, mercifully, I began to change back. By some miracle I found I still had the strength to fight the wolf, when it should have been the stronger under the moon's influence. It seemed the wolf needed the moonlight to gain control; the fact that it was the right time of the month didn't matter, not without the moonlight. The wolf felt cheated, and it fought for as long as it could, until its rage and its strength were spent, and it reluctantly retreated back into our subconscious, where I could feel it brimming with anger. I didn't care. I'd been saved from killing, and I looked to the future with renewed hope. I could learn from this. Closing my curtains in an attempt to hide the moon's light wasn't enough, it was still visible through the thin material, but if I could find somewhere to hide during the full moon, somewhere not even the light of the sun could penetrate, I might be able to remain human and save lives. It was something at least. And even if I failed to prevent any more deaths, I would know I had tried. It was better than standing by and letting it happen at any rate.

Saturday came and I was in a better mood than I had been for weeks past, less sullen and depressed, optimistic for the rest of the winter months at least, while the snow lasted. It seemed to me that while the snow lasted the clouds would block the moon's rays, and none need die by my hand while I remained human. But the snow showers had stopped sometime overnight, and as the day wore on and the cloud cover grew sparser, it seemed fated that I would transform that night, fated that at least one would die to satisfy my lupine hunger. Such dark events I did not see that morning when Mum came to wake me (though I had not been sleeping anyway), not until later in the day. I'd forgotten it was Amy's birthday, and since as far back as I can remember we'd always gone into Mum and Dad's bedroom to open presents as a family. I'd also forgotten one of her friends would be coming over to sleep that night.

"Aw no, I'm not putting up with the two of them giggling all night!" I objected when Amy reminded me. I'd always been against her having friends to sleep. It was bad enough having one teenage girl in the house. I still hadn't forgotten the previous year's party, when there'd been six of the brats. They'd run around screaming like they

147

were still five, giggling and talking about boys and other girly crap. When we were younger I used to chase them, but Amy would have killed me if I did that now she was older. Some of her friends were okay as girls went, but she could be a real bitch depending on who she was with, even more than usual, and they were all annoying in their own way. Not only that, I really didn't want to think about them running around the house screaming that year. The wolf had been cheated out of hunting the past two nights, the only thing it lived for, and its bloodlust grew stronger by the day. Full moon or no, it was biding its time, licking its wounds, the rage slowly building. I feared what would happen when it chose the time to break free of its prison and force me down into the darkness. And young, tender girls would be too much for it. The temptation would bring it out of hiding, whether it deemed the time right or no, and with the smell of fresh meat and the power of the bloodlust, coupled with the time of the month, it might be too powerful for me to stop.

"Don't worry, they won't bother you," Mum said, her voice holding a hint of impatience, like she was tired of my reaction every time. "They'll be in their room, you'll be in yours. It's only for one night."

I swore inwardly and continued to argue, but the issue was evidently not open to debate. It had already been decided a couple of weeks ago, and no matter what I said, short of telling them the truth, there was no way I could convince them to cancel it.

As the day dragged by I had the nagging feeling that darkness hung over our house. It felt like a cursed building and I just knew something horrific was going to take place there that night, something resulting in death for one of us under that roof. The thinning cloud cover did nothing to ease the feeling. As the last of the clouds drifted away, my optimism went with it, gone to the same grave in which one of them would soon lie.

A knock on the door came at about five o'clock and I beheld Mel on the doorstep, her shoulder length brown hair, her blue eyes, her freckly face. She had a low cut top on and I could see the veins beneath her pale flesh... She looked at me nervously for perhaps there was a strange look in my eyes, one of fear and bitterness that could be mistaken for hatred, and beyond that even of hunger from the wolf within. I turned from the door and called up to Amy that her friend had arrived, and then invited her in. Soon the two of them were up in my sister's room and I was left alone, growing ever more uneasy.

Night advanced and I retired to my room, telling them I felt ill again. Mum was growing more concerned as the weeks passed and I only seemed to get worse, but agreed with me that I needed to rest. No doubt she put my gaunt appearance down to Fiona's death. If only she knew that was just the tip of the iceberg.

I fled from them and closed the door. I could already feel the change was not far away and it was too late by then to do anything about it. I'd not had chance to search for somewhere safe to hide away from the moon's light, and there was no other way of preventing the change. I was resigned to my fate as I glared up at the full moon, knowing someone would die. There was one thing I could do though. From the wolf's memories, I knew it would not risk smashing the window to reach the world outside, so I locked it and hoped that might keep it in. The door was closed behind me, and I was confident the doorknob would be impossible for a paw to turn. I prayed the wolf would not risk breaking out again, yet I still couldn't shake the doomed feeling that hung over the house, and a part of me knew it was inevitable. Whether that was true or not, it was too late to do anything else. The change had already taken hold.

When I found no way out of the room this time, I gave up and sank to the floor, whining pitifully and growling in frustration, snarling at my tormentor, the moon. I spent the first half of the night there, fighting the hunger. But in the end the hunger won.

The bloodlust had been upon me for the past two nights and, unable to satisfy it, the craving was becoming more powerful, until it blocked out all else. I had temporarily lost my reason, a kind of madness upon me. As the night wore on, I forgot the threat of the Slayers, and the need for secrecy so as not to draw attention to myself. It didn't matter that I was surrounded by humans, and my growling would attract them like moths to a light. All my senses were dominated by the signs of prey just beyond the four walls of my prison, and instinct had taken control. Bathed in the moon's light, much brighter compared with the previous two months, I roared with hunger. Like a great orb it was, hanging in the sky, drawing its power from the sun.

Hunger drew me to the door, tantalising scents snaking their way into my nostrils from underneath. I reared up on my hind legs and rested my front paws on the white, wooden barrier that stood between me and my prey, sniffing it, trying to find a way to open it as I had with the window. I could find none and I growled with frustration. There seemed to be no other way out and this drove me into a frenzy. Forgetting the door, I ran to the window, hearing a group of teenagers wandering the streets beyond. I tried attacking the glass for all the good it did. My claws slid across the smooth surface, barely scratching it, and I couldn't get my jaws round anything to bite my way through. I threw my weight against the wall it was set in. The glass shuddered but miraculously it held, though I would have broken through eventually if I'd kept on trying. And I would have, if sounds of movement within the house hadn't distracted me. I fell silent, listening intently.

The animal moved clumsily, which could only mean it was human, and its scent reached me from the crack beneath the door as confirmation. I could hear its rapidly beating heart and scented its fear. She was a young female, her smell making me drool. I could almost taste the tender flesh in my mouth.

Minutes passed while I listened to her beating heart, my own pumping faster in anticipation. Slowly, so slowly, after she had stood listening on the other side of the door, she began to open it. Perhaps she had heard me in my madness and was curious, though afraid. Maybe she was worried for the human I had been, thinking perhaps the animal she'd heard had killed it. She was right in a way. I was not entirely sure why, but she crept into the room and blinked in the moonlight. To be honest, looking back now I'm surprised no one else came to check on me, for surely they all heard me raging in there. Although I have learnt humans have a habit of explaining away the supernatural, no matter how unbelievable their explanations might be. Maybe they assumed I was watching a horror film and had the TV on too loud, despite the fact I was supposedly in bed. They'd gone to sleep and thought nothing more of it, until the human before me had woken and decided to investigate. It was as good an explanation as any.

The girl looked at me and went very still, while I had been crouched ready to strike when the time was right. We were both deathly still for a few seconds in which the world seemed to still with us, before I was up and running towards her with a new strength. I could see my prey now and it was as if nothing could stop me. The threat of the Slayers certainly didn't. They were the last thing in my crazed mind as I sprang towards her.

I was upon her almost immediately. She was about to scream for help as my teeth raked her face, and I quickly bit into the soft flesh of her throat to silence her forever. The scream never escaped her mouth. All she managed was a soft gurgle as the blood rushed in, and in those few seconds in which she still lived her hand rose to her throat, feeling it in horror, before falling back to her side. Her eyes had been filled with surprise, mixed with terror and horror since she had first looked upon me, and now would be for all eternity, or at least until they rotted away to nothingness. But such details did not worry me; she was prey like any other. Dragging her back into the room so as not to be disturbed, I ripped into her flesh and began to eat my fill, and there would have been little left when I had finished if it had not been for the return of the snowfall.

Clouds had been accumulating in the sky above, unnoticed by me, and the moon was fast becoming shrouded in those clouds. I had eaten only a few mouthfuls, exposing her organs, when I suddenly felt the agony I had felt but hours before. The few mouthfuls I had consumed seemed to squirm in my stomach as if the flesh were

150

still alive, and it churned in there, so that I had to fight to keep it down. It felt like my hind legs were being pulled at either end as my femurs stretched painfully outwards. Other bones were changing shape, muscles shifting. The human mind was becoming stronger. I roared in pain and anger that I had been denied the chance to satisfy my hunger after all, and struggled with the human for ascendancy. The moon was wreathed in black clouds and yet such was its power that night that still a little light penetrated the blackness. It no longer held its sway over me, but I had not been released from it yet. I had not transformed back completely and I was neither human nor wolf, but a beast somewhere in between, my form truly symbolic of the hybrid I was.

For I had become a beast straight out of a Hollywood horror movie. My head was still lupine, as were my hands and feet, more like paws than human appendages, though they had more dexterity than my paws as a full wolf. My body was humanoid, though still covered in fur and more muscular than my human form, but the spine hadn't straightened out completely. And while I could stand upright if I wanted to, relaxed I was stooped slightly with my knees bent forward, so that my front paws reached down to my knees when I stretched my arms to their full length. I was also stood on my toes like a wolf (and many other predators for that matter), my feet too close to paws to allow me to stand on the flat of them like a human. I still had a tail. And as for my mind, it was suddenly neither human nor wolf, but something of both. For we were both of equal strength in the semi-moonlight and somehow both seemed in control.

And, my reasoning now returned, I looked down at my kill and knew it meant trouble. The police would find it in my room, but worse still, I had no doubt that some of the Slayers were in the police force as well, conveniently placed to hunt us down easier and keep our existence secret at the same time. By killing in my own house, in my own room, I had signed my own death warrant. There would be no question in the Slayers' minds as to the human identity of the werewolf. The hunger would have to wait. I relinquished my hold on our body entirely to the human, in the hope it would know what to do to hide the evidence from the Slayers.

I was sickened to find myself trapped in the nightmarish form between boy and wolf, and tried to force the transformation further so that I could be human again. It was no use, the moonlight was too strong. Even more sickening was the realisation of the blood in my mouth, still fresh and spilling out over my jaws, trickling down my body, mixing with sweat. And with this realisation came the discovery of what lay at my feet, and it was all I could do not to cry out and awaken the others. I couldn't let them see me like this, or what I had done.

The bloody corpse stared up at me with wide eyes, almost accusing to my guilty mind. Blood pooled around it, the torso torn open, organs glistening in the moonlight like a sick piece of artwork. The throat had been ripped apart, the windpipe severed, more blood spilling out of it. Long gashes covered the mutilated face where teeth had torn through the delicate skin to the flesh beneath. It was barely recognisable as Mel, the girl it had once been. And now I had to clean it up. I don't think I could have brought myself to touch it if it wasn't for the thought that if the Slayers found out, it could put my family in danger as well.

Numb with shock, I mopped up the blood with a couple of towels before it could stain the varnished wooden floors. Then I used the same towels to stem the flow of blood from the body. I didn't bother to wipe her prints off the door – if the police knew she'd been staying with us I was confident it would not arouse suspicion. As for my own prints on the body, there were none on the hard black pads beneath my paws. Or at least none that could be identified as human. All that remained then was to dispose of the body and the bloodied towels. Reluctantly, not really wanting to touch it, I picked up the dead weight and slung it over my shoulder. A few specks of blood flecked the painted walls and the floor with the movement of the body, despite the towels I'd wrapped round it, but I'd clean them up when I returned before daybreak.

I fumbled with the window, trying to unlock it. I couldn't grip the key in my paws and kept dropping it, but somehow I managed to open it after several attempts. I shifted my hold on the body and leapt out of the window, landing crouched and cat-like, as I had countless times whenever I'd jumped the last two stairs in our home. But it wasn't a game anymore.

I stood and forced my protesting spine upright and my knees straight, just while I paused to clear my mind. I was vaguely aware of the fact I was naked, and on two legs I was much more exposed than on four. Ordinarily I'd have been embarrassed and would have attempted to cover myself, but I was too lost in my emotions to care. The shock of finding her body lying bleeding at my feet had numbed the pain that was soon to follow, but now the shock was wearing off and I could feel the sadness and despair creeping into my senses, along with the guilt that had been there all along. I didn't want to hide her body. Her family had the right to know what had happened to her, and to give her a decent burial. Instead her parents would have to suffer the agony of not knowing whether their missing daughter was alive or dead. At least Fiona's family had soon found out what had become of her. Mel's family might never know if I hid the body well enough, which was something I had to do for my own survival, and that of my own family.

Gently I let her body slide into my arms and stood looking at her face. When I had beheld her in the doorway earlier that day she had been beautiful, but in death she had become ugly, mutilated. She'd still been warm when I first picked her up, but the icy cold wind was already creeping into her dead veins, flakes of snow cooling her skin. It should have been hours before she was cold to the touch, but the snow was speeding up the process. And then she was so cold, as cold as the snow my feet were upon. The muscles twitched, and I almost dropped her with revulsion, before they stiffened in response to the cold, though rigor mortis wouldn't happen for hours yet. As I stood there gazing into her face, snowflakes collected in my dark fur, tinting it with white. I could see my breath steaming out of my mouth. I had to close those eyes, for I could not stand to look into them and see the horror, the terror, the pain. Minutes passed that seemed to last for years and time once again seemed to stand still. Finally I howled her name into the night sky so that she may not be forgotten, and that broke the spell. I started walking with her, headed towards the other side of town.

As I walked the snow began to cover my bestial footprints. It drove into my face as if it was trying to drive the evil in me from the world, and the wind was strong, trying to force me back. I pushed on, ever aware of the dead weight in my arms. The night was bitterly cold but my fur kept me warm, though I would have rather suffered the cold in human form if I had the choice than spend the night as the monster I was.

Finally I came to the same field where Fiona had died, thinking that if they ever found her they'd assume 'the rogue wolf' had killed her, and that it had taken up residence in the woods. The Slayers wouldn't believe that, and the fact she had been sleeping at our house could not be overlooked, by either Slayers or the police. Unless they found the body and pronounced it the work of an animal, there was nothing I could do to completely avoid police suspicion. I just had to hide the evidence as best I could. But I feared that the Slayers would also not overlook the fact that it had been a full moon when she went missing. If they discovered what I was my family and I were doomed.

The soil was hard in the field, frozen over, and a layer of snow covered it. I had the strength to dig into the soil but long I had to labour to dig down deep enough, and precious time was lost. I was hoping her body would never be discovered, knowing it would inevitably lead the Slayers to me. So I dug deeper than most humans could reach without aid of machinery, and then ripped off the blood

153

soaked towels and carefully lowered her into the hole and laid her to rest. At that point I felt a great hunger that I had not noticed while my mind was bent on hiding the corpse. I looked on her small form and saw her as prey as the wolf had done, not as appetising now that her flesh was frozen over, but satisfactory. This sickened me and then I began to really feel the horror of what I had done. She had been so young with so much to live for, her whole life ahead of her. And because of me she was no more. Roaring with rage at myself, I carefully laid the towels over her small form so that they covered her from head to foot, and began to fill in the hole. Filling it in was easier and soon the snow began to cover it over again, so that only someone looking for it who knew it was there could possibly have found it.

I stood watch over the grave for most of the night, mourning for all those who had died at the jaws of the wolf, including myself. Fiona's body might have been moved, but she had died there. It wasn't hard for my guilty imagination to hear their voices screaming in the howling wind. I can still hear them to this day, screaming in pain, screaming in terror, screaming for the help that never came. Screaming for all eternity as if their very souls were trapped in my head, the terrible sound reverberating endlessly round my skull. I crouched down and covered my ears, whimpering.

"Leave me alone!"

It would have been a scream if I was human, but the sound came out bestial, more like a roar.

"I never wanted this! I never meant to hurt anyone, please leave me alone. I didn't want this, not this."

But I had wanted it. Hadn't I spent most of my childhood wishing I was a werewolf? As a young boy I used to stand by my window, staring longingly at the moon. In all our childhood games I'd been the monster, slashing my friends with imaginary claws, and now it had become reality and I hated it.

"I never wanted to be a killer," I whispered. There was no reply. The wind ravaged me with renewed strength, and I closed my eyes against the force of it. I couldn't stay there any longer. I couldn't bear to listen to those imaginary voices of the dead, and the cold was piercing me to the bone now, despite my thick pelt, driving out the warmth until I might as well have been another corpse lying there.

There was roughly only an hour left till daybreak. I couldn't stay there but I wasn't ready to go home yet either. It would be some time yet before Amy discovered her friend missing. She usually slept in till lunchtime given the chance, and her friends were the same.

I walked off aimlessly, feeling lost with nowhere to go, and alone. Before long I found myself in the park, where there was a horse racing course. There was also a playground, a tennis court, lots of space for walking dogs or playing football, and a lake, large enough and deep enough for peddle and rowing boats, with a small island in the middle for the ducks to nest in. It was by the lake I found myself. I came to a stop at the water's edge, aware that my mouth was still wet with her blood. The lake had frozen over, so I punched a hole through it and gratefully lapped at the pure liquid until the salty, coppery taste went away.

The snow was still falling but a thin layer had formed in the cloud cover. Moonlight shone through the veil, though still weak, as if it was determined to make one last stand before it sunk beneath the horizon and the sun rose to take its place. I saw my reflection in the circle of water I had created in the ice, and looked upon the monster I had become for the first time.

My face held no hint of the boy I had been, all human features gone. The first thing I noticed, as I mentioned before, was my pelt was not one solid colour like the werewolves of films, but a mixture of greys, browns, blacks and whites like a true timber wolf, with the same markings they had. The fur was mostly dark grey on the top half of my face and my head. It lightened to brown on top of my snout, with a dark greyish brown streak running through the middle, down to my black nose, and a light greyish brown around my pale amber eyes. The bottom half was a lighter, dirty white, like the snow I ran upon after humans had trudged through it in the day. It was the same colour on the inside of my ears.

Around my neck it was the same dark grey as my head, with a lighter patch of the same dirty white colour on my throat, ending in a v shape at my collarbone. The dark grey covered my shoulders, the top of my chest, my back and sides, the tops of my thighs and my tail. The rest of my body was a kind of a creamy white. The monster looked at me with sad, empty eyes, lost in despair. But as I looked a change came over those eyes, so quick it was no more than a flicker of emotion, when they hardened, grew colder and full of hunger, and a flash of teeth revealed the other half of my personality. The moonlight had grown stronger again for a second and now that I had hidden the wolf's kill it wanted to find someone else and feed before the night was over. It angered me, and with a roar I swiped at the water, spraying it out across the ice. The reflection was driven away and I turned my back before it reappeared, wishing I could do the same to the wolf.

The moon was breaking free of the clouds and its light was growing stronger again. I wrestled with the wolf's consciousness, but it was no use. Coupled with the smell of blood, it grew too strong for me and I gave up, knowing someone else would die.

I was too hungry to bother completing the transformation. The scent of blood was blowing to me on the wind, calling me to hunt. I obeyed and followed the trail at a run, without thinking.

Drops of blood on the snow, next to a bloody piece of glass from a broken beer bottle, and paw prints. The scent was that of a young bitch, a mongrel, who had evidently cut herself on the glass. From the size of the paw prints she was big enough to be a meal rather than a snack. However, she was not a stray, as another set of prints ran beside hers: her human master. I drooled at the scent of the blood and quickened my pace.

And suddenly they were there just ahead of me, and I was bounding across the snow on all fours, focused on the dog, which was limping, her blood strong in my nostrils, spurring me onwards. The bitch must have sensed me coming, for she was suddenly uneasy and turned her head this way and that searching for a scent, then turned around and saw me. She yelped and strained against her master's chain. He would not release his grip on the lead and by the time he turned around it was too late, I was leaping through the air onto his pet. I landed on her but the man aimed a kick at me and I overbalanced, rolling off. I rose, snarling, and pushed him aside, at which point the dog attacked me and bit deep into my arm. I threw her off and she landed awkwardly on the ground, whining in terror. The man had fallen, but was picking himself up again, and it seemed he would fight to save his pet rather than run. But what happened next was too quick for him, for I was on the dog and had ripped her throat out, and now crouched over her, greedily devouring her flesh.

Within a few minutes I had stripped her to the bone, and then turned to snarl a warning at the man lest he try anything else. He simply stood holding his dog's lead, which I had bitten through, staring at it. I took my leave as the sun was coming up and stood in an alleyway as I was forced to become human again, but the sun was casting a shadow on the snow before the man, and he watched with horror as the shadow changed from something half wolf, half man to the shadow of a teenage boy. And then I realised my error as the human regained control...

Chapter Thirteen - Guilty

I shivered in the cold, panting, aware of fresh blood in my mouth. And my hunger pangs had lessened. I'd killed again as I knew I would.

This information hit me when I suddenly became aware of a voice nearby. I was in a narrow alley with a wall at one end: trapped if I'd been mortal. A man stood near the entrance to the alley. The voice belonged to him, and he was either on the phone or talking to himself. I caught him peering into the shadows and shrank back against the wall, hoping he hadn't seen my face. I heard him ask for the police and give them a description of the monster I had been, claiming that I had attacked his dog. And then nothing – silence save for his rapid heartbeat and his wheezing.

I looked back at the wall and knew I would have to climb it if I was going to escape, but only after I'd satisfied my curiosity. I wondered what the police would do when they heard the man's description of me; whether one of the Slayers within the police force might come out, give me a valuable insight into how they worked, anything to help me survive, and through me my family. I wished they'd hurry up, my feet were going numb.

Soon after the man had made the call the police came to the scene to investigate.

"So tell us again what happened sir," said a policewoman.

"I was out walking me dog and we were just going down this street when she started acting pretty strange. She was, I dunno, uneasy, afraid of something. And then she turned to look at something and yelped. She was panicking, it was a struggle to keep hold of the lead, the pissin' thing was slipping through my fingers. I couldn't understand what had spooked her so damn much so I turned round too and this great big bloody wolf was coming towards us. At least, I thought it was a wolf. The damned thing pounced and pinned her to the ground. That's when I decided it was the beast that's been attacking the town, killing all them people.

"Well I wasn't just gonna stand there and let it eat me dog so I went to kick it. And then I realised it wasn't a wolf. I didn't know what the hell it was at that point. I mean, it was wolfish, but everything was happening too fast for me to get a close enough look. The thing overbalanced and rolled off. It was pissed off then. I thought it was gonna attack me but it just pushed me outta the way and I fell over. Me dog got over the panic when she realised I could be in danger and she bit the thing in the arm. It threw her off and she landed awkwardly on the ground. I stood up again to help her out, like she helped me you know? But it had ripped her throat out before I could react and then before I knew it the damn thing was eating her!

"Well it stripped her to the bone and then turned to me. I stood holding her lead like a fucking idiot, too shocked by what had happened to do anything. Then the sun came up and it walked off into that alley," he said, pointing. "And here's where it gets weird. 'Cause I got a clear view of it see. And I swear to God this is true. It was half man, half wolf! It had a wolf's head and its body was all covered in fur, but the body was a man's, except for the wolf's tail. And the hands and feet were more like an animal, with claws and everythin'. It walked weird too, like it was halfway between walking on all fours and walking erect on two, stooped over like a hunchback with its knees bent. But it had run on all fours when it first attacked. And it gets weirder. I couldn't see it after it went in there, but the sun cast a shadow on the snow at the mouth of the alley. I watched that shadow change shape, and this wasn't no trick of the light. It went from being the shadow of that thing to the shadow of some regular guy! Maybe even a kid 'cause the shadow was pretty small for an adult, but it could just have been the way the sun was shining. Anyway, the alley is a dead end and I ain't seen it come out."

"You were attacked by a werewolf?" she asked him in disbelief. "What kind of sick joke is this? You told us you'd found the man-eater. Now if you're done wasting police time, we could be out searching for the real killer."

"The bastard son of a bitch killed my dog! Look, the remains are over there! Isn't that enough evidence for you? And look at the footprints in the snow!"

"Clearly something attacked your dog but I refuse to believe it was a werewolf, not even if you had some real proof. And the prints are already filling in with snow, it's impossible to tell now what they came from. They look like regular animal prints to me, could be from a large dog. The loss of your pet is regrettable but I assure you we are doing everything we can to track down the animal, whatever it may turn out to be," she told him, her voice holding no hint of emotion, least of all sympathy for the dog.

"You could at least check the alley," the guy said stubbornly.

With a sigh, she came into the shadows. I'd already climbed over the wall, and I stood on the other side, listening.

"There's nothing here," she called out. The guy swore under his breath.

158

The police left after that, but I heard a man approach the dog owner. I hadn't been the only one listening in on their conversation.

"Hey mate, they may not have believed you, but I do. I've seen these things and what they can do. If you say it was a werewolf, I believe you. I've seen them take lives before too. You wouldn't believe how many they can kill in a single night. But they're not invincible; I've killed a few of these things myself. There aren't many left now. In fact, I don't know about any others except for this one – it might even be the last. So now you know the truth, do you want to help me hunt it down and kill it? I'm part of a group dedicated to destroying these evil creatures. I can offer you a place in our group if you're interested. I can teach you more about these things. It's safer than being on your own. Werewolves aren't dumb beasts like in some of the movies out there; the best of them can keep their human intelligence even under the full moon, and the wolf in them itself is clever enough. You've seen it and it'll probably come for you next time to protect itself. It knows we're hunting it see. Will you come with me?"

I had the impression the dog owner had been gaping at the stranger, and after a pause, clearly still shocked by all he had seen and just learnt I heard him say simply "Okay."

Back in my room, I looked down at my blood stained body. I'd been lucky it was a Sunday morning and there'd been no one else about to see me naked and wreathed in death. I wanted to shower, even though I knew it wouldn't make me feel any cleaner, but first I had to take care of the blood that had splattered after I'd moved the corpse. I'd left it congealing on the walls and the floor and by then it was dry and harder to shift. There were a few stains on the wall that refused to budge. I moved a poster to cover it before the police came, planning to get some paint to hide it later. Fortunately they were only specks, and the walls were dark blue meaning they didn't really show up unless you knew they were there. That done, I crept into the bathroom. Once again I was grateful of the warm water running over my body, washing away the crimson stains. The last I would ever physically see of Melissa White and the dog drained away down the plughole. I wished the horrific images that kept playing behind my eyes would wash away with it, but it was never going to be that easy.

No sooner had I stepped out of the shower and dried myself off, the towel wrapped around my waist, than Mum burst through the door, her face panic stricken.

"Mel's missing!" she told me.

Inwardly I cursed. They had to find out sometime, but I was hoping it wouldn't be for a few more hours yet, to give me chance to deal with the horror before I had to face my family, and most of all Amy who would be most upset over her friend's disappearance. Not that it really made any difference in the end. It was going to take a lot longer than a few hours to come to terms with what I had done and to learn to live with it. If I could live with it.

Mum was shocked and full of guilt. After all, Melissa had been her charge that night. How could she face Mel's parents after what had happened? Amy was in tears, already fearing the worst. Dad seemed unaffected though surely the bastard felt something too.

"We've called the police already," he told me. "They'll be coming in forty eight hours to investigate."

Nodding, I sat with them and fought the growing sense of guilt that threatened to rule me, because I had brought this upon them. I didn't want to think about having to face Mel's parents. Our grief would be as nothing compared to theirs. And I didn't want to think about facing the police either. I didn't know if I could keep it together long enough to give them a convincing alibi, yet I had to for my family's sake. They were suffering enough through all this, without having to deal with the knowledge of what I had done. It would probably finish them. Could I hide the guilt long enough to convince the police of my innocence? I doubted it. My days were numbered as a free man. But what did I have to fear from the law? I doubted they had a prison cell that could hold me. I wished they could have locked me up and kept me from killing again, but of course if the police did take me in that would leave me at the Slayer's mercy. I put an arm around Amy's shaking shoulders, her protective big brother, feeling sick with myself.

Two days later the police came and went. They'd searched the place for evidence and found none. Somehow they missed the bloodstains on my wall. But they did take prints and as soon as they matched them they'd know no one else had been in the house except for the five of us, and then they'd be back to question us some more. We'd all given them an alibi. I wasn't sure they'd believed mine. Was I being paranoid? Or did I see a flicker of suspicion in the police officer's eyes? Either way, it was too late to do anything more to hide my guilt.

They searched the town for any sign of Mel but found nothing. They tried using dogs to find her, but the dogs only found my scent on the ground and went wild with panic. If they took them as far out as the fields where she lay peacefully, blissfully unaware of the world above, the fear got to them long before they found the scent where I had laid Mel's corpse while I dug her grave.

Somehow we got through the next few days, though it was hard for all of us. Guilt hung over the household, making us all subdued. Amy would burst into tears without warning. God knows what they thought had happened. No struggle, no break in, so she couldn't have been kidnapped. Maybe they thought she'd run away, but then why would she leave all her belongings?

The police were just as puzzled. They questioned us again as I knew they would, and learned nothing new. If they suspected me there was nothing they could do about it without evidence. The search was growing more desperate. If Mel had been kidnapped time was running out, though I think the police knew she was already dead. And the worst was yet to come.

Mel's parents made an appeal sometime after she had first been declared missing. The appeal was broadcast on TV and I could only watch in horror as they held each other, pleading through their tears for anyone who might know anything about their daughter to come forward. I wanted to run away from the TV screen and hide in my room, as if I could make it all go away, but some invisible force held me there, maybe my conscience punishing me for what I'd done. Dad changed the channel before Amy came down from her room and saw it. It would only upset her.

She was spending a lot of time in her room, shutting out the world. At night I heard her crying herself to sleep. At least those three could find a brief respite in their sleep. I still fought it whenever I could. Reality was preferable to the nightmare world I was forced to visit every time I closed my eyes.

The same night of the appeal, I lay in bed fighting my weariness. I even cut myself when I had to with my swiss army knife. The pain was as sharp as the blade that caused it, small and relatively harmless as it was. It cut through my senses, straight to my mind, keeping it alert, repressing the sleep. Then I'd heal the wound so Mum and Dad wouldn't know I was self harming, in case they took everything even remotely sharp from my room. I'd learnt to cause the wound to heal without bringing on any noticeable changes. Don't ask me how, it just happened when I wanted it to, and it meant I didn't have to face the reality of what I really was every time.

How long had it been since I'd had a proper night's sleep? Too long. My eyelids were drooping for what seemed the hundredth time that night. The blade sliced through my skin, leaving a trail of blood. My eyelids snapped open again. Something happened at a cellular level and the wound knotted together once more. My eyelids started to droop again. So tired. I just wanted to give into it, just once. Eyes closed, it felt good. No! The knife came again, too late, I was losing the battle. My arm fell back down and hung limp over the side of the bed, the knife slipped from my fingers and sleep washed over me.

The nightmares were worsening.

I padded quietly through the building, a shadow in the night. Whether I was human or wolf I knew not, but the stench of blood and death hung heavy in the air, clinging to my nostrils with icy claws, to the exclusion of all else. I was using sight alone for this hunt, following a trail of blood, crimson spots splashed across the cold white tiles. I paused to listen to the sounds of the night, alert to the sounds of danger, but the only company here would never speak again. The silence was interrupted only by the hum of the refrigerators. My breath steamed out before me, measured and slow when I first began to follow the drops of blood, but it quickened in anticipation when the trail became clearer, as did my heart. The blood had pooled in the next room, my prey bleeding more heavily from a mortal wound. The blood was everywhere in that room. It stained my hands and the soles of my feet, and the overwhelming taste stuck to my tongue and the back of my throat, making my mouth water, thirsting for more. I caught signs of movement out of the corner of my eye and glanced at the still shapes hidden beneath white cloth, littering the many tables surrounding me. I turned my attention back to the blood and noticed movement from within the puddle. Drawing closer, I could see there was a heart in its centre, arteries and veins severed where it had been torn out from its owner's body. I stared at it incredulously.

It was still beating.

Blood pumped out of the torn tubes onto the floor, the puddle growing larger by the second until it soaked my bare feet. Here was my prize. I moved forward to take it. The heart was still warm to the touch, despite the cold air surrounding it, and the blood made it slimy – it almost slipped from my hands, almost escaped. Then a noise broke the silence. I spun round quickly, the powerful muscle still in my grasp, still beating. There was a little girl stood there, about seven or eight years old.

"Excuse me Mister, can I have my heart back please?"

And that's when I saw the gaping hole in her chest.

Blood was pouring from the wound, which was partially hidden by strands of torn muscle and sinew, hanging down like a ragged piece of red, bloody cloth. I could see a section of her spine towards the back of the hole, and the ribs and lungs around the space where the heart should have been. I could even see the arteries and veins that should have been attached to the heart, dangling uselessly and spewing out more blood. With every movement she made the torn skin, flesh and tubes flapped loosely.

"Please?" she said, walking towards me. I backed away, my wolf instincts confused, and watched in horror as the shapes on the tables slowly sat up, the sheets falling away. Every victim I had taken was there, each one asking for the return of their missing body parts. I dropped the heart and covered my ears, trying to drown out their voices. A scream tore from my throat as they closed in…

I awoke drenched in cold sweat, shaking uncontrollably, trying to block the horrific images from my mind. What disturbed me most about this nightmare was not so much the corpses of my victims coming back to haunt me, it was the thought of not knowing what I was. I realised what I really feared was the thought of mentally becoming a half man, half wolf monster, the two different parts of my mind fused together so deeply that they became one. At least while the wolf was a separate part of me I would only kill under a full moon or if I ever lost control. If the two halves became one would that be the end of the precious little left of my humanity? Would I kill every time hunger struck? Would I crave raw flesh even more than I did then? Would I crave human flesh? I shuddered at the thought of it. In the nightmare I had been joined with the wolf's mind so strongly that I didn't even know what form I was in. I couldn't let that become reality.

As the days passed I became more withdrawn. Time lost all meaning. My hope was dead and buried and the boy I had once been lay in the grave with it. I might as well have been a walking corpse. People were getting really worried about me. Mum kept telling me I needed help. She only worried more when I didn't reply.

I didn't think my teachers had noticed but one day Mrs Redgewell, my IT teacher as well as our Head of Year, pulled me out of the lesson to talk.

"Are you sure you're okay Nick? You don't look well," she said doubtfully.

I laughed bitterly. What the hell did I say to that? Oh yeah Miss, I'm doing great, just fucking great. If I hadn't been turned into a

163

werewolf and then slaughtered a load of people I'd be even better. I settled for a simple "I'm fine."

"You don't look fine. Can't you tell me what's wrong? I just want to help you," she said, looking genuinely concerned.

"No, I'm fine, just feeling a bit sick," I told her.

We'd gone back into the classroom and somehow I'd felt worse, more alone.

My mates were no longer content to leave me alone. David was still mourning Fiona and hadn't noticed the change in me, but the others had.

"When are you gonna stop pretending you're okay and tell me what's wrong Nick? Stop lying to me, something's up. You've been different ever since that Saturday morning I bumped into you in town," Lizzy said. "I'll keep your secrets for you. You know you can trust me."

She didn't know how much I longed to tell her then, even more than the first time she'd asked. If I could just tell my dark secrets to someone human, it would make everything easier. She could tell me it hadn't been my fault; the wolf was the killer, not me; ease my conscience. I needed that more than I knew.

"I'm fine," I protested.

"You're not fine. Come on Nick, you can tell me."

I shook my head stubbornly. "There's nowt wrong, just leave me alone okay?"

She didn't believe that but she gave up. I think she was hurt that I still wouldn't tell her. And what would she do if she knew the truth? Would she be afraid of me? Would she sell me out to the Slayers? No, I didn't think she'd do that, no matter what I did. Would she even believe me? She might think I'd gone insane, or she might think it was some cock and bull story to avoid telling her the real truth. It didn't matter, I couldn't tell her no matter how much I wanted to.

The depression became too much. Death was more appealing. When I went home that day my family wanted to go out for a meal. I told them to go without me, and then some time after they went I was stood in the kitchen holding the bread knife over my wrist.

And so finally it had come to this.

I should have died the night I was cursed, should have died from my wounds, should have died and not come back. I felt I had been living on borrowed time, or stolen time, stolen from every victim I had killed. So I'd picked up the bread knife from the side of the sink, still wet after it had been washed, and held it over my wrist. I wanted to feel it bite into my flesh and slice into the veins that lay therein.

Looking at my wrist in anger and the veins I could see beneath, I could almost see the life flowing in the blue tubes. I wondered if any would grieve for me. Probably not. Nobody mourns the death of a monster.

The knife shook violently in my hand, possibly with fear, but certainly with anger as I willed myself to do it and end this cursed life that had been thrust upon me.

I imagined slitting my wrist, creating a gaping wound from which blood would seep out, the knife falling to the floor where it would become dull, already stained with my blood. The pain would have been intense but it would have felt good. I imagined falling to my knees and clutching my wrist, watching the blood pumping out, gushing down my arm and onto the floor, pooling and congealing. But it would be too slow, I wanted the end to come sooner. So I brought the knife up to my throat too, imagining slitting that so deep the wind pipe was severed, feeling the blood spraying out, splashing the walls and painting them red. And the wounds would weep, like the families of my victims had undoubtedly done on so many occasions, while I choked on my own blood. I imagined everything seeming to be spinning and then all would fast become black as death drew near. And I imagined my family finding my corpse lying on the kitchen floor, crying over me while others would celebrate. And there my life would have ended, bringing with it the end to my suffering and I wouldn't be here, now, to tell you my tale. But I was not permitted to know peace in death, not permitted an end to the suffering I had known and had yet to know. For I did not have the strength to do it. The knife fell from my shaking hand and I cried out in anguish.

And so I cannot live and yet I cannot die, I thought wretchedly as I picked up the blade and put it back on the side. Why couldn't I do it? The image of my family grieving over my passing had stopped me. I couldn't do it to them. They were already suffering enough after Mel. I really needed someone to talk to then. I fled the house and went to find the vampires in their graveyard.

Lady Sarah, as I had guessed, didn't really understand what I was telling her. "You can't stop yourself from killing now, it's in your nature. You have to learn to adapt, otherwise you will not survive. The Slayers will hunt you down."

Vince was easier to talk to. Lady Sarah went off to hunt, but he wandered the streets with me for a while, waiting to hunt until I went back home.

"It's hard at first," he agreed with me. "Hell, hard don't cover it. You still feel human, I understand that. In time you'll learn to accept what you are. Then you can learn from the wolf and get used to your new senses. I remember the first night after I'd been made a vampire, I didn't want to kill but the thirst for blood was too strong to ignore. It drove me to feed and afterwards I was horrified by it. I learned to live with it but it took time. It'll be the same for you."

I didn't believe him but he was trying to help and I was grateful. I had an idea of exactly what it was for him to delay feeding. The thirst must have been as powerful as the hunger that I felt after every transformation. We talked some more, and then I left him and let myself back in the house. I'd only been gone an hour and my family weren't back. I was glad; I couldn't bear to be near them at that moment, not with the feeling of being so close to them and yet being so isolated, so alone, as if there was a wall between us, keeping us apart. Before this had all started I would have enjoyed the freedom of the house to myself, but I didn't think I could stomach my horror movies anymore. The blood and gore on screen would only remind me of things I wanted to forget. So I sat with Alice until they came home, listening to the King of Shock Rock himself. I didn't used to be into music until I discovered shock rock and heavy metal. Before that I'd mostly only heard the soppy love songs from boy and girl bands of the 90s that I would claim made me want to puke. Then I discovered Alice Cooper and all I lived for were horror movies and my music. But suddenly the love songs didn't seem so bad after all.

I turned off the music, unable to listen to it anymore, and sat in silence, alone with my thoughts, fighting off the sleep that threatened to overwhelm me. When my family came home I told them I was going to bed and took to the streets again, determined to stay awake.

The next day at school I felt like I was close to breaking point. Everything was becoming too much and there was no escape, not even in death, unless I found the strength to free myself. Every time I turned a corner I half expected to see a bloody half eaten corpse waiting for me, and I had to concentrate hard on reality if I didn't want to watch the bloody scenes playing again in my head. I tried to keep my mind on my lessons, dull as they were, to avoid them. It seemed each victim was waiting in the shadows of my mind to lunge at me without warning, forcing me to relive their death. Morning break came and I tried to lose myself in my book. I'd finished the horror story and was onto something else, a story about wolves of all things. I'd started it before Fiona's death, not knowing how much I would grow to hate the damn creatures after what I'd done. It wasn't exactly horror, but the chapter I was on was somewhat horrific, where one of the wolves killed a human hunter in self defence, and I had to put it down, my stomach queasy. It was all too easy for my imagination to convert the scene in the book into another gory memory.

I sat staring into space when a girl's voice called me back to reality. Her name was Grace. She was a church-goer and deeply believed in the word of the Bible.

"How can you like wolves? They're evil creatures," she said with a shiver. It took me a minute to make sense of what she was saying. Then I realised she'd seen my book on the table.

I shrugged as I turned to look at her. "I've always liked 'em, as far back as I can remember. Anyway, they're not evil. No animals are evil, except man."

Even though I had grown to hate them, I still felt some need to defend them. They weren't like the wolf that lurked in me, and they didn't really deserve the bad reputation myth, legend, and the Church had given them, even if a monster like me was descended from them. I didn't voice that out loud. I didn't want to get onto the subject of religion with Grace. Arguing about wolves would be bad enough. She was prejudiced because they were associated with the Devil, and because she was your typical girl, into cute fluffy bunny rabbits and such. She hated anything that tore fluffy bunnies apart.

"Well they're savage."

"So are lions but people don't hate lions like they do wolves," I replied, voice neutral. All the passion had gone from the argument. I wanted to work with wolves once, and I'd been determined to overcome the public's negative views. I used to spend a lot of time arguing with people about this misunderstood animal, but my heart wasn't in it anymore.

"Well I don't like lions either," she told me. "How can you like something that's a born killer? It's evil, the way they kill other animals for food."

I sighed. "They've got every right to survival as much as any other animal. Go ask God, He created them that way. At least they only kill for food. Humans kill for the hell of it. Now that's evil. And we kill to eat too, it's nature. It's God's way, if that's what you believe. Whatever, it's the way the world works. Without predators we'd be overrun with the animals they feed on. And wolves really don't deserve the bad reputation we've given them.

"They live in packs, and they depend on every individual's co-operation within the pack to survive, and the bonds between them are strong, not unlike our own family groups when you think about it. If you knew more about them, you wouldn't hate them so much. They rarely hurt each other like men do, and it's even rarer they attack a human. I only know of one recent wolf attack on a guy camping out in the States, and I've spent a lot of time researching it. Dogs are more dangerous than wolves. They're not always as tame as we think and they've lost their fear of humans. I know about a pack of dogs that savaged a boy's arm for no apparent reason. He wasn't even running past them; there was nothing to trigger the attack. Dogs kill a hell of a lot more people than their wild cousins."

"I don't care what you say, I'd feel a lot safer in a room full of dogs than in the woods with a pack of wolves. I still think they're evil. It's just an opinion, you can't change it."

I shrugged again. "If the world had an open mind, they might accept them. Instead we've hunted them to near extinction. Just don't be so quick to judge, that's all I'm saying."

"Yeah well, you can't defend them after what the rogue wolf has done. Those bodies were horrible, don't tell me the victims died painlessly and their deaths weren't violent."

"That was no wolf," I said darkly.

"Oh, so you've seen the beast have you?" she asked disbelievingly.

"Yes, I've seen it," I said quietly. Every time I look in the mirror, I thought silently.

"So what is it then if it isn't a wolf?"

"It's not a wolf, it's a monster."

She searched my eyes to find whether it was true or not. "Have you been to the police?"

I hesitated, unsure what to say. "I'm not sure they'd believe me."

"Nick, you have to go to the police! It could help them save lives. You have to go to them," she urged me.

Someone called to her from across the room, saving me from answering. She looked at me again, probably unsure of whether to believe me herself, and then went over to her friend. I turned back round to face the table and jumped when I found David stood at the other side of me, a madness in his eyes. I hadn't even heard him come up behind me, too focussed on the debate with Grace.

"You know what killed Fiona." It wasn't a question. "Tell me. Tell me how to kill the son of a bitch. Was it that same beast that attacked us that night after the film?"

I shook my head. "Don't get messed up in this David. Or you'll go the same way she did. She wouldn't have wanted that."

"I have to know what did it," he said, breathing heavily, angrily. I knew he'd taken it badly but I couldn't believe what I was seeing. Had he really loved her that much? Guilt stirred within. What did I know about it anyway? I'd never understood romance.

"A monster, that's all I can tell you. I don't know what it was, but I tell you now it wasn't a wolf. It'll kill you if you go after it David. Please, forget about it. For me. We're still mates aren't we? Fiona's death doesn't change that. Leave it to the experts. They'll already have people hunting it. It'll die eventually," I convinced him. The lies came so naturally, I almost convinced myself. For a second a different reality existed, one where I was human and I knew as little about it as David did. The fantasy faded as soon as it came. David believed it though.

"I can't forget it man," he told me with a shake of his head, and walked back to his seat just before Mr Enderson walked into the room and the lesson started. I soon forgot about him when I was faced with my own pain again. After all, he'd get over her death eventually. He didn't have to deal with the knowledge that he was the one who'd killed her, and a whole lot of other people. He didn't have to face an eternity of blood and death.

Chapter Fourteen – Unholy Night

Christmas came; my sixteenth birthday. It would have passed unnoticed if it hadn't been for the wolf.

My family were trying to make it a festive time, but it was too soon after Mel's disappearance. Her family wouldn't be celebrating. Amy was still grieving. Everyone had given up what little hope there was to start with. Once the savaged bodies had turned up after Fiona's death, there wasn't much hope left for missing people. No one could know how long the beast had been stalking the streets. For that matter, I didn't know myself. Who knew how many the werewolf before me had killed, and the rest of his pack mates when they'd been alive? They might even have enjoyed it. But they'd been better at hiding the bodies than me, otherwise I'd have heard about some kind of wild animal loose in the town, even if I didn't pay attention to the news. People at school would have talked. Or maybe he just hadn't been in the town long before he bit me, and there had been bodies elsewhere in the country. If that was the case I should probably be grateful he hadn't turned up any sooner to pass on his wretched curse.

Mum and Dad weren't too worried about Amy. She needed time to grieve. They were worried about me, and I couldn't blame them. Mum had been really worried when I'd first become so gaunt you could see my skull. It seemed only a matter of time until I wasted away to the point where there was nothing left of me but skin stretched tightly across the bones. They kept threatening to take me to a doctor but so far I'd avoided it. I didn't know how much longer I could go on avoiding it though. I'd worry about that when the time came.

They weren't going to let me forget what day it was. We opened presents as usual and Mum cooked a turkey with all the trimmings. What little I ate I almost threw up again. Even Dad forced himself to stay in a good mood in an effort to try and cheer me up. And all I could think of was the bitter irony of it all for one of the Devil's creatures to be born on the same day as the son of God. I'd never really been religious but I still couldn't help thinking about that, and I was starting to accept the fact that God might exist. Satan did, I was convinced of it.

I was glad when evening came and I was able to escape from them. Even if I wasn't depressed, it wouldn't have felt right, the forced festivities. The day didn't seem that special anymore, and I knew it would never be the same again.

Bidding my parents goodnight, I climbed into bed, but as soon as my head hit the pillow the images threatened to overpower me as usual and make me relive the horrors the wolf had shown me. It was enough to have me wandering the streets again.

As soon as I opened the window I felt the bitter cold invading the warmth of my room. For most of the day it had snowed, and as it grew dark temperatures reached below freezing. I shivered and had second thoughts about the wisdom in venturing out into the cold, but I knew I would rather face the cold than the nightmares, so, after quickly changing back into the clothes I had worn that day and pulling on my trainers, I sprang out of the window and landed on the snow covered ground.

I began walking down the street, the fairy lights on Christmas trees twinkling at me from behind almost every window. The elements seemed set on driving me away again; the howling wind raged against me, driving snow into my eyes and face which felt so cold it stung my bare flesh. Ice lay across the pavements and road where a few people had walked that day, causing me to skid a few times. The snow on the ground was deep enough to slow me down as well, and consequently every part of my body was soon chilled to the bone. My fingers were the first part to become so numb as to be practically useless, and the numbness spread up my hand. If the cold continued to creep up my limbs and into the rest of my body, by the end of the night I would freeze to death. I welcomed the thought of that and pressed onwards.

I had not gone far when a strong scent was carried to me by the wind. I froze as the smell entered my nostrils and travelled directly to my brain, awakening the beast that lurked therein. I was too weak from the cold and weariness to fight back and all I could do was stand there as the inevitable transformation began...

Blood. It called to me on the wind and gave me the power to take control for a while. I tore off the last of the human clothing and stood on the blanket of snow. The toughened flesh of my pads was not particularly sensitive, and the cold didn't bother me as I prowled down the wintry streets.

The hunger was more powerful than usual. It didn't help that the human was not eating. And it made our wolf form gaunter. Fewer muscles rippled across my body and my ribs poked out on either side from beneath my skin.

The scent of blood came again, stronger this time. I bounded forward to explore and soon found the thing that had called me into consciousness.

A newborn baby lay in the snow, frozen over, its skin tinged with blue. There was a deep gash in the side of its head, and, looking closer, I found its skull was smashed open. What I could see of the tiny form was bathed in its own blood, and nuzzling the snow away that had settled on it I learnt that its killer had not been content with merely killing it; it had been tortured first. One arm was broken and cuts covered its body. Its mouth was twisted into an everlasting scream of agony. My hatred for humans grew. They dared to call us evil when they could take an innocent life so cruelly. I touched the small body with a paw as big as its head.

"May you find peace, little one," I said quietly.

I took my leave and went in search of food, but as I did so I vowed never to forget so pointless and brutal an act. I could honour the life that was over before it begun by remembering it. I could do that much at least.

Hunger gnawed at me as I roamed the streets, driving me onwards. Of course, I could have eaten the baby, if it hadn't been for the fact it was frozen over. Besides, even if it hadn't been frozen it would not have filled the gaping pit in my stomach. So I searched for more appetising prey. But there were no humans outside, not on Christmas night, and their pets were inside with them. I wandered every street, snowmen glaring at me from each garden, cold, silent guardians over the households, but my search was in vain. Even the centre of the town was devoid of life, the nightclubs and fast food restaurants shut.

Giving up hope of eating that night, I turned away from the town centre and made my way back home. There weren't even any cars about, just the stench of their foul fumes which clung to my nostrils and lingered there.

Wandering up a street where there was a vets to which the human had once taken its snake, I noticed part of one of the buildings was boarded up. Had it not been for a hole in the wood through which a scent came to me, I would have continued walking without giving it a second glance. But the unmistakeable smell brought me to a standstill, nose twitching.

The floor inside was littered with beer bottles and the smell of the alcohol was almost overwhelming, but just underlying that was the faint smell of prey: a human, male, and very young. My senses told me he was a child, no more than eight years of age.

I could see him curled up in the corner with an old blanket wrapped around him. I didn't know what he was doing there but at that moment I didn't care – the hunger consumed me. However, the hole was too small for me to fit in. I snarled angrily and the boy looked up, suddenly afraid. I could see the terror in his face as he beheld the fearsome sight I presented. My gaping jaws were probably all that was visible to him, drool dripping from between the fangs as my breath steamed out, like a scene out of one of the movies I had watched as a human.

I ripped through the wood to reach him. It didn't take long to make the hole wide enough for me to squeeze into, and I did so eagerly.

The boy screamed and tried to crawl away as I advanced, hoping to slip past me and make it back through the hole and escape, but he stood no chance. I was on him in seconds.

I killed the child by ripping out his throat, and then ripped open his chest, hungrily devouring the flesh and his heart, still warm. I dragged him outside, feeling claustrophobic in the small, enclosed space that had been his home, and continued to feed.

Blood on the snow, staining it red. Other fluids mixed with the blood until the pure white was stained almost black. Humans considered it as some kind of holy day. I knew it would have caused an outrage if they knew what I'd done. Would it anger the Slayers, spur them on to greater efforts to hunt me down? I was lucky not to have come across anymore since the first night I'd transformed. Perhaps Lady Sarah had scared them off for the time being when she killed so many of them at once.

My meal finished, I slunk away. My hunger was not satisfied, but I'd taken the edge off it, and the moon was not full; I was not bound to it. I didn't want to change back so soon, knowing I would face near oblivion until the moon called me back weeks later, but it was safer to be human.

Minutes later I was back in my room, giving in to the transformation.

Chapter Fifteen – Descent Into Madness

People looked to the New Year with hope. Amy was slowly recovering from the loss of Mel. She was returning to her old self. Mum and Dad were hoping the holiday season would have the same effect on me. Pity the boy they knew was dead.

I was angry at the wolf for killing on Christmas night. It made it worse somehow. I might not have believed in the Christmas spirit anymore, but most other people did. I didn't know who or what the wolf had killed that night, I only knew that it had and its prey had most likely been human. It had taken someone away from their family at the one time of year when families came together. If I'd known it had killed a homeless boy would that have made it better? I don't know. I only know that I hated the wolf for making me kill on that holy night, when everyone should have been celebrating the birth of Christ, not mourning the death of a loved one.

Before I knew it, the next full moon was almost upon us. That night, I left the house, not wanting to risk the wolf killing family this time. If the wolf killed one of them the grief and the guilt I had known so far would be as nothing compared to what I would feel at their death.

The change was almost upon me. In despair and depression, I'd even tried turning to God for help, despite what I may have said about Him when I had been human. I'd tried praying to Him, asking for His forgiveness for my sins, asking Him to cure me of my curse and save me from my fate. If He heard, He didn't bother to reply. I wondered if I was being punished for what I'd dared to say to Lizzy before all this had started.

"God!" I roared at the sky while I still had a human voice. "God, are you listening to me? Why have you forsaken me?"

I waited for an answer, but the world was quiet. The sky above was still, dead and empty, save for the moon glaring down at me, devoid of any Heavenly signs.

"God! Answer me! Why am I being punished? What did I ever do to deserve this? Why me? Why must I suffer?"

Still there was no answer.

"Fuck you then," I snarled. "Don't answer. I don't care."

But I did care about this, whatever I may have told myself. If the Devil really did exist, I assumed that meant God was for real too. What had I done to deserve this fate? Was I being punished for something in another life? Or was it that God really didn't give a damn about what happened to us mortals? I didn't know, and I didn't know which I wanted to believe. Then the wolf took over and I embraced oblivion.

The next thing I knew I was lying face down in the snow, feeling the cold slowly creeping up my body, my mouth cold and dry. I could barely feel my fingers stretched out before me, but with effort I managed to flex them, and the movement brought some life back. I couldn't say the same for my toes. I tried to move them but couldn't feel anything. The gruesome thought crossed my mind that they may no longer be attached to my foot. Even more disturbing – or at least it should have been – was the fact that I found I didn't care. They could have been lying by my body in the snow, frozen and dead, and I didn't give a damn. I didn't know how long I'd lain there, but I knew I had to move.

I was burning with hunger. Moving was hard, and not just because of the cold. I felt weak, so weak I could barely crawl over the snow. The wolf hadn't fed that night. It had collapsed where I now lay and the transformation had left me feeling like I was dying of starvation. I hadn't been eating much since Fiona's death, but I'd never felt anything like this. Why had it left me so weak? It didn't matter right then. What mattered was getting somewhere warm before I died of exposure, if that was possible for a werewolf. I already knew I couldn't commit suicide, for my family's sake, and letting myself die out there wasn't much better. I had to at least try to save myself.

I forced my freezing, starved limbs into action. Weakly I managed to crawl down the street. I didn't even know where I was going, I just knew I had to keep moving before the cold robbed me of what little strength I had left.

A car raced past, too fast to see either me or the luckless pigeon in the middle of the road. The front left wheel went straight over the bird just as it tried to fly away, and its life ended in a splatter of blood and feathers, flattened flesh and crushed bones. I stared at the roadkill, ravenous, and without thinking crawled over to it, the smell of fresh death spurring me on. Before I knew what I was doing, I'd pried the body from the tarmac where it had stuck like glue, the flesh almost one with the road. Blood dripped onto the ground as I raised the small chunk of squashed meat to my mouth and bit it in half.

The taste of raw meat brought me to my senses. I realised what I was doing and spat flesh and blood into the snow as if it was poison. I'd involuntarily swallowed some of it. My stomach heaved and I dropped the carcass, retching. The flesh looked worse now it was covered in bile. As soon as I was able, I crawled back over to the

175

pavement and collapsed again, feeling weaker than before. The full realisation of the situation hit me. I was crawling through the streets naked, too weak to stand. How was I going to explain this to any passersby, or my parents if I made it that far? I was lucky it was a Sunday and the world was quiet so early in the morning. At least I knew where I was now. The bird had done one thing for me; it had awoken me to my senses and now I knew I was on my street. My house was just round the corner, though it felt like miles in my weakened state.

Finally I managed to pull my numb, freezing body, which was rapidly becoming no more than dead weight, to the side door so that I was out of sight of the neighbours. The last of my strength spent, I couldn't even raise my fist to knock on the door. I closed my eyes and lay there in the snow, hoping someone found me soon before it was too late.

I think I must have passed out sometime after that, because when I opened my eyes my parent's worried faces swam into view, somewhere above me. I groaned, warmth spreading through my veins, feeling returning. I was aching all over, but the pain was good. I was safe. It didn't matter what happened, I would live.

Now that I was in the warmth, hunger led a fresh onslaught against my stomach. The foul taste of bile and raw meat still filled my mouth.

"Water," I croaked. "Food."

Mum brought me a glass of water and some cereal. Right then I would have eaten anything as long as it wasn't meat. I ate the cereal gratefully, and for once it didn't taste so bad. I could feel my strength returning already. Looking around, I realised I was lying on the sofa in the dining room with a blanket draped over me.

"Are you okay?" Mum asked me uncertainly. "What happened to you?"

"Can't remember," I moaned.

Well it was half true. I knew why I was out there but I couldn't remember exactly what had happened. I don't know if they believed me or not. Dad didn't look convinced and had it not been for Mum he might've beaten the truth out of me. As it was he turned away in disgust and I was left to rest, though I wasn't going to sleep, not if I could help it.

I could hear them talking in the lounge. Mum wanted to take me to a doctor. Dad thought I needed a psychiatrist. Maybe I did, if only there was one who'd believe me, who I could trust not to turn me over to the Slayers or even the police. Since there wasn't, I had to somehow convince them I didn't need any kind of doctor.

Feeling strong enough to walk again, I helped myself to some more cereal and forced it down. Then I went to dress myself and spent the rest of the day arguing with my parents.

"There's nothing wrong with me, I don't need a doctor! Just need some time to get over Fiona, that's all," I told them, ignoring the stab of pain her name brought.

"Amy was never this bad after Mel, what's the matter with you?" Dad said angrily. "You always have to be so damned melodramatic!"

"John! That's enough," Mum said. She looked at me with understanding and sympathy. She'd lost her dad when she was about my age, maybe even younger. I didn't know if Dad had ever lost anyone close to him. "If there's anything we can do to help you, Nick, please tell us."

I forced a smile to reassure her. "I will Mum."

My family were wary around me after that, almost afraid of me, as if they thought I was losing it and they weren't sure how to act around me in case they provoked any more fits of madness. I couldn't blame them, but I hated it. It dug the knife in a little deeper, bringing home the feeling that I was apart from them, and the rest of humanity. I couldn't face their fear, so I was spending more and more time in my room, shutting out the rest of the world. Sometimes I'd play on the Playstation, though my heart wasn't really in it. Other times I'd just sit with Alice, letting the guilt and the grief take over.

Amy came into my room one day while Mum and Dad were out shopping, taking advantage of the January sales. I groaned inwardly. I just wanted to be alone, free of human company.

"Nick, I'm bored," she whinged.

"That ain't my problem. Go find summat to do."

"There's nothing to do, I'm bored," she moaned again.

"Well go watch TV or something!" I snarled, annoyed and growing angry.

"I don't want to watch TV."

"Then go on the computer!"

She shook her head. "I don't want to be stuck at home in front of the TV or the computer all the time, I want to do something different."

"I don't care what the fuck you do, just get the fuck out of my room!" I shouted.

177

"Oh, well I'm sorry for not wanting to spend my life in front of a TV," she snapped, going from cute little girl to pissed off bitch in the blink of an eye.

I completely lost it then. Why couldn't she just leave me alone?

"Get out of my room!" I shouted, standing. I pushed her out of the room. She tried to fight back but I was too strong for her, until she lashed out and hit me between the legs. I doubled over in pain and felt the wolf stir within. Now I really was pissed off, and the wolf responded to the anger. I felt its hunger, coupled with my anger and the need for violence. I wanted blood. Amy ran back in the room just to spite me, ranting about something, mouthing off at me like she did with everyone. She could be a real bitch at times and she was never a good loser, always determined to have the final blow. But not any more.

"Get out of my room!" I roared and punched her right in her gobby little mouth. She fell back stunned, reaching a hand up to her face. I don't think I'd ever lost it so bad before. It wasn't the first time she'd pushed me to the point where I struck back, but never really hard enough to hurt her. I used to be pretty good at controlling my temper as a human; she was the one who'd always snapped first. The shock at what I'd done showed in her face, and the hand came away with blood. Then the pain set in and she started to cry. Blood poured from her mouth where I'd knocked three of her front teeth loose. She fled the room, probably to go crying on the phone to Mum, and I was alone again, fighting to control the anger.

I was panting heavily as if I'd been running. The wolf was pressing for the transformation, and I was struggling to control it. Beneath the anger I was shocked as much as Amy at what I'd done. The nightmare of her wriggling, bleeding body dying beneath me, ripped apart by my jaws, came back to haunt me. The images flashed before my mind until I was screaming.

"No! That's not me, it's not me! Get the fuck out of my head, it wasn't me! I won't do that to her, never do that to her. Not that, not that!"

I sank to my knees, head tilted back, and screamed again until it became a howl, an animal sound that didn't belong to any human. My eyes turned amber and fangs grew. The change was coming whether I wanted it or not. Veins bulged beneath my skin as I fought it with everything I had. I looked back down at my hands and saw the claws forming.

"No!" My voice came out as a growl, becoming more bestial. I dug my claws into the wooden floor and gritted my teeth, the pain of the transformation intensifying the more I fought it. But I couldn't transform there, not with Amy in the house. The smell of her blood excited the wolf, I could feel it, and I knew if I gave in I would never be able to control the hunger. She would die and part of me would enjoy it. So I continued to fight until suddenly, as quickly as it came, the wolf slid back beneath the surface, sinking back into the depths of my subconscious, and the few changes that had taken place reversed. I ran to find Amy, horrified by what I'd done and what I'd wanted to do, and wanting to put it right.

I found her curled on the sofa in the lounge, crying and shaking. The phone lay forgotten by her feet.

"Amy," I said softly, reaching a hand out to her. She whimpered and curled up tighter.

"Amy," I tried again. "I'm sorry, I didn't mean it. I don't know what's happening to me but I can't control it. You have to leave me alone when I tell you to, so you don't get hurt."

She didn't answer, still crying into the sofa. I glanced at the phone.

"Did you tell Mum?"

She shook her head.

I breathed a sigh of relief. "You know you can't tell Mum right? Please? She'll take me to a doctor and they'll take me away. Please Amy. I'm scared. Doctors can't help me. I have to work through this on my own. The more people who interfere, the more people who get hurt. Please, don't tell Mum, for me. It'll be okay, everything will be okay. Just stay out of my way when I tell you to and no one will get hurt."

Slowly she turned round to look at me. I couldn't read her face. I didn't know what she was thinking. I don't know what had made me say the things I'd just told her, but I knew it was all true and that I couldn't go down that route. Doctors couldn't help me. They might even end up dead for their trouble. Or the Slayers might get me somehow, and then I'd end up dead. Maybe not such a bad thing, or maybe I still wasn't ready for death yet. Finally Amy spoke.

"Nick, what's wrong with you?"

"I don't know but you've got to trust me on this. Mum can't find out what just happened."

She nodded and let me clean her up. The blood flow in her mouth was slowing. She was lucky I hadn't hit her with everything I had, or it would have been much worse. She agreed to tell Mum she'd fallen and hit her mouth on the desk in my room, which had knocked her teeth loose. Mum would buy it. But after that Amy was even more afraid of me than before, and my guilt was all the worse for feeling the wolf's hunger directed at my own sister, its need for blood. Recently I'd been trying to pretend it was all a nightmare, that none of this was happening to me, but its desire for flesh had been all too real. And the thought that I'd come so close to killing Amy wouldn't leave me alone. If I'd not been strong enough to fight the transformation... I spent even less time with them after that.

Barely a week later, I was in my room when I heard Mum and Amy calling from the lounge. I started downstairs to see what they wanted when I heard Amy whisper "Nick smells!" from her bedroom. I paused and cocked my head to one side, listening intently. And then I remembered I was home alone. Was I going insane? Was my brain offering me a way out of reality? I smiled to myself. Letting them lock me away in a padded cell for eternity did have a certain appeal about it. It would mean I couldn't kill any more and put an end to the misery. But it wouldn't solve matters. Much as I wanted to run from the harsh reality I had found myself in, I knew I had to face it like a man. I could try running from my fate but there was no escaping what I had become. I was a killer, and even if they locked me away I would kill again, eventually. The wolf wouldn't be caged for long and it certainly couldn't be tamed.

"Nick!"

My name came again, louder than before, more urgent. Slowly I descended the stairs, dreading what was waiting for me at the bottom. The door to the lounge was closed. I paused again with a hand on the doorknob, afraid to go in. My name came again, and taking a deep breath, I ventured inside and a scream tore from my throat.

I'd thought after Fiona and the things the wolf had made me relive, and the incident with Amy, it couldn't get any worse. I'd thought there was nothing worse for me to see. I was wrong.

Mum lay sprawled on one end of the sofa closest to the door. She was just lying there, no reaction as I walked into the room. Was she sleeping?

"Mum, are you okay?" I asked as I drew closer. No answer.

"Mum?" I repeated, shaking her. To my horror her head fell from her body and rolled across the floor, coming to a stop by the fireplace where it stared at me with a wide eye. The other was missing, a fly laying its eggs in the socket in its place. A flap of skin hung down from one cheek, the flesh shiny red beneath, and an ear had been torn off. Amy was curled up on the other end of the sofa. Her head was intact, though it was missing the lower jaw, the tongue hanging out uselessly. One arm lay on the floor; the other bore deep cuts spaced evenly apart, unmistakeably scratch marks. I screamed and ran from the room. When Dad brought home their living counterparts, they found me cowering underneath the table in the dining room.

Back at school, things were getting worse. I'd finally snapped. Friends came to talk to me and all I could do was cringe with fear, seeing my victims coming for revenge, bloody and half eaten and starting to rot. I was convinced I could hear the voices of the dead whispering to me, threatening to drag me back into the earth with them. Everyone seemed to be looking at me, talking about me. Oh God, what if they knew? No one dared approach me though. To my paranoid brain this was proof that they knew, though in reality they were scared of me, either because I was mad or because of what I'd done to Jamie, or both. Then one night after school things rose to a climax.

I went straight to my room, the only place I felt safe, and the voices were getting louder. I fell to my knees and covered my head with my hands, screaming at them, trying to block them out. They were accusing me, damning me to Hell, promising me payment for my sins. When it became too much I ran out into the hall and shut the door behind me, as if I could lock them in there. The voices only grew louder still. They were whispering worse things then, making me see all the gory details again. I ran into the bathroom and stood over the sink, vomiting until my stomach was empty. Then I raised my head and stared at my reflection in the mirror. The image seemed to change before my eyes until I was staring at a wolf's head. It grinned at me, blood staining its fangs, and with a roar I smashed the image with my fist as hard as I could, hating what I saw there. The glass shattered, shards raining down and breaking into smaller pieces when they hit the tiled floor. I'd heard shouts from downstairs but had ignored them, and continued to do so even when my parents came running in. Mum looked at me in horror, while Dad was angry. I didn't even acknowledge they were there. Whimpering, I sank to the floor, still hearing the whispers of the dead. I was vaguely aware of a pain in my hand. Bits of glass were stuck in it but that was the least of my worries. My parents were arguing what to do with me. Mum was afraid of losing me, even though she knew the best thing for me was a doctor. Dad wanted someone to look at me straight away. I think he was ashamed to have a maniac for a son.

They came to a decision and I found myself confronting a doctor. I sat there shaking, refusing to even look at him, or anyone else in the room. He soon referred me to a specialist and before I knew it I was in a mental hospital, surrounded by loonies.

Looking back, it makes me laugh at the irony of it all. I spent my childhood fantasising about being a werewolf and it came true. For more years than I care to remember I'd been telling people someday I would end up in a padded cell, and there I was. Though it wasn't exactly as I'd been predicting for all those years.

In many ways the mental hospital reminded me of the old people's home my Grandma was in. They did have a Seclusion Room which was the infamous padded cell for those who needed it. I spent a fair bit of time there, when my depression would give way to fits of violence, but they never put me in a straitjacket. Maybe because they couldn't force me into one, not with my inhuman strength, all the more potent in my madness.

I had my own room but I didn't feel safe there. In fact it felt like a prison cell. There was nothing personal about it like my room back home. Just four walls, a window, a door, and a bed. There wasn't much of a view out of the window. I spent most of my time in there lying awake on the bed, staring at the ceiling, fighting sleep with everything I had. I refused to eat at first so they had me on a drip, nourishing me if I wouldn't do it myself. I was losing my gaunt appearance again, recovering quicker than a human would have. They couldn't explain that. Nor could they explain why my hand had healed so quickly where the glass had penetrated the flesh. I was soon feeding myself when it became clear that it was either that or the drip, though there was little pleasure in it. Even if the hospital food had been gourmet, there would have been no pleasure in it.

There was also a room where the patients could go to socialise with each other. They had board games and a TV. People encouraged me to go there but I felt better in my room. Whenever I went in there I tended to shrink away from the others, either afraid I would hurt them or afraid that they would hurt me. A few times a patient said something to me and I would start to rage at them, until I was taken away to the Seclusion Room to calm down.

Doctors spent a lot of time with me, trying to get me to talk and work through my problems so I might regain my sanity. It was evident I needed help and they all thought they could give it to me. Shame I was beyond that. Pity no one could give it to me, even if I could be saved. Whenever I recognised them for what they were, rather than mistaking them for a vengeful victim back from the dead or a Slayer out to kill me, or even a potential victim to satisfy my hunger, I just found something to fix my eyes on and stared at it until they left me alone. Sometimes I'd grunt at them if they gave me a question that required a one word answer. For the most part I screamed at them through the horrific hallucinations, and I even attacked a few. The next thing I knew I'd be in the Seclusion Room, screaming at more enemies conjured by my mind. The voices drowned out my thoughts often and I'd rage at them. Sometimes I'd draw myself into a tight ball and lie there on the floor, hands over my head, whimpering, like I had in the bathroom back at home. Other times I was more violent, banging against the walls and door in an attempt to escape from the horrors, unseen by everyone but me. I even ripped some of the padding to shreds. And still the doctors sought to tame me. I've no idea how long it was before they gave up on me. Must have been less than a month because we hadn't reached full moon yet.

My family visited often. I treated them like anyone else. Like with the doctors, if I recognised them I either ignored them or grunted. Mum begged me to let the doctors help me so I could come home again. Dad said little. They didn't let Amy come most times, scared of what she might see there.

And every day I spent there I lived in fear. What would happen next full moon when the wolf found itself in this building, surrounded by prey? There were about thirty patients in residence there, plus all the doctors and nurses. It would be a feast the wolf couldn't refuse, like a fox in a henhouse. And there would be nothing I could do about it.

Chapter Sixteen – The Mating Season

As it turned out, the next full moon was the least of my worries. We were now in February, the start of the mating season of the grey wolf. And the mating season for werewolves too apparently.

I don't know when it was I first noticed. Even if I weren't in my present state of mind, there was no way of telling time in the hospital. As it was, days and weeks had lost their meaning after Mel's appeal. It was all just one continual block of time. Day and night became one. It was hard to differentiate between the two when I was lost in a dark part of my mind where not even the light of the sun could penetrate.

A female nurse came into my room with a tray of food. She was in her late twenties, slim and fairly pretty. But it was her body I was interested in. Her natural scent was more powerful than any brand of perfume she could have worn. She set the tray of food on my bedside and took her leave. Hungrily I followed in her wake.

We were in another patient's bedroom before I realised what I was doing. Feeling foolish, I ran back to my room and wondered what it meant. Sex might have been on my mind a hell of a lot in my teens but I'd never done anything like that. And I hadn't given it much thought since Fiona's death. The constant state of depression suppressed any such desires.

But suddenly I found I could think of little else. The instinct had grown as powerful as the unearthly hunger, and with a jolt I realised I'd been ready to rape the woman. As if I didn't have enough to deal with. I would have found it funny before all this began, thinking it just a new kind of insanity, but I knew it was more serious than it sounds. If I couldn't control myself I was going to be in a whole new lot of trouble. Of course, if I just gave into the urge and found a girl who wanted it, there was a good chance the instinct wouldn't be so strong, though I wasn't too sure about that. For all I knew these instincts could persist throughout the entire mating season. Yet even if the act of mating could help lessen my urges, I refused to give into the beast. It had killed Fiona. I wasn't going to make anything easy for it after that. I was better than the wolf, I was stronger. It wouldn't rule me. Besides, it was pretty sick that the monster considered humans as both prey and potential mates, in the absence of its own kind. I assumed that meant they could bear its children, something I couldn't allow. I didn't want to think about how many people would die if there were more of us roaming the streets.

My will power grew weaker by the day as the lupine instincts grew stronger. Roughly halfway through the month it reached its climax and there was little I could do to fight it. I might have remained human in form, but as the lupine instincts became more powerful, I became more bestial. It was like the wolf had taken over my mind and there wasn't any human left. Some small part of me knew the lupine half of my mind was still separate, but the human half was becoming more like it every day, until the human was dead and only wolf remained.

At first it had been little things that showed signs of lupine behaviour. I grew hostile towards other males, shouting at them if they came too close. I had the urge to follow females around, particularly the nurse it had all started with, though I fought it before the behaviour could go any further. As the days passed, the shouting turned to snarling. Words made little sense anymore. I began to pace my room like a caged animal again. I pissed up the walls to mark my territory, losing the last of my self control, and then before I knew it I was wandering the hospital looking for a female in season. There weren't any. A couple were just coming out of heat, and a couple just coming into heat, but somehow I knew they weren't at the right stage yet to be sure of a pregnancy. So I broke out of the hospital through the window in my room. It was easier than it should have been. The glass wasn't strong enough to withstand a blow from a werewolf, and long before anyone would find I was missing, I was loose on the streets.

Dusk came before I found what I was looking for. The scent was fresh, and I tracked her to a nightclub. I stepped inside but the scent became confused with so many others, lost in a sea of humans, and the sound of the music blasted into my ear drums, the beat throbbing painfully as it had before in wolf form. I howled in pain and frustration, but the animal sound was lost in the noise. Snarling, I backed away and waited just outside.

Hours passed and finally she emerged, alone. She was beautiful, curves in all the right places, her skin pale, her smooth blonde hair flowing down her back like water, spilling around her shoulders and onto her breasts, her blue sapphire eyes gleaming in the night.

I advanced towards her, growling softly with anticipation. She heard me coming and looked round. Spotting me she grinned, probably used to boys approaching her all the time. I paused as she spoke, trying to make sense of her words. Failing, I growled again and she laughed. She came closer and kissed me. She was playing with me but I didn't care. I snapped at her playfully and suddenly she drew back as a male voice called out something behind us.

"My boyfriend..." she gestured.

Though I didn't understand the words, I knew the meaning behind them and snarled, preparing for a fight as a boy advanced angrily towards me, older and more muscular than I was.

"That's my girl buddy, so you can back off," he said, fists raised.

Studying him for a moment, warily sizing him up, I gave no warning when I struck first. I drew back my fist and punched his nose, still snarling. He fell to the floor, crying out in surprise, as the girl stood watching us with interest. The guy quickly got to his feet, his nose a bloody mess, and we circled each other, then he punched me in retaliation but I blocked it with my arm. I punched him again and the fight was over in seconds, the force sending him back to the floor. Then I was standing over him, pinning him to the ground, my jaws around his throat. Terrified, he didn't know what to do and squirmed, trying to wriggle free.

"You're insane! What do you want from me?" he screamed, afraid of what I would do next. Fortunately for him, he looked towards his girlfriend for help but to do so he had to tilt his head to the side, exposing more of his throat and underbelly, a sign of submission to my lupine instincts. I stood up and let him go. He ran off, his girlfriend forgotten, and I turned back to her. She seemed amused by me, and so she led me back to her house. Her parents were out and she had no siblings. We were alone, in her bedroom...

Wolves can remain 'tied' for up to thirty minutes. It didn't last that long.

I nearly lost myself in the pleasure and struggled to remain in human form. As it was, I still couldn't control myself and was more wolf than human. While she moaned with pleasure, I bit her several times, often drawing blood. But afterwards the instinct to mate was satisfied, and gradually I regained what little humanity I had left. I didn't know where I was and had little memory of the past few days, but I knew I should have been in the hospital. When I saw the girl lying in bed next to me I knew what it meant. Confused and afraid, I fled her house, though she begged me to stay.

I had no desire to return to the hospital now I was free of the place. Besides, the moon would soon be full and I'd only escape again. People would die regardless of where I was.

Mum was shocked to find me stood on the doorstep.

"Nick, what are you doing here? Why aren't you at the hospital?" she asked.

"Don't make me go back there Mum, please? I'm okay now, I promise," I said. She looked like she was going to argue but she let me in. Mostly, I think she was just pleased to have me home. Dad wasn't. Either he didn't think I was ready to come home or he didn't want me back. I didn't give a damn either way. I wasn't going back and a mere mortal like him couldn't make me.

Chapter Seventeen – A New Crisis

February soon became March. People had died during the full moon as I knew they would. More disturbing was the fact that the horror seemed to have lessened slightly. It was still there, but numbed a little as if I had taken a painkiller that wasn't very effective. As if I'd taken something just to take the edge off but not strong enough to completely nullify it all.

Back at school, they wouldn't leave me alone. The rumour that I had been taken to a mental hospital had spread like wildfire. Everyone wanted to know what was it like, had I been in a straitjacket, had they sedated me? Somehow they didn't have trouble believing I'd been insane. Some were still scared of me, others found it funny. When I wouldn't talk about it, more rumours spread. They told their mates I'd said what they wanted to believe, and there were more stories flying round than I care to remember.

We learnt we were to have our TB jabs some time that month. They wouldn't tell us when, knowing some of us would have skived to avoid the injections. But we didn't have to wait long, for that Wednesday we were sent to the hall where the nurses awaited us. I felt like I'd seen enough of nurses to last me a lifetime.

While waiting in the queue outside we were given forms to fill in. I was one of the first into the hall. A nurse beckoned me over to her and motioned for me to sit down. She asked me a few questions, like if I had any allergies, was I on drugs, did I drink, and then rolled up my sleeve.

I've never been good with needles. No matter how hard I try not to look, I always end up watching, and even before the needle touches my skin I end up fighting them. Usually I would win unless a couple of people held me down. The odds would be different this time with my lupine strength, though I was hoping it wouldn't come to that. People were already giving me more attention than I wanted; I could just imagine their reaction if they saw me struggling. They'd call me insane and say I wasn't safe, that I should be locked up again in the padded cell. They'd say that I was a danger to them and myself and they would be right.

I took a deep breath and tried to relax. I looked away until I sensed her bringing the syringe closer and my eyes were drawn towards it. The needle drew closer to my arm, glinting in the morning light. I could've sworn I could already feel it sliding under my skin, its contents being forced into my bloodstream. Then would come the unpleasant feeling that the needle was still stuck inside my arm once it had been withdrawn, which was in fact the liquid, slowly dispersing into my blood. This was the point where I usually started to struggle, though I was determined to be still that day. But now I was also half wolf, and I guess the wolf didn't like needles either. It also knew what was coming, and the combined fear almost drove me mad again. With an animal cry I tore my arm from the nurse's grasp and pushed her backwards. She cried out in surprise as she fell to the floor, the needle embedding deep in her thigh. The fall caused it to snap, leaving most of its length stuck in the muscle. I swore, realising what I had done, and ran from the room to catcalls of "Loony!" and the like. Just as I'd predicted, people were already gossiping about it, saying I should be locked away again. It was hard to pick out individual voices in the babble. I didn't know whether my friends believed the rumours or whether they would defend me. I hoped so, otherwise I was truly alone and I couldn't deal with that.

In the corridor outside, I leaned against the wall with my eyes shut, panting, until the sound of someone approaching caused my eyes to snap open again. A girl from my year was coming towards me, one I felt I should remember though she was in none of my classes. But I couldn't put a name to her face. And yet the feeling that she was vaguely familiar would not go away. She obviously recognised me, however, as she walked up towards me and said "I'm pregnant, I thought you should know."

I looked at her confused and asked "Do I know you?"

She sighed impatiently and said "Don't you remember *any* of it? February fifteenth, we met outside a nightclub. You were obviously drunk from the way you were acting. You fought with my boyfriend and then we went back to my place, I'm sure I don't need to remind you of the rest."

"Oh God," I moaned.

"Oh God is right. I checked the dates. You're the father."

"Are you sure you're pregnant?"

"Yes, I wouldn't be here if I wasn't!"

"Then you've got to have an abortion," I told her.

"This is our child we're talking about. I'm not killing it!"

"You must. Trust me on this. If that monster is allowed into the world innocent people will die. You have to kill it!" I was getting desperate, the thought of the trail of corpses it would leave in its wake twisting my guts with fear. "Please, you have to kill it before it's too late!"

"I've no idea what you're talking about or why you're talking like this but I'm not murdering an innocent child and that's final!" she said.

189

"I don't know why I bothered telling you. You're all the same, you only want one thing! Then when you get it you want nothing more to do with us." She walked off.

"Please, don't do this!" I called after her. "You'll regret it! You think you'll be able to love it? You'll hate it. You have to kill it!"

She shot me the finger in reply and disappeared around the corner. I couldn't believe the wolf had picked someone in school. It couldn't have picked a complete stranger, someone I would never see again. I could have been blissfully unaware of the thing growing in her womb.

She had to think me insane from the way I'd reacted, her and the rest of the school. People were taking the liberty of pointing me out to their friends and whispering rumours to them. I realised I'd blown it. If I hadn't have panicked maybe it would have gone differently, maybe not. There was no way of knowing. But calling the baby a monster sounded insane, even to me. Anyone who didn't know the truth would not understand why I would call it that.

"Shit!" I said and banged a fist against the wall in frustration. And just when I didn't want them to, a teacher appeared.

Needless to say my language didn't go down too well, and the episode with the injections had landed me straight in isolation. Indifferent to this latest dose of school discipline, I followed the teacher up the stairs to the IT floor and into the isolation room. I was sat at a desk with wooden boards either side of me so that I couldn't see or talk to the other students, and given some work to do.

The time passed slowly, my mind on the girl and the monster I had spawned. I realised I didn't even know her name. Not that it mattered; the thing she was carrying was all that was important. I had to find a way to get rid of it before it was born, but if she refused to have an abortion how could I kill it? I could see no way to force her without showing her what I really was, which was suicidal if I didn't want the Slayers to find me. And now I had something to live for, I wasn't going to let them get to me first. I had to kill that baby somehow. If I left it until after the thing was born, it would be virtually impossible. Unless the Slayers would do it for me, but if its birth went unnoticed until the first few bodies started turning up it would already be too late. No, I had to take care of this myself.

The girl wouldn't let me near her again after the way I'd acted, and she'd be in a hospital surrounded by doctors and nurses when the baby was born, too many witnesses. Once she was home there might be a chance, if her family disowned her, disgusted at her for getting pregnant while she was still a child herself. But I'd rather not leave it that long. That left only one other option: kill the girl before the pregnancy could reach full term and the unborn baby would die with her. That was something I knew I couldn't do. There was always the chance of a miscarriage but I didn't hold out much hope for that. Unable to see how to resolve the problem, I decided to follow her over the next nine months and do what I could, and if no other way presented itself I'd be forced to kill her and the monster we had created, though the thought of this filled me with little comfort. I'd be killing one to save many but I didn't know whether I would be able to kill in cold blood when it came down to it. I could plan to do it if I became really desperate, but actually doing it was another thing entirely. Still, I could follow her for the time being and hope a better idea would present itself.

My mind made up, I began to follow the mother of our child whenever I could, starting as soon as I got out of isolation. Or that was the plan, but she'd already gone home. I couldn't remember the way to her house and I still hadn't learned to pick out her scent amongst the hundreds of others. How I had done it that night when I first found her I had no idea. I'd been more animal than human, otherwise I would never have been able to find the right female to mate, let alone tracked her down. My sense of smell was still pretty overwhelming. Sound I was learning to deal with, but without the wolf's help I wouldn't be able to make the most of scent. It might seem easy to you, but imagine being in a crowd of ten thousand people, all shouting and screaming to each other, and then imagine trying to pick up a single voice from the other end of the crowd. That's what it felt like. If I'd really taken note of her scent earlier that day, maybe I could have tracked her without the wolf's help, but by then the trail would be faint and lost in all the other scents. I had no choice but to go home and spend another sleepless night worrying about the monster she was soon to bring into this world.

The weeks passed, the full moon came and went, and it became clear the thing would be born, regardless of how much I pleaded with her to be rid of it. More worrying, the pregnancy was already far more advanced than it should have been, or so it seemed. She already had a noticeable bump. If I was going to do something I would have to do it much sooner than I had expected. God knows what the hospital thought, assuming she'd been for a check up.

So I awaited the fated day with growing dread, so afraid of what would be spawned that day that I barely noticed the deaths I had caused at full moon. That should have bothered me too. Maybe I was just too afraid of the new evil soon to enter this world, or maybe I was too distanced from the pain to care. Even now, I'm not sure which it was.

And then it came, on the twenty second of April, exactly sixty three days since it first began; the gestation period for most species of wolf.

She was aware of me following her that day, and doubled back down an alley in an attempt to lose me. She'd already threatened me with the police once. And there I emerged from the shadows to find her bent over in agony. It had begun.

Chapter Eighteen – Baptised In Blood

Panic taking over, I knelt beside her, both hating and pitying her in that moment. Hating her for putting us both through this, which could only end in death, pitying because she probably didn't even know what was happening to her, it had come so soon.

"I think my waters have broken," she gasped through the pain.

I did not reply, but decided to stay by her side until it was done, and then I would kill it, the thing we had created. She would not be able to stop me, I would be too strong. I only hoped I had strength enough to do what I had to. Then I would get her to a hospital and leave her in peace.

Screaming in pain, hours went by as she fought to give a monster entry into this world. She pleaded with me to take her to a hospital. Nothing I said could calm her, and she even tried to crawl away for help before the pain became too much. She didn't get far but it worked to our advantage, as she was better hidden in the shadows. It was a miracle no one had heard her screams and come to investigate. If anyone else came down the alley it didn't matter how well we were hidden. They'd hear her panting, screaming, straining to bring this baby into the world. But somehow we managed to get through those hard few hours without being disturbed. I held her hand, ignoring the pain when she squeezed as hard as she could in response to her own agony, and stroked her face, forgetting my hate. And then, long after nightfall, as the contractions were growing shorter the blood began to flow, blossoming out onto the pavement, soaking into the dirt. Was there meant to be this much blood?

And finally, followed by the blood, came our offspring. Not one but three, each more hideous than the last. But something was wrong, the girl was still screaming in pain even though they'd been born, the placenta with them, and more blood was flowing out. She was growing weaker by the second, I could almost feel her life draining from her, could hear her heart beat slowing, weakening. And then she gave a final shudder and lay still.

I turned back to look at the three scraps of life she had died giving birth to, thinking that her death had been in vain. I stared at the tiny, ugly creatures lying in the pool of blood, sickened by them; two boys and one girl. One of the boys and the girl appeared to be almost human, though I knew they were not, and they were smaller than babies born at the end of a normal nine month pregnancy. But the third one, the other boy, he was far from human. It appeared to be a normal wolf pup, blind and deaf and naked, completely defenceless against the cruel world, crying out for its mother. The other two were fairly quiet, limbs waving helplessly in the air, covered in their mother's blood. I turned away in horror, knowing what they would become if left alive. I couldn't bring myself to kill them after all, but I knew they would not survive alone. Leaving them to their fate would be slightly easier on my conscience, and I was convinced there was no way they could survive with their mother dead and the streets devoid of human life.

So I left the scenes of death behind me and headed for home, though the horror was fading already. I didn't feel much else after that, as if the guilt that had stained my conscience the past few months had finally been lifted. There was a vague sense of relief that at least that horror was over. The monsters would die alongside their mother; they would not grow to be killers. Other than that there was nothing and I wondered if I was becoming even more of a monster than the three I had just condemned to death.

What became of the bodies I don't know. It was probably in the news, unless the Slayers had hushed it up, but even then I didn't pay attention to the media. My prints were on the body but the police never questioned me. That was strange, since they probably already had me down as a suspect for Mel's disappearance – probably had my family down as the leading suspects, even though they couldn't find evidence against any one of us – though I didn't give it much thought at the time.

Tensions were growing at home. Dad hadn't been pleased when I'd come home so late the night my children were born.

"What the hell do you think you're doing staying out so late? Do you know how worried your mum and I have been? That's it young man, you're grounded!"

"You don't know the half of it! Why can't you leave me alone?" I had yelled back at him, suddenly feeling tired, more so than I had ever felt before. I was not in the mood for his temper tantrums, just because something was bothering him. It was a different excuse every bad year of his cycle; work, stress, boredom. Those were the usual ones.

"Don't you take that tone with me, son! What's wrong with you anyway? You're always going out on your own for no reason while we're left to slave around in here! It's time you started to help round the house. If you don't buck your ideas up soon I'll…"

I didn't give him chance to finish.

"You'll what?" I shouted. "You'll what, Dad? You couldn't make my life any worse than it is already!"

He mouthed at me wordlessly, but I'd heard enough. I ran off up to the sanctuary of my room and went straight to bed, fuming. Ironic that he used to complain about how much time I spent inside on the computer or the Playstation, and now he was complaining I spent too much time outside!

And it only went downhill from there. We were now in May. Dad was finding more excuses to shout at me than ever. His favourite one was spending too much time on the computer. He'd even restricted me to an hour a day! That really pissed me off. I didn't spend half as much time as I used to since becoming a werewolf, mostly because computer games just weren't as fun anymore after everything I'd seen and done, but just recently they were helping to take my mind off everything. I didn't know what I'd do without them, and one hour a day was hardly enough. Then one day Mum stood up for me, unable to watch me suffer any longer, and I was more grateful than she ever knew.

"Why do you always have to take the kid's side, Emma?" he asked angrily.

"I don't at all. I agree with you. He shouldn't spend too much time on the computer; it's not good for him. But I'm sure longer than an hour a day won't harm if he has a break in between each session," Mum said, her own temper having finally snapped. "You go about things the wrong way, John. He's just lost his friend. He needs our help to get through this. You shouldn't be so hard on him all the time; it will only turn him against you and make him more rebellious."

"That was half a year ago! I don't have to listen to this Emma. He'll do as he's told, and he should be grateful he's allowed on it at all, the way he's acting."

The bastard wouldn't leave me alone from then on. Everything I did was wrong in his eyes, one way or another. He hated the way I spoke, the way I dressed, the way I ate. He hated it when I used slang, snapping at me to "Speak properly!" every two minutes. If they took me out for a meal I was never dressed up enough for him. He always wanted me to wear my smart shirt and trousers we'd bought for someone's wedding, even though he went in jeans and a t-shirt. I ended up looking overdressed. And when I ate, I'd developed a tendency to rip into meat with my hands and teeth rather than using a knife and fork, and he usually ended up sending me to my room because I wasn't civilised enough. He even shouted at me once for singing! I could tell you countless incidents about the arguments we

195

had, most of them petty. Now I look back at it, it all seems so pathetic and childish, but that's what he was like. Some of the arguments sound stupid now though they weren't at the time.

The horror and the guilt were gone, even after I killed again that month. For a short time I felt nothing at all. I was more of an empty shell than ever. Then the arguments started and rekindled feelings that had lain dormant. Admittedly the anger and the hate were nothing new, but in the past few months every emotion I'd felt had been directed at the wolf. Now old feelings were awakened, feelings toward the bastard who dared call himself my father. Somewhere around the start of May the anger stirred whenever he was being completely unreasonable. Then it reared its ugly head every time he shouted at me. By the end of May it had begun to claw its way out of the dark pit of despair it had briefly been trapped in.

One day I sat reading while Mum cooked dinner. My grandparents on Dad's side had come over to see us, and Dad decided reading while we had guests was rude, despite the fact Amy was on the Net and he was reading Teletext. I'd already sat with them for a bit, what more did he want? So I told him I'd talk to them again when I finished the page.

"That's not good enough, Nick. You'll do as you're told. Put the book down."

"Yeah, when I've reached the end of the page," I replied stubbornly.

"Put it down now and go see your grandparents." Most people's eyes narrow when they're angry, yet his dark eyes always seemed wider with it. The look on his face was close to madness. Eyes wide, nostrils flared, temples throbbing, he would have been right at home in the mental hospital I'd been sent to. The hatred I felt for him whenever he did that face was more than words can describe.

"Are you deaf or are you stupid? I said when I've finished the fucking page." He didn't take that too well.

"That's it, go to your room and you'll do without any tea tonight!"

I turned my back on him and walked away. I wasn't afraid of him. Even if I'd been human, I was too angry to be afraid. But that time I felt he'd gone too far. He'd forbid me to play on the computer or any kind of console games whenever we had guests, but he couldn't expect me to just sit there while they talked about grown up stuff for hours on end. I was damn sure he wouldn't have done so when he was my age. He was probably out playing with his mates, and wasn't that worse? At least I was still in the house with them. So I went up to my room, letting the anger take over, stomping up the stairs as loud as I could. I slammed the door behind me and glared at my bookshelf in a rage. There was a photo album on one of the shelves. I grabbed it and looked through the pictures. Every time I came to one of him I ripped it up. It helped vent the anger.

It was almost free, that anger. It had reached the top of the pit and had found the final barrier it had to overcome before it ruled me. My self control had grown weaker since that day in April. After everything I'd done, what did it matter if I killed more? There was no going back now. I felt distanced from the pain. When I looked in the mirror cold, dead eyes stared back at me, almost completely emotionless except when anger flared up in them. The eyes of a killer. There was no point fighting it. I'd lost. I was more of a monster now than I had been when I killed Fiona. The only thing that remained for me was the anger, and once it was free I knew I would be unstoppable. The last of my self control was in place for my family's sake, because the last remnants of that fear that had ruled me for the past few months said that if I gave in to the anger, the beast within, I might not care who I killed. And the bastard wasn't helping matters. I was sick of the way he treated us, sick of his stupid rules, which half the time didn't even apply to him. I challenged him every time he gave me a bollocking and in turn that made him angry. So far we'd avoided a physical confrontation, but the rage was building between us and it was only a matter of time before it exploded.

Chapter Nineteen – School's Out

Meanwhile, everyone else in the normal, human world I used to belong to had exams to prepare for. I should have been revising along with the rest of them, but doing exams no longer seemed right. I was beginning to realise it was only a matter of time before I was forced to leave humanity behind me, and I wasn't going to waste my time revising. Even if I'd still been human, I would probably have settled for some last minute revision and that would have been it. We were about to go on study leave, and I would have found better things to do with all that free time than hours of revision each day.

Before we left, we had a leaving assembly. We sat with our forms while Mrs Redgewell and some other teachers high up in the hierarchy system made some pretty boring speeches, talking about our future, wishing us luck in the exams, and droning on about how proud they were of our year group and how much they'd miss us. To the monster I had become, it was all bull. Although some part of me, some part of my old self that I had thought dead, was enjoying himself immensely. He was about to be released from school forever and he wanted to celebrate. He was just waiting for the doors to open to freedom.

After the speeches they played some music and they let us wander round the hall to spend time with friends we may never see again after the exams. Each form had chosen their own song to be played in the assembly. Not one of them had chosen the perfect song for the occasion; Alice Cooper's legendary School's Out. That would have been my choice but no one listened to me, so instead I was subjected to all kinds of rubbish. I let that last part of my old self rule me for the rest of the day, and he decided to sing his own lyrics to our form's choice.

"I won't survive," I sang. "I won't survive. I'm gonna slit my wrist tonight, I'm no longer alive. I've got no more life to live, I've got all my blood to give. And I won't survive. I won't survive."

I was sat with Becci through that song. Becci thought it was funny, while the girl next to her gave me a look of disgust. I think she might have suggested it, thinking it was fitting somehow. I guess in a way it was because everybody has their own problems to deal with in high school. I just had more problems than most. But I still thought School's Out would have been better.

After the song Becci went off to find Ava. I went to find Lizzy, but I was soon distracted by the table of food at the back of the hall, the highlight of the entire event for me. I'd been able to ignore the enticing scent of the selection of cakes and biscuits for the most part, until I went too close and it was overpowering. Lizzy would have to wait.

I was busy eating when she found me. Most people were in tears by that point, something I struggled to understand. They couldn't possibly enjoy school, could they? I was suddenly pulled into a hug by my closest school friend. Still eating a biscuit over her shoulder, I patted her back uncertainly, while she sobbed over mine, tears running down her cheeks. I supposed they were all mourning the end of an era, the end of a life that had been all they'd known for the last five years. That life had long since been taken from me by the wolf, but for them it was only just ending, and perhaps some were caught up in the emotion of its end, coupled with the uncertainty of what the future held. Whatever the reason, it was a human experience I couldn't share in and I felt out of place once more.

Finally the doors opened and we were free to go when we were ready. I was the first out. I walked through the gates singing the chorus to School's Out at the top of my voice, to a chorus of more tears. On the other side of the gates I turned and gave school the finger. Then I turned away from the hated building that had brought me much misery and boredom over the years and never once looked back. Well, except for when we had to go in for exams. Being a werewolf didn't get me out of sitting them, even if I wasn't going to bother to try and pass. While I was still living in the human world it was better to avoid the trouble of not turning up.

Minutes later I sat in my room blasting out my music. I was home alone; Mum had to carry on working at the school until they broke up, and then she had to do an extra ten days at some point over the summer holiday, while Dad was in Leeds for the day. I raided the fridge and took a couple of bottles of beer. I really wanted to get drunk, but it would only make things worse with Dad. Part of me wanted an excuse to fight him, yet if I did there was no guarantee I could cling to the last of my self control, and all three of them might end up dead. I couldn't let that happen. Besides, I wasn't entirely sure it was possible for me to get drunk even if I wanted to. My body had changed in ways even I didn't understand. For all I knew my liver had become so efficient at cleansing my body of poisons, all the alcohol would be driven out before it could take effect.

I spent the rest of the day on the internet and the Playstation, knowing full well it was probably my last day of normality. Soon I would be forced to give up humanity completely. It had already begun. Once the anger was free and I embraced the beast – not the wolf but the darkness in all of us – I really would be a monster. That anger had driven me to kill a rabbit and beat Jamie to a pulp. There was no telling what it would do if I fully embraced it. I only knew that it would make me no better than the wolf itself, and then there would be no going back.

Chapter Twenty – Darkness Eternal

Dad came home that evening in a rage. He noticed the missing beers and went ballistic. He said I should have asked him permission since they were his; he'd bought them with his money. I pointed out that actually they were Mum's because she'd bought them with her money. He didn't take too kindly to that. He was always shouting at me for answering back. I think it angered him more than anything else I could do. But I couldn't help it: it was in my nature to argue. I couldn't keep my mouth shut when he was being unreasonable. Needless to say, he sent me to my room where I sat with Alice, trying to calm myself. I blasted out my music again, playing the ones about necrophilia and other such morbid subjects, knowing how he really hated that. They didn't bother me anymore, like they had at the height of my depression. I didn't even have to deal with any mental images of my victim's corpses being defiled.

Mum called me down about an hour later. Dad hadn't wanted to end the punishment so soon but Mum stood by me and he backed down, fuming on the sofa in the dining room while he watched golf. Sending me to my room wasn't much of a punishment anyway, since my Playstation was in there, and all my books and my music.

Later that night I went into the kitchen and put the kettle on to make a coffee for Mum. Amy never had to do anything around the house, and I would normally have complained, but I owed Mum for sticking up for me.

Dad was in his favourite chair watching the news about football, when the noise of the kettle boiling rose above the TV and he commanded me to turn it off.

"So football's more important than your own family?" I snarled, the anger flaring up inside. The next thing I knew, he was stood before me, hands wrapped around my throat, his own anger taking control of him.

"You ungrateful sod," he said. "I'll knock your head off!"

I yelled at the top of my voice, in shock more than anything. I knew it would come down to a fight eventually but I hadn't expected him to go so far and it had caught me off guard.

"John!" Mum had come running through from the lounge. She didn't hesitate before she reacted. She ran over to us and pulled us apart. I stood glaring at him while Mum fought to keep him from hurting me, and the bastard kept shouting over and over again "I'll have you son! I'll have you!"

"Nick, go to your room," Mum said.

"I don't need your help Mum, I can handle this," I argued.

"Just go Nick."

I swore loudly but did as I was told. Mum didn't bother to tell me off; she was too busy telling Dad to calm down. I could hear everything from my room and my hatred for him grew every time I heard his voice.

"The bastard! I'll kill him!" I growled under my breath. "I swear I'll kill him!"

The anger was free at last.

"I'll kill him!" I roared to the empty room.

Then I turned and, with my palms facing upwards, watched my fingers curl into claws. I looked up at my reflection in the window. If anybody else had seen me then, I was a fearsome sight. Anger blazed in my murderous, amber eyes, face twisted in a bestial snarl. It was not a human facial expression. My canines had lengthened and I had barely noticed, both top and bottom, until they were unmistakeably lupine. With another roar I turned and slashed the wall, the claws biting into it as if it were as soft as flesh and causing five long, deep gashes. Man, that felt good. I could feel the wolf beside me and I didn't fight it, though I didn't let it take over either. Just knowing I had all that strength and power at my command made me feel better. The knowledge that I could literally rip him apart limb from limb was enough, at least for that night. I wanted blood, but I could wait for it. I bowed my head and closed my eyes, fists clenched by my sides, trying to calm myself. When I raised my head and opened them again, human eyes stared back at me out of the human face in the window, though they were bloodshot, and some of the anger still lurked behind them. Later. I would call on that anger later, and then we would have blood.

Shadows danced across the ceiling, shapeless things called into life by a combination of the moonlight, streetlamps, and car headlights filtering through the curtains. Somewhere below raised voices argued about their marriage. Footsteps sounded on the landing where Amy crouched, straining to hear everything that was said with her weak human senses. Images lurked just behind my eyeballs, nightmares waiting to ensnare me. I would face them when I was ready. I wasn't afraid of them anymore, and yet they would not leave me alone.

Restless, I rose from the bed and went to join Amy, though I could hear every word from my room. We sat in silence while the argument raged below. Mum questioned Dad about what had happened with me in the kitchen, asking him what it was really about. He couldn't answer her. I was willing to bet he couldn't even meet her

202

eyes. She told him he needed help. At the very least he needed some coaching in anger management. He agreed, but his voice sounded hollow, as if his heart wasn't really in it. Did he regret what had happened? I wasn't sure. Then Mum asked him why he was in a mood all the time. He made some poor excuses about how they never did anything together as a couple and they lived completely separate lives, but what he was really saying was that he'd grown bored. Amy turned to me, a look of horror on her face.

"Nick, they're talking about divorce!" she whispered fearfully. Of the three of us, I think Amy would have suffered most if the family broke apart. I'd been hoping it would happen for years, feeling certain we'd have been better off without him. Not that I really believed they would ever separate. They'd talked about it before and in the end always made up. It was part of the cycle Dad put us all through. But Amy believed, and beside the fear there was a pleading look, as if I could say something and make it all better.

The anger growled hungrily, and I felt a fresh wave of hatred towards the bastard for putting Mum and Amy through that. All it needed was a spark now and the rage would drive out the monster in me.

I didn't want to lose control at home where Mum and Amy might get hurt. I needed something else to direct it to, someone else. Someone outside the family I could kill and feel no remorse for, someone who would feed the anger before it controlled me. And then I remembered the Slayers. I could shed their blood. They were nameless, faceless people to me back then, and they were the enemy. And in a way, they had made me what I am. For if they hadn't hunted us to near extinction they would not have driven the werewolf to share his curse and I would most likely still be human. I may have got through a mortal life without ever being bitten and eventually died a natural death. The Slayers had taken everything from me.

Amy was still looking at me, still waiting for an answer. I turned away. Mum and Dad's marriage was not my problem anymore. None of it was. We were at war, and I had found a reason to fight.

Lady Sarah sat on a coffin singing to herself, her voice high and unnatural, but more beautiful than any human voice I'd ever heard before. I wondered what the vampires did in their spare time. It was easy to imagine Vince enjoying human activities, but somehow I didn't think Lady Sarah had much to do with the human world. She had to do something other than hunt, otherwise how could she bear to go on through eternity?

"Hey," I said. "You sing better than me. Didn't recognise the song though."

She smiled. "It is something I wrote centuries ago for the vampire who made me. I have only seen him once since that night, and our time together was brief, though it was enough to know I love him. I will find him again someday, when the war is over and the world is safer for our kind. Until then I could not find him even if I wanted to. It is easier for those with more power to hide from the world. He may even be living in the human world as Vincent chooses to. For him it will be easier to go unnoticed. Vincent has much to learn, even after all the centuries he has seen. Time has yet to bring him wisdom. But you did not come here to talk about my singing, nor my love life."

"No, I didn't," I agreed. "For the past few months I have been fighting the wolf, but I'm losing and I want blood. You told me we are at war, and I am finally ready to fight."

I was vaguely aware I was already beginning to talk like the vampire, that I was losing my humanity even quicker than I'd first thought.

"You should not seek to fight. The war will find you eventually and once it does you can never again have the life you have known. Are you willing to give that up so soon? I would encourage you to embrace your other half as I have said before, and do not fight the urge to kill, but you do not have to go to war for that. The longer you avoid the Slayers the longer you can live among humans," she said. "I know how much that means to you, even if it does not seem like it sometimes."

"I've already crossed the line. I can't live as a human anymore. And what if it's too late for that? What if the war has already found me? They tracked me down on the first night I changed. I've seen into the wolf's mind. They would have killed me if you hadn't killed them first. Why haven't they come back to finish me off? Why haven't they hunted you down in revenge? Something is not right. They may not know who I am, but they know my wolf form. I should be dead by now. It doesn't make any sense now I think about it. After all the bodies started turning up they knew it was a werewolf so they should have tracked me down. I even saw one of them take in a guy who witnessed me as a half man half wolf. They know I exist."

Lady Sarah was silent for a moment before answering. "I cannot give you an answer to that. I do not know why they have not attacked again, unless they are hoping to learn your human identity so they may kill you in human form when you are less dangerous and unprepared. I just do not know."

I didn't like her answer. The more I thought about it, the less it made sense. The Slayers were up to something. But I had other questions. I was curious about Lady Sarah. She had been alive for centuries, longer than I could even begin to imagine! "So what role have you played in this war? Do you remember the last battle when there was an army to fight for us, before they began to pick us off one by one?"

"I fought in that battle. I have fought them many times, when I've had to. Often times for survival, and also for revenge on occasion. And other times purely for the love of killing and feasting on their blood. They have not given us any choice. If it weren't for them we would be far more numerous, and the human population would not have increased so drastically over the last century. Though if it weren't for them perhaps the war between my kind and yours would still rage on, keeping our numbers in check as well.

"I have had many reasons to fight the Slayers, but they are too numerous and we are too few to fight the battles of times long past, so the war is reduced to small skirmishes whenever we cross paths. With today's technology only the most powerful stand a chance, and even then they would rather hide than risk death," she told me. I liked this answer even less. The odds didn't look good. "Your race is nearly extinct. They wiped out zombies. We are but a shadow of what we once were. Every undead race has suffered at the hands of the Slayers."

"Tell me about zombies."

She shook her head. "Not now. I have to feed. And Vincent is out there somewhere. I need to watch him. If he grows careless again he not only endangers himself, but every other vampire nearby. Somebody has to look out for him, for our own sakes as much as his."

I knew better than to argue. I went straight back home and lay in bed, thinking about what she had said. We were both right in a way. The war had found me the first night I became a werewolf, but in some ways it had yet to find me. The fighting had not truly found me yet. Lady Sarah had made it her fight when the Slayers first attacked me, and since then they had not so much as threatened me. But surely that could not last. The day had to be coming when they would make their next move. And then, for me at least, the war would really begin.

Over the next week whenever the anger possessed me I went out and killed. The third time I found that I liked it.

Dad drove me into another rage that night, and the desire to kill took over me once more. I hadn't been letting it drain away since I had last spoken with Lady Sarah. No, I took to the streets and let the anger feed my bestial nature. I let it burn inside and mix with the wolf's unnatural hunger and my newfound thirst for blood.

There was a man stood waiting at a bus stop. He lit a cigarette as I approached him, briefly illuminating his face. The anger flared up. In the darkness, he even looked a little like the bastard, with a bit of imagination. I smiled, and it wasn't friendly. The first two times I had strangled my victims and felt nothing, except for the feeling of the anger retreating, satiated, waiting to be called upon again like the wolf in some ways, and very different from it in others. This time it was different. The wolf had had no part in it before, but as the full moon drew nearer, the wolf grew restless, and it hungered.

The man glared at me with hostile eyes, though he didn't know anything was amiss, unable to see well in the darkness. Once my eyes turned wolfish, the night became almost as clear as day and it took a greater effort of imagination on my part to see my father stood before me. I willed myself to believe it was Dad glaring at me in the darkness, and it fuelled the anger, the wolf rising with it. But I didn't grant my lupine side control.

I let my canines lengthen. At first they could have been mistaken for a vampire's if it wasn't for the ones on my lower jaw, until they took on the unmistakeable shape of a wolf's fangs. My nails became claws, though that was as far as I let the change go. Then without warning, before the guy knew what was happening, I knocked him to the floor and fell on him like the animal I was. He screamed as fangs pierced the flesh of his neck, burying themselves deep, until with a backwards thrust of my head and a spray of blood they came free, taking the flesh with them. His throat torn out, he made gurgling noises, trying in vein to breathe through his torn windpipe. I had taken out enough flesh that you could see a section of his spine at the back of the wound, before blood filled the place of the muscle and cartilage, and the extent of the damage was no longer visible.

I had finally freed the monster that lurks in all of us, the darkness at the heart of mankind. Not the wolf. This monster was different to the wolf. It enjoyed killing in a different way to the canine within me.

No creature on Earth other than man could ever know of this monster. It likes to kill, enjoys it above all else. It lives on death and destruction, not flesh and blood. The wolf had always killed to feed and to survive. The monster killed for the hell of it. I killed for the hell of it. I had become the monster. I had fallen into the void made of our own evil, lost in the darkness, fallen for all eternity into a place that had never known the light.

The wolf didn't like it. I was wasting life, the thing that is most precious to the universe. It didn't like watching things die for no reason, and part of it had no desire to even share a body with the human in us, while the other part fought to change and feast on the flesh, the smell of the blood like a drug. It wouldn't be long before I would welcome the change, but the desire to kill had been satisfied for one night. I licked the blood off my teeth, enjoying the taste. Crimson spots dotted my body and my shirt, congealing to a darker red, almost black. I didn't care. I'd wash them away later, not because they horrified me anymore but to hide the evidence. I couldn't let the police or the Slayers find me like that, after all.

I licked off what I could and walked away, leaving the man dying in the road. Minutes later his bus came. A crunch and a splatter of blood meant the driver hadn't seen him in time to stop. He was dead anyway, and now there was nothing to tie the body to me. I glanced back to see it flattened against the road. It was just another roadkill now, only this one was bigger than the others and there was no fur or feathers, just a mess of blood and flesh. His face had been pressed into the pavement. They'd need DNA or something to ID him. And then I was gone, leaving humans to clean up my mess.

Chapter Twenty One – Prom Date with Death

While the death toll continued to rise, the time had also come to sit my exams. I wanted to laugh at the absurdity of it. I didn't belong there, and yet there I was. I didn't need them marking by examiners to know I hadn't done well in any of my subjects. I hadn't bothered to revise, and my mind had not been on my work all year. I only remembered scraps of the knowledge our teachers had tried to impress upon us, maybe enough to scrape passes, but probably not. I would have said I did worst in the year, if it wasn't for the guy across the room who fell asleep in his Geography exam before he could answer a single question. It was good to know I wouldn't have the lowest marks in the school (at least not in that subject), even if it didn't matter anymore. I don't know why I cared; it just meant something to that last part of my old self that had enjoyed the leaving assembly.

We put our pens down and closed our exam papers for the final time and left the school for good. Some people worried about their results, others didn't. Talk turned to the prom at the end of July, only a week away. People asked me if I was going. It would be a full moon that night, so I couldn't go even if I wanted to. It wasn't my thing anyway; I couldn't dance for a start and I had no girl to take with me. I didn't know why they were so surprised when I said I wasn't going. I doubted they'd miss me. But no matter how disappointed any of them might be, there was nothing I could do to change the timing: there was no way I could go and that was final.

The night of the prom I left the house long before nightfall and found somewhere safe to transform, plus a hiding place for my clothes until I was ready to retrieve them at dawn. Since I'd decided I wanted to be part of the war, I'd been doing some thinking. Every time I changed in my room, there was a chance someone could see. And whether any potential witnesses were one of the Slayers or not, it wouldn't be long before the Slayers found out, one way or another. My curtains weren't great at blocking out the light, and you could probably see my dark shape through them. And even if I couldn't be seen through the curtains, someone was bound to see me leaping through the window in wolf form eventually. I was lucky I hadn't been seen already. So that night I left before the change could take hold, telling my parents I was sleeping over at a friend's.

I had enough time to reach the woods near where I'd killed Fiona before night fell and the full moon rose. I didn't fight it anymore. I hadn't done since April. In fact, now the monster had awoken and the anger had taken over, I embraced it.

There were no humans in the woods and I had no desire to hunt animals. The anger that lived in the human part of me wanted to taste human flesh, and it had grown stronger than the instinct to feed. Even if that meant suffering the hunger for the best part of the night, only human prey would satisfy. That left me with two choices: either head back to the town and hunt there, or go through the woods. I knew there were houses on the other side, and a bigger building, some sort of hotel. They were playing loud music there; I could hear it from where I stood – the prom.

Since the anger took hold, the human had allowed me closer to the surface than before, and I had been listening to its friends. A large gathering of human youths would present the perfect feeding ground, even if I didn't understand why it was so important to them. I don't think the human part of me did either. I could feel its confusion over why girls went to such great lengths for one night, why they had to have the best dress and why it had to be different to everyone else's, and so ridiculously expensive. That didn't matter. All that mattered was the hunger, the need to kill, both physically and mentally, and the desire for warm flesh between my jaws. I was going to the prom after all. And if only they knew, I could have won the award for the best entrance.

Limousines filled the car park. A yellow taxi, like the ones they have in America, pulled up and four girls spilled out of it. One couple even arrived in a tractor, and a boy named John Smith brought a case of beer by the same brand name, all trying for best entrance. I could hear it all as I ran towards the feast that awaited.

I didn't fear the Slayers in that moment. The need to kill was too great, and I doubted they would be near the prom. They probably didn't think we were foolish enough to feed in somewhere so crowded.

Music blared out from inside. It was a posh hotel. They probably had their own ballroom. Over the music I could hear human voices. I could pick out individuals, people's voices a part of me recognised. Adam, the boy from Science the human didn't like. Lizzy, David, Becci, all its friends. Those who used to bully it before they learned to fear us. And any one of them was mine for the taking.

The woods thinned as I reached the end. I knew better than to even attempt to go in the front way. The people on the door would sound the alarm the minute I stepped out onto the road and it would cause too much panic too soon. Men with guns would appear before I even had chance to feed.

A shadow in the night, I slunk silently along the border between woods and tarmac, weaving in and out of the trees just far enough from the road to go unnoticed. I crossed over once I was confident I was out of sight and made my way round to the back of the building.

It was built on large grounds, and there were just as many people outside at the back as there were inside. I crouched behind the other side of the wall ready to pounce, enjoying the sounds and scents carrying to me on the light summer breeze. Most powerful was the scent of human bodies sweating in the heat, and beneath that the smell of burning flesh from a pig being roasted, and the sickly smell of some sauce they would drown it in. Why did humans always have to spoil a good piece of meat? That was something I couldn't understand. The sauce took away the taste of the meat. Roasting it was bad enough, but whatever sickly sauces and flavourings they added to it was sacrilege. The scent of the meat didn't excite me at all, not like the live prey surrounding it.

Once I judged most of them were outside, enjoying their cooked meat, I leapt with all the strength I had. The wall would have been too high for a mortal wolf to cross, unless it was able to scrabble up, but I cleared it with that single jump. I landed on the other side and roared, almost like a lion rather than a wolf. That was the human, voicing its anger. It had fought with its father again that day.

Pandemonium ensued. Screams almost deafened me. They started to run, all in different directions, panicking, remembering the pictures they had seen of my other victims. A girl tripped and fell on a dress that had no doubt cost her hundreds of pounds, and now her life. She cried out to her boyfriend. He started to run back to her.

I was on her before anyone knew what was happening, and the boyfriend hesitated. I moved too quickly for them, and I was just suddenly there, stood over her, drool falling from my jaws and spattering her face. For a second I saw her as her boyfriend saw her. I didn't need the human to know she was considered beautiful among others. Blonde hair framed the perfect face, which could have been sculpted by a god. It was hard to believe it was the mere creation of random genes thrown together from her parents. The skin was smooth and pale, the lips round and full, just the right size for her face, the nose small and straight, everything in proportion. Green eyes like emeralds looked up at me, filled with shock and terror. If she'd had fangs she could have passed for a vampire. No living creature should have been that perfect. And she was mine: her life was mine to take.

I could take her beauty as easily as her life. In that first moment I couldn't do it, but then she screamed and tried to crawl away, and the moment was gone. She made a pitiful attempt to escape and found it was too late. She was helpless when I started to feed, helpless when my teeth pierced her soft flesh, bit into that perfect face. I savaged her, lost in the bloodlust. No inch of her body was spared. The face went first, my fangs gouging deep lines in the heavenly sculpture. If I wasn't ruled by the hunger it would have seemed an act against God. Or at least to the human part of me it would have, once when I had been truly human. But no longer. I could hear its thoughts: God never did anything for it when it cried and begged for His help, so why should it spare her? To me, she was just another animal trapped inside nature's vicious cycle, her life forfeit so I may continue my own. That didn't mean her life was

210

not sacred. I understood that better than any human. I did not kill so freely as the human part of me, at least not on my own. The human was with me that night, and we were closer to becoming one again than we had been since I first heard the call of the moon. Only then, when I was truly awake, did we begin to separate, to become two beings living in one body. The male vampire had hinted that we needed to become one again if we were to survive eternity. And he was right. But I did not like it. I only killed for food or to protect myself. The human wanted to kill to feed its anger, and I did not want to be a part of that.

Her blood flowing into my mouth brought me back. I ripped some more flesh from her face and moved further down her body, like a sick, perverted nightmare of two lovers, except I brought the kiss of death. I left blood and gore behind whenever my mouth touched her.

I tore one of her breasts off and ate what flesh I could from the ribcage, though I left the organs beneath intact. Her stomach split open and I bit into the liver. I swallowed and went back for another bite when something slammed into my side and we rolled away from the dying girl.

Her boyfriend had leapt on me in a desperate attempt to save her. We landed in a tangle of limbs and I breathed in his scent. It was the boy the human didn't like, Adam. He was trying to pull away, fear chasing away the last of his nerve when he realised his act of bravery may have cost him his life. Still under the influence of the bloodlust and the moon, I snapped at him, straining to reach his throat. But we were locked too close together for me to twist my head round so I could close my jaws around his neck.

He fought against me, determined not to end up a mangled corpse like his girlfriend. He slammed a fist into the side of my muzzle. I growled, the blow frustrating me more than anything else. When he realised he couldn't hurt me, he drove a finger into my eye, struggling to be free at the same time. We disentangled ourselves just as my eye exploded with pain, and I fell back, yelping, while he got to his feet and ran over to the girl I had mauled. Something wet and sticky dribbled down my cheek, matting my fur. The eye had burst, and half of the world turned black. Somewhere inside the human screamed and I felt its fear and anger rise up simultaneously, one step closer to the thing it feared the most. He would pay for that.

With another roar, I pounced and ripped out Adam's apple, all in one movement. He was dead before we hit the ground. His girlfriend was also dead by then. I looked at that face, so beautiful in life, yet in death there were no distinguishing features to set her apart from the rest of humanity. She had been the envy of the school, almost a goddess among them, worshipped by her fellow students. In death she was nothing. Just another carcass in a world filled with the dead.

Her emerald eyes would have sparkled in their sockets, before death dulled them. The rest of her face was gone, so badly mutilated that without the eyes it would have been unrecognisable as a face at all. Just another lump of meat, glistening wet in the moonlight. Her figure, conformed in the shape every female died

211

for, gone. She didn't curve in the right places anymore. The missing breast made her lopsided, ugly. I'd managed to bite into one of the hips before Adam had distracted me from the kill, and the bone had shattered, on the opposite side of her body to the missing breast. Nobody wanted to be her now.

Movement behind me made me turn. I lost interest in the dead, my attention on the living. The bloodlust wanted more lives. The hunger didn't care whether the meat was living or dead. If I had been a true wolf, there would be no bloodlust and I would be content with the meat from the dead. But I was a monster and killing was in my nature. The part of me closest to a true wolf didn't want to kill more than was necessary, but the part bound by the curse needed fresher blood. The dead would not satisfy.

People were still running in panic. A girl stared at me in shock. The human knew her as Kerri. She was the next victim, gutted like a fish, and still I hungered. One boy was not running. He stood watching me with a mixture of horror and hatred. I glared at him with my good eye, readying to attack. The human knew this one too, and now it decided to interfere. No, not this one. David. The name came to me and it meant something. The boy was nothing to me, no more than prey, but the human fought me, and there were enough potential victims that I gave in. I turned away, catching a glimpse of his puzzled expression as I went for someone else. He knew he should have been dead once I'd turned my sights on him, and he couldn't understand why he had been spared.

I forgot him as I feasted upon the fourth body that night, the most I had ever killed at one time.

I plunged my snout deep in her innards as I had with so many of my kills before, when I became aware of a shadow looming over me. I looked up to find another familiar face. Like David, this one was not running, but she was not held in place by shock. She'd taken advantage of the chaos I had created to draw a gun. I don't know enough of guns to tell you what model it was, I only know that it had been concealed somewhere on her person, small enough to fit on the inside of her trousers. And finally she'd revealed herself as one of the Slayers, as I had known all along.

I had smelt her on the others who had attacked me the first night I changed. To me, that made her their leader. Wolves rub their scent on other pack members to identify each other as pack, to mark them as belonging to the pack. Her scent was on them and her scent alone, and to me that meant they belonged to her. Of course, she wouldn't have touched them in the way that wolves do to bond, and it wasn't sexual, but her scent had been there. She was high ranking among them, and I feared her. That's what the dream had meant of hunter and hunted, back in the classroom, months ago. The human hadn't realised what it meant, but I knew. Maybe the human could have worked it out, if it hadn't been lost in its own horror. If it had known, we could have killed her long before that night. But we had not, and there I stood, snarling at her with fear, knowing the gun could end my life.

212

And yet she did not shoot. She could have killed me then and I would have been powerless to stop it, just as my victims had been. And she knew it. I could see it in her face, the smugness about the eyes and the mouth, the cruelty glittering in the soul that peered out from behind those eyes. She could have ended it, but she did not and I knew in that moment she wanted me alive, though for what reason I couldn't say. And I wasn't staying to find out.

Once I knew she would not kill me, I slowly backed away. She aimed at my front leg. Not a killing shot, but it would slow me down long enough for her to catch me. I didn't know how she would do it with so many witnesses. They thought I was just an animal, a large wolf gone rogue. People would want me dead, either in revenge for the lives I had taken or to prevent more deaths. And if the authorities were called in they would see to it that this man eater terrorising the town was killed. They would not let civilians take me. Perhaps this Slayer had already called in the reinforcements. Perhaps they would bring guns loaded with tranquilliser darts to sedate me, and take me away under the pretence of being professional animal handlers sent to transport me elsewhere. Whatever their plans, I couldn't let it happen. They would take what they wanted from me and end it. Handing myself over to them would only delay the inevitable, they would kill me eventually.

Her aim never wavered as I continued to back away. Those pitiless eyes just watched me, maybe reluctant to shoot before the others arrived. It would draw too much attention to her. But it wouldn't last; she would have to shoot me eventually. I didn't really have a plan. I just knew I had to get away from her before more of them arrived, and I had to do something soon before she was forced to shoot.

Confident in the knowledge that she would not kill me, I turned my back on her and ran. She pulled the trigger, but for some reason she'd panicked. The shot had been wild. She hadn't given herself chance to adjust her aim after I'd moved, and it thudded harmlessly into the wall beyond which was freedom. I bounded over to the wall and threw myself at it, but fear clouded my brain. I hadn't judged the distance as well as the first time, jumping just high enough to hook my front paws over the top. My back legs scrabbled against the brickwork as I fought against gravity, pulling myself up, but it took precious time. It gave her the time she needed. The next bullet buried itself in my back leg. I yelped, and the shock and the pain almost caused me to lose my footing. But somehow I managed to keep hold and pull myself up before I slid back down. I heard her cursing behind me as I limped away.

Some time later, I lay hidden in the undergrowth of the woods, blood leaking into the soil around me. I could only hope they wouldn't find me. I'd tried putting weight on the leg and it had collapsed beneath me. I'd had to struggle on three legs to find somewhere safe to wait for dawn, when the change would heal me. If the Slayers found me before then, they would take me. Without the use of my back leg, I would not be able to escape them a second time, not if they had more guns. As it was, I

213

was lucky I was much stronger than a mortal would have been after the blood loss I had suffered. And not even I knew if the eye would heal or not. Only time would tell.

Morning came and the moon sank beneath the horizon, driven away by the sun. They'd been searching for me. I'd heard them crashing through the undergrowth, stealthy for humans but clumsier than any other animal in the woods. It had been a long night, and I almost welcomed the change back to human.

Pain spread through my body. Limbs shifted. My paws shrank and separated until they formed outstretched fingers, the claws shortening, going blunt, until they became harmless. My canines shrank and extra teeth I didn't need as a human melted back into my gums as if they had never been. Guts reformed within, changing size and shape. My tail was sucked back into my spine. I cried out with the pain, forgetting the danger of the Slayers. The noise started out as yelps and yips but soon became human screams of agony uttered from a shrinking snout, reforming into a human mouth. My ears became rounder and moved back to the side of my head. One eye turned from amber to greenish brown, while the damaged one repaired itself. I felt the human's relief as it came to the surface, pushing me back into oblivion. And then I knew no more.

Pain. Overwhelming pain as I became human again. Not only the agony of the change, but the searing pain in my damaged eye as it reformed, swelling up like a balloon, filling itself again with more of the gunk that had spilled onto my cheek. I rolled it around its socket to test my vision. It seemed to be working as well as it ever had, thank God. The one thing that truly scared me was the thought of being blind. I'd always felt I'd rather die than live without my sight but, judging from the events that night, it was something I no longer needed to fear, thanks to my lupine blood.

My leg throbbed to greater heights of pain while the damaged tissue changed and tried to repair itself. Just as the pain became unbearable I could feel something being pushed out of the limb, and then felt the small hole close over and heard something small and metallic fall the short distance to the ground. Finally the pain ended and I was fully human, where I lay in the soil, shaking from the after effects of the pain, naked and bloody. Something glinting in the dirt caught my eye and I found the bullet that had been embedded in my leg for most of the night. I didn't know what had happened, but I knew what it meant. The war had found me, and I welcomed it.

From then on, I couldn't go anywhere without being followed. I first noticed when I walked into town to meet up with Lizzy. I heard footfalls somewhere behind me. Whenever I stopped so did the footfalls, only to start up again as soon as I did, matching my pace. Yet when I turned round there was no one there.

I had to get into the habit of doubling back on myself and circling my destination, taking the longer route until I could lose them so I didn't lead them to my friends or my family. I was hoping even though they knew who I was, they still didn't know where I lived. Otherwise they'd have killed me in my sleep, wouldn't they? I could see no reason why they wouldn't have killed me already if they knew where I lived, since they had people in the police force to cover their arse when it came to the legal stuff. Hell, they were the police force from what Lady Sarah had told me, or enough of them were. For all I knew they could have members in the government too, and they probably had judges sympathetic to their cause in case it ever went to court. So I let them follow me when it suited me, and slipped away from them when I was sure they would cause no one else any harm. As long as they were only following me, there would be no bloodshed, no matter how much I thirsted for blood. I would let them make the first move, just to be sure this wasn't some kind of trap. Of course, they could still spring a trap even then, but from the way they were simply following me and hadn't yet attempted anything more, even when they'd had plenty of opportunities, I couldn't help feeling it was a trap they wanted me to walk into. I stuck to crowded places as much as I could, hoping they wouldn't risk anything with so many witnesses around. Surely they couldn't be immune to the law, even with a number of their people in high places.

Whenever I was forced to go somewhere quiet, or even deserted if I had to, there was little I could do to protect myself from their guns. I'd have slipped into wolf form, making it easier to dodge a bullet, but then I would have had to feed and that would have made me vulnerable too – they could track me down and shoot me while I fed.

They were biding their time, waiting patiently. I knew their patience wouldn't last forever, and the odds were stacked against me, though I wouldn't go down without a fight. The only questions were when would they strike and how many would die?

Chapter Twenty Two – Victim of War

Sweat trickled down my body in the summer heat. I forced one foot to move after another, my legs heavy, my body feeling like one awkward lump of flesh, melting under the blazing sun. I always hated the summer. I hated the heat, the long days and short nights, and all the bugs buzzing around. And judging from what Lady Sarah had said a couple of nights ago, she didn't think much of it either.

"Bah, the worst time of year for vampires. We have less time to feed and are forced to spend more time in the sleep of the dead. There is little time for anything else. I will welcome winter upon its return."

Well, people always associated the winter months with death. I wondered if that idea was more to do with the undead, rather than the natural world dying as people in more recent times took it to mean. In times gone by when people knew of our existence, they knew exactly what the longer nights meant; the greater numbers of deaths it brought under the longer hours granted to the undead to roam the earth. The undead ruled the winter months. Death ruled the winter months.

Vince had little to say about it. He'd said "Yeah, it's a bummer not having as long to do stuff, but it sure beats the hell out of spending eternity truly dead. Immortality comes with a price and I don't regret it."

People think of spring and summer as the time for new life. In that heat I wasn't so sure. How could anything survive the intensity of the sun beating down so hard on the land? Try as I might, I just couldn't keep cool. It was unbearable.

I reached my destination. It had felt like the longest walk to town I'd ever put myself through but it would be worth it. Mum and Dad were going out that weekend and I was stuck babysitting Amy. I'd complained about that, knowing I might not get any peace if she was feeling that way out. Though after the incident earlier in the year, I hoped she'd give me more space and find something to amuse herself with that didn't involve me. Mum had given me some money for a DVD as compensation. There were a couple of shops in town that sold nothing but DVDs and video games. My favourite of the two specialised in horror movies.

Fans beat the dead air, trying to breathe some life into it. Compared to outside, it was heavenly. For that reason alone I spent over an hour in there, looking at every movie the shop had to offer, before finally choosing Mary Shelley's Frankenstein. I almost forgot about the Slayers following me.

When I left the shop, a pleasant breeze had picked up. It had grown misty too, which seemed odd after the way the climate had been an hour ago, but I assumed the mist had blown in from the sea or something like that. I wasn't an expert on the weather so I didn't dwell on it for long.

The Slayers were quick to find me, even with the mist clinging to everything. It had grown so thick that if I reached out I could see my hand in front of me, but little else. Buildings suddenly loomed up ahead when I was within a few feet of them, only to disappear again moments later, swallowed up by the gloom. It didn't seem real, more like a dream world than reality. There could be anything hiding in the mist, waiting to jump me. It wasn't a comforting thought. Not after the bullet wound to my leg on the night of the prom.

A dark shape lurked somewhere up ahead. It came closer and I tensed, ready to fight. Then the mists parted and Lizzy stepped into view.

"Nick, I came to warn you. Do you know you're being followed? You didn't tell me you had a stalker." The last sounded like an accusation. Once again I was sorry I couldn't share my secrets with her. If only she knew. But she was human and this wasn't her world. I wouldn't drag her into my mess.

"No, I guess I forgot. Just some freak who's obsessed with me, nowt to worry about."

She shook her head. "I don't believe you. What's going on, Nick? You've been acting strange all year. I thought it was just Fiona's death, but it's more than that. Something's up."

I sighed. "Look, this is all I'm saying. I've changed more in this year than you can ever imagine. I'm mixed up in something I don't want you getting into, for your own safety."

She opened her mouth to argue but I held a hand up to stop her. She closed it again and let me finish. "I know you want to help me, but you can't so there's no point endangering you an' all. I've been dragged into a nightmare world of shadows. I know what lurks in the darkness. I'm learning what humans are capable of, what I'm capable of. I've seen things kids should never see. Don't throw away your childhood, your life, for me. Thanks for warning me, but you want to help some more? Then go home, you'll be safe there."

"No Nick, I'm not leaving you here," she said stubbornly. "What kind of trouble have you got yourself into?"

"Go home Lizzy, this is not your fight," I told her.

"No."

"Go home, you'll be safe there."

The footsteps of my pursuers were drawing closer. Was it meant to be a threat? This was the first time the Slayers had drawn so close. Usually they kept their distance.

She hesitated, uncertain.

"Go!" I roared, afraid for her.

She turned and ran. I nodded to myself, satisfied. I'd lost one friend to the wolf. I wouldn't lose anymore. I watched her retreating back until it was swallowed by the fog, whispering "And by God if I am destined to die today, I will take them with me."

With that I walked off, safe in the knowledge that at least if they got me, they wouldn't get Lizzy.

Screaming in the mist. I came to an abrupt halt, fear pounding my heart against my chest, so hard it hurt. I listened intently for anything else, but there was nothing. The screams came to a sudden stop, almost as if they mirrored my movements.

"Lizzy?" I whispered her name into the mist uncertainly, afraid that they would hear. Fear was taking over, twisting my guts into a painful knot. There was no answer. Only the unnatural fog, and the memory of the screaming long after the sound had died. Was it the last cry she would ever make? With a sudden certainty I knew what it meant.

"She was one of my closest friends," I said softly, anger clawing its way out again. I fought it back down, feeling it was not the time to give into my rage.

I should have felt sad at least, if not the horror that had been there when Fiona died, because in a way, this death was my fault too. And Lizzy had been even closer to me than Fiona. She truly had been there for me when I really needed her. Of all of those I considered friends she had been the only one to stick by me when death seemed certain at the jaws of the werewolf that fateful night, the only one who'd been more concerned with saving me than saving herself. But there was nothing, except the bitterness in my voice at the unfairness of it all.

"She was one of my closest friends," I repeated. "She was… She is dead."

I bowed my head, fighting to control the monster inside. The monster looked out through my eyes for a brief moment and it spoke, pouring all its malice, all its cruelty and all its rage into one sentence.

"Someone will pay for that."

Then it was gone, locked away again, to be called on when I needed it. It wanted blood. It didn't care whose. It didn't care so much about revenge, it was just the need to kill and it had been given the perfect excuse. I would kill again, and it didn't matter whether they were one of the enemies or an innocent bystander. And I would enjoy it, though revenge would be sweeter than a random death. Whoever had killed her would die by my hand, and I would enjoy that all the more.

Chapter Twenty Three – Prepare to Battle

"They killed Lizzy," I said, my voice dead and emotionless.

"Who?" Lady Sarah asked, face blank, impossible to read. We were in the graveyard and it was some time after midnight. No more than twelve hours had passed since Lizzy's death. Both vampires were sat on coffins in the mausoleum. I remained standing, pacing.

"Lizzy, the girl from your school?" Vince asked. "Your friend?"

I nodded. "It was me they were after. They know who I am. They've been following me, but until now they haven't even attempted to kill me, though there's been plenty of times when they could have shot me easily and got away with it. Then today, for whatever reason, they decided to do it, but it was misty and I think maybe they mistook her for me. Maybe they saw someone coming towards them and they panicked before they could see who it was. I don't know the reason, but Lizzy's dead and it should have been me."

"That does not make sense," Lady Sarah said. "I have never heard of them stalking a victim unless they intend to kill them that same night. For that matter, I have never heard of them attacking in a public place in daylight. And they do not allow for mistakes. The only humans I have known them to kill are those connected to the undead, through more than friendship. This does not make sense, why go to the trouble of following you if they do not intend to kill you?"

"Who cares why they did it, they have to pay," Vince said angrily, and I agreed with him. "I'm sick of running from them. We've spent centuries running. It's time we stood and fought them one final time, because time is all we have left and they'll even take that from us eventually. They chase us from our territories and we are forced to scavenge on animals, become animals ourselves. I don't mean changing shape, I mean the way they force us to live. We were not given the gift of eternity to spend it like this. Now they're coming for us, hunting us down like dogs. We can't keep running. They're gonna find us eventually and kill us. Well I ain't going down without a fight."

He fell silent and I took up the argument for him. "What does it matter if they kill us today or tomorrow, or in years to come? We'll be dead all the same. If we want eternity we have to fight for it. You told me once a great battle was fought and we lost. The survivors fled and lived to fight another day, but how many of them have gone down fighting since then? Too many. Those who went into hiding, like yourselves, may have survived longer, but it can't last. Now the time has come for another great battle in which the undead must either win to carry on the fight, or die and be lost to eternity."

"I told you, we are too few for another battle. They would slaughter us all," Lady Sarah argued.

"We have no other choice," Vince said. "The werewolf is right."

"And who will lead us?" she asked. "None of us here are powerful enough to lead what others we can gather. We will fight amongst ourselves and do more damage than the Slayers before the battle has even begun. Ever has that been our downfall; it is in our nature."

"Worry about that later. A natural leader will rise when the time is right," I said.

"Even so, we will be outnumbered. They will wipe us all out easily. Better to take the time we have left than throw it all away for nothing."

"We might as well be dead if we have to spend the rest of our time running. Besides, can you not make more vampires? There may be no more werewolves after I'm gone, but there will always be more vampires. Not even the Slayers can stop that, can they? And there must be more kinds of undead than vampires and werewolves. Both you and Vince mentioned zombies before. Are you sure they're all gone? And what about ghouls, ghosts, wraiths? Are they all myths?"

"They exist," Vince said quietly, as if he'd rather not talk about it.

"Yes, they exist. But it takes a powerful necromancer to raise the dead, especially as many as we will need for an army. There were free roaming zombies, but the Slayers wiped them out. Ghouls, ghosts and wraiths cannot be controlled so easily. And we could not make enough vampires in time. The Slayers will recognise a corpse destined to become a vampire and stake it long before it ever has chance to rise again. Even if we stole the body, it would raise suspicions."

"So we'll find a necromancer. We'll raise an army so terrible no one will dare to look upon them. The dead will fight for us, and think of the possibilities! The dead will always outnumber the living. Billions have died over the millennia, billions more than there ever will be alive at any one time. And for every Slayer we kill, we will add to our ranks. There must be someone you've met somewhere along the line who has the power."

"There is," Vince said. "And she's standing in front of you."

"What?" I said confused. "You can raise zombies? Why the hell didn't you tell me before?"

"It is not a power I wish to brag about. Some vampires have the power, as do some humans. Vincent is jealous, because we are descended from the same line, yet I was granted this particular power and he was not. Zombies are bound by the power that raised them. They are forced to obey the one who brought them back. That is, unless the necromancer has not the power to keep them under his control. Some are strong enough to bring back the dead but not to bend them to their will. Sometimes the zombies fall back into their graves, dead once more, but sometimes they have been given enough power to cling to their new life. I could raise the entire graveyard but that does not mean I could control them. They could turn on us. They would overwhelm us through sheer numbers and there would be nothing we could do to stop them from ripping us apart."

"It's a risk we have to take," I argued.

She looked unhappily from me to Vince, then finally bowed her head, admitting defeat. "Very well, I will do what I can."

Vince stood. "It's decided then. We'll call a meeting for other vampires and together we must convince them to fight. I'll see what I can do about ghouls and wraiths. For ghosts we need a psychic who can speak with the dead. Give us some time, I'll send word to you when we're ready to meet again."

"If we have time. If the Slayers decide to strike sooner we're screwed," I said.

"Wait, are you sure you were not followed here?" Lady Sarah asked.

"Nah, we would have heard others coming. They're only human," Vince replied.

"You are right, I am growing paranoid. Until the next time we meet," she said to me.

"Until the next time," I echoed. Now I knew I could avenge Lizzy's death, it was time to worry about my next trial: Saturday night.

Chapter Twenty Four – Heed This Warning

"No arguments while we're out, I want you both on best behaviour," Mum told us, the sentence punctuated by a roll of thunder. I could hear rain pounding the ground outside.

"Mum, we're teenagers now, not kids anymore. We'll be fine. Just go and enjoy yourselves."

"Don't be staying up too late and don't wait up for us," Dad ordered. A flash of lightning lit the night sky.

I rolled my eyes. Would they ever leave?

"Okay, well have fun while we're out," Mum said. "We'll be back around midnight."

And finally they walked out the door with a last goodbye and darted through the torrents of rain lashing down on them, into the car. I locked the door, then Amy and I stood at the window to watch them leave, a flash of lightning illuminating the scene for a brief second as they waved goodbye and drove off around the corner, and then they were gone.

I turned to Amy and said "I'll be down here, go please yourself and go to bed when you're ready."

"I'll be down here too," she replied, adding quickly "And I get the big screen!"

"No fair, you always get the big screen. I'm the oldest, that means I'm in charge so I say I get the big screen."

"Says who?"

"Says Mum and Dad."

She turned on the cute act. It really was an Oscar winning performance, but it didn't work on me. I gave in only because I knew if I didn't let her have the big screen she'd annoy me all night, and I'd never get through any of the films I planned to watch. Besides, after a month or so, depending how quickly the vampires spread the word and which way the battle went, I might never see her again. And it wasn't far off nine thirty already; I wouldn't have time for even just one film if I didn't start soon.

"Okay, you can have the big screen," I sighed.

A smug look spread across her face as she strutted into the lounge. I shook my head and went into the dining room.

I sat on the sofa by the patio door and pulled back the curtain to look out for a moment, though even with my superior night vision I couldn't see much. It was a dark moonless night, the black storm clouds hiding the stars and making the land pitch black. The only light came from the occasional flash of lightning, followed by the rumble of thunder over the ever constant sounds of the rain thundering against the glass and the howling wind, driving the storm onwards.

I let the curtain fall back over the door and turned back to the DVD I'd bought. Amy was scared of the dark and insisted on having the lights on throughout the house, but it just wasn't the same for watching horror movies. So I'd closed the door separating the dining room from the hall, shutting out the light. Without the lights on, the room was as dark as the black night outside, until the film started, and the light from the screen illuminated the area around the TV.

Amy came in after a while and sat with me, afraid of the storm. I sighed in frustration, wishing she could have slept over at a friend's house. I didn't like being disturbed when I was watching my movies, and of course the light had to be on while she was in there. When I realised there was no chance of watching the movie in peace I sought to comfort her, though I'm not sure I did a particularly good job. I had little comfort to give, so dead inside as I was, and I found it hard to act human. It was something of a relief when it reached ten thirty and she was ready for bed. She wouldn't go up on her own, so I walked her up the stairs to her room and tucked her in bed, wondering if it was the last time I'd ever play the role of the protective big brother. It was a role I was no longer suited for, and perhaps it wasn't a bad thing that it was one I might not have to play for much longer.

As I walked back downstairs I heard her breathing growing heavier and smiled to myself. She was already drifting into sleep. The house was mine. I could watch anything I wanted without being disturbed.

I sat back on the sofa and started watching the film where I left off.

It had just gone ten to eleven when I heard a scratching sound at the front door. I stiffened, wondering what the hell it could be. It sounded like something, possibly a large animal, trying to get in. My imagination turned against me, conjuring up images of zombies crashing through the glass panes on either side of the doorway and ripping their way through the internal door, ripping away what was left of the thin piece of wood that was the only remaining barrier between them and me. Then I reminded myself I was the monster, so why was I worrying? I was the one who was meant to be scratching at people's doors. I realised it was probably just a tree branch or something clawing at the door in the wind, so I relaxed and thought nothing more of it, until another sound came to me above the howling winds.

What was that? I could have sworn I heard something that wasn't caused by the wind. And then it became more noticeable, a distinct knocking on the patio door, loud enough to be heard above the sounds of the storm. There was something out there that didn't belong in our garden. Something was lurking in the dark, something that wasn't troubled by the harsh weather. And it was waiting just on the other side of the glass.

Heart beating faster, I threw back the curtains to reveal... nothing. The night was as black as ever, impenetrable without some faint light for my eyes to see by. I might have better night vision than any human, but I still needed some kind of light to see by, and there was no moon, no stars. There was only that blackness, deep enough to drown in. We had an outside light but when I tried the switch nothing happened: the bulb had gone. I decided I must have imagined the noises and closed the curtains again, going back to the film.

Minutes later the knocking came again. I froze and the hairs on the back of my neck began to stand on end. There was definitely something out there. And the most terrifying thing was, it could be *anything*. I of all men knew that. It wasn't an animal. Animals didn't knock on the glass like that. It was either a fellow member of the undead, or a human. But what was a human doing out at this time of night, in this weather? And why would they be in our garden? Could it be a Slayer? Or some other enemy that Lady Sarah hadn't told me about? I didn't know. I couldn't see anything when I looked out again, no matter how hard I strained my eyes.

The third time the noise came it was much louder.

A loud thump and I was sure the glass must have shuddered under the strain. I was on my feet for the third time and threw back the curtains a final time. A bolt of lightning flashed overhead, bright as day. It illuminated the thing that was lurking in the darkness and I fell back with a cry of horror.

The lightning died and the thing was hidden by darkness, until another flash revealed it again. And there, pressed against the glass, was the mutilated corpse of what appeared to be a man.

Another flash and this time, now I was over the initial shock, I came forward to examine the corpse that had been thrust against the door. Most of the skin had been removed from the face so that the muscle beneath showed, and even the bone was visible in some places. I wasn't sure if it had been disfigured to make it unrecognisable, from torture, or to scare me.

I stared into that mutilated face, and dull eyes stared back, but what really caught my attention most was the victim's teeth. The lips, and the flesh just above and below the lips, had been completely cut off so that the whole of the gums were visible and the teeth became more obvious. My eyes were drawn to the long canines. I'd thought I was looking at a man, but he was not human. He was a vampire. Or rather had been a vampire before they took his life, reducing him to just another corpse.

All went dark again and I could hear the body sliding down the pane of glass. The next flash of lightning revealed the blood smeared over the glass where the cadaver had slid down a little way, and I began to notice more about the vampire's corpse, which was naked to show the wounds he had suffered.

A network of wounds surrounded his body; some were mere flesh wounds, others deeper and damaging the internal organs beneath. I noted that part of his chest had been cut away to reveal his heart, which had a hole in it where a stake had been driven through, and his muscles were clearly visible in many places, like partway along what remained of his arms and legs. Some of the muscle itself had been hacked away from the lower half of each of the limbs. The feet and hands had been cut off. He was also missing most of his manhood. And I knew all of this was probably done while he was alive, since vampires can survive torture for longer. He would have even survived such extensive damage, if it weren't for the damage to his heart. And then with the next lightning flash a piece of metal caught the light and my heart stopped. A pendent with a strange symbol on it, and yes, next to it, there was the fang, where it had always been. *Vince!* First Lizzy, and now they'd taken Vince too. I tried not to think about what they might have done to Lizzy. At least she was human; there was only so much she would have had to endure before she died. She couldn't suffer as long as Vince had.

There was no doubt in my mind who was responsible. When I first saw the body I'd thought the Slayers wanted to scare me, and they'd succeeded. It was more the shock that had got to me rather than horror. After everything I'd seen and done I was beyond horror. But when I was over the shock the anger bubbled up, until the second shock hit me with the realisation of who this corpse was, and I felt numb. I could still feel the rage building somewhere inside, but for the most part I was numb. They'd killed two of my friends. Who was next? Family? And what did they want from me? My life? They could have that, it was in ruins anyway. Why not just shoot me? Could it be that they thought I had information? Maybe that's why they'd tortured Vince so badly, but if he didn't give them anything they'd be looking for someone else to question. Whatever the reason, it seemed they were making a point that they knew where I lived. I decided the mutilated corpse was probably meant as a message, or rather a warning, amongst other things. And I knew how I was going to respond to that message. I would have revenge for his and Lizzy's deaths.

I couldn't leave Vince's body there in that state. A part of me refused to believe it was really him. Just days ago I'd seen him, spoken to him. Did Lady Sarah know he was missing yet? I needed to tell her, but first Vince deserved a decent burial. And I had to remove the corpse before my parents came home, since it wasn't exactly something I could explain to them. But I was aware there was a chance the Slayers could still be out there somewhere. What if it wasn't a message at all, but a trap which I was about to walk right into?

I hesitated, unsure what to do. They'd already taken two of my friends. If I was stupid enough to go out into the night they could take me too. Was it worth the risk of capture by the Slayers, or was it better to risk my parent's wrath? Dad would try and blame it on me. There was no reasoning with him through a bad year. It would be my fault and I'd probably be grounded again. Not to mention they would send for the police and it would raise further suspicions, even if the Slayers intervened. It seemed I must choose between my life or my freedom, a tough choice.

Rain lashed against my face so hard it hurt. Within minutes I was soaked to the bone. It dripped off my face and my hair, the ends of my fingers, the strings on my jacket. I squinted my eyes to protect them from the rain and waited for another lightning strike. I was blind out there. There was still no natural light to see by and none of the neighbour's outside lights seemed to be working either. The glow from the street lights round the front was not powerful enough to reach the back garden. And the rain drove away any scents the wolf could have used to help us find our way around, as well as rendering my acute hearing all but useless. Even when the thunder wasn't growling above, the other elements combined made it hard to hear anything else. I might as well have been human; my heightened senses were of so little use that night. Finally the lightning came and I approached what remained of Vincent Desmodontidae.

Darkness fell once more and I was left to grope the body in the dark, which sounds somewhat perverse but there was nothing sexual about it. Even if I'd really been interested in the dead like I had so often joked about, I wouldn't have wanted a male corpse.

I got a grip on a pair of limbs. Whether they were arms or legs it was hard to say with the mutilations. He'd been dead at least a day because he'd already gone cold. I felt something moving in the flesh, probably maggots. That spurred me into action. I dragged the corpse backwards, nearly tripping at the edge of the garden that formed a kind of a step up from the patio. I slipped twice in the mud.

The next lightning flash showed I had reached the end of the garden. It would have been easier to dig a grave in wolf form, but that would mean I had to feed and hunting would be hard in such harsh weather, not to mention time consuming and I only had so long before my parents returned. I let my nails become claws and struggled to make a hole deep enough for the corpse, trying hard not to think about who it was. I was lucky it was raining so hard, otherwise I'd have had to wash the blood away too. And it made digging easier in the soft earth. It wasn't long before I was able to climb out and roll the corpse into the hole. Somehow I managed to snag part of it on the hedge that formed a borderline between our garden and the fields. I fought to pull it free and fell back into the grave with the corpse on top of me. The impact made me curse without thinking. Phantom Slayers moving through the darkness silenced me. The phantoms I thought I could see weren't really there, it was just my eyes straining to see something in the blackness. But that didn't mean I was alone.

When I climbed out for the second time I stood, dripping things thicker than blood. After I'd filled in the grave I made my way back to the house. I didn't like leaving Vince in an unmarked grave, but it was the best I could do for him in the circumstances. Besides, he was just as dead, either way. He didn't give a damn. He was beyond caring, and even if his spirit lived on in some other place, he wouldn't be visiting his own grave, so what was the point in marking it and leaving flowers? He wouldn't appreciate them.

Once inside, I slammed the door shut and locked it. Then I stood for a while, soaking from the rain, covered in blood and dirt, my back pressed to the door and panting heavily, relieved to be back inside and safe. Or at least it gave me the illusion of being safe. If they really wanted to, I knew there were enough Slayers out there to force their way inside to get at me, and they'd hurt anyone who got in their way.

And while I stood there I thought of Vince and Lizzy and their cruel fates. There was no grief, just anger. A year ago I'd have been devastated at Lizzy's fate. She'd been one of my closest friends. But I'd changed since then, and it seemed there was no longer room for anything other than anger, though maybe there was sadness somewhere inside that small part of who I used to be, the part that had survived long enough to make an appearance at the leaving assembly. Maybe there were other emotions, all lost in the anger and the numbness that had taken over my soul. If I even had a soul anymore.

Mum and Dad found me slumped against the door, lost in my own thoughts. That was as close to mourning as I ever came for those two lives. Mum believed me when I said I'd been out to bury a dead animal before it upset Amy. Dad refused to talk to me. So it was Mum who helped me clean up before I went to bed. No surprises there.

The horror lay buried at the end of the garden, but I couldn't keep the nightmares away. It was as if the horror called to them, reaching out with cold, bloody fingers, dragging me into the darkness of my mind. A new nightmare started, one I'd never had before, and all I could do was ride it.

I was inside a large building, walking down a corridor. I hadn't been there before but it felt like some kind of a prison. Official looking men in military style uniforms stood outside a door, looking straight ahead. They were armed and could have stopped me if they'd wanted, but the guards took no notice of me. I went through the door and I knew in the dream they couldn't see or hear me. There was a girl tied to a chair inside, head bowed in despair as if she'd given up hope of being rescued.

Aughtie stood in the room with her, sharpening some kind of tool. It looked like a torture device, and when I looked back at the girl I realised that was exactly what it was. She was wearing a t-shirt and jeans, and I could see her bare arms were covered in cuts and bruises. It looked like somebody had been beating the shit out of her, and now they were going to try the torture device. But I couldn't let them do that. I didn't know who the girl was but I couldn't just let them hurt her for no reason. Maybe she was a criminal, but no prison I knew of allowed this kind of thing to go on, at least not in the UK. So it probably wasn't a prison, and she could be an innocent.

The girl didn't even look up when Aughtie started walking towards her, brandishing the torture device threateningly, and I couldn't take it any longer.

"No!" I yelled.

At first I didn't think they could hear me. Aughtie certainly couldn't, and neither could the guards outside, but the girl finally looked up, a mixture of pleading and hope in her blue eyes staring at me through a thick curtain of bushy light brown hair, and I realised I did know her. The hair hid most of her face, but I still recognised her.

"Lizzy?" I whispered, unable to believe it.

Then flames swallowed up her face and the dream changed, and that's when it really became a nightmare. Lizzy was suddenly reaching to me through flames. Then we were on a battlefield. No, I was on a battlefield. Lizzy had vanished. Zombies surrounded me and other things I had no name for. I tried to make sense of the sudden change of environment. The zombies were fighting humans, Slayers I presumed. And Aughtie pushed her way through to me. She could see me now. I don't know what happened next, she was just suddenly there in front of me, raising a sword. The next thing I knew, I felt a great pain in my chest and time seemed to slow down, though it was never real to begin with. I looked down at my body to see the sword submerged in it. Aughtie began to laugh as I fell to my knees, hands clutching at the cold metal in vain, trying to pull it out, blood staining my bare skin. I opened my mouth as if to speak, but only more blood came out. The dream world turned black, my life draining away…

I woke clutching my chest. The dream had been so real it was as if I could feel real pain where the sword had pierced my heart. And Lizzy, I felt sure she was real. I remembered what Lady Sarah had told me of dreams and I knew what it meant.

Chapter Twenty Five – The Beast Breaks Loose

"Lizzy's alive," I said.

"What?" Lady Sarah asked, distracted. I'd found her feeding in a dark alley, her fangs buried deep into a boy not much older than I was back then. She'd looked to be enjoying it more than the boy; her face full of pleasure and hunger and something else inhuman, while the boy had clearly been terrified, but she'd done something to him, so that he couldn't scream. Even as he lay bleeding to death he couldn't scream.

"Lizzy's alive," I repeated.

"You're sure?"

"Yeah, and I have to save her. She'd do the same for me."

"No. If the Slayers have kept her alive, it is a trap. Wait until we have gathered the others, then if she is still alive we will go for her."

"What if it isn't a trap? She may not have that long," I argued.

"She does not know about our world?" I shook my head. "Then she has no valuable information to give them, thus there is no other reason for them to keep her alive. You will be killed if you go alone."

I opened my mouth to argue but she held up a hand to stop me and I let her continue. "You are no good to her dead. Give me a couple more days to contact the others, then we will take those that wish to fight and there will be enough of us to rescue your friend."

I still wasn't convinced. I'd never been good at waiting and there was no way I was going to wait around for the Slayers to kill Lizzy. But I didn't tell the vampire that.

"Lady Sarah, there's something else. Lizzy's not the only one they took." I told her about Vince's grim fate. The boy started to convulse, unnoticed by the two of us.

"No, it cannot be," she whispered, staring into space, shocked. "He cannot be gone."

"Are you okay?" I asked. I knew it was a stupid question but I didn't know what else to say.

She drew in a deep breath and pulled herself together, though I knew Vince's death was affecting her more than she'd ever let on. Maybe she'd even cry for him when I left. I didn't know how close they'd been, but on some level she was deeply shaken by his passing. "I will be alright. Is there anything else I need to know?"

I hesitated. I'd planned to tell her about the rest of the dream, but after the way she'd taken the news about Vince, I didn't want to give her any more shocks for the night. Still, she needed to know. "Lizzy's alive, but that's not all. Even if I wait until we are ready for battle, if I save her, it means I'll die."

That's what the dream meant. But it didn't matter. I wouldn't leave Lizzy to the Slayers. I wouldn't let them do to her what they'd done to Vince. I'd tried to protect her from being dragged into this mess and I'd failed. But unlike me she could still get out. I was in it now until I died. She was still human and hopefully still ignorant of our existence; if she got out now she had a life to go back to. I couldn't stay in the human world any longer. Her life was worth more than mine in the circumstances.

"Nothing is certain. Many will die in the coming battle. I hope you are not one of them."

With that comforting sentence she spared the boy a final glance and was gone. He died seconds later. I didn't know how much blood she needed to survive, but either she preferred to take it from the living and this victim was no longer any interest once he was too far gone, as he had been once we'd finished talking, or she was already satisfied. Or perhaps she hadn't gone in search of more prey at all, perhaps she'd gone to contact other vampires, or maybe even mourn Vince. After nearly a year she was still a mystery.

I sighed and started walking aimlessly. I hadn't really expected help from the vampire. I'd had to do something though. After the nightmare I couldn't sleep. Lizzy needed me. So I'd gone to find Lady Sarah, knowing I had to tell her about Vince as well as Lizzy, and received neither comfort nor knowledge for my troubles. I was hoping Lady Sarah might have at least given me something to go on, like where they might be holding her. Perhaps she didn't know herself.

I had one last hope of finding them. Aughtie had been in the dream. It had been so realistic I didn't think that was a coincidence and that could mean only one thing. She was a Slayer.

I'd been surprised that she'd been in the dream and now I'd realised what it meant, I couldn't help feeling shocked that she was one of the Slayers. It made sense though; that was why the wolf had been so scared in that first English lesson if it already knew, and why she'd been the hunter in that one nightmare that had triggered the change. It must have come across her that first full moon and recognised her scent. I just hadn't thought they'd be anyone I'd know. In my imagination they'd always been shadows in the darkness with no names or faces, as if they were the monsters, not us. But if I was going to help Lizzy, I didn't have time for shock.

I went to the same deserted part of town I'd used before and changed to wolf form. Then I ran back to the school, not caring who saw me. If the Slayers found me first I'd force them to take me to Lizzy. I didn't think they'd shoot me on sight. They'd passed up too many chances to kill me, which could only mean they wanted me alive for something.

When I reached the school and broke my way into the English classroom, I touched the wolf part of my mind, tentatively at first, afraid it would take over and start to hunt. I could feel the instincts there and I used them to help pick up Aughtie's scent. It took a while, since I'd never tried anything like this before, but I found it easy enough in the classroom, though I felt uneasy there. I felt like I was being watched. It was like Aughtie spent so much of her life there, her presence could still be felt, even when she was miles away. I lost the trail in the corridor outside and couldn't pick it up again. Growling in frustration, I left the school and searched the grounds. There was no hint of her in the car park or on the field, and I realised she'd probably left by car. It was useless. I had no way of tracking her. After crossing the field several times I was ready to give up, when I heard someone behind me. I started to turn when something smashed against my skull and I fell to the ground, unconscious.

When I slowly began to regain consciousness, my vision was slightly blurred, probably something to do with the blow to my head. Judging from my other senses, I was lying on a hard, cold metal floor, which I was soon to learn made up the base of a small cage, only just big enough for me to stand and walk five small paces from wall to wall as a human.

The cage was in a large room, which I guessed from the reinforced walls and doors was some sort of compound, and it seemed the walls were soundproof since my sensitive ears couldn't pick up any sounds beyond the room I was locked in. Probably so the public can't hear the screams, I thought bitterly to myself, knowing who my captors must be. Lizzy was probably nearby, for all the good that knowledge did me. I couldn't do anything for her while I was stuck in a cage.

My vision had not completely cleared, but I became aware of human scents within the room, and with the wolf's help, could pick out five males, each holding a piece of metal which I could only be a gun. So someone had placed guards around the room, more than I'd seen with Lizzy in the dream. Either the dream hadn't been accurate or they were afraid of me. I was willing to bet on the latter. The number of guards seemed a bit over cautious, though I couldn't blame them if they'd seen first hand all the damage I'd caused. Still, it was a shame they'd chosen to exercise so much caution, as the guards would complicate things when it came to escaping. But I wouldn't give up so quickly. There had to be some way out, some weakness somewhere, and I'd find it.

I stood silently, able to see properly again, and took in as much of the dimly lit room as I could before the guards noticed I'd regained consciousness. The guards were stood with their backs to me as if they were waiting for something. I could also make out a thick metal slab along one wall with chains built into it. Some sort of torture device? Or was it used for some kind of experiment? I realised there was a dark stain on the floor around it. Blood. It was too old for the wolf to learn anything from the smell, but I guessed it was from another undead, maybe a werewolf or maybe something else. I couldn't know if the room had been specifically adapted to hold werewolves or whether they were all like that, built to hold almost anything.

Having learnt as much as I could from my surroundings, with no way of knowing where the compound was, or how far from home or the nearest town I was, or even whether it was day or night, I leaned forward on the bars, hoping to learn something more from the guards before anyone else came into the room.

But as soon as my hands touched the bars a burst of electricity jolted through my body, throwing me back against the wall with a yelp, and filling the room with the smell of burning flesh.

Two of the guards looked around and smirked, but the others were more disciplined and didn't even flinch. Grimacing, I looked at my hands and saw the skin had been burnt off, though it was nothing a quick transformation wouldn't heal. Then I remembered I'd been a wolf when they'd caught me. It seemed I'd transformed back to human at some point. I hadn't even known that was possible while I was unconscious, but I was wishing I'd have stayed in wolf form. Two transformations without feeding in between had left hunger ravaging my innards, so powerful it was nauseating. While I had the chance I started to change, concentrating on my hands. I watched as they healed over, hardening into paws, and then reversed the transformation. I wondered why I wasn't being electrocuted on the metal floor, until I noticed the plastic casing round the base of the bars. So I'd learnt I couldn't break out through those bars, something that had obviously been taken into consideration when designing the compound. There was no window, no other weak points that held any possibilities. It didn't look like I was going anywhere soon. Damn.

I was contemplating my fate when none other than Aughtie herself walked into the room.

She swaggered over to the cage to taunt me. I watched her with hungry eyes, feeling my tongue slide out, wanting to taste her sweet flesh, dripping and wet with blood. But I couldn't harm her while I was behind bars and she knew it.

"So we meet again, Nick," she said.

I didn't answer but met her gaze. I didn't let on that I couldn't remember the last time we'd met outside of school, when there'd been no pretence of who either of us truly was. Since I'd been in wolf form when they caught me it meant I was naked in front of her, but it didn't bother me like it would've when I'd been mostly human, and I no longer bothered to cover myself.

"I hope the accommodation is to your liking. It's such a challenge to keep any of your kind captive, but I feel the electric door is a nice touch, a stroke of brilliance if I do say so myself," she said, gloating at her own masterpiece.

"Shouldn't you be out teaching Shakespeare somewhere to someone that cares?" I asked. Maybe it wasn't wise to goad her while I was at her mercy, but I couldn't help it. She was my English teacher for God's sakes; she didn't belong in this world, in this war. But then, neither did I. In many ways I was still just a kid, even though the curse had forced me to mature faster than other teenagers. I hadn't known what I was asking for when I'd wanted to be one of the monsters. And now I was one for real and all I wanted was my humanity back, though I knew it was too late for that. Even if someone freed me of the curse, I'd already become a killer. And there's no going back when you cross that line.

"Teaching is what I do for a living, but this, this is my great purpose in life."

That statement didn't inspire me with much confidence. It seemed I was dealing with yet more insanity. She really believed it too, I could hear it in her voice. She really thought her crusade as a Slayer was what she was meant to do, why she was put on the planet. She droned on for a bit about serving God, ridding the world of evil, and something about being chosen to be a leader of this great army. I soon lost interest and gave her the same treatment I'd have given any teacher in any situation. I switched off. My blank face was turned towards her as if I was listening, but no one was home. I hid somewhere inside my skull and watched a few of my own fantasies while her voice washed over me, a few of them involving her screaming in pain. My mind was still reeling slightly at learning the leader of the Slayers in the area was my English teacher. It felt like something out of a B-movie.

When I thought she was going to go on forever I said "Oh please, God doesn't give a damn, otherwise why would He suffer us to exist in the first place? Okay, so some guy wanted to be a hero and put humans back at the top of the food chain, so he created his own little army to kill us all off and make the world a better place. That's all down to humanity. God had no part in it, if He even exists. Besides, I didn't think you believed in God. From the way you go on at school, I thought you worshipped Shakespeare and all those poets you go on about."

She didn't seem to know what to say to that, but I'd succeeded in angering her.

"You know nothing of us or our history. If you knew, you would not talk about the first of us with such disrespect. That's what this generation needs. Respect. Yes," she whispered the last, a dreamy look passing over her face, before she pulled herself together. "But enough of this, there is time for idle talk later. We know you are gathering an army for some kind of last stand. Werewolves alone can walk in sunlight and we believe you are the last. So your army needs the cover of darkness. Give me their daylight resting places and we will release you, unharmed."

I said nothing. Even if I had known any more about the army the vampires were supposedly gathering, I would not have betrayed them. If the Slayers had gone to such lengths to capture me for questioning so they could massacre our army while they slept through the day, then they must be growing desperate. They must have felt we posed a real threat to them if they were trying to avoid meeting us in honest battle. So they'd wanted me alive to put a stop to the battle, but as soon as they learnt I didn't know anything I had to assume that meant I would no longer be of any use and they would just kill me. I had to be careful not to reveal how little I knew, or my cage would quickly become my tomb.

"How many are there?"

I stared stubbornly at a brick in the wall just above her head, trying not to give anything away.

She sighed and I wasn't sure if it was in frustration or to do with pleasure. "I didn't think you'd be so cooperative to begin with. But what if I told you we have developed a cure for the curse? Think about it, Nick. You can walk away from all this; go back to your human life, a normal teenage boy again. They need never know you betrayed them and they'll no longer be a threat to anyone after we've finished with them."

She was lying, I could see it in her eyes. Still I said nothing.

She sighed once more. "If that's the way you want it to be then fine, we'll do this the hard way. We have other ways of making you talk. I will break you if it comes to that. And one way or the other you will tell me everything, then I will force you to watch as they all die."

"And afterwards?" I asked, undaunted, finally breaking my silence.

"Let's just say I've got something special in mind," she whispered so that only I could hear. Raising her voice again, she commanded "No food unless he talks!"

She was about to go but then, with a smile, she added "I'll visit you again when you're in a more talkative mood. No food is just the beginning, think on that."

With that she swaggered out of the room, leaving me alone with the guards and my thoughts. Watching her go, I noticed she pressed the palm of her right hand onto a small panel before the door opened. So if I did find a way out of the cage I'd need someone to get me out of the room. Were the guards authorised to open the door or was it restricted to their superiors? Surely they'd have to change over at some point, but would someone escort them through the compound or could they come and go freely? I hoped they'd be able to open the doors, because even if I somehow broke free of the cage, the chances of someone like Aughtie being in the room at the same time were minimal.

I sank to the floor. No food. To a werewolf that was the worst possible torture and Aughtie knew it, especially when I could smell prey just beyond the bars of the cage. I wasn't sure exactly what effect starvation would have on me, or even whether I could die of starvation or not, but I remembered that one winter night without feeding that had left me as weak as if I'd been starving for months. Granted I'd been eating little, but the wolf had still fed when it was allowed to roam free, other than that one night. For some reason after the two transformations that night I'd been captured I was much stronger than the last time in winter, but I knew if I didn't feed soon I wouldn't have the strength to change and that would make it harder to escape. And even if starvation couldn't kill me, I knew enough about myself to know it would exact a heavy toll upon my mind if nothing else.

Did anyone know I was missing yet? Were the police looking for me? Or did the Slayers have enough hold over them that there would be no search party, no rescue from the authorities? I wondered what they'd told my parents. Maybe my body would turn up days later from some tragic accident and no one would ever know the truth. The thought didn't give me much confidence. I didn't want to die there, at the mercy of the Slayers. They could just shoot me through the bars and there was nothing I could do about it. I hated that. If they killed me I wanted to go down fighting, not caged and powerless to even defend myself. Maybe it was years of bullying, but the thought of being at anyone's mercy awoke the anger. And I knew if I was going to escape I needed that anger, but not yet. I had to save it, let it take over when the time was right, and if I let it grow strong enough I'd be beyond pain.

Maybe the vampires would realise I was missing and help get me out, but until then I was on my own. If they came at all, which I knew I couldn't rely on. Would they risk their lives to save mine? We were allies, yet I realised we hardly knew each other. Lady Sarah remained much of a mystery. Sometimes it was easy to forget Vince was a vampire. He was just another one of the guys. But both of them had been around for centuries and I'd barely scratched the surface. They'd told me a bit about themselves but I didn't know enough about them to call them friends. I'd trusted them because I'd had to, there'd been no one else there for me once I'd become a werewolf. It had been nearly a year and I still wasn't sure whether I could count on them or not. Of the two, Vince was probably more likely to want to bail me out than Lady Sarah, I felt. And then I remembered Vince was dead. If I failed to get out on my own, Lady Sarah may be all that stood between life and death, my last hope. Another comforting thought. I was doomed.

So, no food, that meant I was stuck in human form for the time being. I couldn't waste energy transforming needlessly, and as I'd already accepted, I might not even be strong enough after a couple of days. I had no idea how quickly the hunger would weaken me. Perhaps the full moon had made it worse last time, I just didn't know. Or maybe it was the fact I'd barely been eating in between the full moon nights whereas more recently I'd been feeding well. The more I thought about it, the more convinced I became of how that must have something to do with it. It was only logical.

Regardless, I didn't completely understand the way my body worked. Biology had been hard enough to understand to begin with, thanks to Brewins, without the complication of being a werewolf adding to that. The transformation I underwent every month should have been physically impossible, so God only knew what happened inside my body since I'd turned.

Somehow I was betting I only had one chance at escape. If I failed they'd either kill me or they'd take greater security precautions. No doubt they'd kill me eventually, once they knew I was useless to them, it was just a matter of time. With that cheerful thought, I closed my eyes and let sleep wash over me, saving energy for when I would need it. I'd come up with a plan at some point, but until inspiration struck I might as well get some rest. At least I tried to tell myself that. My mind was blank and I knew I was probably fucked.

The first thing I was aware of when I awoke was the hunger. It had long since passed the point of becoming unbearable. The guards were no longer another obstacle to overcome, after the electric bars of the cage. They had begun to smell like dinner. I listened to their hearts beating and dreamed of their warm flesh between my teeth, their blood running down my jaws. I groaned while my stomach gurgled and tried not to think of food. After a while I slipped back into sleep.

The next time I opened my eyes it was to find Aughtie watching me on the other side of the cage. I felt like a zoo animal. Actually that wasn't a bad analogy. Things were getting worse, now there wasn't only the hunger to greet me when I awoke. I needed to pee. And there was nowhere to go, save a small drain in one corner of the cage, and no privacy. If I didn't come up with an escape plan soon, I was starting to think that maybe I should just kill myself and save the Slayers the trouble. It'd be less painful and it'd take care of a few problems.

I stood up, stiff from sleeping on the hard floor, and tried not to show any of my discomfort.

Aughtie watched me with those cold eyes and finally she spoke. "You must be hungry. Tell me where your allies are and I'll give you fresh meat. You can choose anyone within the compound, and once you have eaten your fill I'll set you free."

"Yeah right, like you would sacrifice one of your people and then just let me walk out of here. I'm not that stupid."

"My people are nothing to me, just pawns to serve my greater purpose."

"Okay, so maybe you would feed me. But I know I'm not getting out of here alive," I said.

"Perhaps not," she agreed. "But I could make you more comfortable before the end."

I snorted disbelievingly. "Next you'll be trying to tell me you've found a cure again."

"Do you know what happens to a werewolf when they're deprived of food? Have you ever wondered why you are always hungry after a transformation, or why you kill so many in one night to fill the wolf's almost insatiable hunger, or how you can eat so much? Or why you are left so weak if you do not feed, having become a wolf and changed back to human again, and vice versa?"

I frowned. It seemed she knew the answers to the questions, and I had to admit I was curious, but then, she always had that air to her that she knew everything. Haughty Aughtie my Mum called her, and it was true. She treated everyone as an underling. She always made you feel like she knew some great universal secret, and that made her somehow better than you.

"I still don't know everything about the curse," I said carefully, not wanting to reveal how little I knew. For all I knew, my ignorance could give her some sort of advantage.

"As technology evolved, so did we. Our methods have changed. Scientists are constantly searching for answers, and we are no different. It has proven useful to learn about undead biology. Before we drove werewolves to the brink of extinction, we learnt what we could from them. Now we know that to become a werewolf you must already have wolf blood running through your veins, though you cannot transform until you have been bitten by another werewolf. The transformation relies on DNA. Direct descendants of wolves can revert to the form of their ancestors as they have already got a small percentage of wolf DNA, whereas direct descendants of apes cannot, because they were not wolves to begin with.

"When a wolf descendant is bitten, more wolf DNA is somehow passed on, thus heightening the percentage of wolf DNA within the victim. We still do not know exactly how this works. We do know that the bite kills the victim, as with vampires, and the wolf DNA reanimates the body, but we're still not sure after that. One theory is that every cell in the body mutates and the DNA within the nucleus changes, causing the victim's genetic makeup to change until it becomes closer to that of a true wolf. Whatever may happen, the victim then has a higher percentage of wolf DNA which allows them to change form. We're not sure why it happens involuntarily during the full moon, but we think this time in the lunar cycle has some significance to the lupine part of the brain, making the percentage of wolf DNA stronger, so that it asserts itself over the human DNA and causes the victim to change form. It also awakens the lupine instincts trapped within the victim's subconscious, thus causing them to lose control and become wolves both mentally and physically.

"After a werewolf has changed, it must feed. The change itself requires energy, more than the body can cope with, and the werewolf has to eat much more than a mortal wolf could stomach to support the change back to human, and still they will be hungrier than usual through the day. If the werewolf fails to feed, the transformation back to human leaves it weak, most of its energy gone. You should have been too weak to stand when you regained consciousness, if it hadn't been for us. I had you hooked up to a drip so I could draw out your suffering until the end. How long can you survive without food? Months? Years? At least I can offer you a quick death if you tell me what I need to know."

Amongst all the science there were some good explanations for what was happening to me. And believe me, that's the simplified version. It explained a lot, and from what I understood, it was easy to see why there was no cure, for how do you possibly reverse a mutation like that?

"I'll be just as dead, no matter what I tell you. What's a bit of suffering before the end? A bit of pain then an eternity free of it. Sounds good to me."

"Fine, have it your way," she said. Her voice was calm, but I could see a muscle twitching round her eyes. I'd pissed her off again and if I wasn't more careful, I was sure I'd be dead by the end of the week.

I was left alone once more, except for the guards, with nothing to do. I slumped against the wall and tried to ignore my full bladder and empty stomach. Eventually I fell asleep again.

Time passed. Every time I awoke the hunger seemed to increase, while I grew steadily weaker. And every time Aughtie was there waiting for me, growing a little more impatient, offering me food and freedom. I couldn't be bothered talking to her anymore. I think my silence only angered her further.

Water was pushed through the bars from time to time. It was in a plastic bowl to get past the electric bars. But it was meat I really wanted.

It got to the point where the hunger was taking over everything, sapping my strength. The same hunger that had almost driven me to dig up the graves after the first time I'd changed was taking control again, and this time the only meat available was my own. I think it would have driven me to eat the flesh off my own limbs if I didn't have the strength to fight it. I might have done, if it wasn't for the knowledge that it would take more energy to heal the wounds than I would take in from my limbs. It was getting to the point where I would eat anything though.

The hunger was quickly becoming all consuming, as if it now defined me and I would be nothing without it. I could feel my sanity slipping away again. It was like when I'd gone through the mating season; instincts ravaged my brain until there was nothing left, except for a beast more primitive than even the rage driven monster. God only knew what I was becoming. It wasn't wolf and it wasn't human, that much I knew.

More time passed. I was losing my humanity more and more by the day. I couldn't even keep hold of my human form anymore. I felt things transforming, slowly because there wasn't enough energy for it to happen and I was still trying to fight it, but it was happening all the same. Eventually I'd reach wolf form, and I didn't think I had the energy or the sanity to change back. I'd spend the rest of eternity as an animal, or even worse as a monster, depending on how much of my brain survived. If I didn't die first.

One of my eyes was the first thing to go, the left one. It turned amber and there was nothing I could do about it. Then my right ear became pointed and furred and travelled up to the top of my head, and my teeth were starting to grow longer and more pointed. My face became a mess, becoming more bestial, like a gargoyle. If it hadn't been for the ear or the eye there would be nothing in my facial features to define what I was becoming, but anyone looking at me would know it wasn't human.

I was growing hairier and I had a tail. My nails were more like claws. I needed help and fast, because I knew, if I completely lost my sanity, I'd lose any hope of escape.

I awoke to find I wasn't alone in the cell. I blinked in confusion, and reached out a hairy hand to the girl stood beside me, to see if she was real. It was Grace.

Thinking had become difficult. There was no need for it anymore. The hunger truly was everything and instinct had almost completely taken over. But somewhere in the chaotic mess better known as my brain there was confusion, because the human left in me knew she shouldn't be there. She couldn't be there. Was I losing my sanity quicker than I thought?

I opened my mouth to speak, frowned, trying to find the words, and finally managed her name. "Grace?"

She nodded.

I tried again. With effort, I could reach beneath the instincts, and find the thoughts and knowledge that made up my humanity. Once I'd accessed that part of my brain talking grew a little easier, though my speech was slurred slightly, as if I'd been drinking. I felt drunk. Everything was confused. I couldn't even remember what I was supposed to be, human or wolf or something else.

"What you doing here?" I asked.

"I came to keep you company, take your mind off the hunger."

"Help me," I pleaded. "Need get out. Need food."

She shook her head. "I can't help you. You have to do it yourself."

"Then kill me."

"You want to die here? Alone?" she said, shocked.

I laughed madly, fighting off the drunken feeling for the time being, my speech becoming better. I was able to form proper sentences again. "Alone, surrounded by people, what does it matter? We're all alone in the end. It only takes seconds and then you pass away and there's no one there for you. And anything's better than this. Look at me. I'm a mess."

"You can't lose hope. And when you die, you won't be alone. God will be waiting," she said with feeling.

"No He won't. God doesn't give a damn about us," I spat.

"You're wrong. He waits for all of us on the other side, so that we may never be alone again," she said, her conviction immune to my pessimism.

"Oh yeah, like He's here for us in life when we need Him most? Like He's here for me now?" I sneered. She'd touched a nerve and my instinct was to lash out in retaliation, fighting pain with pain. A year ago I would have kept my silence, regardless of my thoughts and feelings, but a year ago I wasn't half wolf. "You can pray all you want in that empty building but He ain't listening."

She turned away, tears in her eyes, refusing to believe me.

"Why are you really here Grace? I don't want to listen to your religious crap."

"It is all I have to offer," she replied.

I frowned again, and struggled to think. Understanding dawned. "I get it, you're a hallucination. You're me keeping me company. But why you? Why didn't I hallucinate Mum or Amy, or a closer friend? Sure, we talked in school but I barely know you."

"Your brain picked me for a reason, think on that. Perhaps you have more faith than you think," she answered.

"Well thanks brain but I don't need an imaginary friend," I said and closed my eyes. Maybe this was my brain's way of trying to keep me sane, a way to cling to my humanity, but I really didn't want to discuss religion with Grace, real or imaginary. When I opened them she'd gone. I smiled and lay staring at the metal ceiling, ignoring the guards laughing at me. If I got out of there they wouldn't be laughing for long.

243

Aughtie visited me a few more times. She seemed to find everything fascinating: the transformations, both mental and physical, my way of dealing with it, my stubbornness, refusing to talk when there was a chance that would save me. I watched her hungrily, and as my mind became more primitive I even tried to lunge at her through the bars. Electricity travelled through my body and I fell back with a yelp, the smell of burning flesh and hair filling the room again. Aughtie just laughed. I licked the wounds but couldn't transform to heal them that time. I was growing weak, and if I didn't get out soon I'd be in the same state as that winter morning after the full moon. If it went that far I would be beyond escape.

Eventually the transformation reached the same halfway point I'd been stuck in the night I'd killed Melissa White. It was roughly the same half man, half wolf form as before, though my hands were still basically hands, just furred and clawed. They definitely weren't closer to being paws like they'd been before; I'd retained my opposable thumbs. One eye was still human while the other was lupine, but the rest of my head had become a wolf's.

The primitive brain didn't have much use for eyesight. It smelled the guards, heard their breathing, the beating of their hearts, different men to those who had been there last time I lay down to sleep. My mouth watered and I dreamed of ripping apart their soft flesh, the taste of blood and raw meat, the smell of it. A growl escaped my throat. The guards raised their guns in alarm, the noise breaking the silence, the only sound I'd made in what must have been days. They relaxed when they saw I was still sat hunched over, ape-like, in a corner of the stinking cell. The beast didn't care about relieving itself in privacy.

The room wasn't as sound proof as I'd first thought. I cocked an ear at the sound of someone walking down the corridor. More prey. The beast knew better than to lunge at the bars this time. It had learnt touching the bars meant pain, though I'd been wounded a few more times before the lesson stuck. Burns covered my arms and chest where I'd thrown myself against the cage door. I listened to the prey until the walls muffled the sound, and then licked my wounds. They were healing faster than if I'd been mortal, but the transformation hadn't been quick enough or complete enough to completely heal them over. There was nothing left of the human. All I had was the hunger and the pain. The beast had learnt to accept it. So I sat there, no thoughts running through my head except for instinct and a few vague images of blood and flesh.

The lights overhead flickered and died, plunging us into darkness. I cocked my ears and scented the air but there was nothing to hear or smell, though somehow I sensed something was different. Something had changed.

One of the guards said something and I smelt his fear. Panic spread to the others like wildfire, and then they all fell silent, breathing hard, hearts pounding when they heard my low growl.

Chapter Twenty Six – Escape

I threw myself at the bars and they bent with the force, but nothing else happened. I hit the cold metal again and there was no pain, no crackle of electricity. In my weakened state it took two more attempts before the bars broke from the force and I was free. I burst forth from my prison to the sound of gunfire. The guards were blind in the darkness but they'd all heard the bars rattling. They weren't taking any chances.

I was hit in the arm and anger flared up inside. I barely noticed the pain in the face of the hunger, and now rage was building. Soon I'd be beyond pain and nothing was going to stop me, except for a lucky shot through the heart or the brain.

The guards might have been blind but I had no trouble locating them in the darkness. I didn't need sight. Scent and sound led me to them and I fell upon the nearest one. More gunfire punctuated the sounds of his screams. I dragged him off towards the torture table, making it harder for the others to hit me, devouring him in minutes. I ate two more and the hunger was beginning to die down, while my strength was returning. The remaining two men were still firing into the darkness at things they couldn't see, until their guns clicked empty. I heard a scream of frustration and someone banging on the door, trying to get out. One of them started to cry.

I went for the man by the door first since he was nearest. He felt my breath on his neck as I closed in and drew a knife. He plunged it blindly into the dark just as my clawed hands grasped him and I fell back with a yelp, the blade deep in my shoulder. I crashed down onto the crying man. He screamed and I turned on him, ripping him apart.

Seconds later I felt a second blade pierce my back, just beneath the ribcage. Another lucky strike, but the man's luck was running out. I grabbed hold of him again, one hand around his throat, one around a leg, and twisted. There was a sharp crack, barely audible against the man's screams and I dropped him bodily onto the floor, where he lay still, spine broken. Unable to escape, completely paralysed from the waist down, he lay helpless while I ate him alive. He was still dying when the lights came back on, revealing scenes of gore and horror.

Most of the corpse's faces were frozen in silent screams, though one had been literally smashed in, the bone exploding inwards, shards of his own skull sticking in his brain the thing that killed him. I'd been too greedy to completely strip them to the bone. Organs lay strewn across the floor, most bitten through, some half eaten. Blood pooled on the floor, and pieces of flesh lay scattered around like gruesome jigsaw pieces. A couple of limbs lay a few metres away from their owners. I picked up a leg and gnawed on it like a dog with a bone. Then the hunger was gone and the beast grew docile. And somewhere, deep down in my brain where I had been more than instincts before the hunger took over, I knew I had to escape and I was dimly aware of what to do.

I crawled over to one of the men and ripped a hand clean off the arm without any effort. With the power back on, I was able to use it to open the door. The hand left a bloody imprint on the panel Aughtie had used before, but the door opened and I was on my way to freedom.

The corridor outside was deserted. I scented the still air and smelt more prey to the left. There were no clues as to the way out so I ran towards the humans. The hunger was satisfied for the moment, but the primitive brain liked blood and violence. That belonged to the human alone, and somewhere deep within the wolf growled in disgust.

The metal floor turned to a blur beneath my feet. I was spurred on to greater speeds by the smell of blood up ahead, and then there was the sound of more gunfire and I raced towards it. The two humans, a man and a woman this time, had heard me coming, but they hadn't had time to aim before I was upon them. They shot at me in desperation, but luck was on my side now and I avoided being hit. I took both down at once and crushed the man's neck before he even had time to scream. The woman I ripped apart like the guards outside my own cell. The latest victims had been guarding a door, and beyond it lay the smell of blood. I went through and was met by yet more gunfire. They'd all heard the woman screaming before she'd died of her wounds, and they were all afraid, I could smell it. They were too scared to aim properly and most were just shooting wildly and backing away from the door. Behind them humans in white coats cowered behind their equipment with no way of defending themselves and no escape, waiting for death.

As I walked further into the room, one man shot at my head, aiming for the brain, but he was shaking so badly the bullet grazed my cheek. Almost in unison, another man tried for my heart, and it went too high, embedding itself in my shoulder. Anger reacted to the pain and I roared as rage took over again. Before they knew what was happening I was before them, and with a single swipe I sent one man flying into the wall across the other side of the room. He hit it so hard his neck snapped on impact. Other bones broke but he was already dead, beyond the pain.

More bullets thudded into my chest, though I barely noticed. Thanks to the rage I too was beyond pain, and the bullets didn't even slow me down. I killed the others, thirteen in total, until the room was almost silent, my ears still ringing from the gunshots and the screaming. Almost silent, if it hadn't been for the scientists, most of whom hadn't moved throughout the onslaught. One had tried to sneak round me while I tore the limbs off a guard but the movement had caught my eye and he now lay dead with the others, in pieces. One of them clutched a phone to him, his last lifeline. He'd been screaming into it minutes earlier. I turned my attention from the scientists to the source of the blood I'd smelt outside. There was a vampire chained down to an operating table. They'd cut him open, apparently to do some kind of tests, and he was still alive, despite the fact I could see his beating heart and his lungs, swelling every time he took a breath.

Looking beyond the vampire, I found jars full of some clear liquid, with organs floating in them. Something about this disturbed the beast, and I fled the room.

Footsteps sounded down the corridor, somewhere behind me as I entered another lab, much like the first, only a young boy lay in this one, no more than eight or nine, and he wasn't a vampire. He was alive, barely. He looked at me with pleading eyes, wanting it to end. Little dots of blood covered his right arm, just above the veins where needles had been plunged beneath the skin; the other was missing. His stomach had been cut open, though his chest lay untouched. His legs were intact, though the skin had been scraped away in places. And sickest of all, a wolf's head had been grafted to his neck, for no apparent reason. There was no reason for it, just man's ego, torturing things because they can. The glassy eyes looked out on the world, unseeing and definitely dead. If they'd tried to reanimate it they had not succeeded. Or perhaps it was merely somebody's idea of a sick joke.

The lifeless flesh of the second head had started to decay. There were bald patches in the fur where the skin had rotted away exposing bare flesh, flakes of it falling to the ground, curling like greying rose petals. The jaws gaped open, the tongue hanging out between a gap in the teeth. Maggots ate away at the flesh on one cheek. Some of them had spread to the boy's head. As I watched, one crawled into his ear. The boy couldn't have much longer to live. Once they were inside his head, it couldn't be long before they wriggled their way through his brain and ate him alive.

He made a weak sound, a cry for help, and I reached out to him, whining softly. The boy's eyes widened and I turned and caught the arm of another scientist, just as she was about to plunge a needle into

248

my neck. She screamed and I roared with anger. The beast didn't like what they'd done to the boy. It was angered by the gruesome experiment. I'd thought I was the last but I was wrong. There was at least one other survivor, one other living werewolf, reduced to a plaything for the humans to butcher. I roared again and ripped her arm off. Blood spurted from the wound, running across the floor to mix with the boy's blood, and my own.

I hadn't noticed the blood dripping from the bullet and stab wounds, but my fur was soaked with it. I had yet to pull the blades out so that stemmed some of the blood flow from those two wounds, but the bullet wounds bled freely. If I'd been mortal the blood loss would have finished me off by then. After the prolonged starvation it should have made me weaker again, but if it did I didn't feel it. The anger gave me strength and I pulled the woman's head off her neck like I'd seen my sister once do by mistake to one of her dolls, though this was considerably messier, but just as effortless. Blood jetted out in a high arc from the stump of her neck and it dripped from the severed head, jaws wide with the scream that she had never had time to make, eyes wide with shock and horror. Tendons and ligaments hung down from the head, and part of the spinal column snaked out beneath it. Reinforcements were coming down the corridor. I threw the head at them and followed in its wake.

Once they were dead I turned back to the boy. The beast didn't know what to do for him, so it helped in the only way it knew how. I took the boy's head in my hands and twisted. There was a sharp crack and the boy lay dead, free of suffering at last. I left the body in search of more death.

After I'd worked my way down the corridor I was on, through more science labs and a couple of empty holding cells like the one I'd been in, leaving a trail of blood and death and destruction wherever I went, I finally came to a torture room. Excitement coursed through the beast's mind, through my veins, as I smelt yet more blood, lots of it in there, some old, accompanied by the smell of old death, some fresh, still spilling from the living. It was growing hungry again.

There was something familiar about this room, though the beast knew it had never been there before. It crept towards the room, the faint sense of recognition making it wary, despite the bloodlust.

No guards stood outside. They'd probably followed the rest in an attempt to stop me, and lay dead somewhere with the others. As for the room, it was empty except for a girl tied to a wooden chair in the middle. If they had any of the big, medieval style torture devices they must have been in a separate room. A few handheld devices lay scattered on the floor. The beast didn't know what they were or what each one did, but it smelled the blood on them and knew what they were for. It snarled and stalked further into the empty room, closer to the girl. Blood dripped down, the wood soaked and stained with it, the floor slick with it. Her bare wrists bled where the rope bit into them, the skin rubbed away where she'd struggled. One eye was bruised so badly she couldn't open it. Her nose was broken. Her ears bled where the earrings had been ripped from them. Blood trickled from the corners of her mouth and her lips were red with it, cut to shreds. The little finger had been clipped off her left hand, the stump glistening with congealing blood. I could see the severed digit lying at her feet. There were a few deep cuts over her body that would scar, but it didn't look like they'd had chance to use many of the torture devices yet.

The beast drew close enough to touch her, hunger pounding its stomach, and brought its bloody snout to a wound on her neck. It sniffed the wound, drooling, and opened its jaws, as if to finish her. The girls eyes widened with fear and pain, when it drew back, some form of recognition keeping the hunger at bay. I looked at her with my mismatched eyes and whatever was left of the boy I'd been knew we couldn't kill her. Pity stirred deep inside, alien to the mind of the beast. The human inside me rose up, resurrected by the sight of the girl, and slowly intelligence started to seep back into my mind. Whining in sympathy, I pulled the ropes apart and, free at last, she fainted from loss of blood and fear. She didn't understand what was happening, and she didn't know who I was. All she saw was the beast I had been, the monster I still was. I caught her as she fell forward and carried her in my arms, much like I had with the body of Melissa that winter night, knowing I had to find a way out.

I walked back through the bloodbath, careful not to trip on any corpses, and searched for a way out. Now I was able to think more clearly, I saw that the corridor had been sloping downwards. That made me think I was in some kind of underground compound, a short stop along the way down to Hell, hidden from the rest of humanity. Which meant I'd been heading deeper into the compound, so I needed to retrace my footsteps, back upwards towards the light and the entrance above.

I followed the corridor upwards until I reached a point where it branched off to the left. If I carried straight on I'd be heading down again, while the other corridor was level. I turned left and continued down there until I was faced with another decision. I tried to keep heading upwards but eventually I reached a dead end, and when I tried to retrace my steps I found my sense of smell was no good, the scent of blood drowning all else out, and there was nothing to see or hear. Before I knew it I was lost. Anger and frustration bubbled up, threatening to turn into rage again. Lizzy needed to go to a hospital, the sooner the better, and I was lost. I was angry with myself but I was angrier with the people who had done this to her. So when I came upon Aughtie while exploring more rooms for any clues as to where in the compound I might be, and how close to the surface it was, it wasn't surprising the rage took over again.

When she saw me stood in the doorway she began to back away, until she was pressed against the wall. She flattened herself against it as if she wanted to fall into it to escape me, her face full of unconcealed terror instead of her usual haughtiness and superiority. A part of me was pleased I could inspire such terror in even the leaders of the Slayers, and who could blame her? I knew I must make for a fearsome sight as I advanced towards her, threads of blood and saliva hanging down from my gaping jaws, my tongue and teeth stained crimson with bits of flesh caught between them. My breath must have stunk of raw meat and viscera. I fixed my mismatched eyes on my prey and watched her quail before the anger burning in them. My muscles rippled beneath my fur with every movement as I gently laid Lizzy down on the floor and then charged my enemy, coming to a stop with the end of my snout inches away from her face. I'd knocked a tray of some unknown liquid in test tubes to the floor while I'd run. The glass had smashed and the liquid caught fire the minute it was given chance to react with the air. I didn't care, and Aughtie was too scared of me to notice. She screwed her nose up at the stench of the warm air coming out in pants from my nose and mouth. I rested my hands on the wall either side of her, digging my claws into the metal while I tried to control the rage. I wanted to kill her, but I needed some questions answering first.

"How did you know it was me?" I snarled.

"What?" she said, pressing herself against the wall so hard I could see her knuckles turning white.

"The last 'rogue wolf' that's been terrorising the streets. How did you know it was me?"

A sly smile crept over her face as she answered "I would have worked it out for myself of course, but I was saved the trouble. Imagine my delight when my contact told me they had not only discovered who the new werewolf was, but they had met him and even gained his trust."

251

"What are you talking about?" I asked, confused.

Some of her usual smugness crept back into her voice when she spoke again. She ignored my question and went on to say "I had my suspicions after you fell asleep in my lesson, but without the information from my contact I couldn't have been certain until you were admitted to the mental hospital, where we had chance to study your behaviour. You showed all the signs of a newly turned werewolf: increasing violence, increasing aggression, unprovoked rages, insomnia, restlessness. And then you were taken over by the urge to mate and there could be no doubt."

"Then if you knew what I was all along, why didn't you just take me when you had the chance?" I chose to ignore what she'd said about a contact for the time being.

She was about to answer when Lizzy groaned, regaining consciousness. I turned to look at her and Aughtie took the chance to slip past me.

"No!" I roared. With one powerful leap I pinned her to the ground, one hand wrapped around her neck. She cried out as she fell face first, the skin ripped from her knees. "Who was the boy? What were you doing to him?"

"What boy?" she said, stalling for time. She must have thought the longer she kept me talking, the longer she lived. But maybe I'd just kill her and ask someone else if she didn't answer me quick enough. As it was, I wasn't in the mood for games. With my long fingers I was able to put pressure on her windpipe until she started to choke. "Research. We needed to know more about your kind, that was how I came to know so much about you. We hoped to find a cure, impossible though it was. Still, it proved useful. We used it to find more efficient methods of torture. We discovered more about vampires too. Over time the knowledge will prove invaluable when we uncover a way to rid the earth of the undead forever. The dead should stay dead."

"And the boy, who was he?" I asked again, ignoring the bit about making us extinct. Actually, I agreed with her. The dead should stay dead.

"Why do you care? How many men have you massacred today? What's one more life to you?"

Why did I care? It was a good question. I supposed it was because the sight of the boy had disturbed even the primitive beast I'd temporarily become. And more than that, he was like me, and he probably hadn't asked for this life either, but he'd been dragged into it all the same and had then become just another casualty of war. And because I needed to know, feeling it was important somehow. It was important to the wolf. I could feel it in there, mourning the loss. It still felt the need for a pack and beneath all the horror and the anger it felt cheated of the pack it could have had, if it hadn't been for the Slayers. How many more like the boy had there been? How many had they killed? I felt another surge of hate towards the wretched woman, and I squeezed her neck a little tighter. "Just answer the damn question."

"My nephew," she spluttered. I released my grip in shock. She rubbed her throat, still coughing, and repeated "He was my nephew."

"No," I said. "No, he can't have been your nephew. You idolised him. You never stopped talking about him, about how proud you were of him, how good at English he was."

"Yes, and then he was bitten," she spat. "Cursed for eternity to be undead like the rest of you. He died a long time ago. That thing you found was not my nephew. I gave it over to our scientists for research and in that it proved most useful, enabling us to kill off the rest of your wretched pack. And just when we thought we'd exterminated them all, you surfaced. He was the last free survivor, the werewolf who bit you, and when we hunted him down and he impaled himself on the railing trying to escape, we thought it was over. I could not believe the curse lived on. For years we have been employing midwives to test newborn babies for the presence of the wolf genes passed on to them from their lupine ancestors. Every child that tested positive we killed. It was hard to keep what we were doing from the world, but we managed. We had to hide the bodies in lorries, where they could be taken to be burned. You were a mistake. You should never have been allowed to live. How you passed us by unnoticed I'll never know. I should have killed the boy too, but I had hoped the wolf would never be awoken within him since lycanthrope numbers were decreasing."

I couldn't believe what I was hearing. She'd tortured her own nephew! I didn't care if she said it was in the name of science, it was still torture. And I'd thought I was evil. And all the babies she'd killed! I tried not to imagine a lorry full of tiny corpses being sent to burn to ashes. I wondered what they told the parents and how they got away with taking the bodies from them. Then I decided I didn't want to know. And I had more pressing questions, questions that needed answers. Flames were rising higher around us. They'd spread to some paperwork that lay scattered on the floor, greedily eating their way through months of research. Time was running out.

"Why did you take him and not me? He was your own nephew! I'm nothing to you. Why didn't you take me when you had the chance? And why take Lizzy?"

She sneered at me and I was about to beat the answer out of her like she'd tried to do to Lizzy, but a door burst open on the other side of the room that I hadn't even noticed was there and more guards appeared. They opened fire and reluctantly I left Aughtie where she was, untouched. One of them hit some kind of gas tank, and it exploded in a ball of flame. The fire raged to a greater inferno, given new life. Still the guards fired, more afraid of me than the flames. I didn't want Lizzy caught in the crossfire, and if I didn't take her to safety she really would be swallowed up in the flames as I had seen in my dream, so I picked her up, semi-conscious by that point, and shielded her with my body as I ran from the room.

Bullets followed me out into the corridor, but no one came through. I heard them retreating but didn't look back. My eyes were stinging from the searing heat. If I didn't find a way out soon the whole compound could go up in flames. Most of it was made of metal and there was a good chance it would be contained in that room, but I wasn't going to take that chance. If the flames came into contact with any more of that liquid, or the gas... God only knew what they kept in their laboratories. They were probably experimenting with different substances, looking for new ways to kill us. I wasn't going to stick around to find out.

Smoke snaked beneath a door further down the corridor as I passed and rose up, slowly becoming a deadly cloud above. I ran blindly in any direction. I had no idea where I was going, just as long as I kept moving. If the smoke was anything to judge by, the fire was indeed spreading, though what was fuelling it then was anyone's guess. I'd only seen a small section of the compound. I didn't know how much of it was flammable. I tried not to think about the vampire chained to the operating table, still alive but not for long. There was no time to save him.

I kept running until finally I came to a staircase leading up. I fled upwards and was relieved to find the faint smell of fresh air. The exit couldn't be too far ahead.

Another staircase and I came to a trapdoor in the ceiling. If I'd been human I'd have needed a ladder to reach it, but in my current form that wasn't a problem. I gently laid Lizzy on the cold floor. She stirred and her eyelids fluttered, but she had yet to completely regain consciousness. Maybe she was vaguely aware of what was going on, maybe not. I didn't think she'd remember any of this later on.

I jumped up towards the trapdoor and dug my claws in the ceiling. Then I was able to pull myself up and push the trapdoor open with my feet. I swung back down and held Lizzy in one hand, using the other to pull myself up towards freedom. I hung below the exit while I lifted Lizzy up to safety, and then clambered out after her. The hunger came back again and I was starting to feel weak from the loss of blood, once the anger and the adrenalin had worn off. I used the last of my strength to take Lizzy to a hospital, where I lay her just outside the entrance. Keeping to the shadows, I knocked on the windows until someone came out to investigate. It didn't take long and Lizzy was rushed inside. Once I knew she was safe, I crawled away, pushing my body to the last of its limits. Somehow I reached the graveyard, and I thanked God Lady Sarah was home, before I collapsed, exhausted.

Chapter Twenty Seven – Betrayal

I floated between sleep and the waking world in some kind of dream state, feeling at peace for the first time in months, safe in the knowledge that Lizzy would soon be back among her family and the Slayers had been forced to flee. I couldn't remember where I was but that didn't matter. Nothing mattered except the need to sleep. Or at least not until someone forced my jaws wide enough to pour blood down my throat.

I was brought back to reality with a sudden jolt, almost choking on the blood. The full force of the hunger hit me and I greedily latched onto a chunk of meat offered to me by Lady Sarah, despite the fact I was still spluttering from the warm fluid at the back of my throat.

It didn't take long for me to devour the still warm flesh. Lady Sarah waited until I finished and then said uncertainly "Nick?"

She looked into my mismatched eyes and I could feel her concern. I remembered her warning not to stay in wolf form too long. She must have thought the wolf was taking over.

"Nick, you have to transform back to human form, can you do that? You need to heal your wounds."

"Don't worry, I'm still in here. The wolf hasn't won yet," I growled, and did as she said, though it took some effort. The hunger was still there and I could feel the wolf fighting to take the transformation the other way, to hunt. In the end I won, and within minutes I was human again. Even my eye had changed back to its normal colour. Bullets and the two blades still stuck in my shoulder and back thudded to the floor.

"What's happened to you?" she asked.

I gave her a quick run through of my stay with the Slayers, as much of it as I could remember.

"You're lucky to be alive," she told me when I'd finished. "You're even luckier to have kept your sanity. Most undead would not have survived the torture of starvation with their minds in tact."

"Lucky, that's one word for it. So how long was I gone?"

"Just over a week; nine days to be exact."

Nine days! It had taken only nine days for my mind to reach near breaking point. It had felt like longer. Nine days. How was I going to explain being missing for so long to the human world, and most of all to my family? Out loud I said "So, now the Slayers have been forced to flee their main base in this area, we should strike. Did you get in touch with any others?"

She nodded, her voice dead when she replied, devoid of emotion. "In Vincent's absence I contacted others. There are wraiths who will fight with us, those who seek revenge on the Slayers. I only know of one psychic, and she was out of town when I sought her, but I convinced a number of ghouls to join our cause though I warn you they are impossible to control. I cannot guarantee their support. They are an animalistic race, driven by a base desire for flesh, both of the living and the dead. Once lost in their bloodlust they will attack anything, and they could just as easily turn on us."

"So they're like zombies in a way, only they're not raised and bound by a necromancer's will. Awesome."

"In the circumstances I believe the risk is worth it, as you yourself pointed out. We will still be outnumbered as it is. As for other vampires, they were considerably harder to persuade. Most will not hear of meeting the Slayers in open battle, deeming it suicide. I convinced a handful to at least hear us out, and we can only hope they are persuaded to fight once they learn of the horrors you have witnessed. Of the slaughtering I knew, but not of the experiments you described. I am certain many would find it preferable to die in battle than meet that particular fate."

"And what about the zombies, will you raise them?"

"I will try, but I cannot promise you what the result will be. They present just as big a risk as the ghouls," she warned me.

"If there are too few of us we'll die anyway. What do we have to lose?" I replied, trying to sound confident. In truth I was uneasy knowing the chaotic force we were gathering could just as easily destroy itself as the army of humans we were supposed to be making a stand against. But even with all our supernatural powers, the humans would have the advantage through sheer numbers, especially if the Slayers had chance to call on their forces from the closest base to the one I'd destroyed. That was a possibility that couldn't be discounted, though I hoped we would be facing them in a weakened state after the damage I had wrought on the compound they had briefly kept me in. We had to assume we'd be facing hundreds of Slayers, so we needed every undead creature still walking the earth to join the fight, no matter how great a danger we posed to each other as much as to our enemies.

"I will do what I can."

"Okay, so where do we meet and when?"

"There is a place on the outskirts of this town where fields meet woodlands, do you know it?"

Images flashed before my mind of Fiona dying in a pool of her own blood. I nodded. "I know it."

"Then we will meet there. It's just on the border between territories, thus it was the only place I could get the vampires to agree to come to," she said. "We agreed on three nights from now."

I opened my mouth to argue but she held a hand up before I could say anything and told me "It was the best I could do. And if we can persuade them to help let us hope we catch the Slayers unprepared and still recovering from their losses. Then we will hunt them down, until we have cleansed this town of their evil."

I nodded reluctantly, though I couldn't help feeling by then it would be too late. My gut told me we had to strike sooner if we were to catch the Slayers off guard and weakened. Still, what could they do in three days? Their base lay in ruins, their numbers down. They needed time to recover and three days wouldn't really make that much difference, would it? I hoped not.

Lady Sarah looked up at the sky.

"Dawn is coming," she said. "Will you be strong enough to walk back to your home alone?"

"Yeah, I'll manage thanks."

I took my leave, mind racing with lies to tell my family, each more unbelievable than the next, desperate to find an excuse that would explain why I'd been missing for nine days. In the end I decided to tell them I'd been sleeping at a mate's house, but I hadn't told them because I was mad at Dad. It wasn't the best story I could have come up with, but in the circumstances it would have to do.

As it turned out they were too relieved to have me back to notice I was lying. They were ready to accept anything I told them, just as long as I was okay and unharmed. When I hadn't been in touch they'd started to fear the worst, and Amy had been worrying about all the bad things that could have happened to me, from being eaten by the 'rogue wolf' to being abducted by a psychopathic murderer. I tried not to laugh. She hadn't even dreamt of anything that came close to the truth. It was just another crazy chapter in the insane reality I'd found myself in.

As for Lizzy, the hospital had called her family shortly after they'd found her. I don't know what she'd told them, but I hoped she didn't try the truth. Her version of events wouldn't be as insane as mine since she didn't know about the undead, but there was a chance she'd remember the beast I'd been stood over her. If she described a werewolf to them she'd find herself in the same mental hospital I'd been taken to. And then there was the dream. So far it had been true. The room where she had been held had been just as I'd seen it in my dream. That's why it had been vaguely familiar to me when I came upon it in the compound. And if the first part had been true, there was a good chance I was going to die in three night's time. I had three nights left on this Earth, and I intended to make the most of them. I had to try and talk to Lizzy before then and settle things with her. I wanted to make sure she would be okay after I was gone. And I'd make an effort not to argue with Dad. I didn't know if my family could survive losing me a second time. The least I could do was leave them with happy memories of our final days together. In a way I supposed I was lucky; most people don't know when they're going to die. Mum had lost her dad just after they'd had a big argument, and she'd always regretted never being given the chance to say sorry. At least I knew when it was coming, and I had chance to make ends meet. In that respect I felt I was luckier than most.

Night wrapped itself around the world, tight as a snake, slowly squeezing out the light. The darkness was so thick you could choke on it. Shadows pressed against the eyeballs, sight becoming useless. But there was movement in the blackness.

Tarmac cut its way through the countryside, a long forgotten road, rarely used and deserted. Out there the darkness was complete. There were no streetlights to give the illusion of lasting daylight, only the light of the moon, and the faint light of the stars overhead, hidden by clouds on this night. A faint breeze stirred the grass, ghosts whispering in the wind, before it died, leaving the surrounding area still and dead around it, save for a pair of field mice that had dared to make their home there, as nature slowly reclaimed it.

The mice crept through the grass, searching for food, when one of them froze, ears pricked, listening to a new sound in the distance, one that didn't belong there. Sound rolled out over the grassland, and the mice fled.

The roar of an engine and the glare of headlights disturbed the night. A lorry sliced through the darkness like a blade through flesh. The driver stared out at the road ahead with grim determination, wanting only to deliver his cargo and go home. It had been a long day, but it wasn't a bad job. He could be worse off. They paid him well, and the actual cargo itself didn't bother him. He had no conscience, the very reason why he was so valuable to them, him and the other men in this business. He knew what he was carrying, even if he didn't know why. He didn't ask questions.

But the cargo in that dread lorry would have made any sane person sick with horror. Tiny carcasses lined the inside of the vehicle, too many to count. The corpses of newborn babies, eyes glassy and lifeless as a doll's, all that remained of each new life stolen before it could truly begin. And somewhere in the stinking heap there was one survivor, by some miracle. It was too weak to cry, barely strong enough to move, but some instinct drove it to crawl its way slowly to the top. It should have been crushed by the press of bodies around it, suffocated by the stench of the rotting shells. The lorry stunk of death, old and new, each carcass in different stages of decay. Tiny limbs, fragile in life, more so in death, snapped off, until it became impossible to tell who they had belonged to. It didn't mean anything to the survivor, too young to understand what was going on around it. It continued to claw its way to the top, until it was too weak to go on and finally it died, its very existence lost to the rest of the world.

I was jolted into the waking world, the gruesome images still playing in my mind. And the worst thing was I knew it was all true. Out there somewhere, at that very moment, there could be a lorry like the one in my dream. Or maybe there were too few of us left for that, maybe I really was the last of the wolf descendants, though I didn't want to believe I was truly alone. There certainly weren't any survivors once they were thrown into the lorry, all those potential new werewolves exterminated long before the curse could take hold.

It occurred to me my family ought to carry wolf blood in their veins too, on one side or the other. My wolf blood had to come from somewhere. But the wolf had never attempted to bite them so I had to assume for whatever reason they didn't have a high enough percent of wolf DNA. Not that I wanted to bring them into this cursed life.

It was still dark, and I still had one night left before the battle that would supposedly result in my death. I didn't feel much like sleeping after the nightmare. I still needed to talk with Lizzy, though I doubted the hospital would allow visitors at that time of night, but I decided to try. It was better than returning to the nightmares.

So, half an hour later I stood outside the hospital, wondering how to find Lizzy and how I was going to get into her room without being stopped by anyone. Finally I decided to just slip in and see what happened. If they threw me out I'd come back later that day, no big deal. More than anything I just needed something to do to keep me awake.

All I had to do was follow her scent, with the help of the lupine half of my brain, and slip inside her room when no one was looking. Luck was on my side, since I managed to avoid all the doctors and nurses floating about. At one point I'd been distracted by a car crash victim and the overwhelming smell of blood, but I'd made it and I was glad to see Lizzy was looking a little better already for the medical attention.

She had been asleep when I first found her. I'd tried shaking her gently, for all the good it did. At first I'd panicked, wondering if they'd drugged her to help her sleep, until she finally opened her eyes and looked at me, confusion plain on her face as she fought to wake herself.

"Nick?" she whispered. "What are you doing here?"

"I heard about what happened so I came to check you were okay," I said, careful not to let slip I'd been there too. I was hoping she wouldn't remember much of it.

"I'm fine." She smiled, but it slowly turned to a frown.

"So, what do you remember?" I asked. "What did you tell them?"

"I came to warn you about those people following you. They knocked me unconscious then when I woke up I was tied to a chair and they were asking me all these questions. They hit me when I wouldn't answer them. Aughtie was there. And they kept asking me about you."

"Shit, I'm sorry. You shouldn't have got mixed up in this; it was me they were after."

"You want to tell me what's going on?" she said.

"I can't. Trust me, you're better off not knowing."

"These people kidnapped me Nick. I want to know why."

"I can't tell you that," I insisted.

"Are you going to the police?"

"No, we can't."

"They kidnapped me. We have to go to the police, Nick. They could have killed me!"

"We can't go to the police. Some of them are involved in this. They won't help us."

"I don't understand you anymore, Nick. And I don't know what shit you've got yourself into, but I wish you'd tell me. You know you can talk to me. I'm here for you. And I need to understand. I need to know why those people took me. If you won't tell me I'll look for answers elsewhere, but either way I need to know."

"No, the less you know the safer you'll be. Please, just forget about it. For me, for whatever remains of our friendship, just forget it," I pleaded.

"I can't."

She wouldn't say anything else after that unless I told her the truth. She hadn't mentioned any monsters at least. I was hoping she didn't remember that much. I hated to leave her like this when it might be the last time I ever saw her, but what more could I do? I couldn't tell her anything else in case it put her in more danger, and she ignored me when I tried talking to her about other things. I had no choice. I just hoped she'd forgive me after I was gone and that she wouldn't regret leaving it like this for the rest of her life. At least she would be okay. I was pretty sure once I was gone the Slayers would leave her alone since she'd be no further use to them, and I convinced myself she would never find any answers without me. She'd be okay.

The next day passed quickly. I spent most of it with my family, trying not to think about the fate that awaited me that night. I tried to make things work with Dad but I ended up just avoiding him so we didn't argue. It was the best I could do when he was being so unreasonable. He was going away that night anyway, to work in some other part of the country for a few days, and he went early evening.

When darkness fell I left the house as soon as I could. I found somewhere safe to transform and headed towards the meeting place, carrying my clothes in my jaws. I ran most of the way, late as I was.

There were more than I had expected waiting for me. Lady Sarah took me to one side before I could do anything else, and waited for me to transform back and dress. I needed to feed but it would have to wait. The starvation the Slayers had put me through seemed to have strengthened me. I wasn't weak like I had been the first time I'd undergone two transformations without feeding in between, though it had sapped some of my strength.

"They are growing restless," she said. "I have tried addressing them but they would not listen to what I had to say. If we are going to convince them it has to be now."

I nodded and turned to face the crowd, made up of roughly ten vampires, twenty ghouls, and five wraiths. I had to shout to be heard above them. From the looks on the faces of the vampires it seemed each one was voicing their doubts. The ghouls were just looking forward to flesh, and the few ghostly figures I could see shimmering in the moonlight, who had to be wraiths, were ready for revenge.

The ghouls stood out among the vampires, since they looked like rotting corpses, too skeletal to ever be mistaken for a vampire. Their skin was greying and stretched tight across the bones beneath, their faces little more than skulls, noses missing. Ribs were obvious beneath their chests and their nails were more like claws, making it easier to rip apart the flesh of their victims. Some of them were covered in tattered remains of the clothes they had been buried in. The wraiths looked similar, except they were like ghouls made of something as insubstantial as mist.

"How many of you have been hunted by the Slayers?" I roared. I was never much good at speeches, and I didn't have time for pleasantries. Nobody answered me but at least I had their attention. Silence had fallen, and every face was turned towards me, the vampires regarding me with disdain, the ghouls with interest, and the wraiths with indifference. The wraiths at least would fight for revenge with nothing to lose, for only the wraiths were beyond further harm. They were deader than any of them. That didn't mean they couldn't be stopped, just that stopping them didn't involve harming them like it would for those of us with corporeal bodies.

"How many have suffered at their hands? I look out at you now and I see a dying race! Look at me. I may be the last of my kind. The Slayers know who I am. They've already captured me once and I am lucky to be alive. We have become the hunted, the night no longer ours. Our time is running out. Do you want to spend it cowering in the shadows? Or will you fight? Yes, we are outnumbered, but humans die far easier than we do. And if we are going to die anyway, what do we have to lose? At least this way we have a chance of survival, and if not at least it is better than waiting for the slow process of extinction."

"This is madness," one vampire shouted. Others agreed with him. "Many of us have survived for centuries, even with the threat of the Slayers. We still have our lives, our eternity! Would you have us cast them away like so much worthless junk? Are they nothing to you? Well I for one will not throw that away to save one doomed werewolf."

All the vampires were shouting at me then, and even a few of the ghouls, and looking out at their angry faces I couldn't help feeling it was hopeless. Nothing I could say was going to convince them. Still, I had to try.

"Life," I laughed, the shouts dying down to angry muttering. "You call this life? What life is this for us, we who are the greatest predators ever to walk this earth? Mankind used to fear us! What life is this, living in fear of them, they who should be no more than prey! Were it not for the technology they hide behind they would be no match for us. Are we so afraid of them we won't even fight to take back what's rightfully ours? Will we not make a stand like the great predators we are, instead of running and falling into extinction?"

"You're talking about a fight we cannot win," argued another vampire. "Better to stay in the shadows and continue to elude our hunters, than throw away what years remain to us in one rash move."

"Tell them what you witnessed after they captured you," Lady Sarah said to me with a quiet urgency, aware it wasn't going well.

She wanted me to shock them with what I'd seen, so I searched my memories of the experiments I had happened upon after I'd broken free of the cage I'd been kept in. Most of those memories were vague, but one came to me, sharper and more graphic than anything else from the night I'd escaped. If this didn't convince them to fight then nothing would.

"You think you can survive much longer?" I tried again. "You think you will live out the rest of your years in freedom? When the Slayers took me they starved me to the point of madness, almost to the point of no return. But I escaped and I destroyed their base. And while I searched for the way out, I saw enough to know I was one of the lucky ones. Did any of you know they've been capturing us alive so they can experiment on us? A vampire lay on an operating table, his chest sliced open, his heart and lungs visible. A young boy, possibly the only other living werewolf besides myself until I freed him from his suffering, had been sliced up in a similar way, but they'd sewn a rotting wolf's head to his neck. Maggots were eating the rotting head, and as I watched they spread to living flesh. They were eating him alive, and the Slayers had scientists making notes, testing how much he could endure. They were testing things on him, things I have no name for, trying to find the best way to kill us, the best methods of torture. Will you stand by and let this happen? If we do nothing, you could face the same fate. If we are truly doomed, is it not better to die fighting than spend the last of our days, maybe even years, as playthings of the Slayers?"

Finally I had their interest. It seemed I had succeeded in shocking them. Some of the vampires still looked scornful, but most of them seemed more willing to listen.

"Well spoken, Nick," said a familiar voice, one I knew I'd heard before but couldn't quite place. It sounded familiar yet different to how I remembered it. Where had I heard that voice before? "But you know there is another option. All you offer is death. I can offer you more, all of you. You can still have eternity, if you are willing to make a few changes, to embrace the new world and let go of the past. The world of men is changing as technology takes over, and we must change with it. I offer you a third choice, one which guarantees your survival."

A dark figure walked towards us from the direction of the woods. The shadows stretched outwards from the trees, but they didn't quite reach our gathering. Closer to the woods the world was black, but it was more a darker shade of grey where we were, the moonlight softening the blackness. He had been shouting to be heard above the

264

others, until silence fell. The last was a low hiss, yet it carried to us on the still night air, as he emerged from the blackness. "Join with us!"

Lady Sarah gasped. I gawped stupidly at him, taking several minutes to recover enough to find my voice. "They killed you! I buried your body. How can you be alive? No one could survive what they did to you."

The vampire looked at me and laughed, and I couldn't believe I hadn't recognised his voice sooner. "Ah, so young and foolish, how could you ever think you could lead us into another battle against the Slayers? You are still a child. None of us can stand against them. No mate, they did not kill me. The vampire you buried had just died after we'd tortured him, and it was my idea to put the pendant on the corpse, knowing you would assume it was me. You're still too human to ever survive this war, even now. If only you'd embraced your lupine side you'd have known it wasn't me. And that little mistake almost cost you your life."

"You," I said, understanding dawning. I'd let myself forget what Aughtie had said about a contact since I'd escaped, but her words came back to me as I fought to make sense of what was happening. "It was you who told her what I was."

"Yes, me. I betrayed you to her. It was I who set up the little trap with the mist. An old power of mine, controlling the weather. We didn't expect to capture your friend instead, but it worked just as well. I brought the storm that night when you discovered the corpse and I caused the bulbs to blow in the outside lights. And now I have brought the Slayers to your little gathering. Join us, or die. There is no escape."

I looked out into the darkness of the woods and saw more figures moving towards us. "Don't listen to him! The Slayers want us dead. If you join them they will only betray you! Now is the time to fight, your lives depend on it."

That brought the crowd out of their confusion. They hadn't really been following the last few minutes, but they knew Vince for what he was then, a traitor, and they were looking at him with disgust. He knew they were never going to join him and hissed "Fools!" before melting back into the shadows, though I knew we hadn't seen the last of him that night.

The Slayers were drawing closer. A gunshot sounded and a bullet thudded into a vampire's shoulder. She hissed, baring fangs, and ran at the humans with unearthly speed. The other vampires and the wraiths followed, until the two armies clashed. Ours was considerably smaller, if it could even be called an army. It seemed Aughtie had managed to bring in reinforcements from other parts of Yorkshire, as there had to be over a hundred of them. The ghouls joined the fray at the first spill of blood, where they ripped apart the wounded and fed. We were stronger than the Slayers – they were only mortal after all – but they had greater numbers and guns. If they didn't panic all they had to do was shoot our hearts or heads and we were dead before we had a chance to get to them. Bullets wouldn't stop the wraiths, but somehow I didn't think they were enough to win the battle. Could they even harm the living? As Lady Sarah and I watched the battle unfold, not yet joining the fight ourselves, I soon had my answer.

Even wounded, that first vampire had proven too fast for the Slayers to land a killing shot. Flashes of gunfire lit the darkness as the humans tried to fell the undead charging at them, but we were simply too fast. There were a few sprays of blood as a handful of bullets hit a vampire or a ghoul, but they were merely painful rather than deadly and only served to heighten the bloodlust of our army. Guns clicked empty and the Slayers dropped them and drew their blades, knowing they would never have time to reload before the life was ripped from their vulnerable mortal bodies. Armed for battle, these humans carried not only knives in their belts but also swords.

Some bullets tore through the wraiths but it seemed no mortal weapon could harm them. The first bullet to pass through a ghostly skull caused the form of the wraith's head to briefly explode into shapeless mist, but seconds later that mist gathered itself back into its form of an ethereal skull. Bullet and blade alike passed right through without even slowing them. And once those tormented spirits reached the humans they felt had wronged them, it was over for their victims. Ghostly skeletal hands reached into the chests of their enemies, three squeezing the life out of their victims, the other two ripping the beating organs out in a spray of gore.

I was about to ask if the wraiths were seemingly unstoppable, why not let them do all the killing for us, but then a sword cut through one of the wraith's outstretched hands, temporarily preventing it from killing its victim. A man produced a book from an internal pocket in his jacket and began to intone some kind of incantation, causing the wraith to utter a terrible shriek born of centuries of pain and torment. As if the pain had suddenly become too much for the vengeful spirit to bear, it withdrew with its ghostly skull in its skeletal hands, floating backwards across the battlefield. Thus repelled, the wraith was rendered useless. There were a handful of other Slayers working on repelling the remaining four wraiths, and I had to wonder if I was witnessing a few of the last witches and warlocks left in the modern world. I felt a wave of despair as I watched them choosing to use their powers to serve the Slayers, no doubt in exchange for their own lives, just as Vince had done. I just hoped these were the only humans with supernatural powers in their service which Aughtie had summoned for the battle. If not, if there were groups of them in each area throughout the country, or even the world, and we faced witchcraft as well as human technology, then it seemed ultimately we really were doomed.

The vampires also realised the threat the spellcasters presented. Most of our army fought with our bare hands but three of the vampires had swords of their own. Judging from their skill with a blade they were from a time before guns, when cold steel was all they had to rely on as humans. One of those vampires I recognised as the first who had spoken out against facing the Slayers in open battle, and he cut his way through to the man who'd repelled the first wraith. The warlock, if that's what he truly was, had no choice but to abandon his chanting and turn his attention to the vampire advancing towards him. As soon as his spell was broken the wraith was able to rejoin the battle. I would later learn wraiths could be banished from the mortal realm, but it was not an option in the heat of battle so repelling them was the best counter available to the Slayers that night.

I was beginning to feel the battle would go in our favour. In that initial charge we'd already killed around thirty of the Slayers, while they'd only felled the female vampire who'd already been shot, and a handful of the ghouls. That first vampire to die had been weakened just enough by her wound for her movements to slow and present the Slayers with a chance to finish her. She'd also wielded a blade and had been locked in combat with a human, but slowed as she was she couldn't cut him down as quickly as she could have done if she'd had chance to heal. While she was focussed on parrying his blows, another of the Slayers who'd had chance to reload his gun got a clear line of fire and was able to put a bullet through her brain. A couple of the ghouls had also been shot and a few heads had been severed by the swords of our enemies. Perhaps we didn't need to risk raising any zombies after all. I readied myself to join the fray, about to rip free of my clothes and embrace the full power of my lupine side, but Lady Sarah placed a hand on my shoulder.

"Do not be so quick to count on our victory," she said.

And as I watched with dismay the vampire facing the first of the spellcasters raised his sword to strike with all the fury and inhuman speed of their kind, but the warlock had quickly begun to chant a new incantation, one of his hands outstretched with the palm face up. Suddenly the blade fell from the vampire's hand and he sank to his knees in agony, clutching at his head. Blood leaked from the orifices in his skull; crimson rivulets flowed out from his ears, his nostrils, his eyes and his mouth. Before any could go to his aid, the warlock finished his chant and closed his outstretched hand into a fist, and as he did so the vampire's head exploded. Gore splattered against the warlock and a few of his fellow Slayers, as well as two nearby ghouls, while the headless corpse fell to the ground. The ghouls lost control to their hunger and bloodlust and attacked the corpse in a feeding frenzy, ripping and tearing with their bony claws and teeth. So intent on their meal as they were, they became easy targets for the Slayers to pick off. Their corpses fell on top of the vampire's, a woman placing a bullet in each of their frenzied brains.

"Damn it, all that combined supernatural power and it's still not enough," I growled. "We have to raise the dead or lose."

"I fear you are right but I know not if I have the strength to raise the whole cemetery, especially as I have yet to feed tonight," Lady Sarah replied. "And not every corpse is capable of becoming a zombie. It depends what happened to the soul. Some face oblivion, though we do not know why. Most move on to whatever the afterlife holds for them, but some vengeful spirits become wraiths, while others are trapped on the Earth, some able to manifest as ghosts, some too weak to do that. It is they who reanimate their own bodies for as long as the spell binds them to their earthly remains, although I have heard stories that some are drawn back from the afterlife if the call is powerful enough. I will do what I can but I fear we will not have the numbers we need."

"I should help the others while we wait for you to bring reinforcements," I said.

Again she held me back and I growled irritably at her. The smell of blood was calling to my own hunger.

"Come, I need you with me."

There was no time for questions so I reluctantly joined her as we slipped away from the battle and ran towards the graveyard she called home. I had trouble keeping up with her in my human form and was again ready to rip off my clothes to transform, but as if she read my thoughts she slowed and bid me to wait.

The streets were deserted of human life. I wondered if the Slayers had managed to impose some kind of curfew to keep innocent bystanders away, no doubt using the threat of the rogue wolf as an excuse. Or perhaps people subconsciously sensed the danger of so many predators nearby and were hiding behind locked doors of their own accord. It meant we had to feed on a large stray dog but it did help replenish our strength, even if it wasn't our desired prey. The flesh was dry and chewy once Lady Sarah drained the animal of most of its blood, but I forced it down, even though it was far from palatable. I needed the energy for the fight still ahead of me, and to support at least one more transformation.

We entered the graveyard together and Lady Sarah explained why my presence was required.

"Necromancy demands a blood offering. It must be human blood, which is where you come in. My own blood is too far from human, but yours is closer than mine in your human form. It should be sufficient."

I had little choice but to trust her to slit my wrist with her nail and lick the wound, the same coagulant bats have in their saliva preventing it from healing. When the blood started to drip down into the soil she began to speak the words of some long forgotten language that would awaken the dead. Once she fell silent she spoke again in English.

"Now you may transform and let the wound heal."

So I finally ripped off my clothes and let the transformation take hold, but I only took it halfway, becoming the wolf man again. The wound closed on my wrist as I changed, and as my senses grew sharper I became aware of something happening in the graves.

A pair of eyes snapped open in the darkness beneath my feet. The darkness - all consuming and smothering in its intensity, pressing against the eyeballs until they must surely pop. Hands clawed at the coffin lid. Panic took hold. Lungs gasped for what little oxygen existed there. Panic turned to fear. The need to get out, the urgent need to breathe, it was overpowering. Hands continued to claw at the coffin lid, desperate, strengthened by that fear. They succeeded in breaking open the lid but dirt fell in, burying them. They did not give up the fight to be free, legs kicking in panic, whole body thrashing urgently, lungs burning for oxygen.

On the surface I could see the earth moving over one of the graves. Suddenly a hand broke free of the dirt and reached upwards, as if trying to grasp the sky. Seconds later another hand reached the surface, and then a head. The corpse pulled itself out of its grave and stood, inhaling the oxygen in some echo of life, as if mocking life itself.

All around me the dirt writhed as the dead pulled themselves to the surface, more than I had dared hope for after what Lady Sarah had told me about the souls of the dead. My worst nightmares had come true, for there stood all my victims, their dead eyes glaring at me with hatred, bound only by the dark magic which had brought them back from the grave, the only thing preventing them dragging me down into the eternal darkness into which I had sent them. I looked at Lady Sarah nervously. Vengeance is a powerful thing. She controlled them but for how long?

She ordered them into battle and they had no choice but to obey. We returned with the dead to find the tides had been turned and the Slayers were winning. Casualties from both sides littered the ground, but we had been outnumbered to begin with and the most deadly of our enemies, those capable of witchcraft, were still among the living. Our force was reduced to six vampires and around half of the ghouls. The rest were dead or dying. They'd taken down a respectable number of humans with them but it wasn't enough. Dozens of the Slayers still remained and there were enough of them to protect their spellcasters, who were once more focussed on keeping the wraiths at bay. However, as we drew closer to the fallen Lady Sarah's necromancy was powerful enough to raise many of the dead humans and add them to our ranks, but not the vampires and the ghouls who would never rise again.

The zombies moved towards the Slayers in a cascade of maggots, each in various stages of decay. The new dead walked almost like humans. The older ones limped, their muscles stiff and almost useless. Some were reduced to skeletons, Lady Sarah's power the only thing binding the bones together. Some had died in the last world war, their legs long since blown off. They dragged themselves along with their hands. Some groaned. Others were silent, their vocal cords rotted away years ago. Few of them were whole, but they didn't need much to kill. One of them even had a head missing, but it seemed to be doing well enough without it. They pulled their victims apart with inhuman strength. Some of them tore through flesh and bone with their teeth. And they were virtually unstoppable, much like the wraiths without the interference of witchcraft. Lady Sarah later told me the only way to stop zombies was to either kill the necromancer that raised them, assuming they were still bound to that necromancer, or vaporise them.

Faced with this new horror, the Slayers were starting to panic. One weapon they lacked was fire, and even if witchcraft was capable of producing flames, it seemed the spellcasters were too focussed on maintaining the incantations to repel the wraiths to be able to perform any other magic. Without flamethrowers or any supernatural power to defeat the reanimated corpses, the best they could do was to hack them to bits, until they were left in too many pieces to do any harm. Then a Slayer came at me with his sword and I was forced to take my eyes off the zombies to join the fight at last.

The human swung at my head, so slow, so clumsy. I dodged it with ease and drove a hand into his gut. I pulled out his entrails and left him dying on the floor. The bloodlust was taking over again. A man had just succeeded in knocking one of the vampires to the ground and was about to blow his brains out. I killed him before he even had chance to turn and rose to face another one…

Chapter Twenty Eight – Death

I killed a Slayer who charged at me and felled another one in my way. The boy I had been would have loved to have taken up one of the blades of the fallen but my bestial nature had no need for tools. My own teeth and claws were the only weapons I needed and I slashed and bit my enemies, tearing flesh and breaking bones as I raged through the battle.

But it was Aughtie's blood I really wanted. I knew she would be there somewhere, and occasionally I picked up her scent, before I lost it again in the overpowering smell of blood and death. I was losing control of the wolf. The bloodlust was upon us and it was taking over. A man ran at me and I pounced on him without even thinking. He wasn't a Slayer: he had no weapons and he was dressed differently to the rest of them. No, he was just the one unfortunate bystander we encountered that night who had got caught up in something he didn't belong in. I could even see his car on the distant road. He'd stopped for a break on the way to wherever he was going, and I could only assume the sound of the fighting had drawn him to the battlefield to investigate what was going on. I'd like to think that it wasn't until after I killed him that I realised I knew him, but I know to tell you that would be a lie. In truth the human's rage merged with the bloodlust of the wolf and we savaged him. And God help me I enjoyed it.

I ripped open his stomach, blood blossoming over his white shirt, and spilled out the entrails while he screamed and thrashed beneath me. He kicked out with one leg and I grabbed it in my jaws and ripped it off. It came clean out of the socket with a wet sucking noise, as if his body was trying to suck it back in. His arms flailed weakly against me. I ignored them. I dropped the leg and took hold of his head in my jaws. Teeth sliced into flesh. I shredded his face until it was nothing but bloody tatters. Then a zombie lurched forward and pulled him away from me.

"No!" I roared. I fought to drag him back, but his body could not withstand the pull of two creatures with supernatural strength. The other leg came free of its socket, as did the arms. What was left of his mouth formed a scream that was quickly cut off by death itself. And then he was dead, and the zombie ate what was left. I looked at what had been my Dad and in that instant felt no grief, only the anger. I'd killed him just like I'd sworn to and in my anger I felt he'd deserved it. All he'd ever done was make my life a misery, and I felt I wouldn't miss him.

Leaving the zombie to its meal, I went back to join the fray. I'd regained control for the time being. I needed to keep a clear head just long enough to find Aughtie, so I transformed back to human. I looked up, the change complete, and went in search of the hated woman. But someone else found me first.

Vince reappeared from the shadows, fangs bared, holding a gun. He had the same bat-like face as when we first met.

"Why, Vince?" I said, controlling the anger long enough to get some answers.

"Why?" he spat. "I never asked to be this way! The vampire created Lady Sarah out of love. I was a mistake. I lay dying in his arms as the bastard drained me of my blood, my fucking life. I wasn't ready to die so I stabbed him in the chest with a dagger I'd stolen earlier that day. And his cursed blood made me into this! At first I decided death would be better, but the thing that kept me alive was the need for revenge. I wanted to kill the bastard for what he'd done to me, and I didn't care how many others I killed along the way. I hate us all! Centuries I've searched for him with no luck. Then Aughtie found me, and made me an offer. She hates us as much as I do. I joined them and I helped her kill and torture others. I enjoyed it. I helped her invent new methods of torture. I helped her find more effective ways to kill us. And it was I who brought your kind to an end. That fang on my pendent was from my first kill. And it was I who was hunting the werewolf that night he bit you. I didn't realise my mistake until later, but thanks to Lady Sarah I was able to correct it. I delivered you to Aughtie in the end."

"Why didn't you set a trap for me sooner when you knew it was me all along?" I growled.

He shrugged. "You're just the right age to want to fight the Slayers. I knew you were the one as soon as I laid eyes on you at Halloween. We have been waiting for you for years; the one who would bring the last of our kind out of hiding and lead them into destruction. Once you had served your purpose, then we set the trap. The first one was never meant for you. Originally we intended it to be a threat, to scare you into taking action. And then a girl who I knew was a friend of yours happened to be nearby. You were taking too long. I had to push you further so we took your friend. Aughtie wanted to take you from the start, but I told her to let me bring you to her in my own time. You needed time to accept what you were before you would fight. And I enjoyed the control I had over you. I could have killed you anytime I wanted and you never knew it. And perhaps you reminded me of myself in the early days of becoming a vampire."

"I am not like you," I growled defiantly.

I vaguely wondered why they'd felt the need to capture and question me at all, rather than just kill me. Surely he'd learnt all he could from Lady Sarah before faking his own death, so what other information had they possibly thought I could give them? But the one thing that was becoming clear about the Slayers was their blind hatred for the monsters that preyed on them. For many it seemed joining the cause was personal, and they agreed to become a part of the Slayers to seek vengeance for lost loved ones taken from them by members of the undead. Most of them were so driven by hatred, they didn't need a reason to inflict as slow and painful a death as possible. Hunting and killing us wasn't enough, so they'd built compounds like the one I'd been captured in to satisfy their own monstrous needs. Aughtie hadn't really been interested in any information I might have had about the army Lady Sarah had been gathering, she'd just wanted to torture me for her own dark pleasure.

Vince ignored my protestation and carried on as if I hadn't spoken. "And imagine my disappointment when you escaped from the compound. Still, now I have you."

He was about to attack when Lady Sarah appeared.

"How could you?" she asked, bitter tears in her eyes.

He snarled but didn't answer this time.

I stepped back. This was Lady Sarah's fight.

She was faster than Vince, more powerful. The fight was over in seconds. She punched a hand through his chest. Her fist came out the other side with the heart clutched between it.

"Now Vince, remind me how you kill a vampire again?" I said while I watched. "Oh yeah that's right, take out the heart and cut off the head."

Vince looked down at his chest, surprise plain on his face as if he hadn't expected her to really do it. Then he grinned, still very much alive, even after Lady Sarah withdrew her arm, as impossible as that was from what I knew of our world. She crushed his heart until it was nothing but a bloody mess. Vince watched but made no move to stop her. He aimed the gun at her head, but she knocked it from his hand before he could fire and it landed somewhere near my feet. Vince's eyes followed it, and I tossed it away into the woods before he could make a grab for it, while Lady Sarah proceeded to take out his brain. She could have done it quick and relatively painless if she'd crushed the skull in one go, but she wanted to make him suffer. I understood; it would be the same when I went up against Aughtie.

What happened next was a blur. Lady Sarah's fist connected with Vince's face and he fell to the ground. She bent over him and hit him until blood seeped from his eyes, nose and mouth. She kept hitting him until his face literally caved in. Shards of bone stuck into the brain. It began to ooze out from the force of the impact, and parts of it were already crushed. When there was nothing left of his face to punch, she tore out the brain and shredded it. Vince ceased struggling as soon as his brain was removed from his body. For good measure she pulled his head clean off his shoulders, or what was left of it, and then he was truly dead. There could be no way for him to come back again. He was gone, and I can honestly say we never missed him, though I think his betrayal left its scars on Lady Sarah. For my own part, I hadn't known him long enough to be too upset once the initial anger had subsided, but Lady Sarah had known him for centuries. What she was feeling in that moment I wasn't sure. I couldn't read her.

With Vince dead, that left Aughtie, and she was mine. I left Lady Sarah to her feelings, whatever they were, and continued my search.

I walked back into the battle, killing a couple more Slayers who got in my way, but grew wary as I neared one of the spellcasters. This one was a witch, and like the man who'd destroyed the vampire earlier she immediately broke off chanting the incantation repelling the wraiths to face me. It seemed witchcraft relied on incantations and, with that in mind, I knew I had to prevent her from chanting anything else.

Aware that I would never have time to transform again before she could start a spell, and that the bloodlust would most likely overpower me if I did, I tried taunting her first. Slower and less powerful in human form, I felt my chances were slim of reaching her in time to forcefully keep her from speaking the words of any spells, so I had to hope I could keep her distracted until another option presented itself.

"So, it seems you witches and warlocks lack any kind of honour, since there's a few of you here. Was it that easy for you to betray the supernatural world you were a part of?"

She didn't rise to my bait, beginning a new spell before I could do anything else to stop her. I tried to lunge at her the moment the chanting began, but I only managed a step before I found myself paralyzed by some invisible force. The air around me grew warm and my flesh began to burn, but I was powerless to even scream. Of all the pain I'd endured over the last year, in many ways that was the most intense. Skin melted away, the heat stripping my flesh with its barbed tongue. In its wake it left a stinging pain, sharp and immediate as nerves reacted with the air. The damage crept deeper and the pain changed, evolving into an entirely different sensation, one of a deep ache and steady throbbing, pulsing rhythmically like a second heartbeat, as if the pain had a life of its own.

Exposed muscle, wet and glistening, began to appear in patches, my body quickly being reduced to a useless lump of meat. I tried to fight the force holding me in place, tried to push my body to transform and heal the damage, but the spell was too strong. I was beginning to think I wasn't destined to die with a sword piercing my heart after all, until suddenly the pressure lifted and I fell to the ground, shaking uncontrollably from the pain. I rolled my eyes towards the witch to see a giant vampire bat on top of her, its jaws clamped around her throat. The witch had not had time to chant anything else that might have saved her, and she died within minutes. The bat looked over to me and as I watched shadows gracefully seemed to shift as it took on the form of Lady Sarah. It was much quicker than my own transformation, taking only seconds, and I was given only a brief glimpse of her naked form before she'd retrieved her black dress and stood before me looking the same as ever, concern etched onto her beautiful face.

I let my own transformation begin in order to repair the damage, but I reversed the changes as soon as my body was fully healed. I still needed a clear head to find Aughtie, determined to repay her for the torture she'd put both me and Lizzy through.

"That's the second time you've saved me," I said. "Thanks."

She nodded and turned away, still battling the emotions Vince's betrayal had awoken in her. I was just glad she'd been able to put aside those emotions long enough to take note of the danger I was in and to act quickly enough to save me, before the witch's spell could finish me off. I assumed she'd taken her bat form so she could swoop across the battlefield to reach me in time and take the witch unawares, which was more than any of my other supposed allies had done. Maybe they'd just not noticed I'd been at the witch's mercy in the confusion of battle, or maybe they'd not wanted to risk their own necks to save me. If I'd had time to dwell on that I might have begun to feel lost and alone once more, or perhaps it would simply be something else to feed my rage, but we hadn't won the battle yet and I was forced to turn my attention back to the fighting.

I felled three more Slayers foolish enough to get in my way, and then suddenly she was there before me.

Aughtie dispatched a ghoul as I watched, a madness in her eyes not unlike the rage that burned in my own. Each of us was bent on taking revenge upon the other. She no doubt wanted to make me hurt

276

for the pain I'd caused her in the compound and the damage I'd done to her base, and perhaps she also wanted to see me suffer purely because I was a werewolf. A part of her probably wanted to punish me for the lycanthropy that had taken hold of her beloved nephew, even though I was not the one who turned him.

"Now you're mine," she snarled.

Her gun had long since clicked empty so she swung her sword in a high arc intended to cleave my head in two. I dodged the blow and grabbed a sword of my own, though it felt long and clumsy in my hand. I really wanted to transform again. Having found her, there was no more need to keep a clear head and I could give in to my rage and my bloodlust. But once again I knew I would never have time to change whilst being attacked, and a part of me knew I'd been foolish enough not to return to the wolf man form while I'd had the chance. In my human form I was just about fast enough to dance around Aughtie and avoid her silver blade, but I felt it would be hard to close the distance between us to deal any damage. She was careful not to leave herself open to attack, and though the bestial side to me had no need for the tools of man, in human form it seemed necessary. So I parried Aughtie's blows as best I could but I was no swordsman. It didn't take her long to disarm me, laughing contemptuously at how easy an adversary I was. She stabbed forward just as another Slayer stumbled behind me, causing enough of a distraction that meant I was too slow to dodge.

I felt a great pain in my chest and time seemed to slow as I looked down at my body to see the blade submerged in it. Aughtie began to laugh while I fell to my knees, hands clutching at the cold metal in vain, trying to pull it out, my skin slick with fresh blood. I opened my mouth as if to speak, but only more blood came out. Breathing was difficult. I was close to death for the second time that night, only this was the end I'd seen in the dream and I knew there would be no Lady Sarah to rescue me once more. The mud, stained with the blood of both friend and foe, would be my final resting place, where I would be forgotten in the midst of the battle.

But something was wrong. The sword had been driven through my chest and out the other side, and yet there was still a heartbeat. It seemed luck was on my side as I realised the blade had narrowly missed piercing my heart. It had gone through a lung and cracked a rib but I would survive. I looked back up at Aughtie's gleeful face, the battle around her forgotten. She was focused entirely on me, wanting to see me die. I watched as the glee turned to horror when I pulled the sword out of my flesh and thrust it into the ground. Then, weak from pain and loss of blood, I leaned against it and waited for the change to happen. Slowly at first, the wound began to heal over. The severed veins fused together and the blood flow began to stop. Muscle stretched and joined once again, and flesh rolled over to cover the hole. Finally the skin stretched across, leaving nothing of the wound that had nearly taken my life, not even a scar. The other changes came more quickly once the damage had healed, but Aughtie was weaponless and didn't stay to watch, knowing she wouldn't reach a weapon quick enough to strike me a second time while I was vulnerable, and that once the change completed she would face the same destructive force that had almost been her end in the compound. She had already begun to flee towards the woods as my teeth lengthened, my ears becoming pointed. I watched her go as my eyes turned amber, willing the change to come quicker, wanting it to make me stronger again.

No matter how far or how fast she ran, Aughtie had no chance. I was going to have my revenge for Lizzy, and for the boy, her nephew, and everyone else who had suffered at her hands. She was no better than we were. The Slayers claimed to be ridding the world of evil, but they didn't care who they had to hurt to get to us. Perhaps that made them worse than we were. At least we only killed to eat, to survive, for the most part anyway, but they murdered any of their own kind that got in the way of their quest to hunt us to extinction.

Moments later I gave chase, swifter than she in full wolf form, my paws surer on the earth they bounded over, my senses focused solely on her. It was fitting that, after years of hunting down my kind, one of our kind would finally hunt her down.

When I caught up with Aughtie she was already slowing. She'd not gone far into the woodland before she could run no more. I thought she was going to collapse, but she faced me, trying to hide her fear. I slowed too and transformed back into the half man half wolf monster once again, ignoring the hunger. I could see the terror in Aughtie's eyes as she scanned the trees for the help that must surely come. Wasting no time with words, I struck her to the ground, Lizzy's injuries fresh in my mind, and Dad's death. The bloodlust had worn off for the moment, and in the absence of it there was guilt, something I had not felt for months. Guilt not so much at what I'd done, but at what it would do to Mum and Amy. I wasn't sure if they'd survive losing him. At least they wouldn't lose us both.

I directed the guilt at Aughtie, turning it to hate. If it hadn't been for her we wouldn't be there in the first place and Dad would still be alive. I would enjoy killing her.

She hit the ground and tried to crawl away. Bent on vengeance, I picked her up and threw her bodily against a tree. How I managed it without breaking her back I'll never know, but she hit the ground with a whimper and tried to crawl away again. She wasn't going anywhere, but I wasn't going to kill her quickly either. I wanted her to feel the same pain her victims had known over the years. So I kicked her over onto her back and placed a clawed foot on her chest, temporarily restraining her. I had no rope to tie her with but I soon solved that. With a single claw I made a huge gash in her belly, and then I widened it into a hole. I submerged one hand into the hole and felt around, her screams of pain bringing me a sick pleasure. I wondered if she had felt the same when she had tortured her nephew, and all the others. When I found what I'd been searching for, I withdrew my hand, bringing her intestines with it. I used these to bind her hands and feet so there would be no escape.

I doubt the gut would have held her, had it not been for the pain itself. She began to cry, the pain so overwhelming that she lost all sense of time and place. She cried, this evil spawn of the human race. People would say that she wasn't human, that her actions were inhuman, yet I knew different. She was very human. For only humanity is capable of the horrific acts she had committed. And I was half human, which made me capable of becoming every inch the monster she was. It had already begun. I was also half wolf, but no evil lurks in the lupine heart. The wolf had no concept of killing for fun. It despised me for it. No, the wolf killed to eat or to defend itself, nothing more. In my rage it was the darkness that lies in every human heart that took over. The wolf had nothing to do with it.

That evil at the heart of humanity made me dig my hands back into the hole I had created. I didn't do any more real damage, not yet, I just wanted to make it hurt more. Her screams pierced the night, and much as it gave me pleasure, I didn't want anyone to find us before I'd finished. She needed silencing, so I stuck my bloodied claws down her throat and slashed her vocal cords. Not content to stop there, I ripped out her tongue. Blood gushed down her throat, making her retch. I watched her closely, not wanting her to choke on the blood and die too quick. The more uncomfortable she was before the end the better.

Next I skinned various parts of her body, knowing the pain that would cause after experiencing losing patches of my own skin to the heat of the witch's spell, and I punctured a few organs. I reached back inside the hole I had made and ripped out a chunk of flesh and bone containing a large bunch of nerves we learnt about in biology a while back. I forget the scientific name for them, but I felt since nerves register pain it had to cause a considerable amount of discomfort for her. Unfortunately that meant she wouldn't feel the pain in her legs anymore, but maybe that made her suffering worse.

"You never did smile enough," I snarled, the only words I spoke throughout the torture session, and with that I used a claw to slice through her flesh to the bone, drawing a line from the top of her ear, down underneath her cheek bones, underneath her nose, and back up to the other ear. I worked away at the flesh around her ear for a few minutes and finally lifted it up enough to get a good grip. Using the small strip of flesh I had lifted up, I slowly tore off all the flesh beneath the line I had drawn, exposing her bare jawbones and giving her a permanent grin. Then I sliced off her ears and burst her ear drums. Next I punched her nose, hard enough to leave it a bloody mess and permanently damage her sense of smell. After that I gouged out her eyes, tears of blood flowing down her face as she was plunged into eternal darkness. My anger and bloodlust spent, I finally cut her bonds and left her.

Miraculously, she was still alive for several minutes after my gruesome work was done, and I sat and watched her drag herself painfully away, devoid of all senses save for a weak sense of touch, her guts trailing behind her, legs useless. I wished I could make her suffer like that for all eternity, but I came to realise those few minutes would seem like eternity to her, spent in a Hell of her own making. It would be time enough to dwell on all the evil sins that she had committed. She came to a stop a few feet from where I sat at the end of a bloody trail. Her hand reached up towards the night sky, as if seeking help from above, or perhaps to try and reach something that would pull her out of the Hell I had sent her into. Then it fell pitifully to the ground and I heard her heart beat its last. Satisfied, I turned away and stared into space, utterly spent.

Chapter Twenty Nine – Love Lost

The last of the screams tore from the throats of dying men and then there was silence. Lady Sarah found me sat between the trees, the mortal remains of Aughtie lying a few feet away. She seemed to have regained control of her emotions, though I doubted she would recover fully for some time, if she ever recovered at all. I didn't really know enough about their history but it seemed as if she and Vince had been close friends at some point in their long lives, even if they'd drifted apart nearer the end.

"The battle's over," she said. "They're all dead, except for the spellcasters. After I killed the witch and the Slayers' defeat seemed certain, the others fled. We lost a few more, and there are casualties, though most wounds won't cause permanent damage once there's chance to heal. I broke the necromancy spell before I lost control; the zombies are just corpses again."

"Good," I said faintly, not really hearing what she was saying. "What happens now?"

"There are still many more Slayers in other towns and cities. Those who fought tonight have agreed to go out into the world and attempt to make more of us, as well as meeting with others to try and persuade them to join the fight. We will build a bigger army for the battles to come."

"You too?" I asked.

"I do not know if I will leave yet. Perhaps I will make more vampires in this town. With the threat of the Slayers gone from this area for the time being, they could develop in safety, and once they are powerful enough they can join the fight. And you?"

What would I do? I hadn't expected to survive the battle so I hadn't thought about what came after.

"I can't go back home," I said, realising it for the first time. "Life can't go back to the way it was, no matter how much I want it to. I can't be among humans, not anymore. And I think Aughtie was smart enough to have sent my identity on to other bases. The police will have my name. They're probably looking for me if they can tie me to any of the deaths. I can't stay here. I don't know where I'll go, but I can't stay here."

The recognition I had to leave was a hard one, especially after letting myself think I could go back to my family and help them through Dad's death. That was, if my guilt would have allowed me to return to them. But in reality it would never work. My time amongst humans was over. I belonged to the world of the undead now.

"Then we should leave now before you change your mind again," she said.

"Wait, you said you were staying. You're coming now?"

She smiled. "You still have much to learn. You would not last long on your own. If you are to leave the human world behind, you must learn to live in our world. I will teach you. You cannot simply wander around on your own. The vampires here today will not forget you, but there are others who would harm you. You may be the last of your kind, and I will not be responsible for the death of your race."

"What about making more undead round here?"

"One of the others can stay behind and make the most of the absence of the Slayers in this area, for as long as it lasts."

I nodded, and was secretly grateful she was coming. Eternity was a long time to be alone. "Before we leave there's some things I have to do. Wait for me back at the graveyard, I won't be long."

Alice watched me with his cold black eyes as I walked into my room for what was probably the last time. There was no way I could take him with me, much as I wanted to. Mum wouldn't look after him, but I knew she'd find someone to take him in. To my family I'd be dead. They'd hope I'd come home again after a few days, but as the days became weeks and the weeks became months, they'd lose hope and finally come to accept that I was really gone. It pained me to think about what they would go through, but what choice did I have? They were in danger as long as I lived with them. I wouldn't be the one to get them killed.

I knew I couldn't take anything with me, tempted as I was. In leaving I was sacrificing a lot, but then, I had eternity. Maybe some day when the war was over I might enjoy human pleasures again, but until then I had to leave it all behind. I wasn't human anymore.

I walked around my home for one last time, remembering the good times, trying not to think about the bad, and listened to the soft breathing of Mum and Amy in their sleep. I didn't want to leave, but dawn was not far off and Lady Sarah would need to sleep soon. We had to be out of the town by then. So I bid them a silent goodbye, and took my leave.

I was on my way to the graveyard, when a figure stepped out of the shadows. A silent tear slid down my face at the thought of all I had lost that night and what I had been forced to leave behind, and I raised my eyes to the heavens, thinking what now? I'd had enough shocks for one night. What else could fate possibly have in store for me? Whoever

282

it was that time, I would not let them see me cry. I pulled myself together, pretending to rub my eye while I wiped away the tear on the back of my hand.

The figure came into the light, a boy who thought he knew me once, a gun in his hand.

"Put the gun down David," I said calmly.

"Give me one good reason why I should," he said.

"You'll live to regret it mate."

"Don't call me mate!" he screamed, sobbing uncontrollably, the gun shaking in his hands. His finger was dangerously close to squeezing on the trigger. "I'm not your mate! You killed Fiona. I know it was you. You knew something, so I followed you until I learned the truth. It was you all along, you were the monster! I loved her."

"Ha! Love. She never loved you," I told him. I'd just killed my own father. Of all the deaths I had caused his had affected me most deeply, for no matter how much I had hated him, I couldn't kill my own flesh and blood and not be affected by it. I don't know what I was feeling; my emotions were in turmoil and my soul was almost consumed by darkness, and there was David, weak and afraid and angry, and I didn't care if I hurt him. I didn't even care how he knew it was me who had killed her. I remembered when he'd confronted me at break just before Mr Enderson's lesson, when I'd told him to forget and he'd said he couldn't. And then I understood. It hadn't been the Slayers following me all that time, it had been David, probably following me in the hope that I'd lead him to the monster. And I had led him to the monster. At some point he must have seen me transform.

"Yes I killed her. So go ahead and shoot me but it won't solve anything. You're not a man yet, just a scared little boy. You know nothing of killing and revenge. You don't have it in you. You're not a killer David. Put the gun down. She never loved you. The sooner you get that into your thick skull the sooner you can move on with your life. She never loved you and she never will, in this life or the next."

At my words, he collapsed into a pathetic heap on the floor and wept. The gun lay forgotten by his side. I left him to mourn her and went to the graveyard, where I cast away the last shreds of my humanity.

Minutes later I walked away into the night with Lady Sarah by my side, into a new life in an uncertain world beginning to go through a transformation as dramatic as the one I faced every full moon. I was done with humanity. With my father's death I could not be a part of the human world any longer and it was time to move on. I was truly one of the undead now, and it was to their world I must go. We had won the battle but the war was not over. There was much work to be done.

Chapter Thirty – Beyond The Grave

Deep in the bowels of Hell, screams of the damned sounded endlessly, echoing around dark caverns and black pits, their suffering, tortured, mutilated bodies illuminated by the burning fires that consumed everything. Demons tormented them, feeding off their pain and despair, most too busy with the lost souls of the damned and the sinners to take an interest in events up on Earth, and the lives of those whose souls were still connected with their body. But one demon sat apart from the rest in a lair He had fashioned for Himself, a dark place where nightmares were made.

Stony walls rose up around Him, souls He had claimed for Himself chained all around, each one suffering their own unique torment. He knew what lay in the hearts of men and beast, both living and dead, both damned and pure, and He could feel their fear. Each soul strained against the chains, desperate to be free, each mind in a state of terror, each body in agony. Blood pooled on the floor all around Him. He liked blood. It gave Him sustenance and strength.

Bones lay dotted about, the flesh long gone, littering the floor when He'd finished gnawing them. A throne made of body parts rose up in one corner, where He liked to sit and watch them suffer. But not now.

A fire burned in one corner of the lair, the only light in the darkness, and He crouched on the floor, hunched over it, watching through the flames as a werewolf and a vampire left behind a trail of carnage and set out on a journey that would change the world.

His dark form was very much like that of an over-sized werewolf with black fur. Shifting position slightly, He unfurled His bat-like wings and spread them out behind Him, stretching them before curling them around the flames as if to shield the view of Earth from the others. His arched back was torn open along the spine, bone protruding through the muscle. Each bone in the spinal cord had been moulded into a spike, curved like shark's teeth. Flesh clung to the base of the bones, covering the ribs, glistening and wet with blood.

A hand that was somewhere between being wolf and human, almost a paw, splayed out beneath Him, supporting His weight, long claws gouging scars into the rock beneath. Along the knuckles He bore a similar wound to that along His spine, more bone protruding from fur and flesh.

His face was hidden by darkness, but a flame rose up as if to lick its master, and briefly illuminated the long snout and razor sharp fangs. Again and it revealed more wounds on His face. A large cut over the right eye extended from the top of His forehead to the top of His muzzle, and there were four identical gashes on His left cheek, each one roughly just over a centimetre wide and a centimetre apart, as if they had been caused by large claws slashing across the flesh. These four wounds were deep and stretched across His face, running right across the jaws. The flesh had been completely ripped away, including the gums, giving Him a lopsided, skeletal grin, one fang at the top and one at the bottom partially visible in the first three wounds, and part of the cheek bone and the lower jaw visible in all four, the bone marked with a long scratch in the middle of each cut. Blood red eyes with slits for pupils glowed in their sockets, both fixed in the center of the flames where the events on Earth were visible.

His chest rose and fell with a slow rhythm as He deeply breathed in the putrid air around Him, each lung visible, swelling with air and emptying again. The whole of the chest had been ripped open, just above the diaphragm. Not only were the lungs visible, but also the rib cage surrounding them and part of the heart, the organs and flesh riddled with maggots.

Movement in the darkness as the head of a huge boa constrictor swayed in the dancing light, resting on one shoulder. The rest of its body coiled around the muscular, torn chest, its tail extending to the top of one thigh, while a tarantula crouched on the other shoulder, completely still.

Shadows shifted and the beast was gone, replaced by a man with black hair and the same blood red eyes. He bore the same wounds, though now on His face the cut over the left eye extended from the top of the forehead to the bottom of His nose, and the four gashes revealed the whole of one tooth at the top and one at the bottom. The bones along the spine were now human, no longer spiked, though they were no longer visible in the darkness. Only His face remained visible, the rest of His body hidden entirely in the suffocating sheets of black that engulfed Hell.

He grinned as He continued to watch the werewolf and the vampire, and whispered into the darkness.

"And so it begins."

Epilogue

I fall silent. You look at me expectantly, wanting me to continue, oblivious to the fact that it is growing dark, and that the storm is long since passed. But I shake my head. No friend, I must leave it there for now. For a full moon is rising and the transformation begins. I must conclude the first part of my tale to feed.

You look on with horror as you realise it really is all true. You stare with grim fascination as my face bulges outwards into a snout filled with razor sharp teeth, and you look on at death, realising your mistake in coming here with me.

Bloody images flash through your mind of everything I have told you. Panic takes a hold again. You wish you were home already, safe behind locked doors. Where is home? Can you remember the way you came?

A smile would curve my mouth now, if I were still human. I feel better for talking about my past, though it doesn't change the fact I am still alone. No matter, that is a human need, and my humanity is fast disappearing again, falling to the onslaught of the beast. Perhaps it will die along with you, memories I have recovered lost again, maybe for eternity this time. Or maybe not. I've been at this point so many times before, and a part of me wishes I could forget, just become an animal and join the natural world where the laws of survival are simple. I was so close before you made me remember, but I can never truly belong to that world. I will always be a hybrid, belonging to both worlds and yet a part of neither. There is only one world to which I truly belong and it abandoned me. Eternity is a long time to be alone. My sanity is slipping once again.

Grim fascination wants you to watch the man become the monster, but you know to do so is to forfeit your life. So you flee the cave, but everything looks different in the darkness. In the heart of the woods the only light is from the moon overhead, the very thing that will kill you, yet it could also be your saviour. By its faint, ghostly light, you can just make out a path between the trees. Did you come that way? It must eventually lead out of the woods, right? It's your last chance, your last lifeline. You run along it, straining to hear the animal sounds behind you, aching to know how close I am in pursuit.

A howl rings out from the natural shelter, the transformation complete. I follow, swift and silent as death.

You push yourself to greater speeds and know it will not be enough. Your legs burn, your heart pounding against your ribcage as if it's trying to escape, your lungs demanding more oxygen. You already feel exhausted, but fear keeps you going.

Salvation! You find the main pathway and up ahead you can see streetlights, and hear the sounds of civilisation. If you can just reach them maybe the werewolf will pick someone else.

How close am I now? You turn your head just enough to see behind you and a sob escapes your throat when you see me closing in. You're too busy watching me to see the thick tree root barring your path. You don't know to lift your legs higher to clear it, and consequently you trip, your momentum carrying you crashing to the floor.

"No!" you scream in frustration, voice high with fear. The lights are so close now, so close and yet so far.

You twist round onto your stomach to see me pounce and scream again, praying someone will hear you, something will distract me and I will take someone else instead. But you know my secrets now: it has to be you who will feed me tonight. And I will not waste energy on another when you are such an easy kill.

My front paws land on your chest, knocking the air out of your lungs. My jaws lower, my mouth encasing your head, my fangs the last thing you will ever see before they gouge out your eyes and drive deep into your brain, ending it. You have no breath left to scream. You will die here, alone in the woods, and no one will ever know what became of you. You feel a brief sensation of intense pain, the last thing you will ever feel, as you are plunged into darkness, and finally the last thought dies in your head, my teeth in your brain, soon to know no more.

Your brain is dead, but your body has yet to realise it. You twitch beneath me, limbs convulsing violently, while I gorge myself upon your mutilated corpse. In time I will continue my tale where I left it when I find another fool to listen, another easy meal. Not that you care. All that you ever were and all that you may have become leaks away through your ruined eye sockets and the puncture holes in your skull, and then you are no more. Your earthly remains will soon be long gone. As for your soul, only you know what will happen to that. If you're lucky you may reach Heaven. Or you could face an eternity of wandering endlessly, trapped in a shadow of your former life, or worse, an eternity of pain and suffering in the fires of Hell. Or perhaps worst of all you could cease to exist, lost in oblivion, never to know or see or hear or think ever again.

Or perhaps you will rise as one of us.

Those last few seconds of your existence trickle away. It's growing cold, so cold, and the world is getting darker. You're alone, lost in the void of the great beyond, all alone. The pain is fading as your brain dies and then it's over. Frightening, how one second you can be here and the next gone. But it awaits us all. And in the passing of a second you cease to exist.

Biography

Nick Stead began writing at the age of fifteen. His love of horror and werewolves in particular led to the creation of Hybrid, following a brainstorming session with his cousin to get him started on the first three chapters. Twelve years later at twenty seven and after two major redrafts, his dream of seeing Hybrid published was finally realised. He lives with his two cats in Huddersfield, England, where he is hard at work on the next book in the Hybrid series.

For more information about Nick, Hybrid, and other works visit: www.nick-stead.co.uk.

Lightning Source UK Ltd.
Milton Keynes UK
UKOW01f1638071016

284690UK00002BB/40/P